THE
HIDDEN
VECTOR

THE HIDDEN VECTOR
A SPY THRILLER

by Mathew Snyder

The Hidden Vector
A Spy Thriller

By Mathew Snyder

ISBN: 978-1-7355793-1-3

First Edition: October 2020

For James V. Snyder,
my father and steadfast lover of adventurous books

CONTENTS

"He that dies pays all debts."
—*William Shakespeare, The Tempest*

PROLOGUE

DEBTS PAID

Tbilisi Airport, Georgia
7:33 p.m., Sunday, May 4

KAMRAN KHORASANI sat in a first-class seat, awaiting his escape down the nearby runway while the sickness hiding in his blood threatened to devour him from the inside. He glanced at his watch and counted again the time past departure, just as he had while waiting for takeoff in Novosibirsk, then Yekaterinburg, then Moscow. With each race down those runways, the tension in his chest lessened, only to return like a vice around his heart when he handed over his passport to the dour and suspicious Russian border guards who rifled through his medicines and asked crude questions about his health.

Why must it take so long? He tugged at the loose gold watch band around his wrist and glanced again at the dragging minute hand.

A pretty Georgian woman sat next to him tapping notes on her phone to someone. She wore American blue jeans and a bright shirt with splashy slogans he couldn't understand. When she had taken the seat beside him, she had smiled but said nothing. He shifted as close to the window as possible giving her every centimeter of room. He knew he looked frightful and disheveled. He smelled worse. That morning in Moscow, he had splashed water on his face and arms. His face was haggard and dark with patches of stubble, and his shirt bore clumsy stains and spots of sweat. He had checked his eyes for the first traces of blood. Exhaustion weakened his immunity, but he saw no symptoms of the Marburg virus he had injected into his bloodstream at the lab in Koltsovo.

It was a desperate measure, but he had no choice. The Russians could not find what he did not carry. Only his treatment, which looked like aspirin tablets, in a vial prescribed with his name. He had created the antivirus himself, but it wasn't sufficiently tested. It was a risk, but he could wait no longer. A woman journalist who spoke exquisite French would meet him in Istanbul. He would tell her his story, and he would be free of them. Free from the guilt. From everything.

Out the window he hoped to see the flight crew waving the jetliner away from the gate. There was no commotion, no more thumping as the crew tossed bags into the belly of the plane. To the east, night crept behind the mountains far beyond, and he longed to hide in that coming darkness.

The girl spoke to him in Georgian. He looked at her and wondered about the French journalist he would meet soon. Kamran shrugged meekly and wondered why someone as lovely as she would speak to him. His seat mate tried again in Russian.

"*Are you from Istanbul?*" she said.

He shook his head. "*Iran.*"

She seemed surprised. "*Is that so? I thought you might be going home.*"

He could never return home. Not with what he had done to the Russian lab where he worked until two days ago. Now the virus within him was his only insurance, but going home would never be part of any deal.

"No. I am visiting."

"Me, too. I'm Ana." She smiled at him and made a timid wave with her hand.

"Is it always like this, Ana?" he asked, tapping his watch.

"Yes, yes. Always." She sighed and rolled her eyes.

He checked his watch. A minute passed, then another while he fidgeted with the slack gold band. Perspiration beaded in the small of his back. He closed his eyes and breathed, hoping to pass the time peacefully. He felt his face and forehead for any sign of fever. No, it was only his ragged nerves.

Chatter erupted from the rear of the plane, racing among the passengers to his seat near the front. Georgians and Turks and a half-dozen others barked to one another about a commotion out on the tarmac. Kamran leaned forward to peek through a sliver of window far on the left side of the plane.

Bearded men with rifles poured out the side door of a Russian armored carrier—an eight-wheeled beast that looked like a great steel caterpillar. The turret spun leftward, then froze menacingly at the Tbilisi terminal. Pieces of a mangled wire fence hung from the front of the monstrous vehicle from where it had burst through the airport perimeter.

A pair of armed men raced beneath the plane and up the steel stairs to the gangway.

Screams erupted around Kamran. Some passengers jumped from their seats and clawed at overhead bins in a panic.

The attendants shouted at the frantic passengers. "Sit down! For the love of god, do not move!" One raced to the open cockpit door to alert the pilots. The other moved to the aircraft's exit and pulled it shut in a panic.

Kamran remained silent in his seat, frozen in terror as the chaos tumbled around him. Time moved slower still for him as his pulse pounded in his ears. He felt sick, but he lost all thought of the virus. *How could they know? The border guards seemed too suspicious. They are not coming for me,* he assured himself. But the thought faded, and he sank into his seat. He didn't want to die.

Beside him, Ana whimpered a mute phrase. A prayer perhaps. Her hand trembled, and then she gripped his arm in white-knuckled fright. Her strength surprised him—hurt him, even, and shook his senses.

At the front of the cabin the flight attendant stared through the closed door's window at the pair of armed men. One of them held a young man, a member of the ground crew he'd dragged up from the tarmac. The other man pushed the barrel of his rifle to the man's temple, then pointed at the attendant, motioning for her to open.

"Do not open the door!" her fellow flight attendant screamed from the cockpit door. The pilots echoed her as they leaned out the cockpit shouting.

The flight attendant screamed. A splatter of blood hit the window as the young man fell away from the window.

More armed men appeared on the gangway. They brought with them another crewman. Again, the man pushed his rifle's scalding barrel to the young man's head and motioned through the bloody window for her to open the door.

"Do not open! Don't do it," said the pilot. He stepped back into the cockpit and murmured something into his headset.

Kamran leaned forward and saw the men press the crewman against the aircraft door, their rifles now aimed at the back of his head and into the cabin. The attendant stared at the crewman, and their eyes locked in terror for a moment. She reached out, first at the crewman's face, then with a shudder of hesitation at the door latch. Kamran wanted to shout to her, to plead with her along with the crew. He could see it was too late. She wished to save the man, but it would doom everyone on board. Resigned, the weeping attendant opened the cabin door.

The men moved quickly. Six of them entered, shuffling past the attendant, who had pressed herself against the forward wall, loathe to touch the killers. They blocked Kamran's view, standing in a huddle with the attendant now between them and the open door.

Kamran heard the unmistakable crack of a Kalashnikov rifle. He had heard it enough over the years. In his home in Iran, even for a wealthy family like his, it was a sound as familiar as thunder. Ana dug her nails into Kamran's left arm. The flight attendant lay bleeding, abandoned on the gangway next to the dead crew man. The cabin door shut.

One of the men grabbed the intercom transmitter and spoke in rumbling Russian.

"We commandeer this plane for the Chechen nation. Remain calm, and there will be no more problems."

Nervous chatter died down in seconds to a tense calm of tiny gasps and whimpers. The speaker scanned the cabin as his men spaced themselves down the aisle, rifles tucked under their arms. He wore camouflage fatigues with no insignias and a short-brimmed hat. His beard was neatly trimmed, and the shape of it lengthened his pudgy, weathered face and squat nose.

The Chechens gave Kamran little to hope for. *Surely, they are not here for me,* he thought again. This was not how the Russians would take their revenge on him. But he would die just the same. The vice in his chest tightened again. He felt like crying, but the thought of it shamed him.

Behind the bearded Chechen near the cockpit door he saw another man dressed unlike the others. He wore a long, dark jacket and carried no weapon that Kamran could see. He dropped a bulky duffel bag, which he unzipped and from it removed a black harness. When he turned slightly to whisper to the leader, Kamran saw his face, clean shaven and sallow, his scalp cropped close with blond stubble. He was no Chechen. That much Kamran knew from his Slavic steel eyes and paler face and hair. He was subtler and more unassuming than the rugged Chechens, his movements quick and precise. Kamran's unease deepened, and at that moment he sensed this was no ill fortune interrupting his escape. That man had come for him.

The bearded leader entered the cockpit with his rifle at the ready. *"Take off. Immediately."*

The pilots raised their hands and talked over one another, protesting his command.

"I have just given you all the clearance required," the leader said. *"Now."*

Defeated, the pilot adjusted his headset and argued with the airport's controllers. Behind him, the Chechen stood in the doorway motionless, his head cocked back, his eyes fixed on the frantic pilot. The engines whined, and the plane lurched and rollicked, then rolled backward.

Kamran watched from his window seat as the concrete rolled beneath the plane. Small crowds of people had gathered outside the fence to watch while a pair of policemen waved helplessly to herd them out of danger.

Their faces faded, and the world pulled away with them. Kamran felt locked in place, at the center of a whirlwind that pushed everything from focus. In a crescendo of keening engines, the earth and dry grasses sped by ever faster and then fell away from below, disappearing in terrible minutes under the dark wisps of clouds.

With the cabin leveled after takeoff, the crouching Chechens in the aisle stood upright. One let out a cheer praising Allah, and the others joined. They seemed to relax, becoming at once more jovial and more brutish. The men tossed bottles of water to one another from the rear of the plane. One old Georgian man's disapproving glare won him sharp strike to his head with a rifle butt. A trickle of blood dripped down the man's forehead, and he ducked lower into his seat, hands raised.

The whimpers died down, and the passengers' whispers quieted too low to hear. Many minutes passed with only the grind of the engines in the cabin. Beside him, Ana said nothing. She released her grip and curled herself into her seat. She pulled her arms within her colorful shirt sleeves and wrapped them about herself in a futile cocoon. Kamran wished he could say something to her and allay her fears. But what could he say? Every doubt crept in his mind as it did always with women. They wanted nothing to do with any man like him. They thought him too strange or weak willed. He manufactured every reason to avoid those women who drank champagne from the bottle and laughed in the chill night air at Koltsovo.

A voice spoke Russian, interrupting his anxious thoughts. "*Dr. Khorasani?*"

The Slavic man stood before him. He held a crumpled piece of paper, a printout of Kamran's face from a security photo taken years ago. In his other hand dangled the black harness he had pulled from the bag, similar to the one the man now wore himself. "*You are Kamran Khorasani?*"

Kamran could barely speak. "*What is this? Who are you?*"

"*Get up. Come with me.*" He motioned to the rear.

Kamran hesitated, then stood. Ana sat up, wide-eyed. How he longed for her easy smile now to allay his own terror. They had come for him alone.

He anticipated the pain, and that itself was a kind of agony that drained him of any will to resist. His father would be ashamed of him. But he would not be surprised.

"*It is all right,*" Kamran said to Ana. "*It will be all right.*"

It wouldn't, but he thought of nothing else to say. At least he had said something to her.

Kamran maneuvered down the aisle with his captor close behind. He squeezed past the leering Chechens and climbed over panicked passengers' legs to the rear near the bathrooms and drink cart.

"*Put this on.*" The man shoved the black harness into his chest. "*Like this.*" He motioned with his legs.

"*Are you insane? I'm not doing that. What is this?*"

The man shrugged. In a blur his hand reached out and clutched Kamran's throat. The crumpled photo fell to the floor as he tightened his grip.

"*Listen to me, doctor. I don't fucking care what you will and won't do. You're putting this on and will do what I say. You can go willingly, or I can beat the life out of you and drag you instead. You should be so lucky to leave,*" he said as he tossed his head back toward the other passengers.

Kamran gasped for air as he stared at the man's face. He nodded in a panic. He stepped through the straps of the harness. While he did, the man pulled a band of explosive charges from a satchel and pasted it on the rear door. He signaled to the Chechens, who passed word to each man down the aisle up to the cockpit. Moments later, the engine's pitch whined lower and lower. Kamran's ears popped. His stomach lurched into his aching throat as the plane descended.

"*This can't be right. We'll die,*" Kamran said.

No response came. The man tugged at Kamran's harness and pulled the straps snug. He shoved Kamran back into the aisle and followed, ducking behind the rear bulkhead. The bearded Chechen met them and crouched to speak.

"*Andrei, my old friend, we are ready. The plane is ours, yes? As agreed. With old debts paid, it is time to say goodbye.*"

"Do svidaniya, dukhi," Andrei said.

The Chechen let out a belly laugh and slapped Andrei on the shoulder. He shouted something to his men, and they all crouched low in the aisle.

From behind him, Andrei lowered a pair of goggles over Kamran's eyes, then snapped several carabineers locking the two men together. The man's breath heated the back of Kamran's neck. It reeked of tobacco.

"Hold on to something, doctor."

Kamran gripped the seat in front of him. A sharp crack compressed the cabin air and ripped into his ears. The sudden burst shook the cabin with less force than he expected, but it was no less terrifying. The plane shuddered and dipped leftward. Air rushed through the cabin toward the rear. He fought his heaving stomach.

"Move," Andrei shouted into his ringing ears.

Kamran trudged to the rear again, half carried by Andrei. The door was mostly intact, though the window had cracked and a smoking hole no larger than his fist smoldered near the center. With a violent tug, Andrei pulled the lever and heaved the door outward.

The rushing air knocked Kamran from his feet. Air sucked from his lungs in a scream that never reached his ears. He tried to stand. With another shove, Andrei pushed them both out into the night air.

Somewhere behind and above him the engines pealed in a steady roar. Below him yawned only bleak darkness. There were no pinpricks of light or signs of civilization. Together the two men tumbled through a windy void, invisible and silent. He was too terrified to scream anymore.

Andrei tugged the ripcord, and the harness holding them together snapped tight against Kamran's chest and groin. The upward gale ceased, and they glided through the quieted air, spiraling slowly downward.

Behind him, Andrei reached into a chest pocket and pulled out a small transmitter. He waited, scanning the sky above, then pressed the button. Aboard flight PC463, now almost fourteen kilometers away, a canvas suicide vest laden with explosives lay hidden in Andrei's duffel bag. The signal from the device triggered an electric charge to a detonator, and the daisy chain of explosives ignited. The plane and its occupants disintegrated.

Kamran lifted his head to see the vibrant orange and yellow explosion far off and above, beyond thin clouds. He knew what he'd seen and cried out. The pretty girl Ana and the old Georgian man—all of them gone in milliseconds. All dead because of what he carried out of the lab in Koltsovo. Blood for blood.

Andrei said nothing as the pair glided down for minutes. Kamran saw a faint glint of moonlight on an uneven plane of roiling black glass that rose up before him. They splashed into the Black Sea, frozen by the dark water but alive.

PART I

The Passenger

CHAPTER 1

CHASING PHANTOMS

Tbilisi, Georgia
7:54 p.m., Monday, May 6

Ethan Pierce stepped down from the agency Learjet and scanned the terminal at the far side of the Tbilisi Airport runway. Two-hundred yards away, twin gangways stretched out over the tarmac. A roaring jetliner parked at the end of one gangway awaited passengers who moved like little quivering shadows behind glass. At the end of the other, tatters of yellow tape whipped in the hot wind. Georgian police had removed the two bodies that had lain there barely twenty-four hours earlier—one a crewman, the other a young flight attendant who made a terrible choice. Now 183 people were dead, and Ethan had to find actionable intelligence before more died.

Two fellow CIA officers followed behind him, shielding their eyes from the glare of the setting sun. Wade Dixon squinted, batting away the hours of sleep from the flight, as he took in the scene. Wade could sleep through anything, a knack he'd learned in the Marines. Ethan once spent a long night with Wade after a failed agency operation in an Afghanistan village during a mortar attack. Wade had snored for two hours while Ethan waited out the explosions on his haunches, shivering and starting at the delayed bursts of mortar shells in the nearby neighborhood.

The new face that trailed behind was Marcus Eldridge, a young language officer who three months ago was still training at the Farm. But Eldridge spoke Russian fluently with a passable handle on Georgian. They needed his expertise for this operation, but Ethan didn't need another unknown in the form of a rookie. Marcus surveyed the scene and whistled. No one else could hear him amid the drone of taxiing jetliners, but still the reaction grated Ethan's senses.

There wasn't much to learn from the scene at this distance. Wade's eyes were sharper than his, but Ethan could still see the baggage carts parked at awkward angles below the empty gangway. The dead passengers' luggage spilled out on the ground. Next to them the eight-wheeled BTR towered over the scattered luggage. More shreds of yellow tape surrounded the armored personnel carrier, as if to pen the thing in with the feeble strands. Georgian soldiers walked lazy circuits around the vehicle. Its side door hung open, a last and lingering sign of the hijackers' deadly plan.

They moved to a vacant hangar that swallowed up the sounds of the airport and echoed with the squeaking of their shoes on the epoxied concrete. A checkerboard of lights reflected on its surface, shifting as they crossed the expanse. Two men in suits stood at the far end waiting for them, standing like untouched chess pieces in their black and gray wool. The taller man greeted them with a curt handshake for each.

"Gentlemen." His mouth barely moved.

"You must be Alan Sanger," Ethan said. "Paul Corso says hello."

Alan was Chief of Station in Georgia, a veteran Agency man who had risen through the ranks over years of maneuvering in a tumultuous country up against the hard edge of Russia and a stew of ethnic tensions. Ethan's supervisor, Paul Corso, had warned him about Sanger—his exact words were *horse's ass*. What he meant was that Sanger would resist the team's need to move quickly.

"I'm sure he does," Sanger said with a slight frown. "Is Corso still burning the midnight oil trying to save the world?"

"When he has to."

"He's got more reason than ever now. Follow me. We'll take you to your flat where you can all settle in."

Outside, a conspicuous Chevy Suburban with windows as dark as its paint waited with the engine purring, heat emanating from beneath the vehicle in a visible blur. Wade carried most of their gear. He heaved his bulging duffel bag into the vehicle's rear with ease, along with Marcus' knapsack, while Marcus climbed into the rear seat row.

For his part, Ethan traveled light. When Corso had called him at his old apartment just twenty hours earlier, he had stuffed two wrinkled shirts, a toothbrush, and his holstered Beretta into a small duffel bag. From his half-empty dresser he had grabbed a newly minted passport with the name Ryan Sawyer and a recent photo of his dark hair growing over his ears, an affectation he'd acquired more from idleness than fashion on his last excursion in Istanbul. He left behind an older photo, one he kept in a frame atop the dresser. Then his hair was shorter and lighter, and Sarah still smiled next to him, locked in a moment that seemed like someone else's life. In a way, it was. Leaving the quiet apartment for Tbilisi was his duty, but it came as a needed relief.

"So, what have we got?" Ethan said once he stowed his bag at his feet.

Wade took the seat next to him and shut off the hum of the engines outside. The Suburban left the airport gate and merged onto a busy highway that flowed into the heart of the city. Sanger sat in the front passenger seat. Ethan watched the balding spot on his head as he looked up into the visor mirror to address them, his face sober as a tomb.

"I want to make one thing perfectly clear to the three of you. Georgia is my responsibility. This thing is more volatile than you realize from both sides of the border. You're not going to come in here and scare off what my teams have worked a long time to build just to placate an over-eager deputy director."

"This isn't our first day of school. We know how it works," Ethan said. That was mostly true. He didn't want to mention Marcus, and he hoped Sanger wouldn't push it. He hoped even more Marcus was smart enough to stay quiet.

"Look, I don't know you. My people don't know you. You're here because Corso thinks you can do something we can't. I doubt that's the case. But we're all batting for the same team here, so my people will assist you," Sanger said. He turned from the mirror to face the three of them in the back of the Suburban.

"But do not get in our way. You do not come and go as you please. You stand out too much here. Just work with our agents under my officers' supervision. You don't talk to the Georgians without my say so. None of you so much as takes a shit without my approval. Do we understand each other?"

Ethan understood very well. Like all station chiefs he'd worked with on operations, Sanger protected his turf—and his dominance. Ethan had no time for it. Corso's comments about Sanger echoed in his mind. He envied his boss' ability to cut agency politics to the bone, and he fought a smirk, then matched Sanger's glare with an expression as stern and stubborn.

"Understood," he said, tilting his head. "Now what can you tell us?"

Sanger calmed slightly. He turned again to the front as the Suburban wove among speeding traffic headed into downtown. Ethan had called his bluff for now.

Tbilisi lay ahead, thickening with more modern buildings hemmed in by steep foothills covered with trees and looming electrical towers. It was a city shedding its old skin, trying and frequently failing to slough off the troubles of the old empire and enter a new world. Ethan sensed more trouble lurking somewhere ahead of him. The trick was finding it before the trouble found them.

"They briefed you on Pankisi Gorge, I take it?" Sanger said.

Ethan knew the place by reputation. He'd read more than twenty briefs alone on the flight. Jihadists had been crossing the border from Chechnya there for years, and the traffic steadily increased since Chechen strongman Ramzan Kadyrov had clamped down his domain to the north to curry favor with Vladimir Putin. The valley had become an artery of rage, exporting violent men into hotter war zones across the Middle East.

"That where we're headed?" Marcus asked.

Ethan winced, trying to avoid Sanger's notice as he glared in the mirror.

"Settle down, Rambo," Sanger said as he scowled in the mirror at Marcus, then shifted his ire again to Ethan. "This is what I'm fucking talking about, Pierce. I'm not putting up with Corso's antics under my watch. I will put you back on that plane right now."

Ethan leaned back, waving his hands casually. "You're right. That's not the plan. We just want to get pointed in the right direction. Marcus is just eager to do the right thing here. We all are. So, tell us what your teams are reporting, and we'll figure out how we can help."

Sanger sighed. "We have a promising lead for you. We've been chasing phantoms in the gorge for years. In the last twenty-four hours, we reached out to every agent we could. Two of them pointed to the same contact. A smuggler in Pankisi Gorge."

"Does this phantom have a name? Any verification at all?" Ethan said.

"*Al Jamal.* It's a flimsy *nom de guerre*. Not much else on the individual's identity. But it matches earlier activity. We've known about this one for a while. The Georgians have apprehended several smugglers in the last couple years. Arms dealers, human traffickers, sympathizers, that kind of thing. *Al Jamal* has eluded them."

"For now," Wade said.

Sanger shook his head—a slight tic that Ethan almost missed. Wade had scanned out the window since leaving the airport, his head swiveling at every curve of the road and turn of the city's structures. Wade seemed to ignore Sanger's ranting, but Ethan knew he heard every detail.

"We suspect the hijackers were in the country for at least a week, which means *Al Jamal* probably sheltered them, and probably knows more about them," Sanger said.

"Then we need to make contact," Ethan said.

Sanger chuckled. "The Georgians can't even seem to do that. We need to tread carefully here, or we'll scare him away."

Marcus spoke up again. "*Al Jamal* knows you. Knows all your agents in the field. And the Georgians most of all. He doesn't know us."

"He knows you're American. That's all that matters."

"So, I make sure he thinks I'm Russian. That I can do," Marcus said.

For the first time since meeting him, Ethan sensed Marcus relax. His voice grew louder, his pace slower and less anxious. Sanger hadn't intimidated him either, and Ethan now saw what Corso had seen in him. He might just work out after all.

"You said *Al Jamal* eluded the Georgians," Ethan said. "You didn't say anything about him eluding your officers. It's not much of a lead if you don't have anything to give us."

Sanger paused, considering the next move. Ethan guessed Sanger would either open up to them now or shut down their operation before it started. He let the quiet fill the air—he'd already pushed Sanger's pride too much.

Sanger finally spoke. "One of our assets provided a number," Sanger said. "We shared with SIGINT, but there's no activity since the hijacking."

"Then we start some activity. My team makes contact, offering to arrange an arms deal attractive enough for him to listen. You supervise. Loop in the Georgians, if you think it will help. Just let us get started."

Sanger grimaced. "All right. But you go with my officer. And Georgian intelligence. They won't let this one go."

"Fine by me, but my team makes initial contact."

Sanger made a call while the driver knifed his way through the city's center. They cruised along the river, where a postmodern government building shaped like a clump of white mushrooms glinted in the morning sun amid the older buildings and church spires. Next to Ethan, Wade kept quiet and still save for his fingers tapping on his thigh like a hidden code. From the back, Marcus whispered ideas in Ethan's ear while he nodded, trying to listen as Sanger grunted commands into his phone.

They coursed north of town near the U.S. Embassy. The driver pulled behind a sleepy apartment building filled, Ethan knew, with embassy staff. Some lounged on narrow second floor balconies drinking beer, smoking from their stocks of American cigarettes.

Wade grabbed their gear from the back while Ethan met Sanger at the passenger window.

"I'm giving you more leash than I'd like," Sanger said. "Don't make me regret it." He flashed his phone to Ethan, then rolled the tinted window up without another word.

"Can't say I'm sorry to see him go," Wade said. "You get the number?"

Ethan nodded. "Find our car. You and Marcus trade it with someone. Get us something that blends in better, especially out of the city. We leave tonight."

Marcus gaped at the change in plan. "He won't like it," he said, motioning at the fading break lights of the Suburban.

"No. But Corso will," Ethan said. "Let's go."

* * *

By Wednesday evening, Ethan perched low on a ridge in the Pankisi Gorge watching for a target whose identity he still didn't know. He peered through small binoculars ill-suited to the range. Nothing stirred below, and he wondered not for the first time if they had been played.

Wade lay in a stand of long grass beside him surveying the nearby valley through a heavy scope mounted on a Dragunov rifle. The old Soviet weapon wasn't Wade's first choice. He was particular about his firearms, though his days as a Marine taught him to go with rugged and reliable. Firearms were almost as easy to acquire here as the car, and in this case the quality was equally lousy.

Long shadows fell into the valley as the sun set behind them and the mountain air cooled. The valley stretched north and south where sparse village lights dotted the shallow banks of the Alazani River. The gorge was home to Kists, a little-known minority of Chechen Muslims from centuries-old wars. Their modern counterparts now found refuge among them, driven out by back-to-back wars in Chechnya and the hard hand of Kadyrov. Somewhere among these dispossessed was *Al Jamal*. Somewhere too,

Ethan knew, were the answers Corso demanded—the jagged pieces of a puzzle scattered from here to the bottom of the Black Sea.

"What do you think?" Ethan asked. He talked into his sleeve.

"I think this is bullshit," Wade said.

"Maybe. You think Sanger's source is playing us?"

"You think too damn much. What's bullshit is getting plopped right down here, and I haven't even had time to sight this piece in. It's like trying to score on an ugly ass blind date set up by my sister."

"My heart bleeds, big guy." Ethan said.

"It might if I have to cover you with this thing."

Below their position was a ramshackle farmhouse nestled at the western edge of the valley floor, far away from the nearest village. Its paint had faded and chipped away from long years of neglect, and the broad, low angled roof lacked tiles in places. At its side was a shed almost the same size as the house and in poorer shape. It nearly leaned against the house, its sideboards angled and askew under the curl of the corroded metal roof. Twin doors of dry, gray wood clasped together clumsily with a wooden latch. Yew trees sprouted up between the house and nearby road, and a low stone wall provided some privacy to the small yard where nothing moved. For Wade, the yard was an ideal position. A near perfect kill zone, but resorting to that meant their operation had failed. Worse, he and Marcus would have nowhere to go. Ethan didn't like the risk, especially with an inexperienced officer at his side. For them the place was a trap.

He heard the whine of the old Mercedes from far down the road. The car was the best Marcus and Wade could find back in Tbilisi. They needed a car for amateurish arms dealers, not intelligence officers masquerading as diplomats. It was plausible enough for Ethan's plan, so long as the engine kept running. The car's screech warned of imminent malfunction.

"Here he comes," Ethan whispered. He patted Wade's shoulder. "That's my cue. I'm headed down for the meet."

"You think he's ready for this?" Wade said.

"He's ready."

Wade nodded without taking his eyes off the farmhouse. He nibbled on a long stalk of grass, but the rest of his body lay flat and almost perfectly still.

Ethan crouched low and moved away from Wade's position. He slid down a slope and found a steep path that lead to a small pasture north of the yard. Below him, the Mercedes wove down the rural road, then groaned as Marcus slowed to await his arrival. Ethan climbed in, and Marcus turned on to the long farmhouse lane. Once inside the stone wall, Marcus killed the screeching engine. They waited. Nothing. Marcus opened the car door and stood in the yard, his hands open and at his side. Ethan followed, staying on his side of the car. He'd let Marcus do the talking, as they had planned.

A man appeared in the doorway. He shined a bright light on them. It wasn't yet dark, but the light stung Ethan's eyes. The man approached with the flashlight aloft. It was a simple trick, disarming and clever. Ethan couldn't see any of the man's face, and he held his hand high to block the glare. The man spoke as he came forward.

"*You are the Russian from the phone?*"

"*Konechno,*" Marcus said. *Of course.*

"*Where from?*"

Marcus shrugged. "*Stavropol.*"

"*You don't seem much like someone from Stavropol.*"

"*And you don't seem much like Al Jamal.*"

The man lowered the light and his revealed face cracked an amused grin. Lines stretched across his leathered face. He appeared as broken down as his weary abode, worn from living between nations and eras. Nothing about the man alarmed Ethan. He seemed fixed here as though part of the scenery. He wore a checked shirt that tugged and bulged around a pot belly, partly untucked from his brown trousers. He was an unkempt, if well fed, local in a dilapidated house. Only his mischievous grin suggested otherwise.

He scratched the back of his head and said, "*Let us see what you have for us.*"

These were the old man's last words. The flashlight fell to the ground, distracting Ethan from watching a single wound tear through the old man's neck. In the span of a half breath, the report of the rifle shot punctuated the quiet evening. Marcus lunged instinctively toward the Mercedes as Ethan crouched around the rear. He heard a second shot as he rounded to Marcus' side of the car. Blood already swelled at Marcus' side. Stunned, Marcus slid to the earth.

Ethan called into his radio. "What the hell are you doing? Hold fire!"

Wade's voice crackled a reply in Ethan's earpiece. "Negative. Wasn't me. We got another shooter, long way off southeast. I can't spot him. Looking …"

In the dim light he saw the outline of the old man slumped in the yard. Beside him, Marcus leaned against the Mercedes with his hands clutching his left side.

"Marcus," Ethan yelled at his comrade. "Marcus!"

Marcus stayed silent. It wasn't panic in his eyes. It was disbelief. In the waning light, the blood on Marcus' hands looked like black oil. The blood consumed light, ever expanding in a dark pool on the ground around him.

"Marcus, listen to me," Ethan said. "You're going to make it. Hold on, chief."

He wasn't so sure. Marcus didn't need to hear that now. Blood pumped out of his side, spilling on the ground. Ethan tore off his own shirt and balled it up to staunch the flow. He pressed it into Marcus' side.

"Oh shit …" Marcus moaned.

"Easy, chief. Hang on." He tapped his transmitter again. "Marcus is down. Repeat, man down."

Again, Marcus tried to speak. "It's not *Jamal* …" His words fell away.

A grinding noise came from the farm shack where an old engine roared to life. Headlights streamed between the sagging doors' planks. Ethan looked up just as a car burst through the doors and launched into the yard. It swerved to miss the old man's body. Ethan piled on top of Marcus to get out of the way. He caught a glimpse of the driver, a slight silhouette covered with a patterned scarf. The car spat gravel and dust into the air, then raced toward the lane.

Wade's voice filled his earpiece. "I'm taking the shot."

Wade fired from his position, but the round flew high. The car kept moving, veering for the lane. Another shot punched a hole just rear of the driver's side, and the car bounced down the lane.

"Damn it!" Wade shouted over the radio.

Ethan focused on Marcus. The young man's eyes drooped, light fading from them rapidly. He coughed. It was a sputtering, useless thing to do. Ethan stared into his eyes thinking all the while how miserable it would be to drown in one's own blood. He fought a wellspring of rage that came up from his stomach into the back of his throat. This was his op, ending in disaster before it started. The thought took over his mind. He glanced at the dead old man, then at a far hillside where the killing shot came from. He turned to spot the car down the lane. Marcus had tried to tell him. This op wasn't over. It was getting away from them.

He settled Marcus to the ground. The makeshift bandage soaked through with blood and seeped onto Ethan's hands. He leaned over, his ear close to Marcus' mouth. Only short breaths teased his ear. Ethan pressed Marcus' own hands to hold the shirt to his wounded side. There was little strength left in them, but it would have to do.

"Get down here," he told Wade over the radio. "*Al Jamal's* getting away from us."

Wade replied between breaths. "Already moving."

Marcus' chest seized in short gasps. His eyes widened in desperation. Ethan mumbled something to comfort him. What could he say? He hardly knew the man. Where he was born, who his parents were. If he had a wife somewhere. But he could see something of himself in Marcus then and the eagerness of his younger days. Behind him, Ethan heard the car racing down the rocky lane, and he made the calculation to leave the dying man alone.

"He's fading. I've got to leave him. I have to do this."

"Do it. I got this," Wade said. "Go."

He climbed in the car, stepping over Marcus' shivering body. The engine sputtered, then howled defiantly as he put the car in gear. As he closed the door, Ethan saw Marcus staring up at the twilit sky in a strange country. He sped away from the yard with Marcus' face burned in his mind's eye.

The car whined and roared as he hit uneven mounds along the lane. The motion tossed him high in the seat. He shifted gear. His eyes darted for sign of the other car, but he saw no lights or movement. Past the yew trees he spied a fading wink of red to his north. Ethan dimmed the headlights, hoping he could close the distance with *Al Jamal* unaware of his pursuit. He veered onto the road and accelerated.

A half mile ahead, the taillights turned toward Birkiani, the nearby village. Once there, his quarry was lost. Ethan knew he'd turn to allies to hide. Even if he did overtake *Al Jamal* there, he could do nothing alone with hostile witnesses all around.

He pressed the wailing car, ever closer to the target. Now he could see the other car's silhouette. It was one of the old Fiat-based models from Soviet days. At this distance, there was no point in hiding. The noise from the Mercedes' grinding belts would give him away from a hundred meters or more. He flipped on the lights and kicked the dimmer switch. Ahead, the car swerved, and the driver spun around to spot him.

The faded yellow lights of the village shone barely a kilometer away. Ethan pulled within a car length. He veered right. Just a little more to nudge the back wheel. He clenched his teeth anticipating the collision.

Al Jamal veered hard left. Tires skidded across the broken asphalt. The little car bounced into a shallow ditch, then mounted over it again onto a barren field. Ethan turned hard on the wheel to follow when his headlights passed a painted sign. A skull and bones in a red triangle flashed in front of him.

"Oh shit," he said aloud.

Land mines—no doubt part of *Al Jamal's* contingency plan. Maybe the field was a bluff, a smuggler's trick to shake Georgian authorities. Either *Al Jamal* knew the course through the field, or there were no mines at all. There was one way to find out and avoid letting Marcus die for nothing. Ethan shifted to reverse. Gears ground in the bowels of the Mercedes, and the car shuddered. He steered the car at the gouges in the roadside where *Al Jamal* had entered.

He found the taillights again, moving almost leisurely through the field. He drove toward the lights directly, with no other option and bare hints of tire tracks to trail. It was reckless, and he knew it. The night had run far past reckless. This was stupid. Only Corso could approve.

The little car kept rolling, but Ethan gained. He downshifted as the engine protested again. Ethan rammed straight into the car, shoving it forward slightly. His head snapped back. Steel hammered on steel. Ethan bit his tongue and tasted copper.

The front car shook from the impact, and both vehicles twisted to a halt in the desolate middle of the field. The Mercedes creaked, and the engine finally died. Ethan gripped the wheel with one hand and stared at the driver. He felt for his sidearm, then climbed out of the car, one cautious foot at a time. Ahead, the driver door opened, and a slim figure emerged, still covered with the scarf.

Ethan raised his Beretta and shouted in broken Arabic, a phrase he'd memorized more than understood. *"Don't move. Show me your hands!"*

The driver raised a pair of delicate hands that reflected bright white from the Mercedes' headlights. A high voice tinged with anger called out. "Is that how you treat women in America?"

Before him stood a woman. She spoke English well enough. She was a slender thing with an oval face and pouting lips. Her eyes squinted in the light as she wrinkled her nose—at him or from the glare, he wasn't sure. Her lips parted as she stared. She wore snug, black pants and a plain, collared shirt. The scarf covered much of her head, but strands of a pair of dark brown hair dropped down the left side of her face. He stared at the face of an exquisite doll, the most remarkable phantom he'd tracked in nine years.

"You're *Al Jamal*?"

"*Jamal*? *Jamal* is camel. I am *Jamila*," she said, pointing at herself. "It means beauty. Now, please, put your gun away and we go out the way we came in. Then we discuss a deal, yes?"

CHAPTER 2

TIDAL ECHO

McLean, Virginia
6:48 p.m., Wednesday, May 8

OVER THE course of eighteen years, Paul Corso kept track of time in his head out of habit. Even a glimpse of daylight through a courtyard window had less effect on his mind than a glance at his watch's minute hand and an instinctive adjustment for time zones halfway around the world. Seven hours ago, it was sundown in Pankisi Gorge. Six hours ago, he lost an officer.

The light inside Langley never changed. A permanent fluorescence filled the labyrinthine halls and glinted off rows of closed doors. He stood at the door of his supervisor, Suzanne Tasker. When they spoke on the phone earlier about Marcus Eldridge, she had asked two questions. Does the operation still have cover? And did Eldridge have a family? More questions awaited him. He had some of his own, and he wasn't going to get many answered from Georgia where it was almost 3:00 a.m.

Suzanne's assistant smiled meekly when Paul looked her way. Twelve minutes ago, she had greeted him with a quiet hello. "She's on the phone with Director Drummond," she had said.

She went back to her screen, and the faint hum of white noise filled the empty distance between them. He couldn't recall her name. Like everyone,

Corso had acclimated to seeing strangers in the hall over and over again. He recognized most people by their habits and hairstyles, left to wonder about their names. They were younger and younger. Some barely older than his boys. They didn't speak much in the halls, and over the years the distance between personal and professional lengthened.

The door opened, and he met Suzanne face to face. She looked as freshly made up as she had at the 7:00 a.m. meeting, a mask that never faltered and never revealed its secrets.

"Paul, come in."

She waved at her assistant, who gathered her things to leave while there was still daylight left. The same languid fluorescence filled her office, which occupied an ample space in the middle of the old building, insulated from the luxury—and intolerable risk for the Director of the National Clandestine Service—of windows. Paul slumped in one of the cushioned chairs positioned in front of her desk.

"What's the latest?" she said.

Too impatient for pleasantries, he noted. The door closed.

Paul shared what he knew. His voice rasped, though he hadn't had a smoke in two years. Somewhere in the base of his brain the urge lurked. He fought it back amid the noise in his head and kept talking.

"Alan Sanger managed to get our embassy to step in. They've got a consular officer escorting Eldridge's body to a Tbilisi hospital. We fly him home in a few days, God willing. It's going to take some work to keep a lid on a murder investigation, so Sanger's pushing the cover a little farther in hopes it will stick."

"Which is?"

"Officially? Marcus Eldridge was a young engineering student who took a little evening trip to score some recreational drugs. The deal went south, and he got shot by dealers."

She narrowed her gaze in thought. "That's not going to do it."

"No. It's pretty thin. We've got a dead local and an empty house. We're going to have to lean on the Georgians to keep their eyes on the prize."

"We don't have much of a prize, Paul. I have to tell you, it's three days out. I just got off the phone with the Director. You've got four teams running around, and everyone in HUMINT is knocking on doors. Your crew here looks like amateur hour. Now we're spending time covering their tracks and wasting valuable time in getting to the bottom of this Chechen group."

Her ability to keep calm astounded him. Yelling he could handle. All of her predecessors were yellers. She seethed, and he loathed the tightened look on her face. He tugged at his collar. He had removed his tie around noon when Pierce updated him on Eldridge.

"Suzanne, with respect, it's not amateur hour," he said.

"Really? I expect better of you. I mean it. I understand you want to defend your guys, but this is … this is unacceptable, honestly."

Her rebuke stung, and for what seemed like the hundredth time he thought about losing Eldridge. *What the hell happened?* Something wasn't right.

"There is some good news," he said. "Pierce pursued the asset. Picked her up in a mine field."

"Her?"

He fought back a smile. "That's the part that surprises you about what I just said?"

She waved his comment off with a flick of her hand. "Anything from her yet?"

"Not much. They're moving her to a house for now. One of ours. She had a nickname that covered her identity pretty well." Corso didn't share that the intel got the Arabic wrong. "She's from Chechnya. That's pretty clear. Pierce thinks her name is …" Paul fetched a pair of half-rimmed glasses from his breast pocket and glanced at his notebook. "Seda Alaskhanova. But she had three passports."

Suzanne nodded. "That's fine, but we need leads on our perps, not her. Pierce is with her now?"

"Yes. And Wade Dixon."

"Anyone else?" she asked.

"Sanger's got an operations officer on the way."

With her elbows propped on the desk and her hands folded, Suzanne leaned in intently.

"Drummond seems to think we have more to gain cooperating with the Georgians. Hand her over to GIS. They'll cooperate on our little situation here, and we can pick up the pace. This op is over, Paul. Focus on your other teams."

"Christ, Suzanne, that's a fantastic way to avoid amateur hour. Are you kidding me? Oh yes, the almighty has spoken, and we need results. Does anyone honestly think we're going to move faster now with this brilliant stratagem? Do you? We've been on the ground three days, have a target in custody, and we're not moving quickly enough? And now with the best lead … no, the only lead we've got, Drummond tells you to pull the plug and hand her over to the Georgians? Push back, damn it."

"Save it," she said. "Get it done."

Paul stomped out of the office without another word. He paced down the halls, retracing his steps to his teams' operations center. He had to give her credit. She didn't lose her cool. She was dead wrong, but at least she didn't take his bait to argue. Some day he might like that about her. For the moment, he hated every well-creased bone in her body.

The operations center filled a large room on the third floor of the old headquarters building. It was his own domain where he tugged on the strings of clandestine teams across the world. His days in the field were in the last century, though the places and faces remained vivid memories. But here in the air-conditioned room he accomplished more than he had ever thought possible in the back roads and alleyways of Colombia and Venezuela.

The place had calmed since midday, when four staff operations officers and their analyst counterparts had hovered around an island desk in the center of the room. Each officer sat transfixed by twin monitors, enrapt by their headsets. Now, three of them lounged in their chairs, hair tousled by hours on the headset. Half a world away, Georgia slept. Little activity buzzed across their stations. A pair of analysts sat at desks around the perimeter mining for details that someone might have overlooked.

Paul curled a finger at Kay Linh. She coordinated Pierce's op, and she had been on duty since early morning. She wore a pair of stylish thick rimmed glasses that perched atop her button nose. The lenses reflected the glare from her computer screens. She stood up and walked over to him with a confused and exhausted stare.

"They made it to the house," she said as she yawned. Her voice was almost a whisper.

"We've got a problem," he replied. "How long until Sanger's people get there?"

"Two or three hours, maybe. Why? What's wrong?"

"Call Pierce. I need to talk to him directly."

"I think he's asleep."

"Now."

She shuffled back to her desk and tapped in Pierce's number. A muffled voice responded into her earpiece. "Dodger, this is Hourglass. Stand by," she said and handed the headset to Paul.

He held the tiny wire mic close to his chin, his voice grating as he spoke too loudly. "Wake up call, Dodger."

Pierce's voice became alert. "What's wrong?"

Good boy. He knows something's up, Paul thought.

"Home office says we give the asset to GIS. Got it?"

There was a pause and a breath of exasperation. "Understood."

"Dodger?"

"Yeah?"

"You've got two hours to consider options."

The line clicked, and Paul handed the headset back over to Kay. She looked up at him with her head tilted.

"Are we coordinating with the Georgians, then?" she asked.

"Not exactly."

"But we need this woman's intel. We need it," she said through clenched teeth.

"This one comes from on high."

Kay chewed her manicured thumbnail in frustration. The ruby enamel had chipped and worn throughout the day as the operation unraveled. She was a perfectionist, a trait she claimed to inherit from her Vietnamese mother. He needed her perfection right now. Pierce needed her even more.

"Where are the pics from the airport?" Paul asked. He fumbled around on her desk where she had neat stacks of thin folders marked in her own delicate handwriting and a fresh label that read TOP SECRET // SAR-TIDAL ECHO.

"Please, I have these there for a reason."

Kay pushed his hands away from the printed files and nodded at the screen. Resigned, he raised his hands and backed away. Kay opened several images on one screen, each virtual snapshot stacked on another.

"Does Pierce have these?"

"Yes, they're on his phone. Sanger has them, too."

"Good."

She paged through the images. He'd seen them at least a dozen times since Sunday. The photos were stills captured from security cameras at Tbilisi Airport. One angle recorded from the building showed each man, some in pairs, as they crossed the pavement from the BTR to the gangway. The camera was high up and several yards away. Their bodies blurred in motion, their faces inscrutable shades of black and brown. The whole world had seen the photos every ten minutes on news cycles since Monday afternoon.

But another camera in the gangway gave closer glimpses. Georgian intelligence wasn't sharing these with the media. They were closer shots of the men's faces, though some were obscured by military caps. A pair of faces caught the camera dead on. They were bearded men with dark pools for eyes that stared like ghouls at the camera eye. Behind them was a face in profile emerging from the stairway. He looked different from the others dressed in a dark jacket. His face was clean-shaven and pale, his nose hawkish. *My money's on him,* Paul thought.

"So, we're not coordinating with GIS. What exactly are we doing?" Kay asked.

"That's up to Pierce. Unless I miss my guess, we are letting her go."

"What?" Kay's voice rose an octave and stole attention from everyone still left in the room.

He gave her a sour look and waved his hands for calm.

"Think about it. You're Pierce. You've got an uncooperative target in custody, and you need intel in less than two hours. Then she's gone, and your mission is dead ended. What are your options?"

She looked through him, thinking. In seconds she focused again. "He needs leverage."

"Right."

"So, he cuts her a deal. There's no time for anything else."

"Right again. And the deal is?"

"The deal is … give us some names and you avoid worse interrogation?"

"Now you're getting it."

"But how does Ethan know anything she tells him is reliable?"

"It probably isn't."

"Then what's the point? We're no better off." She crossed her arms.

"It's not the intel she spills. It's where she goes next."

"Risky."

Paul shrugged. "Risk is what we do."

"Fine," she said. "Too risky then."

"It's what we've got. He and Wade will need to keep track of her. Help them figure something out. I'll see you in two hours."

She stared at her screen, ignoring him as he walked out.

Paul strolled outside to clear his head. In the old days, he'd take a smoke break near the old auditorium dome. Lately, he settled for an apple or candy bar from the cafeteria. Today it was an apple too small and tart to enjoy much. From the new building, he had to walk around the whole campus to get where he was headed—the Memorial Pool. The water was still enough to reflect the evening sky in an eerie dark green. He watched the reflection as the clouds tumbled by thick with the coming spring rain, rolling like the thoughts in his head about the past hours.

Marcus Eldridge was the first officer he'd lost since taking this job. He knew a few others lost in the field over the years. Who didn't after this long? This was different for him. He thought about Janey and the boys. Wednesday meant Janey played bridge tonight. She'd be home late, but even then she wouldn't wait up for him. The boys were out there somewhere living more normal lives than he ever knew. They'd start families of their own soon. The thought made him feel old.

He wanted to write Eldridge's parents a letter. He might even do it. They'd never receive it, of course. The standard letter explained nothing about how their son got shot in a Georgian valley trying to apprehend terrorists who blew up a jetliner. Eldridge would get a star carved in stone in the lobby of the old building and maybe his name in a handmade book.

He tossed the apple core into the bushes and wandered back to the op center, wondering if Pierce got the message. The man was good at reading in between the lines. It's what made him a good targeting officer. One of his best. Pierce had to get the message, or they'd all have a long and unpleasant vacation.

CHAPTER 3

TANGLED WEB

Telavi, Georgia
4:20 a.m., Thursday, May 9

ETHAN PACED through the dark of the tiny safe house to shake off jet lag that stirred in his head like a drug. Corso's call mingled with it, his scratching voice still swirling inside Ethan's head. He stopped in the narrow hallway between the spartan bedrooms and leaned against the cool plaster wall rubbing the sleep from his eyes.

Two hours wasn't enough. He buttoned his shirt in the dark, feeling each button with his fingertips from habit. She wouldn't tell him anything. Corso had to know that. He ran fingers through his greasy black hair that lay flat against his head. He couldn't remember when he last ate. His mouth was dry. *This is a lousy place for interrogation.*

In the next room, Wade kept watch over the feisty woman he now knew as Seda Alaskhanova. She had said nothing as Ethan rifled through her belongings in the car. He found three passports tucked into a canvas shoulder bag. One was Russian and poorly made. The photo wasn't even her. Too round faced and heavy. Of the other two Georgian passports, one was an excellent fake. When he read her name aloud, her eyes shifted subtly at his. He took it as confirmation. Her name was Seda.

Ethan's eyes adjusted to the dark bedroom. Wade stayed awake, his eyes locked on Seda. She sat up on the bed, her wrists zip-tied to the steel-gray bed frame. Wade sat in an old kitchen chair leaned up against the wall on two legs. The thing creaked under his brawny bulk.

"She's awake," Wade said.

"She say anything?"

"Not really. Mumbled something a couple times. I don't think she likes me much."

"We need to talk," Ethan said.

"Okay. She's not going anywhere. Are you *Jamila*?" Wade patted the bed as he stood, and she shied away.

They stepped outside into the silence of the dead town's outskirts. The hum of an electrical box that occupied the heart of a tangled web of wires over the roadway filled the air. A light fog had settled down from the mountains nearby, and they stood close in the cool damp to whisper.

"Corso called," Ethan said.

"Yeah, I heard. What's the word?"

"He said we're done. Langley doesn't like losing a guy. We surrender her to GIS. They're pulling us out."

Wade was quiet. He snorted through his nose as he shook his head.

"I don't like it either," Ethan said. "But that's the official story. Unofficially …"

"Here we go," Wade said nodding rapidly.

"Unofficially, I don't think that Corso thinks we're finished. We've got about two hours until Sanger's people show up with Georgian intelligence."

"There it is. Damn." Wade sighed as he crossed in the small patch of yard. "Man, that isn't enough time for anything."

"It's enough."

"What are we supposed to do with that? We are not getting tough on that woman, no matter what happened to Marcus. Hell no. And then just hand her over? This op is all kinds of fucked." Again he crossed the yard in frustration. Gravel crackled beneath his boots.

"Not if I'm right about Corso it's not. Look at it from her perspective.

Why talk to us, right? So, we make a deal, just like she said. She gives us some intel. Something to go on."

"Like what?"

"Doesn't matter. Think. That's for her benefit, not ours. She's off the hook. She goes to her people. She calls her family. Whatever she does, we're right behind."

Wade's eyes opened wider. "Tracker."

"Get her phone and get it done. Get another one on her bag. The kit's in my room. I'll talk to her and make the deal."

Ethan returned to the room and turned on a lamp atop an empty dresser. Seda sat up, squinting at the yellow light.

"You understand who we are?" he asked.

She scowled. He pulled a knife from his trouser pocket and unfolded the blade. She whimpered. Ethan leaned over her and passed the blade in front of her face. He smelled her faint perfume, more musky than sweet, mixed with her sweat. With a flick of his hand, he cut the zip tie on her left wrist. It snapped loose with a crack. He leaned away and cut the right. Seda closed her eyes and rubbed her reddened wrists.

Ethan put the knife back in his pocket and sat on the opposite bed.

"You said we can make a deal," he said.

Seda turned calmly, still rubbing the raw skin on her arms. She sat at the edge of her bed with her shoulders thrust back and faced Ethan with a sneer of defiance.

"I said we discuss deal," she said.

"I need names." He held up his phone where the screen glowed with the visage of a burly, bearded man. It was an image from the hijacking. "This man," he said. He flicked his finger and another face appeared. "Him. This one." He paged through more images. "All of them."

Seda studied the photos. She shrugged with each flick of his finger.

"This is deal. What do you give me?"

Her accent drenched each word, but the message was clear enough. Ethan admired her audacity. No doubt it was how she prospered as a smuggler. This was his only shot at leverage. He had to take a harder tack.

"Let me explain something to you. In about two hours, my colleague will walk through that door with some friends from GIS. You know GIS?" He paused, wracking his brain to recall and spit out the unfamiliar words for Georgian Intelligence Service. "*Sakartvelos Dazvervis Samsakhuri?*"

She nodded, her eyes now focused on his.

"They are going to have many questions about how you helped these men come into the country and kill 183 people on that airplane. Do you think they're going to ask you very nicely?"

She glared at him.

"So, you give me names, and we let you leave before GIS arrives. Or you can make a deal with them. Your choice."

Her lips tightened, then she gave him a nod.

"Take another look." He shoved his phone in her face, flicking again through the images. "I need names. I need to know their leaders."

She pointed at the phone, to the heavy-set Chechen with a beard like a lion's mane. "Khasan Kagirov. He is leader. No other leader. He is strong Muslim. *Mujahid.*"

"Kagirov?"

"Yes. This one is Abdula Islayev. How you say? Cousins."

"And you know them? You helped them across the border?"

"Of course me. Who else? Men not do. Khasan not like much help from a woman." She smirked.

Ethan showed her more photos, more faces, watching her intently at each turn. She shook her head. His last photo showed a pair of the hijackers on the gangway, and a profile of a third man behind them. She covered her mouth with her hand and shook her head again. Her eyes flared for an instant, and he knew she lied. She feared someone in the photo. *Or was it fear for someone?*

"What about others? Are there more in Chechnya like them?"

"No more names I know," she said. She crossed her arms. "Now we deal. I want car."

Ethan looked at her quizzically, head tilted. Seda stared back. Her lips were broad, unsmiling. With him, she was stern. *Was she like this with Kagirov and the others? Were those even their names?*

She had panache. As crazy as it seemed, letting her take the car was probably the better option. If they let her walk, the GIS crew would track her down right away. She couldn't get too far. She was bold, not stupid, and she knew her phone was a liability. The car less so. The Mercedes was as good as hers, he just needed to bargain a little more to maintain the ruse. Then he'd have to explain it all to the Georgians. They wouldn't like it.

"You want the car, you need to give me more."

"What more?" she said. Ethan had her then. Her face lifted, and he knew she was in her element as a bargainer. Time to close the deal.

"You tell me. Where did Kagirov get explosives? Who did they work with? Are there more attacks planned?"

"I do not know this."

"Fine. No car. It's a long walk home."

Seda cursed at him, then tapped her finger against her lips in thought. Ethan waited. Behind him, Wade entered the room. She glanced at him where he leaned against the wall, but she failed to notice him drop her shoulder bag on the floor beside the dresser.

"There is bomb maker. In Chechnya."

She explained rapidly. Her clumsy English tumbled out to explain there was an old Saudi bomb maker with one hand missing who made many kinds of bombs for *shuhada*. He knew she spoke in half-truths and local lore. There probably was a bomb maker. He might have been Saudi. And maybe he really was hiding in some mountain village called Shatoy. Ethan couldn't dismiss it all, not entirely. It mattered more that she accepted the deal on its face.

He nodded and said, "The car is yours."

Seda stood. The corner of her lips curled into a wry smirk as she rubbed her wrists again. At the door, she gestured to her bag at Wade's feet. Once he moved, she muttered something as she rifled through it.

"Chill. Everything's there," Wade said.

She seemed satisfied.

"Keys?"

She held out her hand.

Wade fetched the single tarnished key from his pocket. "Hold on now. We've got to get our things out of the trunk."

Outside, the rising sun tinged the broad valley pink and orange. Mist still clung to the wooded lots around them. Seda crossed her arms at the open driver door while Wade pulled his unloved Dragunov rifle wrapped in a coarse blanket from the trunk. When he slammed the trunk hatch, Seda started the car. The Mercedes protested with its familiar screech that broke the morning quiet like an alarm.

Ethan watched from the doorway as Wade eyed him, nodding slightly. The car's tires spit gravel at them, and she sped off to the northwest. They would see her again soon—safe and unharmed, he genuinely hoped. He hoped much less for the Mercedes.

* * *

Ethan and Wade waited in the main room of the squat safe house for Sanger's officer and the GIS escorts to arrive. There was nothing to eat. Wade had found some stale crackers neither of them would try. A stained coffee kettle with no coffee in the cupboards teased them, so they simply sat in the morning light practicing their narrative of Seda's wild escape.

"Our story is I'm watching her while you're sleeping," Ethan said.

"I'm sleeping. You're on watch?"

"Right. Look, you want to look like the jackass here?"

Wade's grin broadened. "No, go on. I'm loving this so far."

"I look out that back bedroom window, and she hits me from the side. I'm down, she runs for the car."

"Okay, okay. What about the key?" Wade asked.

"She gets it from my pocket."

"And we already emptied the trunk when we got here."

"Right."

Wade looked out the window, thinking. "What about your sidearm?"

"She left it. No. It was on the dresser and she ran out without realizing."

"Okay. And I'm still sleeping until that damn car starts up. I think that covers it okay.

"Agreed." Ethan nodded.

"Except one thing."

"What?"

"She hit you, man. Hard enough to put you down."

"Do it," Ethan said as he turned sideways. Wade knew how to hit. He spent five years as a Marine scout. Before that, he'd had his share of fights on the streets of Houston. This was going to hurt. Ethan winced and shut his eyes.

Wade's smile faded. "Sorry about this, man."

Wade's fist ignited a bright light in Ethan's head. He stumbled from the blow. The pain burst beneath his eye and a wave of heat surrounded his head. He felt his pulse pounding on his cheekbone, and he grunted through gritted teeth.

"Son of a bitch that hurts."

Wade's smile returned, and he doubled over in high pitched laughter.

"Remind me never to piss you off again," Ethan said holding his cheek.

Within the hour a pair of silver sedans arrived at the house. Ethan stood to let them in, but the door opened without his help. A blonde woman wearing aviator shades and a dark blazer entered. She moved with confidence, her hair tied tight against her scalp in a ponytail. He recognized her as one of Sanger's operations officers.

"Maria Hessler." She held out her hand. "Jesus. What happened to your face?"

Ethan shook her hand and winced. Another man, well dressed and portly, filed in behind Maria.

"This is Giorgi Gelashvili, Georgian Intelligence Service," she said.

"Please. Call me George," he said shaking Ethan's hand. He bowed slightly to Wade who rose to greet them both.

"So, where's the asset?" Maria said.

Ethan and Wade eyed one another wearily.

"She's gone," Ethan said.

"What do you mean gone?" said George.

"Escaped," Wade answered. "She got loose and knocked the hell out of Ethan here. She got the key and took off in the car. You know, the one you didn't see outside anywhere?"

Maria stood with her hands on her hips. "My god, you're really not joking, are you?" She tilted her head and removed her sunglasses as she examined Ethan's face more closely. "More than you bargained for, huh?"

Ethan raised his eyebrows, though the effect was lost some with the swelling bump under his right eye.

George interrupted. "Which way did she go? We must find her."

"West, I think. She's probably going back up the gorge where we found her. Maybe to make a move for the border," Ethan said.

George was already out the door. Outside he chattered in Georgian at his three comrades, pointing at the cars and then westward. They stood stern faced, glaring at the Americans as George rattled through the explanation. In his gray suit and bulging belly, George seemed out of place amid the operatives in their rolled-up sleeves and denim pants.

Ethan followed Maria out of the house. She spoke into her phone, already sharing the bad news with Sanger.

"Too little time for introductions, I am afraid," George told Ethan. He gestured quickly at the men. "Rezo, Levan, and Ioseb. These are my finest men, you will see. Now, let us get in the cars quickly and hunt our ... what is the word?"

The one called Rezo responded coldly. "Prey."

"Yes, prey. Let us hunt our prey before she gets into the mountains. We have two cars, and two of you who know her face. We can hunt two times."

Maria pocketed her phone. "He's right. Looks like you've got a temporary reprieve. You and Wade are the only ones who can identify her. You ride with me. Wade, you go with Giorgi."

Ethan wanted to object, but splitting with Wade now became part of the plan. They would play along and keep in contact however they could. Still, despite his aching cheek—or maybe because of it—he felt better with Wade around.

* * *

Ethan sat in the back of the silver Toyota alongside Maria as they scoured the outskirts of Telavi with their Georgian counterparts in front. Ioseb drove, Levan twisted his head looking for the dark blue Mercedes. Telavi was a scenic mountain town. Manicured shrubs sprouted between the quaint little houses with broad roofs—much like the safe house he'd just left, though better kept. They passed the train station but found only arriving morning travelers. Row after row of grape vines passed by his window as they drove past rustic stone chateaus on the far side of town.

Maria spoke some with Ioseb and navigated from the back seat. Levan joked with her about it, but Ethan couldn't follow. Georgian was impossible for him. He spoke Russian well enough. Georgian sounded nothing like that, and he understood almost none of it. They drove on, scanning the roadways.

"I'm sorry about Eldridge," Maria said.

Ethan stared out the window at the passing vineyards and side roads half-heartedly looking for the Mercedes. "So am I."

"Alan isn't happy about last night. You three really kicked a hornet's nest. He had some choice words about the whole idea. He doesn't like this situation any better. We can't afford to lose this asset."

"I don't work for him," Ethan said. "I don't need the lecture."

"I wasn't lecturing you. Trust me, you'd know if I was. Call it a suggestion."

Ethan looked at her askance. The gold-rimmed shades concealed her expression, but he read her anyway. She and her sharp jawline were all business. She provoked every man around her, in every way a confident and attractive woman could. He knew women like her. He'd married one. At home she was someone else. She had something to prove every minute on this job.

"You're never wrong, are you?" he said.

She huffed. "Are you?"

"Not usually."

"I'll bet. Look, it wasn't a good day. Now is your chance to fix it."

On that count she was right. Still, he didn't trust GIS enough to admit they were tracking Seda electronically. He had to think through this. He closed his eyes and thought of Seda. What would she do? She was too smart to use the phone. Maybe once to call for help, then she'd toss it. She'd probably do the same with the car as soon as she could find another ride. This wasn't just a deal gone wrong for her. She couldn't lay low and let it all blow over. He saw it in her face in the bedroom. Seda knew this changed her whole scheme. She had to disappear. She had to know Kagirov and the others were up to something drastic. Why take the risk? He doubted it was the money. Maybe she was closer to these men than she let on. Or closer to one of them.

"I need a map," he said to Levan and Ioseb. "You guys have a map of the area?"

They handed him a folded roadmap from the glove compartment. The map was older, the paper brittle, but all he needed were highways. Mountains forced Seda into only a few options. He studied the serpentine lines and the curling Georgian script.

She wouldn't use her regular routes up through Chechnya, he reasoned. Seda had to leave the country or face the wrath of the men in the car with him and the rest of their comrades. The downed airliner was a black mark on their country. They would have no patience with her and less kindness. His eyes scanned the snaking roadways of the north country. She needed money, a new vehicle, and a route that no one would expect. He found a little airplane icon on the map just north of Telavi. He showed Ioseb the map. "Here. Go north."

He couldn't call it a plan, really. The trick was staying on Seda's trail without putting her in the hands of GIS. He could send them north, somehow, so he could pursue his best guess on her actual direction. It wasn't a plan, it was a gamble with too few cards left to play.

Within a half-hour, they approached a lone airstrip barely a mile long where it shot out to the west from a cluster of small buildings and a rust-eaten metal hangar. A bulky Soviet biplane with a broad yellow stripe poked its nose into the air outside the hangar. Several trucks and a handful of cars were parked near the hangar entrance, but he saw no sign of the Mercedes.

"What's that you said about not being wrong?" Maria asked.

As they passed the hangar, the dusty Mercedes came into view parked next to a stand of beech trees, its trunk wide open. Two men inspected the vehicle. One wore coveralls splotched with oil.

Ethan tapped Maria's thigh and smiled at her as they pulled up alongside. She shook her head in disbelief and exited the car.

Levan and Ioseb accosted the men, and the two mechanics waved their hands and shouted back as the argument grew. Ethan paid them little attention while he inspected the car. There was no sign of Seda. She left nothing behind. *At least she took the bag.* Ethan wandered around the car, kicking the dirt and grass. Behind him, Maria joined in on the argument. Ethan looked in the nearby trees. There, on the ground, he caught a glimpse of silver-gray—Seda's phone. Ethan picked it up and walked back to the group.

"They're saying she traded the car for an old truck. She woke them up and gave them 200 Lari. Then she took off," Maria said.

"Found her phone. I'll see if I can get any recent calls. My money's on her heading north for the border."

"Of course she is," Maria said. "She's a smuggler who knows the terrain up there. Let's go."

Except Seda wouldn't go north. Not if his hunch was close to right.

"I'll stay here and wait for Wade. He's got our gear and can help me with the phone. Hopefully, we can get something useful out of it. Then we can catch up with you."

"What? Not going to happen. Get in. Sanger will send us both home if I let you out of my sight. Besides, you have to identify the target, remember?"

She called for Levan and Ioseb, and they climbed in the Toyota.

Ethan crawled in the back seat and tinkered with Seda's phone, careful not to reveal what it held. Ioseb turned the ignition. Ethan looked out the window at the mechanics who ran away from the car, their eyes wide with alarm. Ethan followed their gaze. The exact twin of their Toyota charged directly at the left side. For a fleeting second, he stared at the oncoming driver and recognized Rezo's face.

Glass exploded around him. Ethan slammed into Maria and his vision went black. Maria screamed. He tasted blood.

Ethan lay staring at the car's ceiling. A horn sounded steadily, faintly, as though it were miles away.

"Rezo?" he heard someone say. "Rezo *ratom*?" They were shouting.

A shot rang in his ears. Two more, and another. Then silence.

He couldn't move.

CHAPTER 4

OTHER PLANS

Telavi, Georgia
8:22 a.m., Thursday, May 9

ETHAN LAY across the Toyota's back seat with Maria twisted awkwardly beneath him. She moaned, but he couldn't hear her words over the buzzing in his ears and head. Pain surged up his left arm into his shoulder. *Move, damn it.* He brushed pebbles of glass from his chest and tried to lift his head to look outside. His vision narrowed. Dark blurs swam outside a pinprick of light. *Move.*

Out the windshield he spied Levan's body in the dirt. He looked for others. He wondered about Wade for a moment, then fumbled for the Beretta. *Faster.* He saw another body close to the hangar's side door and thought it might be Ioseb.

Maria opened the car door. With a quick lunge she collapsed to the ground, rolling away as she hit the dirt. She grunted something he still couldn't hear. With his left hand he flicked the Beretta's decocker. He could do that in the dark without thinking. Now the motion came clumsy and slow with the pain and numbness in his arm.

Ethan focused on the hangar door as he scooted out the vehicle. Rezo appeared, his face like a stone. He ejected a spent magazine from his pistol and placed it carefully into his pocket as he walked toward the car, then loaded a second magazine.

From behind, Ethan heard his name. He shielded himself behind the car door and looked to Maria. She kneeled behind the car. A smear of red spread from her cheek to her neck where she had wiped at a bleeding cut from the collision. She pointed to the far side of the car where the second Toyota still honked and steamed.

Ethan nodded. He leaned out and fired. Rezo returned a volley of jacketed lead that shattered the glass above his head. Another round slammed into the steel door. He had slowed Rezo's advance, but it couldn't last. He shuffled to the rear of the car then lay on his belly, wincing from the effort.

Maria ran to the other car, crouching low for cover. Rezo fired again and again at her. The bullets ripped into the ruined car and shattered glass. She raised the Toyota's trunk, giving herself a little cover as she ducked inside.

Ethan waited, both hands gripping his pistol tightly. Too tightly, he worried. His vision brightened bit by bit. It had to be enough. He heard the crunch of Rezo's cautious steps on gravel and dirt. Rezo's boot appeared between the tires. *One more step.* Step by step, Rezo fired again at Ethan, coming ever closer.

Ethan squeezed the trigger and sent a bullet through Rezo's ankle that shredded blood and bone. Rezo collapsed as his ankle buckled, firing in a rage. Ethan shot again but missed as his hands shook from too much pressure. His target scrambled away, moaning in pain as he limped.

Ethan lost sight of him and pushed himself up to peek through the car windows. He saw Rezo approach the hangar door. Once inside, he'd have the advantage. Ethan stood at the rear of the car and fired in rapid succession, each shot wilder than the last. He had lost any sense of focus. Adrenaline coursed through his body. His vision narrowed, darkness crowding in. His hands shook. He didn't have time to think. Rezo ducked instinctively at the flurry of gunfire, then fired back twice.

The slide on Ethan's Beretta stuck open—empty. He ducked down and reached to his belt line for another magazine, but there was nothing to grab. Both magazines were in the car. He swore quietly. He had to get around to the car's open door, which put him in Rezo's line of fire. Rezo tilted his head and sneered at him. He moved toward the car, limping as he came. There was no route to the car door now. He could run or launch himself at Rezo. He didn't like either desperate option.

Rezo rounded the end of the car and stared at Ethan. The Georgian sneered. "Scorpio send its regards." He raised the slim-nosed Makarov pistol toward Ethan's head.

A shot exploded much louder than the pop and crack of their pistols. It reverberated from Ethan's left, off the metal hangar, rolling away in every direction like a distant storm. Rezo fell to his knees with a hole blown in his sternum. He struggled to raise his pistol once more as another booming shot fired into his chest. He toppled forward onto the dust and gravel.

Ethan turned to see Maria shouldering Wade's Dragunov rifle. She had pulled it from the trunk.

"You all right?" she said. She lowered the rifle and rubbed her mouth with the back of her hand, leaving another thin smear of blood on her chin and lips.

He panted and let out a low whistle. "Thanks. Wade will be jealous you actually hit him with that thing."

He ran to the other Toyota and opened the rear door. The seats were empty. He dove in, looking for any sign of his partner. In the front, he found spent casings on the floor from the Makarov and a stain of wet blood in the seat. On the backseat floor, he found Wade's phone. *Where the hell are you, buddy?* He inspected one of the casings.

"What did he say to you?" asked Maria.

"I don't know. I thought he said something about Scorpio. Does that mean anything to you? Maybe something in Georgian?"

She shook her head. "Ethan, what the hell is going on?"

"What do you know about this guy? Did you work with him before?"

"Never saw him before this morning. Same for the other two. I don't have any reason to doubt Giorgi, but he vouched for these guys. What a mess. I mean …" Her voice trailed as she leaned against the car, her arms at rest on the rifle.

Ethan flicked the casing back in the car and moved to the other wrecked Toyota. From his bag he pulled a full magazine and reloaded the Beretta. Then he lugged the bag over his shoulder and moved to the old Mercedes.

"Let's go," he said.

She jogged after him. "What? We can't leave it like this. Stop. We've got to stay here and wait for Georgian police. I've got to call this in. Sanger's going to lose his fucking mind."

He spun around and gripped her arm. "Look, you're smarter than this. Last night, our guy is shot dead at a couple hundred yards by someone who knew about the meet. The asset knows more than she lets on. Now, Rezo here is cleaning up the trail. I don't know who's behind this, but I'm sure as hell not standing around here to get shot at by the next hired gun who shows up. Let's go."

"Sanger was right about you. Damn it, Ethan, you're making this worse." She shook off his grasp.

"I'd say this whole thing is getting worse without my help. Both of us just about got killed by an enemy we didn't know we had yesterday. And thanks to you, I'm still breathing. I owe you my life. After this, I'd rather have you with me right now than playing negotiator with the locals."

"But we don't know anything. The asset's escaped, and we have nothing to show for it. We're flying blind here."

"Not exactly." He held up and wagged Wade's phone while reaching for his own with a knowing grin. "We tagged the asset."

Her face tensed, her neatly shaped eyebrows arcing beneath a wrinkled brow. "You what? You mean we drove around for over an hour looking for her and you didn't bother to tell me that?"

"Let's just say Wade and I had other plans. Now get in." He sat in the Mercedes and turned the ignition. The car bleated its familiar screech. Ethan shook his head in disgust.

Maria let out an exasperated moan, then sat in the passenger seat. "Don't make me regret this."

"That's up to you," he said.

"What about Wade?" she asked.

For the second time in as many days, Ethan faced leaving an officer behind. Last night, he laid Marcus down in the yard seconds from death. He didn't even have the decency to be with him as he died. Was it Wade's turn now, somewhere down the road dying in the dirt? Wade told him to carry on with the chase last night. He'd want Ethan to do it again. But Wade wasn't Marcus. He and Wade had history. Nine years of assignments together. This was his friend, and he couldn't say that of many people.

Ethan's eyes steeled. "Wade can take care of himself."

* * *

The Mercedes swerved as he drove across a pockmarked highway and looked down at his phone's screen where a tiny map and unsteady dot hinted at Seda's location. She moved west, but she'd already passed the gorge. She wasn't running for home. She was running away, leaving everything she knew behind. He knew the risk in letting her go, but he didn't anticipate Rezo.

Maria updated Sanger again just before her phone dropped the signal behind the low-slung mountains to the south. At least she avoided his rebuke for now. Ethan needed to do the same with Corso, but they had to gain ground first over the mountain roads and switchbacks.

Once they veered south toward Tbilisi, she broke the concentrated silence.

"I was out of line back there. Sanger's wrong about you," she said.

"Forget it. I know what he thinks about me. I've got my job to do. He's got his. That's just how it is."

Ethan sensed her watching him as the miles passed. He glanced her way, his gray eyes darting from her to her legs and down to navigate the phone's map. It had been a long time since any woman looked at him like that.

"You still have blood on your cheek," he said. "There." He brushed his own cheek, scratching away at five day's growth of dark stubble.

Maria blushed and rubbed her sleeve across her face. He locked his eyes back on the road.

"You're not ex-military. How'd you land here?" she said.

"That's your question after sizing me up for the last five minutes?" he asked.

"I've got a job to do, too. I'm good at it."

"I never made it to the service. Wade never lets me forget it. It wasn't for lack of trying. I did ROTC in college. Got into a little accident." He rubbed his right knee. "Change of plans."

"That's why I said Sanger's wrong about you. You change plans. When you have to, I mean. You know how to improvise. You're not afraid to."

The barrel of Rezo's gun flashed in his head. "I never said I wasn't afraid."

"But you aren't. There's a lot going on up there." She tapped her temple. "But you really don't worry about it, do you?"

She was right. Somehow staring down Rezo's barrel terrified him more now than it did in the moment. Nothing about Sanger or Corso or any of the road ahead troubled him. This was a thing for him to unravel, an ambiguous puzzle that he embraced. It excited his mind. He thrived on uncertainty. What he feared wasn't the unexpected. It was an empty apartment back in Alexandria. It was getting lost within himself next to a woman he couldn't reach. That was how he lost Sarah, and it drove him deeper into whatever Corso threw at him.

"I guess I don't," he said with his gaze lost on the road.

Just north of Tbilisi, Seda veered west, avoiding the capital altogether. It was the sign Ethan awaited. She headed for the coast almost 500 kilometers away. They stopped for fuel northwest of the city. Maria played the happy tourist with a gangly attendant who smiled and nodded at her. But he told her he hadn't seen any woman driving a truck.

They followed into the western country. The reek of diesel fuel clung to his hands. He steered along a broad river valley checkered with irrigated fields. A mountain ridge covered with deep green firs rose to his left. Each city followed the next like a shrinking pack of nested dolls. Georgia still straddled the old days of lifeless Soviet planning and a modern vitality draped in bright colors and youthful verve. Near the city of Gori, he answered a call.

"This is Dodger."

A delicate voice replied. He could picture Kay Linh talking into her headset from the command desk. "Hourglass requires status."

"I'm tracking the asset now. Outside Gori."

"Location confirmed. Asset still in transit, tracking … standby … tracking a hundred kilometers from you. Do you have company with you?"

"Yes. Safe and sound. Any word from Nomad?"

"Affirmative. Nomad is with friends and reports trouble with an angry local."

Ethan blew a sigh of relief. Wade knew how to handle himself, all right. He was safe.

"You sound tired," he said. He wondered how long she had been sitting at the desk. If there was someone getting less sleep than him it was Kay. She didn't like it when he went off script.

"Station's hot, Dodger. Local authorities on alert for you two. What happened?"

"Nomad's right. Same local trouble gave us a rough morning. Handled with some big help from present company, and now in pursuit. Hostile's identified as Rezo …"

Maria chimed in. "Kaladze."

"Rezo Kaladze. Probably military background. Tough guy. Need you to chase after anything on Scorpio."

"Say again?"

"He said something about Scorpio. Does that signify anything?"

"Negative. We'll review. Think it's related?"

"No question. We have two names from asset. Khasan Kagirov and Abdula Islayev. Need IDs on the rest, and I'm hoping the asset will lead the way."

"That will make someone we know much easier to be around this morning. Sit tight for updates and keep us close. And Dodger?"

"Yeah?"

"Go light."

"Will do, Hourglass."

With a tick the line to Langley closed. It was good to know Kay kept watch over him, which also meant Corso had his back for now. He'd been reckless, but he needed their support to get through this.

* * *

After six hours of winding down mountain roads and the broad basin to the sea where tea farms and vineyards dotted the land, they hit the coast near Poti. Seda had become a mere point on the map, a dot they chased in slow shifts across the country. The little dot avoided Poti altogether and turned south. Within the hour that dot settled on Batumi.

They followed down the coastal road, ever southward where cottages and getaways overlooked the highway toward craggy beaches. The late day sun hovered over the Black Sea and cast warm light over the winding scenic roads. The small city of Batumi appeared at the water's edge, spreading around a small bay where great tankers lazed. They passed into downtown. A few glistening towers and brilliantly decorated churches and hotels harmonized tradition and progress. Palms flanked the roadside and tourists strolled beneath the already glowing streetlamps.

"It's a beautiful city in its way," Maria murmured as they passed through downtown.

Ethan had barely noticed. Again he checked his phone for Seda's signal. The dot signaling the tiny transmitter in her canvas bag had halted in place on the far side of town near the shoreline. They drove to a neighborhood of cream-colored cottages separated by stone walls and narrow streets. He spotted a rusting old truck parked in the street near one of the cottages.

"There it is."

He drove past the truck around a winding street and parked well away to hide the Mercedes' droning wail. It shuddered to a stop, and they exited quietly.

"We're a tourist couple out for a walk," he said.

He took her hand and felt the warmth and sweat as their fingers intertwined.

"Let me do the talking," Maria said.

She leaned her head against his shoulder.

At the truck, they slowed while Ethan peered in through the grimy side window. The seat was empty, but he caught sight of Seda's bag on the truck's floor.

"She's here," he whispered.

A small car passed, and Maria gave the driver a friendly wave. When the car rounded the curve, they moved quickly to the cottage gate. Ethan pushed the wrought iron gate wide. Its hinges creaked loudly. They paused. A halo of light snuck out from heavy curtains in the cottage window. From within, Ethan heard voices arguing.

"You hear that?" he whispered.

"Shh. I'm listening."

Maria crept into the yard and approached the house. Ethan followed her.

"They're arguing about someone," she said. "Something about where a man is."

Closer now, Ethan could hear the woman's voice. It could be Seda. He wasn't sure. Her voice rose, shouting. She screamed something over and over in a panic. Ethan looked at Maria, puzzled.

She translated. "Tell me, tell me." Maria shrugged her shoulders.

A crash came from inside. Glass shattered. The shouting rose louder and unintelligible.

"What now?" Maria asked.

His training told him they should back off and observe. Seda led them to a source, just as he'd hoped. They had a location, and with it maybe phone records and more surveillance. They shouldn't do this alone. But his instinct sensed that answers lay beyond the porch steps and door. Whoever it was suffering Seda's wrath knew something. Ethan had to know what.

"I'm going in. You head back to the car," he said.

"Absolutely not. You need me."

"You go in there, and you blow your cover."

Maria stiffened. Her mouth tensed tight. "I'm going with you."

He shook his head. There wasn't time to debate. He motioned for her to follow and stepped cautiously on the porch stairs. Old slats of wood creaked under foot, and he paused to listen. The screaming continued. Another crash came from within, and now a man's hoarse voice shouted back. Ethan dashed up the stairs. He placed his hand on the doorknob and drew his pistol from the back of his belt.

He burst into a cluttered sitting room, his Beretta held tight to his chest, scanning for Seda and the man. The screaming came from the kitchen in back stopped abruptly. They heard him. Ethan raced past a short hallway and came into a crowded kitchen. Seda cowered in a corner sobbing with a long butcher knife in her hand. Across the room near a small table strewn with broken plates and overturned teacups a man stood in shock, his flabby arms raised. His bulbous nose poked out above a thick mustache and overgrown whiskers. He wore a worn and yellowed undershirt.

Maria barked something in Georgian at the man. In response, he gripped the wooden table and heaved it at Ethan. Plates and teacups flew through the air and crashed to the floor. In the same motion, the man ran out the back door and down a flight of concrete steps.

Ethan raced after him. The glasses and broken shards popped under his feet as he shoved the table aside to run out the back door. The man ran through a cramped and dim courtyard of houses. He exited a lone iron gate that spilled out into another street at the far end where he turned to the right. The man was older and slow. Ethan knew he could catch him. He ran for the gate in pursuit.

He passed the gate, and a flash of light overwhelmed his vision then vanished into blind darkness. He stumbled, stunned by a painful blow to his head. The old man hit him again with a long board, this time in his chest. The blow sucked his breath away, and he fell, conscious enough to clutch his pistol tightly.

He strained to breathe and listened to the man's footfalls running off into the street. He struggled to stand, too dizzy from the blur in his eyes. The pain set in to his already bruised body. As his vision slowly returned along with his breath, he regained his feet, unsure how much time he'd wasted on the ground. The man vanished.

He staggered back to the courtyard. Light filtered in from the curtained rear windows of the other cottages. From one, an older lady stared out at him suspiciously. He clutched the side of his head and stumbled into a garbage can, spilling its contents onto the cobblestones. Potato peels and onion skins spilled out. Egg shells and papers tumbled onto the ground with wadded up envelopes. He stared at the papers that floated around in the courtyard like so many dead leaves. They triggered something in his head.

He ran back to the cottage's rear steps and found the garbage heaped high in a metal bin. He tore open dark gray plastic bags and dug through reeking refuse in search of more papers.

He saw a shadow from above. Maria leaned out the back doorway.

"What the hell are you doing? What happened?" she asked.

"He got away. Hit me pretty hard with a board."

"The old guy? Are you serious?" she said. She squinted in the dark to see his battered face, then chuckled. "You okay?"

He held up a small gray object—a cell phone caked in greasy break-fast drippings. It had been stomped upon, the gray face and LCD display cracked into a hundred pieces. It was otherwise intact, and he stripped away the rear cover to remove the SIM card.

"I am now."

CHAPTER 5

NOVEL STRAIN

Podgoria Traian, Romania
3:42 p.m., Monday, May 6

KAMRAN HAD no memory of coming to the barren room. An unsettling chill radiated from the cool cellar walls. A single orb of electric light dangled from the ceiling by a stout wire, its glow too weak to reach the corners of the room and the lone cot where he had slept hours earlier. He slumped against the worn brick wall, staring into the shadows across the room.

He recalled the terror of leaping from the airplane before tumbling into the freezing water. The man called Andrei had cut him loose in the water, and he treaded until his arms ached and his thighs burned. Andrei shoved and kicked him to keep him alert. More than once he thought he would drown. When his strength gave out, Andrei grasped his shirt collar and carried him to keep them both afloat. People in a sleek boat arrived and pulled him aboard. He lay in the bottom of the craft gasping for air like a catch of sturgeon. They skimmed across the sea for hours. He drifted in and out of sleep while staring out the back of the boat at a sliver of moon rising on the horizon.

He awoke in the room, unaware of the passage of time. He was simply its occupant. They took his gold watch, and he grasped again and again at his wrist, longing for its familiarity. He longed for anything that would wake him from the foggy nightmare. His head pounded. His body ached. They had drugged him. That much was clear to him, but nothing else made sense.

They left food for him while he slept. He nibbled a piece of boiled and nearly tasteless meat from a solitary metal plate. As he ate, he listened to the sounds of his prison. A steady drip of water hidden behind the brick walls counted the moments. The room stayed dry, but somewhere the water slapped concrete in a constant patter. Overhead, a rush of water filled pipes. A far-off electric motor hummed—a sound he sensed more than heard.

Two men appeared. Kamran stared at them from the cot, then stood, uncertain and afraid. The first man was tall and lean. He pushed open the metal door and stared at Kamran, his expression colder than the room. His black hair was long and slicked back, and he wore a gray sport coat and pants. He dragged a metal chair behind him, and Kamran saw black tattoos on both hands. His companion was dressed much the same, but he was bald and heavier. His mouth hung open in a snarl that barely concealed his tobacco stained teeth. He carried a coil of rope.

They were not Russians, though they spoke and sneered like some Russian toughs he had seen. Their accents differed somehow.

"Sit," the long-haired man said to him as he dragged the chair into the center of the room. Its legs screeched along the floor. "We have things we want to hear from you." He spoke strangely, and Kamran strained to understand.

He sat. The bald man busily tied his arms behind his back. He grunted and breathed behind his ear as he tugged at the knots.

"We will start with something easy, yes? Who are you called?"

Kamran turned to look at the man behind him, but the long-haired man struck him with his fist.

"You are called?" he asked.

"Kamran Khorasani."

"And your job is the one at the Koltsovo? VECTOR?" The word hung on his lips as he pronounced it.

Kamran paused. The man's fist struck again, harder. His ear shot out waves of agony at the blow. Another followed, and his lip split. A bead of blood formed, then spilled warmth down his chin.

"Yes," he said, panting. He could feel the other man looming behind him.

"You see? It is easy."

The bald man chuckled as the interrogator massaged his knuckles. His fingers danced with the tattoos, and Kamran wondered what the inky words said. He recognized one of the symbols that looked like the letter *M* with a tail—the sign of Scorpio in the Western zodiac. The man balled his fists and again beat him. He pummeled his face. Twice he pounded his stomach, just below the ribs. Kamran's lungs betrayed him, and he gasped for air as he had aboard the boat.

"You have something we need. Where are the samples?"

He answered with silence. More fists struck him. More pain followed.

"Do not think that I enjoy this," the interrogator said.

Kamran had no doubt that he did enjoy it. That was why he was there, and the very reason his masters employed him.

The beating continued, but Kamran found each blow somehow less severe as the hurt overtook his body. The taste of blood in his mouth faded away, replaced by an intense ringing in his right ear. He had reached some threshold mingling numbness and pain. The interrogator seemed to tire. Kamran bled, and the man's hands became bloodied themselves. Whatever secrets they sought from him they would discover soon. That lessened the pain for him some. He would have to say nothing at all, but they would know.

They beat him like this for several days. He kept time by their daily visits. The men became less careful. They shed their sport coats and arrived in undershirts and casual pants. Kamran found it a small mercy that they only beat him. The idea of knives terrified him. No electric shocks. No burning. They simply beat him with their hands. When the bald man hit him, he grunted. His fists were fatter, but his blows stronger. Kamran felt the force of them like a rupture in his bones. He cried out as they did this, though he could no longer hear himself.

Kamran withdrew into himself. The beatings seemed suspended in time. He grasped at any thought that raced into his mind and held it. He escaped into his head. He thought of the watch his father had given to him in Paris for his twentieth birthday. He imagined the woman with the dark red hair in Koltsovo. *What was her name?* He wasn't sure he ever knew it. He gave her a Persian name. *Suri.* He imagined her running away with him. He and Suri would go live in the mountains somewhere far away where he could make love to her. He thought of silvery airplanes and a song everyone sang as children and how many steps he climbed every day to his first apartment at the university. He thought of the taste of metal in his mouth that reminded him of his dentist in Mashhad who talked to him about birds while he worked. Wherever his mind wandered, he followed to flee the pain.

He thought of the journalist who wrote him quaint emails in French and spoke to him sweetly on the phone. But she was another dream in his head, and he now knew he had been lured by her voice here to this terrible place.

By the fourth day, his interrogators tired quickly. Kamran struggled to glimpse at their bloodshot eyes, wondering if his secret had spread. They asked the same questions again. Their efforts became labored. Sweat stained their white shirts. They ended much sooner this time and left him to suffer, slumped in the chair until he became unconscious. He woke on the cot covered in blood, pained by every move.

On the fifth day—or perhaps it was the sixth—no one beat him. No one moved him to lay down. He slouched in the metal chair for hours, and his back muscles ached in pain that matched his face and ribs. He thought he had a fever. The virus within him had outpaced his efforts to contain it. If the beatings didn't kill him first.

The door opened, and he knew his secret was revealed. Through swollen eyes he saw people dressed in plastic suits, their faces sheathed in glass, their mouths covered. They said nothing and doused him with lukewarm liquid. It burned his open wounds and washed onto the floor where it pooled. They scrubbed him as they would livestock with long-handled brooms and brushes that poked his skin raw. Then they doused him with a hose and began again. They did this with nervous eyes, speaking only to command one another.

Satisfied, they prodded him with the brooms to stand and escorted him to another room. White tiles covered the floor, and they parked a new chair over a circular drain in the floor. He sagged in the chair unbound and helpless. To his left was a sink with a deep basin. Against the opposite wall and farther away, cracks of sunlight crept in between the panels of an overhead door. Here the lights dangling from the ceiling were brighter. He sat dripping wet, awaiting the inevitable. Pains shot down his back and legs like barbed wires tugging on his muscles.

As he dried in the still air of the room, his skin cooled, and he began to shiver. The pain around his swollen eyes tightened, but through the blur he watched a man enter the room alone. The sleeves of his pin striped shirt were rolled up to his elbows. His skin glistened, and atop his head was a shock of thick and curly white hair, neatly brushed. The man paused to look at Kamran. His lips curled, almost amused.

Without a word, he approached as he pulled on a pair of Latex gloves. He grabbed Kamran's arm gently, turning it as he tied an elastic band. Kamran watched passively as he did this, wondering at the warmth of the man's hands on his skin. The man procured a needle and twin vials from his pocket. With a practiced motion, he inserted the needle and Kamran watched as his own blood filled each vial. The man placed the vials within a plastic bag and bandaged Kamran's arm tightly. He removed the gloves and tossed them on to the tile floor.

He took a step back and spoke with dulcet voice that flowed about the tiled room.

"You are a very clever man, Dr. Khorasani."

With effort, Kamran lifted his head to look at him.

"By now you will have surmised your interrogators are suffering miserably. It is a wonderful method of revenge, I must admit. The pathogen is remarkably unpleasant. And so quick to incubate. I wonder if that was deliberate?"

The man inspected his own hands, staring down his prodigious nose at his finely trimmed nails.

Kamran spoke. "Who are you? Where is this place?"

"You may think of me as your host," the man said. "And you are among august company. You are sequestered where Ovid himself spent out his final days."

Kamran's brow creased.

"All in good time, Dr. Khorasani. For now, I have questions of my own. To begin, can I assume that you exhibit no symptoms of the pathogen?"

"I … I require treatments. Please, I need them," Kamran pleaded.

"And yet you remain contagious. Fascinating. You are, as the Americans say, a Typhoid Mary. You will forgive the expression. I have diagnosed hemorrhagic fever, which was to be expected. After all, we brought you here. Can you confirm for me that this is the family *Filoviridae*?"

Kamran nodded.

"Ebola or Marburg?"

Kamran closed his eyes and whispered, "Marburg. A novel strain."

The man grinned. "How wonderful. It seems the rapid incubation was indeed deliberate. A remarkable accomplishment. More than I expected. You are being most helpful, doctor. A pity you were not more forthcoming."

His smile vanished.

"But this is as old as history itself, is it not? You, a Persian. I, a Greek. Have we not been adversaries across time? Let us expatriates shed these ugly histories and become friends."

He rapped on the door. When it opened, he handed Kamran's blood to a figure wrapped in white protective gear.

"Let us get something more nourishing in you, and we may continue our discussion in more comfort." He looked over his shoulder. "There will be precautions, of course. Your presence makes many of my associates uncomfortable. They know so little about these things, whereas I am quite familiar."

His striped shirt and white hair disappeared behind the closed door, and Kamran sat once again alone in the room, feeling he had lost grip on anything resembling sanity.

* * *

Within an hour, the masked figures returned. While one sanitized and changed the bandage on his arm and a stubborn cut under his eye, the other laid a pair of white trousers and a long tunic in his lap and dropped a pair of slippers on the floor at his feet. From their masks, they mumbled instructions he couldn't understand. They spoke English as the Greek had. It seemed the beatings would end, though any thought of instilling more fear into his captors seemed impossible. As his fear of pain receded, his anxiety welled, and his guts quickened. His breath shortened as they pressed his wrist for a pulse and removed his soiled shirt, which he had worn since he first left Russia.

Kamran dressed with effort. The freshly laundered shirt filled his throat with a pleasant scent, a comfort that made him acutely aware of his own miserable state. Cautiously, he stood and steadied himself as he tied the drawstring at his waist.

One of his masked caretakers shepherded him toward the wall with unintelligible commands. The other placed a covered plate upon the metal chair, then collected his filthy clothes in a black plastic bag. They left, and Kamran approached the meal they provided.

Steam seeped from the plate's rim. He kneeled before the chair and removed the cover. The savory smell of a flank of chicken on a bed of rice overwhelmed him. They left no fork or knife, so he tore at the chicken with both hands and shoved bites into his mouth. Eating stung his swollen lips, but every bit of the tangy chicken was worth the effort. It warmed him and set his nose and mouth to watering. When he had eaten every bite and grain, he gnawed on a thin bone, then placed the plate beneath his chair.

The cracks of sunlight on the paneled door darkened. Kamran wondered at them in a daze as he lay on the hard floor digesting his meal. He wondered too late if they had drugged or even poisoned the food. He didn't care.

With the crank of a motor, the overhead door rose, and long lights and shadows filled his makeshift quarantine. Outside was a paved ramp.

A white van with opaque windows eased its way down to the doorway. Kamran propped himself on his elbows and caught a glimpse of men in jackets and sunglasses wandering at the top of the ramp, their arms resting casually on submachine guns that hung from their shoulders.

The van doors opened. A familiar face with a thin mouth and gaunt cheeks appeared. His captor Andrei leaned out from the rear of the van and motioned to him with a quick dance of his fingers. Kamran shuffled to the van. Along each side of the interior was a flat bench that straddled the wheel wells. A black metal cage cordoned the rear from the driver's cab. Andrei stood near the cage and lit a cigarette. The driver complained to Andrei through the surgical mask that covered his face. Andrei glared at the man and blew gray smoke out his nostrils. He sat at the bench on the right and pointed at the opposite bench for Kamran to sit.

Kamran pulled himself up into the van's compartment with his aching arms. He sat as far from Andrei as he could manage, an arrangement he suspected they would both find agreeable.

With another puff of smoke, Andrei snapped at him. "Are you helpless? Close the doors."

Karman tugged on each door and slammed them shut.

From the rear of the van, he could see nothing outside. Ahead, he stole glimpses of cypress trees that lined a long drive and rows of grape vines beyond. The setting sun faded orange to their left and the van coursed its way onto wider paved roads where Kamran could hear passing vehicles. *I am here just inside this van,* he thought. *Can't you find me?* No one would even know to look. Perhaps his interrogators had spread the virus to others, and they would attract attention. It would explain why they moved him. As his thoughts raced, he realized the consequence of his fanciful hope. Someone else would suffer as his interrogators had and perish in fever and blood. It was better that no one looked for him. A darker thought stirred. Perhaps this was what he deserved for what he had done.

The driver steered toward the sunset on an open highway. They drove until full night consumed the summer sky and the hazy glow of a large city loomed ahead. The driver orbited the city at a distance until he veered from it and the van climbed mountain roads into the immutable dark.

Andrei stayed still, moving only to reach for another cigarette in his jacket. He moved like a snake, slow and deliberate. His eyes were open slits that sometimes shifted toward Kamran. Once past the city, the driver tapped at the radio and discotheque music filled the compartment. At last Andrei spoke, his lips hardly moving.

"Turn off that shit music."

The driver's thick arm reached again for the radio and the music grew louder. Andrei tapped the stub of his cigarette on the bench beside him. He stood to grasp the cab's cage and lean toward the driver. Again he spoke, this time hushed. Kamran couldn't hear him. Andrei returned to his seat and again leaned his head against the van wall. The driver turned off the radio and gripped the wheel tightly, his head focused on the mountain road.

Kamran's eyes fell heavy. The van stopped, and he jerked awake, suddenly aware Andrei was gone. The rear doors opened, and bright light formed a brilliant halo around a masked figure clad in protective gear. Squinting, Kamran followed the figure through a steel door marked with a triangle of warning symbols alerting fire risks, caustic materials, and biohazard. He thought of the biohazard symbol as he entered and how he had become the warning incarnate. The hazard coursed through his bloodstream.

They walked down a long hallway lined with glass windows and dark rooms. Steel doors with slender vertical windows fortified the labs. In each sealed room, Kamran saw a vaguely familiar arrangement of countertops and lab supplies. Behind him trailed the stomping feet of his captors. Andrei entered the hallway carrying a bulging plastic bag at his side.

At the end of the hall, the man in protective gear waved a magnetic card over a gray panel, and the stout door responded with a click. As he entered, Kamran stole a glimpse of his captor's face on the ID card. The tiny photo showed the face of a smiling man in spectacles in need of a haircut. His name was obscured by a blue-gloved thumb.

They had arranged the room for him. The counters were bare, one inset with a single gooseneck sink. Along the side wall was a cot much like the one he slept in the last several nights, though here was a luxury—a pillow wrapped in a vinyl case. The wall showed faint angular smudges where a calendar or poster once hung. Quiet consumed the sterile room, save for the dull thrum of fluorescent lights overhead.

Andrei entered, and Kamran backed away with his arms crossed.

"You will begin your work soon," Andrei said.

He wanted to say no, that he would do no such thing. That they could all rot. That he would rather die. It was, of course, a lie. They would know it to be so.

He nodded.

"What did you think? You and your little plan to run away like a little coward. Did you think there was ever a reporter waiting of you in Istanbul? Did you think no one would notice? That no one would find you?" Andrei laughed aloud and made a little mocking sound. "That part was easy. Like breathing. You are not so clever. Just a coward. And where could you go, huh? To home? To the Paris? You are nothing to them. To anyone, you stinking coward."

Andrei sniffed the air, disgusted.

"If it were up to me, I'd put you back on that plane and let you spread that fucking disease all over the world yourself. For you and everyone to choke on."

Andrei tipped the plastic bag he carried and dumped its contents on the floor. He left, and Kamran heard a click as the door locked shut. The men moved down the hall beyond his sight.

Tears welled in Kamran's eyes. He held his breath and knelt on the cold tiles, fighting his deepening shame. There before him rested his last possessions. They gave him someone else's clothes. Not new, but cleaned and pressed, though now they lay crumpled in a heap on the floor. A new undershirt and his old shoes were scattered nearby, and he scooped them together next to his small leather case.

He opened the case and found within the last vial of his antigen. He did not think he would see it again. He was battered and weak, his immune system susceptible. Never had he experienced stress like this. Without the tablets he'd made himself, he would eventually succumb to the virus. The thought that disease still lurked within him, waiting to attack his body like a carnivore from within, made him tremble. With the medicines returned, he had a shallow hope to survive.

Whoever the white-haired man was that spoke to him, he understood the need. The man said they would talk again. The offering was his work.

Kamran gathered his things around him. Then he noticed a lone object just under the cot. He knew at once what it was, and he crawled over to it. It was his watch, the object of such focus for him as they beat him. He clutched the gold watch in both hands as he leaned into the cot and buried his face into the folded blanket to muffle his sobs.

CHAPTER 6

LONG SHOT

Vienna, Virginia
3:58 a.m., Friday, May 10

PAUL CORSO woke minutes before his alarm sounded and flicked the switch to off before it roused Janey beside him. The alarm hadn't made a single noise in years. His need for sleep lessened with age. By routine, his body had become accustomed to the early hour, his mind plotting out the day as he woke. He sat at the edge of the bed for several minutes, chin resting on the heel of his hand while a dozen thoughts coalesced. Outside his bedroom window he heard the calm rustle of maple leaves. He and Janey preferred the window open as soon as the season allowed. Far off, the beltway awakened with steadily rising stream of white noise.

Downstairs he made coffee from the French press Janey had given him for Christmas last year. He thought of it as pretentious at first. Too elaborate for his needs. But it became his fondest vice, a first and best cup he savored before each sunrise. While the coffee seeped, he thumbed through emails for any updates from Kay. He had left her last night while she coordinated with the Office of Technical Collection on the mobile phone records. Pierce's discovery in Batumi gave them enough leverage for today's briefing to keep the operation alive.

Meanwhile, another team had verified the hijackers named Khasan

Kagirov and Abdul Islayev. The two of them moved together in insurgent circles after the second Chechen war. They still needed to confirm the others in the attack, working back through Kagirov's associates. But that took time. For now, his teams could only gather their intelligence, piece by piece. Everything pointed to the Chechens as fighters, not fanatics. But things had a way of changing in Chechnya, never for the better.

He moved to the office with a steaming mug in one hand and the day's *Washington Post* in the other. He stood in his boxers and wrinkled undershirt sipping his coffee with the paper spread out on his father's old oak desk, a relic from his law firm. Paul's hair was too long—a wiry mess from fitful sleep that he flipped from his brow as he adjusted his reading glasses. He scanned the headlines out of habit. Syria roiled in chaos. News that the president sent a carrier strike group to the Persian Gulf caught his eye. It was likelier to provoke responses from Iran than quell them. He saw the shifting connections between each article, but the piece on Iran didn't even mention the situation in Syria. At least the Giants acquired a veteran receiver who might shake things up.

He looked up to see Janey standing in the hall in her satin pajamas. Her face was pale. Faint freckles dotted her neck. Her hair fell over her eye and down to her shoulders. She kept it blonde, probably for his sake. It suited her, but he didn't mind the gray either.

"Well, what are you doing up?"

He put down his coffee and approached her with his arms wide.

"I wanted to see you." She yawned.

"That's my girl," he said and held her for a while. "Want some coffee?"

"I just might."

They shuffled into the kitchen together and he poured her the rest of his French press.

"You know, you might actually use that robe I bought for you," she said with a sleepy look. "With you strolling around in the house like that, the Ericsons are going to have a good laugh looking in your office window."

"Janey, if anyone's looking at me at four in the morning, they deserve what they get."

"Big day today? Working late?" she asked.

He shrugged. She already knew he would.

"You need to shave." She scratched his chin and then perched on a stool with her mug in her hands.

Paul made them both toast while she planned out her weekend. He would forget most of what she said by the time he got to Langley, but dinner tomorrow after mass sunk in. He marveled at her energy and wondered how he'd ever been graced with a woman who stayed with him through all the years.

* * *

At eleven minutes past the hour, Paul glanced around at the dozen faces that filled the briefing room. Those he knew by name looked bored, some sipping lattes from the Starbuck's downstairs. Those he didn't recognize wore anxious expressions awaiting their debut before the Director and the intense scrutiny of their supervisors.

Next to him, Kay Linh propped her elbows on the long conference table and flicked her pen on the laminate top. She focused on her brief's executive summary, reading it for what he guessed was her fifth time in twelve minutes. Her lips moved as she read. Her black hair had lost its normal lustrous sheen, and she constantly pushed it behind her ear without success while she read. He noticed a white smudge on her slacks and realized that she wore the same outfit from the day before.

Director Frank Drummond entered the room from a side door that set into the wood paneled wall. A polka dot tie wagged before him as he paced across the room. His deputy—a man half again his size—trudged immediately behind.

"Good morning, everyone. Sorry to keep you waiting. Let's pick it up right away." At the end of the table Drummond found a leather chair and propped himself at the edge of its seat, arms spread on the table. "Harley, take a seat."

Deputy Director Harley Gilchrist stood near the back wall. His burly frame nearly blocked a bulletin board covered with photos and placards that a pair of analysts had pinned there minutes earlier. The younger analyst craned her neck to see her handiwork in hopes it wouldn't be lost.

"Sorry, Frank. My back's already sore today. I'd just as soon stand for the moment," Harley said.

"Suit yourself. Suzanne, get us started."

Suzanne Tasker cleared her throat. "Of course, sir. As you know, we have multiple targeting operations in and around Georgia. We have confirmed the identities of two of the Chechen hijackers and identified three others. These three here appear to be related. They're maternal cousins of the apparent leader, Khasan Kagirov. We don't have any names for this fifth man in the photos, but we should be able to connect him to the others. However, this man—that's number six in the images you have, sir—does not appear to be Chechen. We think he's probably Russian, but we don't yet have any details on him. Now, the Georgians have connected some of these men to Doku Umarov and fighting in the second Chechen conflict. They may be one of the many *jamaat* under Umarov's so-called Caucasus Emirate. If so, this is their first action against soft targets in the region."

Drummond pushed a stapled brief to his left. "Why now? I want to know if there's any connection here to eastern Ukraine. Ramzan Kadyrov's got fighters on the ground there now. Were these guys taking part?"

"We don't see any sign of that, sir. These men have no love for Kadyrov."

"Who the hell does, Suzanne?" Drummond grinned, and the tension in the room eased a bit. "But these guys are trotting around with some unknown Russian guy in a major act. It's a funny place. Loyalties shift. I want to know if they were making a play on Ukraine."

"Of course, sir. We will look into that immediately," Suzanne said, nodding.

"It's the bigger picture we need here, Suzanne. I don't need to remind you."

"Absolutely."

Drummond again grabbed the brief and flipped to a page near the end. "What about this Georgian agent?" he said, his pudgy finger stabbing at a photo on the board behind Harley.

"Right," Suzanne answered. "This is Rezo Kaladze. He was in the Georgian military, then transferred to GIS in 2008. He has family in Ossetia, and we think he's retaliating."

Harley Gilchrist spoke up from the back of the room where he stood with his hands on his hips, back stretched upright. "Been a long time coming for that, don't you think?" He spoke with a muted Southern drawl, his words drawn out and slow.

"I guess he knows how to hold a grudge," Suzanne replied.

Harley snorted, amused. Drummond paused and looked at her intently.

"I don't want guesses. I want actionable intel," Drummond said. "You're saying he was working alone. That's not my read of the situation."

"I'm sorry, sir, I did not intend to convey that. Our current thinking is that he's working with someone in his family or friends from South Ossetia. Not with others within GIS."

"But you don't know that for sure."

"No. We're trying to verify with assets in the region currently," Suzanne said.

Drummond smacked the table with his palm. "That's not an answer. That's not what I want to hear. We've got scraps, people. Gaps and more gaps. For all you know there are ten more just like him working right alongside our people."

His voice bellowed in the packed room. Paul watched from across the table as Suzanne's lips tightened.

"Sir, if I may. Suzanne?" Paul said.

Suzanne's expression eased slightly, and she nodded for him to proceed.

"The brief mentions Seda Alaskhanova. She was at the house where our targeting officer located a cell phone from a possible staging house on the coast."

"She's the one who sent your guys on this god damn goose chase. And now she's with GIS, as I instructed?"

"Yes, sir. She provided the first hijacker names to our targeting officer, not GIS. And those turned out to be genuine. At this house, she was hysterical. She went there looking for someone. My officer thinks she was looking for someone related to the hijacking."

"You're talking about Pierce? The one in the shooting?" Drummond asked.

"Yes, sir. Ethan Pierce. He believes this woman can identify our sixth hijacker. The mystery man."

"Where is she now?"

"In Tbilisi. Alan Sanger escorted GIS to the house in Batumi after Pierce and that operations officer he was with called it in. They've got her in a holding facility. I believe you're familiar with that site from previous operations."

"Do we have access?"

Suzanne interrupted. "Absolutely. GIS has coordinated with Sanger, and they will cooperate to provide access directly."

"But we're not interrogating her currently? It's what? Late afternoon over there?"

Without thinking, Paul corrected him. "1831 hours, sir."

"So, nothing's happening?"

"GIS will provide access," Suzanne repeated.

Drummond sighed. "See that they do. And, Suzanne? Watch this one. We can't afford another surprise like yesterday."

"I'll remind Sanger of that myself."

Drummond collected his paper and pushed his chair from the table. "Anything else?"

The room went quiet as nervous faces glanced at one another. Paul looked to his left at Kay. She had remained still throughout the meeting. With the pause, her pen again wagged in anticipation.

"Yes, sir, there is," he said. He patted Kay's chair armrest. "Sir, this is Kay Linh, the Staff Operations Officer. She's been coordinating with Pierce and our other teams."

Drummond shrugged. The bags under his eyes sagged, and he checked the time.

"Yes, hello, sir." Her timid voice faltered, then picked up strength. "I have been working with the technical collections team to source calls made from the cell phone that Ethan Pierce found. There were several calls made from this phone to numbers and towers in Chechnya and in northern Georgia."

"Yes, and I suppose it's too good to be true that these phones identify anyone?" Drummond asked.

"No, sir. I'm afraid they are disposable phones. NSA might be able to assist."

"I see. Harley, let's connect with the Director of National Intelligence on that. Thank you, Ms. Linh." Drummond rose and gathered up his briefing papers.

"Excuse me, sir, I wasn't finished," Kay said.

Paul smothered a grin in his hand. Drummond raised his eyebrows.

"As I said, the phone made several calls to phones in the region. However, it only received calls from two numbers. One call was local. A restaurant in a nearby hotel. But there were six other calls from the same number, each time from a tower in Constanţa, Romania."

"Romania?" He looked around the room. "Who the hell do we have in Romania right now?"

Chatter filled the room as the directors and analysts talked among themselves.

"Walt Russell's there," Paul said over the noise.

"Good. Ms. Linh, none of this intel about the phones is in the brief," Drummond said.

"No sir, I just verified the data prior to the meeting."

"I see." Drummond left the table and crossed the room. "Right, keep at it. I want more on this Romania connection, but I can't take that to DNI. I need more, people. And I need it yesterday."

Drummond left as he had entered, where the door set seamlessly into the wall.

Paul leaned over to and whispered to Kay. "Nice work."

She gripped her pen tightly and let out a tiny breath as the group filed into the hallway.

Paul wound his way through his coworkers who lingered in the hall in whispering conversations. Before he reached the stairway door Suzanne called from behind.

"Paul, a moment please."

He waved Kay away. "I'll catch up with you later."

Suzanne crossed the wide hallway and stood near the door with her memo book clasped between her thin hands.

"You weren't kidding about her," Suzanne said. She nodded toward Kay as she walked down the hall.

"God knows she'll be telling us what to do in a few years. Is this about her?"

"No, she's clearly capable of handling herself."

Suzanne glanced over her shoulder as the impromptu whispering continued. Intense faces closed in to one another, and a trio of hallway discussions hissed on. She tugged at the hem of her jacket, forming tidy lines from her shoulders to her waist. Age had been kinder to her than to him. The skin on her hands wound tight around the knuckles, and there were tiny wrinkles at her neck and the corners of her eyes. She had a runner's shape and a warm glow to her skin. She achieved her appearance through deliberate effort, he had learned over the last few years. Every fold of her charcoal pantsuit was calculation. Her bronze lips had hardened purpose. Everything down to her expressions were a crafted front for command.

"Let's go for a walk," she said.

Paul motioned for her to lead on. Suzanne didn't normally discuss anything with him outside a closed room. He had developed a dislike for her office. She often summoned him with brief and cryptic emails, and he marched to her door and the pallor awaiting within. She liked familiar ground. Going for a walk was new territory.

She made small talk as they headed outside to the back courtyard. She mentioned the warming weather and going for early jogs in the morning. But she avoided anything personal. He couldn't recall her ever asking about

Janey or his weekend plans, and he had learned not to ask the same of her outside the Agency.

They stepped out onto a vacant concrete patio encircled by the newer building. The late morning sun peeked over the roof to the east, but the courtyard was still cool and shaded.

"You heard Drummond's concerns in there. Clearly, our assessment of this situation has changed. We need to ensure that there aren't more complications."

"Suzanne, just two days ago you told me to hand everything over to GIS. At his insistence, as I recall."

"And we can see how well you and your team accomplished that," she said with a scowl. "But I see no reason to believe GIS can protect the asset after what's happened since then. We need solid intel from her if we're going to get anywhere with this."

"There isn't anywhere to go yet. Not that I can see. This one's different somehow. I can't explain it. It's like something stuck in my teeth, and I can't quite get at it. Whatever it is, whoever it is, they're way ahead of us."

"Then you need to get ahead of them."

"What happened to we?" Paul said. He regretted it almost before he had said it.

Suzanne stared at him with her arms crossed. Paul sensed that tension taking over again. Her forehead creased, and her stance stiffened. As ever, her voice stayed calm, but her jawline fixed tight and her voice with it.

"To be quite frank with you, Alan Sanger isn't the best individual for this current situation. In my estimation, he's too close to GIS. I know Alan. He couldn't see this coming any better than they could."

At least she was making some sense for once, but he didn't like where the conversation headed.

"Alan Sanger doesn't know his ass from a hole in the ground. I'm with you there. He's going to play the diplomat the whole way along. And if they are as far ahead of us as we think, we may as well forget about any good intel." Paul's voice rose loud enough to bounce around the courtyard.

"That's not acceptable. You need to find another option."

Paul ran both hands through his hair and sighed. She needed this at arm's length, and this was her way of informing him. She must be getting more pressure than he thought. He had to do the same trick occasionally with his own officers, and they knew how to read him. Pierce knew better than any of them. That was how the game worked, and these were the moves. Pierce knew that game's score, even five thousand miles away. The thought left him uneasy. One mistake, one surprise and the broken pieces would tumble down hill, not up. *Not this time*, he promised himself.

"You talk to Sanger. I'll figure out something else," he said.

"Soon. Whoever is behind this won't wait for you."

He wanted to yell, but it wouldn't matter. He shook his head instead and stared at a seam in the sidewalk.

"You know, for someone not giving any orders, you sure are demanding a lot," he said. "If we don't have any air cover, you know we won't bother to ask for it."

"I expect you not to."

She uncrossed her arms and walked back indoors. Paul put his hands in his pockets and wandered around the courtyard, his mind in motion to formulate some plan.

* * *

Paul returned from the cafeteria with poached salmon sitting uneasy in his gut. In the walkway outside the cafeteria he passed an old colleague. Years ago they had shared a flat in Colombia for five months. The man helped him master his Spanish vernacular. Paul gave him a nod and a steady-handed wave. He smiled in return and on they walked, the silent reunion over as quickly as it began.

At midday, the operation center desks filled as the last few analysts and officers returned from lunch. Paul found the lone empty chair and wheeled it over to Kay's desk where she stared at a jumble of text and numbers on her screen.

"I thought I told you to head home after the briefing," he said.

"So you can call me at home in an hour? No thanks," Kay said, her eyes still fixed on the screen.

"What's this?" He pointed at the screen.

"A long shot." She stopped and twisted her chair toward Paul. "We know there is some kind of connection between our hijackers and someone in Romania, right? I've been working on the Romanian number, and there is literally no activity from that number outside of our Georgian cell. But I noticed something else. Almost every time those calls happen, they bounce off the same carrier tower in Constanța. One or two other times, it's somewhere else in the country. Now, there are always a lot of calls going on. So, I ran a correlation to see if there were any patterns. I think I found one."

"You did that since the briefing?" Paul said.

"I've been working on it since … what time is it now?" She glanced at her screen again. "Sometime overnight."

Paul leaned forward in his chair. "What's the pattern?"

"Almost every time one of the calls between Romania and Georgia ends, a different cell number calls out from the same tower within a few minutes. It calls a few different numbers, mostly in Romania. More pre-paid numbers. But there are two calls to different numbers in Georgia. And one in Cyprus."

"Cyprus?"

"Yes. A posh hotel. It's some beach resort."

"What day is it?"

"Friday," she said, annoyed. "And I'm the one who needs a break?"

"No, Kay. I mean what day is the Cyprus call?"

"Oh." She checked her screen. "May fourth. Around 1900 hours."

"The day of the hijacking. You may not think you need a break, but I think you just earned one. That was the green light. Now, what about the Georgian numbers. Same day?"

"One of them is, yes. Earlier in the day. I've actually got a record on that one. That's what I've been trying to tell you. The number's account lists M. Teklashvili."

The name hung in Paul's ear, familiar but far off. He stared off at the wall and reviewed the week's events. Alone, the pieces made little sense. Each defied the Agency's assumptions about the familiar belligerents in the Caucasus. This was far outside their usual concerns. But, as a whole, something took shape that he couldn't quite see. His assumptions got in the way, and he knew he had to abandon them to see the divergent motives in play. *What in the hell could they be up to?*

"It's Seda Alaskhanova," Kay said. "Remember? It's one of the aliases Ethan found on her. Malika Teklashvili. It's her. She knows what's in Romania. She has to know."

Suzanne was tossing his team to the wolves on a hunch. Now Paul knew her hunch about the woman was right, though he hated to admit it. Whatever this shadowy group's aims, they would make sure that Seda didn't talk. Maybe they already had.

"Get ahold of Pierce right now. Tell him that our asset is at urgent risk, and that he is to secure any critical intelligence from that asset without assistance. From anyone. Tell him to play it close to the vest and not let Sanger know what he's up to. On my direction. And tell him he's got to move fast."

Kay listened intently as he relayed the order. She looked pained as the realization of what he was asking of them set in.

"I still think you need a break," she murmured.

"Just get it done," he said. "Then get some rest while they prep."

CHAPTER 7

OUTSIDE INVOLVEMENT

Batumi, Georgia
5:42 p.m., Thursday, May 9

ETHAN HELD a rag filled with ice to his head. He sat on a threadbare couch in the front room of the little cottage. Seda sat beside him, sullen and despondent. Maria watched over them both as they waited for the Georgians to take custody of Seda and investigate the identity of the old man responsible for the lump on the right side of his head and the ache in his gut.

When the Georgian intelligence officers arrived, Ethan watched from the porch steps as they escorted Seda into an unmarked Toyota Landcruiser. She passed the front fence and turned to look at him wide eyed and desperate, arrested by her fear. Ethan doubted he would see her again. They would truck her back to Tbilisi, where Maria said they had a building near the airport. She knew the facility from prior cooperation with the Georgians. She didn't say more, but he knew she meant rendition.

Despite everything Seda had done, he admired her. If nothing else, she had tenacity in a place where women had nothing. Still, she had much to answer for. She had to know what the Chechens would do. A vivid vision of Marcus Eldridge coughing up blood entered his mind's eye, and he looked away as they pressed her into the vehicle and drove away. He did what was necessary. There was more to this thing than her. More to it than him. Now others would do their part.

He couldn't follow them back to Tbilisi. His head buzzed from exhaustion like he'd been drugged. His body fared no better, and the ache in his limbs weighed him down. He needed rest. He and Maria drove back along the sea road downtown and checked into the Sheraton Batumi. He declined her invitation for a late supper. She smiled, but he wanted to drown out everything in solitude and a hard drink. He left her standing in the hotel lobby, her face a worried puzzle.

In his room, he lay awake listening to the low stir of the seaside from the open window. In the quiet, he thought about Sarah. She would like this place and the view of the dwindling sun on the water. She loved new places or any break at all from her routine in Washington.

He had wanted her to keep that routine. He had wanted—still wanted—to come home to her from days like this so they could pretend to be normal for a weekend watching year old shows and eating pizza. Making love. She couldn't be that for him. She never could, but he realized it months after she left.

He stood in the dark of his hotel room and looked out the window at the water. On the promenade below, the stone path glistened from the light rain that had just passed. A couple walked along the shoreline, leaning into one another under the warm glow of the streetlamps. He needed a drink.

The minibar had a single miniature bottle of Jack Daniels, which he poured into a glass he found in the bathroom. It needed ice, but he didn't bother. The whiskey wouldn't last, and the minibar only offered tiny bottles of vodka and some unappealing chilled wine. He needed just enough to calm himself and get some sleep. The harshness of the whiskey warmed his throat, and for the moment there wasn't any pain. His head buzzed, but the sharper sting between his temples had eased.

He heard a knock. He glided over the floor and he felt for his pistol on the dresser. The knock repeated. He leaned to the keyhole and saw Maria's face staring back at him, her arm raised to knock a third time. He opened the door a few inches and hid the Beretta behind his back.

"Did I wake you," she whispered.

He shook his head.

"Listen, Ethan, I …" Her voice faded. "I wanted to see if you were okay."

"I'm fine. Really."

She had removed her blazer and wore only her tight-fitting tank top. Her dark blonde hair fell in tangles around her bare shoulders. She reached her hand to his face and touched the welt at his head. He backed away, then eased and let her hand touch him.

"After everything today I can't sleep. I was just sitting in my room alone. This job …" Again her voice faded away.

He noticed her lips were a darker rose. She pulled her hand away.

"You know, they don't tell you how lonely it gets in the field. You put on all these masks for the job, and even when you go home at night you're someone else," she said.

"It's hard on all of us," he said.

"It's just, I thought we were a good team today. Right? We watched out for each other. It was the first time I felt like someone understood what it was like in a long time. I don't want to be alone right now. Can I come in?"

He opened the door wider. She pressed herself to him, lunging up where her lips found his, her hands running once through his black hair. Part of him resisted, clinging to a hope he knew was empty and gone. He shivered, and she mistook it for thrill and pressed harder against him. Was it the exhaustion? How had he missed her attraction? He felt her lips and the warmth of her tongue. This woman wanted him, and in that instant he didn't care how or why they had come together. He welcomed it then and thought only of the scent in her hair. He wrapped one arm around her waist. With the other, he placed the Beretta on the sink countertop just inside the room. Their mouths breathed into one another, and he closed the door.

She tugged at his belt and lifted his shirt, then removed her own. In the dim city haze and moonlight, he traced the line of her breasts with his hands and found her taut stomach and a thin scar on her side. His fingers dwelt there, touching the mystery that made her more real. They kissed and again pressed close, their bodies greedy for release. He lifted her against the window with her arms spread against the wall. He teased her belly, her thighs, and slid into her, her silhouette rigid and ecstatic. The cool night tingled on his skin, and the two of them clung together sweating. They moved to the bed together silently, but the tension remained as they strained and pressed against one another. Her warmth intoxicated him. He quickened, her wrists clasped in his hands. She moved with him. Her breath became a moan, barely audible. When it was over, they fell to sleep in the open air.

He woke in the early morning to the sound of her showering. He found his glass of whiskey and finished the last traces while he waited. A shower would do him good.

"Good morning," she said with a smile in the mirror. She wrapped a towel around herself.

Ethan stood behind watching her in the mirror, staring at her shoulders that glistened where droplets fell from her hair. She seemed different to him then, a woman altogether new in the course of a night. He had no real sense whether that was his discovery or her intention. He gave her a wistful grin, and she turned to face him.

"You know, Ethan, it doesn't have to mean anything," she said.

"It always means something," he said.

She kissed his cheek, and he took his turn in the shower.

✳ ✳ ✳

They drove back to Tbilisi in the Mercedes, taking their time along the coastal road and valley highways. Maria spoke to him, and he to her, each revealing too little of themselves to matter. The balance was unfamiliar to him, though he had observed it many times. Fellow officers who, once far from home, found one another for romance without any history or future. It wasn't regret they shared, but caution and self-preservation. A part of the craft that one learned only through intuition.

"How long have you been at this?" she asked.

"A while," he said.

"You really can't tell me after last night?"

He shrugged.

Maria became quiet. She twisted in her seat and stared out the window for several minutes, her face concealed behind gold aviator sunglasses.

"They make good liars out of us, don't they?" she said.

"I think we figure that out all by ourselves. That's not what bothers you about it anyway."

Maria turned toward him once again, feigning shock with an open grin. "Oh, really? Please enlighten me."

"It's not the lying. Lying is what we do, there's no getting around that. You came into this work ready and willing to lie. It's safer that way. Smarter. It's what the lying becomes."

"And what's that?"

"Isolation."

"Is that what you do? Keep everyone away from you?"

"That's not what I meant," he said. The muscle in his jaw tightened, and he avoided looking at her.

"Who is she?"

"Who?"

"Oh, come on. I'm good at this, remember? You're not married. Tell me you're not married."

"I used to be," he said.

"So that's it. And I take it that wasn't your idea?"

"Look, what the fuck do you want from me? This isn't going anywhere. It can't. You've been stationed here for, what, four or five years? Long enough to make inroads, but not long enough to get too comfortable. You don't have any real friends, but you say you love the people. I think that yesterday was the most excitement you've had since you got this assignment. I think you enjoyed every minute of it."

"You're telling me you didn't?" She smiled and reached to touch his arm with the back of her hand.

"It doesn't matter. Tomorrow or next week, we'll both be back to keeping everything at arm's length. Because we have to."

She pulled her hand back. He sensed something stir in her. Her amusement was gone, replaced by a hotter instinct.

"Jesus. Don't you ever let your guard down?" she asked.

He held her gaze for a moment, then focused on the road.

"Not if I can help it."

That much wasn't a lie. Her vulnerability last night and now made him more cautious, not less. *Look where that got me,* he thought. He stared at the horizon where the highway vanished atop a rise, but his mind wandered back home. There was so little he could tell Sarah over the years, yet so much she knew about him. Lying to her was necessary, a routine she tolerated at first. The distance between them was the consequence of his omissions and untruths. When she gave it back to him in kind, he hated her for lying. He knew she would leave, and then she did. He had more than a year to reckon with it. But it was an affliction without cure. She held on longer than he expected. The truth was he deserved it.

They arrived in the city after more small talk and long silences. She seemed undeterred, ever eager to open herself to him.

"What now?" she asked as he drove around in the late day bustle around the city.

Good question, he thought. His driving pattern was erratic, his eyes on the car's mirrors as he worked his way through every familiar seeming vehicle behind them. The last thing he wanted was a tired drive that allowed anyone to recognize them together. Whatever they were up against, it wasn't over.

"Relax," she said. "Just get me back to my apartment. Here, turn left on Pekini. You should stay."

"Thanks, but I need to catch up with Wade."

"Call me before you go anywhere."

It wasn't a question. He nodded, then left her waving at a quaint apartment building with pale yellow walls and wrought iron bars on the windows.

* * *

He met Wade for supper in an American themed bar north of downtown closer to the embassy. They ordered burgers while surrounded by young tourists and NGO workers who congregated on a Friday night for a taste of home. Familiar songs drifted through the smoky air from a gaudy jukebox. Survivor gave way to Katy Perry. There was no sense to it. The young crowd seemed as unaffected by the incongruous noise as they were by the cigarette haze. For Ethan, the atmosphere was a thoughtless mash of nostalgia that reminded him of nothing in particular about home. It was just another bar with a veneer of American gleefulness and outdated beer posters. He and Wade fit in among the crowd unnoticed, themselves only vaguely American, which was all the anonymity they needed for now.

"Nice shiner," Wade said, nodding at the small, dark bruise between Ethan's nose and right eye.

"You should have seen the other guy," Ethan said.

"I heard about the other guy. Old. Fat. Sounds like you missed me."

He just shook his head. Wade didn't look much better. His right arm bore a crisscross of scratches and cuts from his tumble out of a moving car. The arm had barely scabbed over, oozing slightly just beneath his shirt sleeve. Wade didn't share many details. He was in the car with Rezo Kaladze, who got a call and then pulled his weapon. Rezo killed Giorgi Gelashvili in the seat next to him without a word. Wade's instincts kicked in, and he leapt from the car. He paid for the effort with a set of lacerations and a sore shoulder. Rezo never slowed down.

A skinny waitress with bleached hair in braids brought them burgers and fries. She doted on them, practicing her English with each request for ketchup and napkins. Talk of their work fell away and they ate quietly, observing the other patrons who flirted with one another and smoked.

Ethan thought again about Maria and her eager prying. With Wade, he had history. They understood each other, and each knew the other's movements and intentions. They could eat together at ease. They had a kind of professional trust, an unspoken bond. But each kept himself apart for the ugly possibilities their work one day promised. Yesterday, he thought that day had come, but he let the memory drift as Wade drained the last of a warming bottle of Natakhtari lager and ordered another.

Ethan's phone buzzed, and he got Wade's attention by tapping at his breast pocket.

"Home office. Time to go."

Ethan returned the call while Wade drove his newly rented car away from the bar. Wade's Toyota was quieter than the Mercedes, but Ethan still pressed his ear into the phone awaiting a familiar voice.

"This is Dodger," he said.

Kay's voice responded. "Hourglass here, have weekend plans for you, Dodger."

"What did you have in mind?"

"Recent asset now at high risk. Require immediate intervention to secure asset's intel on recent event."

He knew immediately something had changed. Seda was now an active target for someone. But she must be still alive. He ran through possibilities and wondered if the men who took her had done something with her. *Why isn't Corso on the line for this, damn it?*

"What is asset's current location?" he asked.

"No change in status or location. Hourglass requires new intel as soon as possible. Sooner. Your priority here is the asset's knowledge on contacts in Romania. You are to verify without outside involvement."

That explained Corso's absence. The Georgians still had Seda, but the GIS was compromised. Someone in Georgian intelligence wanted her dead. It meant the Agency was pursuing other more official avenues, probably through Alan Sanger. Ethan's assignment was something they could later jettison, along with him and Wade if necessary. The distance between him and Corso right then was a cosmic gap, held together by Ethan's faith that Corso knew something serious enough to eyewash the Georgians and leave him and Wade without any help, but still moving.

Kay's always delicate voice drew him from his thoughts. "Dodger, please confirm?"

He wondered just how in the hell he and Wade could do this. They wanted things tidy so that this mess fit neatly in a briefing, part of a larger explanation for people with larger responsibilities.

"Affirmative. Just weighing the options."

"Understand you are on your own, Dodger." Her voice was weaker still.

"Not entirely. I'm with Nomad now. We're going to need more friends."

"Keep it in the family."

He sighed, but before he could reply the line was dead. He stared at the phone in thought. Corso wasn't kidding around.

"What's the deal?" Wade asked.

"We'll talk at the embassy."

A rare wave of worry took Wade's face. Ethan leaned back in his seat, and Wade ceased his cautious meandering to head directly north for the embassy grounds, muttering under his breath at the clumsy driving of the Georgian youths out on the town.

Ethan shared the news with Wade in a dull meeting room on a lonely floor at the embassy. The offices outside the room were dark and empty, though they kept the door closed.

"The orders aren't complicated," he told Wade. "Seda Alaskhanova knows something about contacts in Romania. Langley wants answers without GIS involved. Soon. Sounds like they don't want Sanger directly involved either, which makes things tougher. Corso seems to think someone in GIS wants her silenced."

"Some of Rezo's friends, I bet. Glad Corso gave us plenty of time for a well-planned operation then," Wade said.

Wade's worry had faded after battling the traffic, and he had recomposed his usual sardonic self, a mechanism no doubt inspired by some ghost of gunnery sergeants past. It was now part of him, as innate as his steady hands and measured breath. Still, after the week's events, Ethan shared Wade's pessimism. They had almost nothing to work with, but whatever else happened from here, he wasn't going to lose anyone in the process.

"Right," Ethan said. "Let's wind it back. You said Rezo got a call before he killed Giorgi. So, he wasn't acting alone. Did he say anything to you in the car?"

"The man was ice cold. I kept thinking I didn't like the way he acted before. He was smug, you know? Just the way he was acting. But then he gets that call, says maybe two words, and then pulls his weapon while he's still driving." Wade's hand formed a gesture like a gun and jabbed his finger at Ethan.

"And who made that call?" Ethan wondered aloud.

His mind again flashed to Rezo standing over him with a crooked sneer. The gunshots echoed in his head, and he closed his eyes for a moment. *My friends at Scorpio send their regards.* Wade was right. Rezo was smug enough to taunt him. Whatever Scorpio was had dispatched Rezo to finish what they'd started with Marcus Eldridge. Ethan couldn't think of anyone that made sense. But that's what Corso wanted him to answer.

"How the hell are we going to get Seda to talk even if we do get access to her?" Wade said. "We couldn't do it before."

"Not without leverage we couldn't."

"Yeah, well, she can have that fucking Mercedes back if she wants," Wade replied. "She can leverage that all day."

"No, think. She has to figure these people want her dead by now. So, if we offer her a way out, she'll make a deal. GIS has her in a building east of the city. Somewhere close to the airport. Maria says she worked a rendition there a few years ago."

"Just great. Sounds like the Ritz," Wade said.

"It's just an old building."

"That's not how it works. I've been to these places before, remember? They'll have it locked down tight, and they don't exactly post visiting hours.

No way we're just walking in, let alone out of there. Especially not with a prisoner."

"We're supposed to have access. That's part of the deal. So, we just need to arrange a meeting to question her," he said.

"Sanger's holding all the cards there," Wade said. "He has all the contacts with the Georgians. I don't think he's going to be eager to cut us in. Not after this week. I can tell you after talking to him yesterday that he doesn't like either of us very much. Especially you."

"I wasn't going to ask him."

"Who the hell you going to ask then, your new girlfriend?"

Ethan shrugged, feigning modesty with a smirk.

"Shit. You think that's going to work? Man, you barely know her. She's a ball buster. How do you know she's not going to go straight to Sanger anyway?"

"I think she and I have an understanding."

"What the hell …" Wade said. "Oh, shit. You did not shack up with her on the job. Tell me you didn't."

"In my defense, she showed up at my door."

"That doesn't make it better, man. You do know that I slept in this very fucking building last night, right? Me and a blanket in a glorified janitor's closet and you were debriefing a very fit coworker at some resort hotel. I'm surprised at you. Not saying I blame you, understand. I'm just surprised at you. Shit."

Wade shook his head.

"Besides, she can shoot straight when she has to." Ethan knew that would get him going.

Wade howled. "Oh, that is fucking low. Man, don't even. She was barely ten yards away from the guy. You really going to kick a man like that when he's down?"

"I had to give you hell for it sometime. At least someone put that rifle of yours to good use."

"I'll remember that next time I'm watching your back."

They laughed it off and continued planning over reheated coffee from a nearby break station. The coffee was bitter and burnt, but warm enough to keep them alert.

"Okay," Wade said, "say she gets us in there. Then what? Seda's smart. She's not going to say shit to us until she knows she's out of there for real. And then what? They'll be right in there with us. It's not like we can just ask to take her for a ride."

"Well, first of all, it won't be us. It will be Maria and me."

"What about me?"

Ethan reclined his chair with is hands locked behind his head. "Well, you're right about GIS not letting her out of there. I think we could change their minds with a little persuasion, and that's where you come in. You can provide a little external influence on our negotiation."

"Like what?" Wade asked.

"Like, do you still have those M83 grenades in your bag of tricks?"

Wade shook his head with an incredulous grin.

"You know, what I like about you is you're crazy. What I hate about you is you drag me into your crazy shit."

CHAPTER 8

CRITICAL WEAKNESS

Tbilisi, Georgia
11:30 p.m., Friday, May 9

ETHAN LEFT Wade in the embassy and wandered outside into a broad yard surrounded by a tall fence topped with razor wire. Clouds roiled overhead, electrified by the city night. With some hesitation, he dialed Maria's number.

"That didn't take long. I'm glad you called," she said. Her voice wound into his ear, simmering and less playful than her flirting banter from earlier. She had waited for him to call.

"It's not what you're thinking, but how's your weekend looking?"

"Better now. That sounds exactly like what I was thinking," she said.

He paused and pressed his fingers against his forehead. "Can you meet us tonight? We need to talk in person."

"Us? Sounds serious."

The sultry act disintegrated. *Good,* he thought. Neither of them needed the distraction.

"Never a dull moment," he answered. "Wade and I will pick you up. The corner just down your street, to the east."

"See you then," she said.

They found her on the street standing across from a bus station where revelers waited for midnight rides to the downtown bars. Ethan sat in the rear and opened the door for her while Wade drove, his window open just a few inches.

"Get in," he said and motioned at her.

She tossed in a beige overnight bag and climbed into the car.

"Let me introduce you to our driver for this evening," Ethan said.

Wade shook his head as he eased into the stream of cars.

"I want to make it clear this was his idea," Wade explained. "Not much of a cover, but it explains the black guy driving Miss Daisy here. Wish I could say it was the first time."

Ethan shrugged. "Don't take it personal. You can drive me around any-time."

Maria seemed amused. "You two always like this?"

"Only on Fridays," Wade said. "By the way, I hear you're a good shot."

"When I need to be," she said, now clearly enjoying herself.

They drove south and east along the river where the city became at once its own and like all cities, a blur of lights and passing cars and people walking along in groups. The light rose up into the hills where the old Soviet era TV tower perched above, overlooking all like the night watchman.

"Now is when you tell me what's going on," she said. She turned to Ethan in the seat next to her.

"We need you to arrange a meet with Seda Alaskhanova. As soon as possible. Tomorrow."

"That's Alan's call, not mine." She cocked her head. "You don't want him to know."

"That's right," he said.

"And that's why you need me." Her amusement lessened with a frown.

"You have contacts in GIS, right?"

"Giorgi Gelashvili was my main contact." She said his name with flourish, her Georgian accent rolling perfectly in Ethan's ears. "But I know some others."

"Others who can arrange for you and me to interrogate her?"

"Maybe so. What's this about?"

His hesitation returned. He looked out his window as they cruised along the river and approached the bridge. Involving her had become inevitable to meet Corso's orders. But his instincts resisted. Something about her made him waver. It wasn't a matter of whether he could answer her question. He had passed that point, and turning back meant failure. Failure meant more people would die, starting with Seda.

The uncertainty surprised him, and he wondered if it was his attraction for her that made him uneasy. This was dangerous work that could end their careers. Or worse. Her eagerness was his liability, and he made it worse welcoming her into his hotel room. Maybe it was something else about her and all those masks she talked about. Something he questioned about her, distant and subtle.

"Ethan, what's this about?"

"We need to get her out of there," he said. "Before whoever wants her dead makes good on their intentions. She's the only real link to the hijacking at this point, and I'll be damned before I let that go."

"Look, I understand where you're coming from here. Really, I do. And I want to help. But GIS is not just going to let her go. Do not underestimate these guys."

"Underestimate who, exactly? It's not GIS I'm worried about. It's whoever Rezo was working for."

"But you don't know anything about them, right?" she said.

Wade looked into the rearview mirror as he drove. "That's exactly why we're doing this thing."

"This is crazy. I don't know what you have in mind, but …"

"I'll tell you if you give me a chance to explain. We have a plan. I wish it was one we had more time to develop. I wish we had more help. But this is the hand we've been dealt. It's not the first time we've made the best with some lousy cards."

"Roger that," Wade said, head rocking as he drove.

"So, right now, we're going to take a look. We need you to get us there now. And then get us in the door tomorrow. We know what we're getting into here."

"I don't think you do." She said it quietly. She lost focus on him, fixed on thoughts tumbling in her head. In two short days he had seen so many facets of her, but it was the first time he had seen her uncertain.

"Well, you said yourself. You understand where I'm coming from. I need to know right now. We need you. Are you in?"

At once her posture straightened and she locked her eyes with his.

"I'm definitely in."

She didn't seem happy about it, but he lost any doubt that she was committed.

They crossed the river and found the Kakheti highway where hotels and shabby gas stations flanked the roadway for several miles. Past the airport, they turned north into a modest neighborhood that devolved into decaying junkyards and rows of rust-eaten metal buildings that glowed dimly white in the night.

Maria leaned between the forward seats guiding Wade to the site. She pointed her long-nailed finger past his ear toward a fenced compound to their left a few hundred yards away. Wade slowed as they observed the place. The fence was chain, but well covered by vinyl strips that concealed the yard and building from the road. Behind the fence was a squat and sturdy brick building with small windows. It was a three-story fortress among the other prefabricated metal buildings around them, towering well above, but still concealed by a long grove of cedars growing at the fence line. Whatever industrial purpose it once served was long obscured. Nearer the building sodium lights still bathed the yard in amber.

"This is the place?" Ethan asked.

"That's it. The entrance is on the west, down that alley ahead." She pointed again past Wade's view.

"What do you think?"

Wade turned his head as they passed the building slowly.

"Can't tell if anybody's home. Let's turn around and take another look,"

Wade said. He followed the road until they passed the site, then found a place to turn around. He waited several minutes before he pulled back onto the road.

"It's bigger than it looks," Maria said. "GIS put quite a bit into the place since the Gulf War. They had a little trouble with the Gldani prison scandal a couple years ago. Sanger seemed to think GIS was using Gldani at the time on the sly, but they quietly moved the operation here. I haven't been there in almost three years now, but one of my contacts says they installed strong security. Rewired the whole place. It's not the gulag hellhole you're imagining."

Wade eased the Toyota along the curve of the road. The tires crunched and popped as he drove half on the shoulder where Ethan spied the entryway from a gap in the fence. He caught the flicker of a lighter and the silhouette of a man smoking near the fence gate. The fence blocked his view of the yard, but he counted six cars parked in line along the lane. Most of the building's tiny windows were dark specks on the brick facade, but some glowed like old gas lamps with panes long covered with smoky grime. He looked for doors, but he saw only an entrance facing the fence gate and the top of a vacant loading dock with a pair of sturdy rolling doors.

"Someone's home," he mumbled. He tapped Wade on the shoulder. "Look, there's a sentry down the lane. If he hasn't noticed us already, he will any second. Let's roll."

Wade drove on and picked up speed as he passed the lane. He navigated the back roads of the area, sniffing out an alternate route on the far side of the facility for himself. He needed an approach and seemed content as he drove around gravel lots and dirt alleys for a quarter hour. Ethan thought through his plan again, picturing in his head the steps he and Maria would take to talk with the guard and the walk to the entrance. He had committed the shape of the building to memory, with help from a map on his phone. He guessed where other exits might be to the east and south. He hoped for east, where they could break away into the cedar trees once they cleared the fence line.

Ethan turned to Maria. "Make the call."

"Now?"

"This late at night, they'll know it's urgent. It buys us an excuse not to wake up Sanger. Get us in there as soon as you can. Tonight, if possible. Tomorrow morning, if not."

Wade said, "Bad move, man. Let's get her back to the office in case they get fancy with a trace. Who knows?"

"Okay, you call when we get back," Ethan said.

Maria offered no protest. She fidgeted with her phone as they reversed their route through the city. Along the way, they all shared observations, exhausting every detail they could and repeating them again. For Ethan, it was a practiced procedure with Wade, and part of every operation they had run together. The careful planning, the repetition, the contingencies. They discussed the alley approach, the lamps above, and the likely placement of cameras. Wade had identified vents on the roof and another near the loading doors. But Ethan marveled how quickly into that rhythm Maria situated herself. She came to it practiced and ready. Again he saw in her a subtle change, another facet.

At the office she made the call while he and Wade examined a pixelated satellite image of the building and the grounds and roads nearby. Maria's voice rolled with the lilt of her fluent Georgian. He understood none of it, but he heard her at once urgent and then contrite. She listened briefly then shouted a string of profane syllables into the phone that seemed to startle even Wade into attention. Just as abruptly, she ended the call.

"That didn't go well," Ethan said, crossing his arms.

"Not tonight. He's calling his supervisor now. We get inside tomorrow."

"When? Every delay, every call up the ladder is a chance for one of two things to happen," Wade said. "Either they get wise and call Sanger, or someone else gets to her first. And I don't like either option."

"No. We're in," she said. "Trust me. I know this guy well enough, and I know he's already convinced."

Wade glowered, then went back to studying the satellite map. The plan was crude and simple, which explained Wade's affection for it. Ethan wondered who had the worse task. He and Maria would enter the place to question Seda. That much the GIS would expect from their CIA allies. He might even run into a familiar face to help ease any doubts. For the two of them, it was a game of confidence. They couldn't let the Georgians sense any trace of trepidation. Wade had to rely on their timing. His task was simpler to the point of absurd, and more brutish. He had to enter the perimeter unseen, scale the building, and drop smoke grenades into air vents they'd seen while scouting the building.

They went over it again. Wade nodded. His demeanor calmed as they talked through the plan, focused on the rote that he committed his attention to in full.

"We have to get her out of there before they have time to think about it. That's the tricky part. We've got to shake them then. Whatever it takes," Ethan said. "Understood?"

With that, he eyed Maria intently, awaiting her acknowledgment. This was the critical weakness in his plan. At best, the two of them would face at least a couple GIS officers. Armed and trained men who knew a different, harsher world. No, he realized the worst was that these men could kill Seda and would not hesitate with either of them getting in the way.

"I get it," she said, without any sign of worry.

As they ran through the plan a third time, Maria got the call. She spoke only in assent, her responses brief. She ended the call and rubbed her lips pensively.

"We're in. Tomorrow morning. 0700 hours," she said.

✻ ✻ ✻

Maria picked Ethan up before sunrise. He stood in the building entrance waiting out of sight but exposed to the cold damp that clung to the ground. He had dressed the part, but the too-snug sport coat he'd borrowed did little to keep out the morning chill. He climbed into her Outlander, and she smiled a morning greeting.

"Wade already left, I take it?" she said.

"Three hours ago," he said with a shrug. "You ready for this?"

"Are you?" She gave him her playful smile.

She awaited adventure. She was here for the thrill of it, which made things more difficult. She'd ignore the subtlest of threats, and he would have to watch their GIS counterparts even closer. Every move, every expression spun into variations he couldn't predict, let alone control.

They arrived at the old brick building as the cloud-filled sky warmed pink and gold. Fewer cars lined alley lane, though the sentries remained just near the gate. Maria approached them, and Ethan followed.

"*Dila mshvidobisa*," she said warmly. *Good morning.* "We are here by appointment. With Davit Kodoshvili."

The guards wagged their heads and waved them closer. She fanned out her passport for them to inspect and nodded at Ethan to do the same. The guard eyed him warily, then Maria, barely noting their identification. These were not men to underestimate. They had learned to be loyal to different leaders and survive the sudden upheavals that came with them, all with a careful eye on neighbors who sharpened knives at their border. They knew what to look for.

The other GIS officer escorted them to the building where they stood before double doors. Bolted into the brick above the door was a camera in a long white casing, and somewhere at the other end was an officer recording their faces.

With a buzz and a click, their escort opened one of the doors and another man greeted them. Ethan recognized his dark buzz cut and heavy eyeglasses from the house in Batumi. This was Davit.

Ethan shook his hand and hurried into the building. "Davit, we met the other day."

He entered the front office, an old brick-walled space where guards watched monitors from behind a high desk.

Davit bowed his head. "Yes, I recall you, Mr. Pierce. We have you to thank for securing our asset. I know you had some help," he said with a smug expression meant to impress Maria.

She missed nothing. "You're kind to say so, Davit. Thanks for arranging this meeting on such short notice. We have some pertinent questions for Seda Alaskhanova. Things that can't wait. You understand."

"I do, though I do not think you will get her to talk. She has been un-cooperative. But these things done properly take time, no?" He sighed. "Now, please. You sign in here, then I take you to our visitor. Your mobiles, please."

The veteran officer produced a small plastic basket, and they placed their phones within it.

"Are you carrying any weapons?"

Ethan nodded. He held up his gray sport coat to reveal his sidearm. Davit smiled weakly as he gestured to receive the weapon. Ethan expected this, and he unholstered the gun and eased it into Davit's hand. Davit took it and frisked him from the ankles up to his shoulders. He felt the empty weight at his hip and with it a sense of insecurity. He harbored no hope of retrieving the Beretta, which he bought eight years ago in Virginia on Wade's advice. Now he relied on Wade to begin a reckless distraction that would make sure GIS had no interest in returning the firearm. It was his sacrifice for authenticity, a small means to gain the trust of the Georgians. There was always another gun.

"Miss Hessler?" Davit said.

Maria shook her head. "Not my style, I'm afraid."

"May I?" Davit asked as he approached her.

"Of course."

She raised her arms as Davit frisked her lean legs and hips. He moved up her ribs and armpits. Maria turned her head away while he ran them along her belly and up toward her breasts. Ethan watched her face tense as the Davit's hands rose up. She held her breath until he shied away. She glanced at Ethan and looked away. She had to know they would do this. *She's acting too anxious.* He needed her calm or everything would come apart.

He got Davit's attention. "Well, where to?"

"This way please," Davit said.

They followed down the hall to an open bay and into a freight elevator. The contraption shuddered as it rose to the third floor with a grinding racket. Davit opened the accordion doors and gestured to the dim hallway beyond. To Ethan's right, doors secured with magnetic locks and steel bolts interrupted the old brick wall. On the left, doors with frosted glass cast a faint light into the hall.

Davit opened the second door to reveal a barren interrogation room. A small table and two chairs on either side occupied the room. Overhead, a haze of fluorescent light chased the shadows from the painted brick walls and corners. There was nowhere to go within the almost perfect cube of a room. Only cold light occupied the windowless room lorded over by a black camera bolted into the far wall.

"Wait here please," Davit said, gesturing. He continued down the hall.

Maria took a seat facing the door, which Ethan left ajar. He pulled one of the metal chairs away from the table, leaving a lone chair for Seda. The chair legs screeched along the tile floor as he dragged it to a corner. He circled the table and leaned against the far wall with his arms crossed.

She spoke to him as they waited, her head still facing the door. "You know yesterday morning? When you said it always means something? It did to me."

"This isn't the time," he said.

The camera hung above his head, spectating.

She turned her head slightly, and he saw her profile, the crease of her eyes straining at him, her angled chin and cheekbones. She bit her lip.

"I just wanted you to know."

She needs to keep it together. She expected the worst. He didn't know what would happen in the next hour, but the last thing he needed was an anxious partner. He spent the last two days trying to make sense of her. She saved his life and then came on to him. He had convinced himself she needed him. She was the first woman since Sarah that interested him.

He now knew her protean personality was her great asset, not her brassy reputation. He found it alluring. In her he had something to discover, and that excited him. But he needed her to be bold. For Davit's sake and Seda's. For his own.

They waited a long while until footfalls sounded down the hallway and the door opened. There stood Seda. Davit had cuffed her hands, and she held them at her waist. The skin at her wrists was still raw and red, and Ethan recalled his own handiwork tying her to the bed in Telavi. She had changed since then. Her once sleek hair fell in tangles around her head and face. The bold color drained from her lips, and dark circles swelled under her nervous eyes. She wore the same clothes he had found her in—black pants and a plain tan shirt. Her scarf was gone, as was any trace of her perfume. She was a woman defeated and exhausted, but otherwise apparently unharmed.

Maria motioned to the chair. "Please sit," she said.

With her head bowed, Seda eyed Ethan at the back of the room. She crept toward the chair and sat.

"Let's get those off her, huh?" Ethan said, pointing to the cuffs. "She's not going anywhere."

Davit stretched a key from a cord latched to his belt loop and unlocked the cuffs from Seda's outstretched wrists. He tucked them in his coat pocket and stood at the door behind her.

"I'm sure you're tired," Maria said. "We have just a few more questions for you."

Seda sat motionless. Her eyes shifted back and forth between her new interrogators. If she was even slightly relieved to see familiar faces, she showed no sign of it. Ethan unfolded his arms and took a seat.

"Hello, Seda." He smiled, but she remained unfazed. "Actually, I have just one question for you. Do you think that you are safe here?"

Beside him, Maria grunted disapprovingly. But he was fixed on Seda's reaction, pleased to see her throat move and her eyes narrow as her brow creased. She didn't expect this, he could see. Behind her, Davit sneered and shifted his stance. Ethan ignored him.

"Because I think you know better than that. Wouldn't you say? Not from a loyal man like Davit here. No, if he were with your friends you wouldn't be talking with us now. Isn't that right?"

Davit interrupted. "Mr. Pierce, may I speak with you outside?"

Ethan waved him away.

"I think we understand each other, don't you? We know how to make a deal, right?" Again he smiled at her gently, but she recoiled.

She broke her silence. "What do you want?"

"How about I tell you a story, and you tell me how it ends? That's what I want. It starts with a Chechen woman who proves to the men she's better than them. *Jamila.* She makes a name for herself taking up her father's smuggling network. And this makes her very different from the other women. She has money. And she doesn't have to care what everyone else thinks. She likes this. One day, she agrees to do something. To help some friends of friends over the border. Some dangerous friends, but they promise more money. How am I doing so far?"

"Brother. Not father," she said with a hint of spite.

"Okay, her brother's business. But these dangerous friends of hers— maybe friends of her brother—bring along a stranger. Not a good Muslim. Someone else. Someone interesting. Someone a little more like her. And he makes many promises. He makes her feel very good. And she does what this man needs. He has even more money. He takes her to the ocean."

Seda's eyes filled with tears. Her chin trembled. "How do you know this?"

Ethan stood and leaned over the table, his face near hers.

"Because I am very good at paying attention. Now, you tell me the end of the story. Tell me about Scorpio."

Seda buried her face in her hands and sobbed. A long moan from her throat filled the room, and everyone began talking at once. Davit pleaded intently with Ethan to discuss things in the hall. Maria yelled at Seda to calm herself and answer her questions. Ethan argued with Davit while he stole a glance at his watch. Thirty-two minutes had passed since they arrived.

A fist pounded on the door. The frosted glass at the door filled with a shadow. Again the fist pounded, and a voice shouted in frantic Georgian. Davit turned and opened the door. A haze of gray smoke hung in the hallway. It seeped in the room, thickening as it snaked its way into the interrogation. Davit raised his sleeve to cough.

The man shouted ceaselessly. Ethan didn't need the words to know they feared a fire and discussed the evacuation of the prisoners. Wade had done his part, right on time. Now he and Maria had to make their move. Maria stood in front of him and he sensed the tension in her body ready to act. The other officer moved on down the hall, shouting as he jogged.

A piercing screech filled the hallway and with it a light strobed within the smoke like lightning. Within the brick room, the wailing sound seemed to penetrate his skull. Davit covered his ears with his hands and turned to give them all directions. *Now is our chance,* Ethan thought.

As though on cue Seda leapt from her chair and thrust her shoulder into Davit. She let out a scream as she drove him into the wall. He grunted, stunned by her ferocity. Maria rounded the table shouting in Georgian and rushed to the struggling pair, feigning help for Davit. She gave Ethan a look, and he understood. He reached up and hung both hands on the camera above him, then pulled down with all of his weight. The casing snapped, and the camera pointed at the floor below.

Davit drove his elbows onto Seda's back. Her screams continued, drowned out by the screeching alarm. Maria wrestled with them both, doing what she could to interfere with Davit's defense. She reached into his belt fumbling for his weapon but found an empty holster on his right hip. Davit shoved her off and raised his arms again to strike Seda's back.

Seda slipped away from them. She raised her arm, and at the end of her trembling hand was Davit's Makarov pistol pointed clumsily at his face. He raised his arms and turned ashen. She turned the gun to Maria and backed away two steps.

"Seda, don't!" Ethan shouted from the back of the room over the wail of the alarm. "I will get you out of here. You know you aren't safe here."

She shook her head, shifting the weapon between Maria and Davit. The pair stood still, panting for air with their hands up.

"Seda, that's why we came. Her and me. To get you out. Scorpio wants you dead, right? Do you hear me? I want you alive. We want you alive. You shoot them, you don't get out alive."

She hesitated.

"Seda, we have to go now. Now or you never get out."

Her face tightened and she screamed. Tears rushed down her cheeks. She looked at Ethan, and he saw the desperation in her eyes. She heard him. He approached her one step at a time with his hands outstretched. She kept the gun trained on Davit. Ethan reached her and placed his hands on her arm, helping her to lower the weapon. She held it tightly in both hands pointed at the floor.

"What the fuck are you doing?" Davit said.

"What I should have done two days ago. Put your hands on the table," he said.

Davit obeyed as he cursed in Georgian. Ethan took the fob of keys from his belt loop. He peeked into the hallway and motioned to both women. The smoke thickened, and he could barely make out silhouettes running to the end of the hall.

"I'm taking her," Maria said. "You take care of him."

"I think there's a stairway at the corridor on the left," he said. "Go to the lowest level and find an east exit. If you can't find that, get out of one of the loading docks and run like hell."

Maria grabbed Seda's shoulder and pulled her into the hall. Ethan watched the women run into the smoke and vanish around the corner. *They'll make it*, he thought. They had to.

In the room, he pushed Davit into the chair Seda had just vacated.

"Sit down," he said. He found the handcuffs in his coat pocket and cuffed him to the chair. "Don't look so alarmed. It's just smoke. A distraction so we can get her out."

He patted Davit's shoulder and received an angry scowl. He left Davit in the room and locked the door. Smoke choked the hallway, and he ducked to avoid it and ran down the left corridor. Maria and Seda had closed the doors behind them. He fumbled with Davit's keychain to open the door.

He heard a shot. The noise rose up from the stairway behind the door. His fingers faltered and he tried to jam another key in the lock. Another crack sounded. A third. His pulse quickened and he pounded on the door in frustration. Another key opened the door, and he leaped down the stairs. No reports sounded from below. Nothing at all. At the ground level he heard commotion in the halls beyond, but he descended deeper.

He entered a shadowy cellar hallway. The lower level had no fire alarms, and the screech sounded far off through the concrete walls like a muted insect. Ahead the hallway split, and he walked pressed against the left wall with nowhere else to find cover. At the intersection he could hear it. From the east hallway came the pitiful sound of labored breathing and a whimpering breath in rapid rhythm.

He peeked around the corner and saw her. She lay on the floor, her chest heaving. He ran to Seda and fell on his knees. Her lips quivered as a bubble of blood formed. She still clutched the Makarov in her hand. Blood drowned her tan shirt, but he could see three exit wounds in her chest. She never fired a shot.

Maria did this. She was already gone.

Seda looked up at him, suddenly aware of his face. Her hand reached up and he took it.

"Seda, I'm sorry. I didn't know. I …" his voice trailed off. Her eyes turned to glass as tears fell down her temples. "I need to know," he said. "I need to find him. Who is the man on the plane?"

She gasped.

"Who is he?" Ethan shouted.

Her voice croaked and she tried to speak into his ear. He pressed close.

"Andrei," she said. Her voice was barely a whisper. "Scorpio."

She died staring up at the plaster ceiling, unable to see the sky.

PART II

The Scorpio Compact

CHAPTER 9

SLEEPER ELEMENT

McLean, Virginia
4:14 p.m., Monday, May 26

PAUL ENTERED Director Drummond's seventh floor office. He had visited the room many times since his arrival years ago in the National Clandestine Service. The room itself bespoke the power of the position. Since 9/11 it had become a conduit to the White House and a medium for the ambitious. The drudgery of government bureaucracy dissolved here, giving way to wood paneled walls darkened with age that warmed in the light from brass sconces.

In his first visit to the room years ago, his chest tightened, and his stomach turned. Three directors and thirteen years had eased him of the condition, but it lurked like a secret knot in his chest. He knew his purpose here. It was like entering a new assignment where he had to master another dialect. He expected a dozen or more of his colleagues talking rapidly over one another, speaking the increasingly familiar language of power and position. Instead, a few somber faces greeted him. His superiors sat around the director's conference table, their mouths flat.

"Am I late?" he said.

"Not at all, Paul," Drummond answered. "Grab a seat."

He scanned the familiar faces. Harley Gilchrist, Drummond's deputy sat at his left. The man was inseparable from his more polished boss and for good reason. His Southern charm distracted some from recognizing the CIA's shrewdest mind. Suzanne, his own boss sat opposite them both. She sat upright in her usual practiced posture, her hair still coiffed at the end of a long day. Something more strained than normal lurked in her face as she ignored his glance.

He paused for a moment at the next face that appeared like an old photograph at the edge of his memory. He hadn't seen the man in person in over a decade. Beneath the grayer hair and behind the rounded jowls he recognized Alan Sanger, recently the Station Chief of Georgia. In a sure sign of displeasure, Drummond gave Alan a lateral move to oversee a team of Russia analysts. He approached the nearest chair and extended a hand.

"Alan. Been a long time," he said.

Alan gave his hand a curt shake. "Paul."

He took a padded leather chair and rolled himself to the table. "What have I missed?" he said. He had several guesses about that already.

"We're discussing the fallout from Georgia," Drummond said. "And I need you to clarify a few things I have concerns about. Pierce's report for a start. This supplements his previous update on the capture of the asset. But it comes several days after the incident."

"The Georgians detained Pierce for five days. Thanks to Alan, they released him on condition he leave the country," Paul said. He gave Alan a nod, who reciprocated with an icy stare.

Harley shifted in his chair. "We all know what happened. I think what the Director is getting at is that there isn't one lick about you or anyone else giving Pierce the go ahead to run her out from under GIS' nose. You didn't give the go ahead for this?"

He let the silence fill the room for a moment, choosing his words carefully. "There was no operation to approve, sir."

"Had a feeling you'd say something like that," Harley said. "I expect it's true as far as it goes, but it's too clever by half. So, you didn't know anything about it? What about you, Suzanne?"

She propped back her shoulders and scowled. "I knew absolutely nothing about it, Harley."

"Look," Paul said. "Do we give our officers latitude to operate, or don't we? Ethan Pierce is one of our best targeting officers, and he acted as he should have given the circumstances."

"Oh, come on," Alan said. His frustration seethed as he raised his voice.

"With respect, Alan, he did. Pierce had every reason to believe the asset was in danger. He believed—he still believes—there was someone inside GIS trying to eliminate her. I think that's the larger point here."

"Well, they sure as hell didn't do anything to her once they had her in custody," Alan said.

"Yes, and now we know who the real threat was," he said coolly.

Alan's jaw clenched. Paul felt a twinge of pity for him. He had clearly suffered a recent momentous lecture, though the move spared him professional embarrassment. Alan wasn't blameless, it was true. He missed much playing the long game, too focused on the Russians. Maria Hessler's betrayal blindsided him. Paul wondered how he would perform in Alan's situation. Better, he hoped, but he didn't envy the man.

"Wait," said Drummond. "You said just now he still believes there's, what? An extant sleeper element in GIS? That is not in this report." He planted his index finger on the report with intense pressure.

"No sir, it isn't."

"Well I don't give a good god damn what Pierce believes he knows. I don't recall him or you explaining to the Georgian ambassador why an American officer shot one of his prisoners dead in a government facility. Or who the hell shoved a bunch of smoke grenades down their facility's ventilation system. A facility we went through great lengths to help them establish. Do you have any idea how much we need their cooperation?"

"I have a very good idea, sir," he answered.

"And your cowboys pull a bullshit stunt like this. What do you have to show for it? A diplomatic mess I don't have time for, for one. And a targeting officer who believes he's on to something."

"He is."

"Excuse me?"

"I said he is. On to something. Sir."

"This better be good, Paul. This better be gold plated fucking sermon on the mount hot shit on a platter good."

The knot at his sternum loosened a bit, and he bit the inside of his cheek. He expected a lecture to match Alan's, and he was a little puzzled it had taken several days to receive it. After dozens of visits, he didn't predict that Drummond—easily the smoothest, most personable director he'd worked under—had such a colorful temper. If he made it through the next five minutes, he'd have a greater appreciation for the man.

"We are looking at a larger network here. A new non-state actor. In this case, we believe there are at least two separate cells, possibly three. First, there's the group who hijacked flight AC 163. Next, this GIS officer Rezo Kaladze goes rogue. Then Maria Hessler kills Seda Alaskhanova."

Suzanne interrupted him. "But if Hessler killed Kaladze, then clearly they knew nothing about each other. We don't even know with certainty if they are connected."

"Fair point. That's why we think there may be three active cells. Pierce believes Hessler acted as a matter of opportunity. She wouldn't have been there to pull that trigger if not for him. His assumption is that she was working to undermine him, not to eliminate the asset. He was pretty clear about that. He recruited her to help, not the other way around. Which means this network had other plans for the asset. I think that's a fair assumption. Think of her move as a precaution."

"A precaution." Drummond leaned back slightly and exhaled. He seemed partly satisfied with the answer.

Harley Gilchrist, sitting heavy in his chair, appeared far less convinced.

"So, you think she was protecting something else. Is that about the right of it?" Harley asked.

"She wasn't protecting herself. She blew her cover. Now she's on the run from us and GIS. Not a good career move."

Harley turned his head. "What do you think, Alan? What's she protecting?"

Alan stared at the tabletop and shook his head slowly. "It has to be the Russians. Who else could have done this to us? SVR must have turned her without us knowing," he said.

"So, you don't agree with Paul's theory about some new non-state actor?"

Alan looked askance at Paul to his left. "I think it sounds a little far-fetched. Nothing the Russians do surprises me anymore."

"Supposing it was the Russians," Harley said. "What's their goal? They get a pack of their least favorite Chechens to blow up a Georgian airliner. They burn an agent to help cover up their involvement. It would have to be something mighty important to them."

"Intimidation, maybe? Paving the way for more action in South Ossetia? Take your pick." Alan waved his arms as his frustration rose again.

"I don't buy it," Harley said. He gripped the edge of the table and scowled at Alan. His Southern charm disappeared, and Alan sunk slightly in his chair.

Drummond leaned in. His voice came level and cool. "After all this, we are coming up short. I don't want to keep saying this, people. Get me answers. You are wasting time."

Paul stood from his chair, and everyone but Harley stood with him. They eyed one another with stunned looks. Drummond ignored them and moved to his desk. He was done with them. Time to go.

"Not you, Paul," Harley said. He sucked at his teeth patiently, his hands still gripping the table's edge.

Paul nodded to the rest as they left the room. Suzanne shot him a stabbing look. She would have more to say sooner than later. He sat back in his chair wondering what mode of displeasure he faced. But Drummond seemed disinterested as he checked his phone and began dialing. Harley looked at him for several seconds as if locked in thought.

"What have you figured out about this Scorpio thing?" Harley asked.

So that was it. Harley waited out his surprised expression. *Remind me never play poker with him,* he thought.

"Not much, I'm afraid. We weren't sure what to make of it at first. Maybe a code name or some *nom de guerre*. Pierce tried it out on Seda Alaskhanova. It's on the interrogation tape the Georgians provided. She loses control when he mentions it. His best guess is that's the mystery man from the hijacking."

Harley opened a folder at his side and twirled a sheet of paper toward Paul. Paul grabbed his reading glasses from his breast pocket and examined the sheet.

"What is this?" he said while he skimmed the document. It listed dates and operations trailing back two years.

Harley pointed his thick finger at the paper. "That," he said, "is the Scorpio Compact. More accurately, a record of the times it's mentioned in reports for the last couple years."

"But my team's been searching those reports. We were looking for this."

"Yes, I know that as sure as I'm sitting here. I had it collected. Then I had it blocked."

"You can do that?" he asked. He didn't like the idea of anyone looking over his shoulder without him realizing. Maybe it was worse now that he knew.

Harley grinned. "Pretty cool, ain't it?"

The list contained excerpts of reports from collected intelligence. He recognized two of the operational reports, including Pierce's report at the bottom. But at least a dozen more were unfamiliar. The reports spanned the globe. Indonesia, Argentina, three in Australia, Tunisia. One caught his eye—Romania. The excerpts mentioned Scorpio mostly in oblique terms, others more directly. Two noted something called the Scorpio Compact. He needed to read more of the reports themselves. The context escaped him. From what he could piece together, the references pointed not to a person, but a group. This was the network, he realized. The non-state actor they'd pegged as the new enemy. They were active and responsible for the deaths of 183 souls on AC 163. They killed Marcus Eldridge. *Christ, they turned Hessler.*

Harley let him read in quiet for a moment while Drummond hunched over his desk muttering into his cell phone.

"Where's the rest of this?" Paul asked.

"You'll get it," Harley said.

"Who else knows?"

"Besides the senior analyst who pulled this together for me, you're looking at them." Harley wagged his head at Drummond who looked up from his phone for a moment. Drummond was listening more carefully than he thought.

"Suzanne's not going to like this," he said. As soon as he said it, he realized Harley's ploy. She would think he was getting drawn down for what happened in Georgia and taking his turn at the whipping post.

Harley shrugged. He didn't care so much about appearances, which was not to say he hated the politics. He'd never be director because of it. Not that it mattered. Drummond needed him, and so would the next director in line. Harley's casual shrug said enough. It meant Paul would have to handle Suzanne himself along with anyone else who pried.

Paul removed his glasses and scratched his temple. "What do you need me to do?"

"For a start, keep Pierce on this one like a duck on a June bug. Work it unilaterally. No involvement from the Romanians or anyone else. But there's a bigger problem. It's a very real possibility this Scorpio outfit has someone inside."

"You mean someone else in the Agency?"

"I mean someone else here at Langley," Harley said.

Paul let the observation sink in, as hard as it was to believe. Penetration was always a risk, but for him an abstraction like some relic of the Cold War. A bogey man from his earliest time at the Agency when the veterans talked about the bad old days. He continued his work and let Counter Intelligence do theirs. His mind rewound the faces he'd seen during the week. The analysts and officers, the supervisors. Losing Maria Hessler out in the field was one thing. Someone here at Langley was another. He felt a rush of warmth to his head at the realization, and he felt a little foolish for it.

Harley watched him absorb the implications and a smirk emerged. Behind him, Drummond finished his call and put the phone in his coat pocket.

He looked up at Harley. "How do you know it isn't me?"

Harley's smirk grew and he let out a bark of a laugh. "Let's just say you don't fit the profile. You and Pierce really stepped in it, didn't you?"

"And what about him? You've got more reason to suspect Pierce than anybody after his contact with Maria Hessler."

"Maybe you're right. You worried about Pierce yourself?" Harley said.

Paul's eyes shot from Harley to Drummond and back again.

"No, I am not."

"Good."

Harley reached across the table and slid the Scorpio summary back to his side. He tucked it into his folder and stood up. Paul stood with him and put his glasses back in his breast pocket. They shook hands. Harley's massive hand engulfed his. Drummond rose and joined them near the door.

"Hessler changed everything, Paul," Drummond said. "This Scorpio group was Harley's hobby. I didn't put any stock into it myself with everything else we're up against. This one snuck up on us. I don't like that one bit. But now it's real, and we've got to get ahead of it. This is your top priority."

"I'm already there, sir."

"Then do more," he said.

✳ ✳ ✳

Paul spent the next four hours reading and re-reading Harley's collected reports on Scorpio. The patchwork of threats bore little connection to one another. They shared connections in the deep web, though he needed Kay's help with the technical details. It was an underground internet where participants could share data anonymously via encrypted relays. An internet outside of the internet. For Scorpio, it seemed to be a virtual recruiting ground for malcontents and radicals.

One report involved Argentine nationals who bribed agribusiness executives to prevent release of a food preservative for produce. MI-6 discovered the cell had retained the molecular details and posted them on part of the deep web.

That same site later posted a bounty for hacking ECDIS, the electronic navigation system for ships. A trio of Filipino brothers earned the bounty after one of them inserted a flash drive into the system on a Malaysian container ship called the *Danum 172*. The virus they inserted did little harm outside of bragging on the ship's consoles until the crew reset systems. The brothers took the money and disappeared until one of them showed up dead two months later in Macau. His ears and eyelids had been cut away. So had his fingers.

The latest, and it turned out longest, plot caught his interest most. Several members of *Ansar al-Sharia* in Tunisia worked for months to earn jobs at a phosphate mining operation. Their goal was gathering enough uranium from the mine's waste stacks to build a dirty bomb. It might even have worked had they more patience and resources. His experience was that fanatics had too little of either.

It wasn't the dirty bomb attempt that caught his attention, though. It was their handler. An Agency asset in Tunis provided intel on the interrogations that followed. At least four of those interrogated admitted working for 'Skorpios.' They described him as a European bomb maker. The details weren't as important to him as the method. The outsider infiltrated a group of Islamist fanatics and built them into a network and operation. Whatever their aim, whatever their purpose, they were deliberate in their method. He saw the fingerprints of tradecraft here—the familiar signs of intelligence building. Each cell had a handler. Each handler, he guessed, a director. If there was a foreign agency building these networks, he couldn't see it. This was a new kind of enemy for the new century.

Each operation alone was a minor real threat. Together, they suggested greater ambitions. He knew nothing about what they wanted or why. Worse, if they built assets as he suspected, then they were resilient. Harley was right to suspect. How much had they already overlooked?

Harley's collected intelligence didn't connect to Georgia. It held no hint even of Chechnya. But the tradecraft was the same. The Chechens weren't the instigators. They were the assets. The sixth man was their handler. And somewhere out there was a director, a mirror image of himself in an organization he knew nothing about.

He left headquarters knowing that on his return tomorrow, everything would change. Everything already had. He nodded at the tall officer at the security desk. He thought his name was Roger, and Paul couldn't count the late nights when Roger had given him a half smile and a nod as he walked out tired and distracted. Over thirteen years he'd observed Roger growing older with him, his black face and beard turning grayer by the seasons. He couldn't recall a real conversation in those years leaving under Roger's late watch. Tonight he no longer saw Roger as blameless—one of his fellow teammates united in common cause. Tomorrow, he would see everyone else, those familiar and strange, as potential betrayers.

They needed to gain lost ground. He'd moved Pierce to Romania, but the man needed rest. They couldn't afford any more lost time, so there would be no rest for any of them.

He drove home with the sunset's glare blazing on his windshield. Light peeked through the trees and wooden fences along Dolly Madison Boulevard as he followed his usual route. He often worked late. He could avoid the rush near I-495 and ease into Vienna without shouting himself hoarse at drivers. It wasn't a long commute. He and Janey were lucky to find a home they could barely afford thirteen years ago. Things were better now. Being this close had been worth it. Janey had friends. The boys thought of it as home.

Old instincts filled his head. Tomorrow he needed to change his route home. He checked his rear-view mirror and wondered what he hoped to find there. He wasn't the paranoid type. What he needed was time to think and plan. Still alert, he pulled on to his street where the maples hung over the road touching branches. He and Janey preferred the older neighborhood. If not exactly quiet, it was a refuge with less traffic and pleasant shade. There was a car near his driveway. Not unusual, really. On a normal day, he wouldn't have bothered to notice it. Someone was inside. A woman wore large sunglasses, though twilit shadows cloaked more details inside her car.

He pulled into the driveway without raising the garage door. Standing in the driveway gave him an excuse to survey the street and the car. Dining room lights at the Bauman's glowed across the street. He glanced at the car, a featureless silver coupe at the edge of the street. The woman opened her door and waited at the corner of his driveway.

He stood with his jacket folded over his left harm. He put his hands on his hips and squinted at the woman. She seemed familiar.

"Mr. Corso?"

It was Sarah Pierce, Ethan's ex-wife. Since he last saw her, she had cut her long brown hair into a neat bob that framed her pointed chin. The sunglasses obscured her eyes and face, but it was her. She was still dressed for work. Last he knew, she had risen up the ranks as a lobbyist for some pharmaceutical firm. From the creases in her skirt, he guessed she'd been waiting for him for at least a couple hours.

"I'm sorry to bother you like this. I know I shouldn't. I just …"

"Sarah?" he said, almost to himself. He glanced down the street, then scolded himself for the paranoia.

"I'm sorry. It's just that I've been trying to get hold of Ethan."

"That's not something I can help you with."

He approached her in the street and stood at the end of the drive where the concrete had buckled and cracked over the years. She had been a guest at his house once. A Christmas party he and Janey threw a few years ago. He had invited a few from the office, mostly people new to the city who didn't have many connections yet. Today of all days, she shouldn't be here.

"I know. But I'm really worried about him. I mean, I know how this works. He's gone for a while, I get that." She shook her head. "God, do I get that. It's just I need to tell him something. And I need to know he's okay."

"Sarah, you know there's nothing I can tell you."

She held her breath and waited.

"Is he alive?"

"I can't say anything to you. I would if I could. I'm sorry."

"I left him a message. Sometimes when we were still together, I'd leave him a message, and he'd leave me one back. He kept doing it when we divorced, but he hasn't left a message in a while. I watch the news, and I know that's where he's involved. I just know it."

Paul sighed and shook his head. Yesterday, he might have let that slide. Today, Pierce leaving messages for his ex was a severe risk. He'd have to deal with it later, but Sarah wasn't to blame. She took off the sunglasses and dabbed at her left eye.

"I need to tell him something," she said. "I need him to be okay, and I need to tell him I'm getting married. The wedding's in less than three weeks."

What could he say? Most Agency divorces he knew weren't quite this endearing. It was low on the list of things he wanted Pierce to be distracted by right now.

"Congratulations," he said. He meant it, but it came out wrong. He wanted to tell her that the concern in her face betrayed her uncertainty about her future. But there was no use telling her that. Behind him, the front door opened. He saw Janey's silhouette in the illuminated doorway.

"Paul, honey, who is it?"

He turned and waved.

"Janey, you remember Sarah Pierce. She's just dropping off a message for me."

Janey's silhouette raised a hand to wave. He thanked her silently for staying in the doorway and turned back to Sarah.

"How does she do it?" Sarah said.

"To tell you the truth, I have no idea. Go home."

He patted her shoulder. It was a feeble thing to do. He wasn't her father. She got in the car and waved. Her eyes pleaded once more, and she drove away.

CHAPTER 10

NO COINCIDENCES

Constanţa, Romania
3:41 p.m., Sunday, June 2

ETHAN SAT at a cafe awaiting his only lead. The chair across from him remained empty, and he scanned the tourists ambling by the seaside for any sign of Nicu Prodan, the customs official he'd groomed for two weeks since arriving in Constanţa.

The outdoor cafe spilled onto the concrete seaside. He had a pleasant view of the Casino, a magnificent edifice that had fallen into disrepair. Arches within arches flowed languorously into a grand edifice whose function had shifted over the tumultuous century. He admired its beauty and its emptiness, but its purpose was lost to him. He gazed eastward across the gray water toward Georgia where he had let two people die—where his reckless operation had disintegrated in an instant. Where Maria betrayed him.

He fit in among the tourists in his faded jeans and black collared shirt that fell too loosely around his torso. Five days imprisoned with the Georgians had a surprising effect on his health. His skin had paled, but his eyes had darkened from lack of sleep. He didn't eat much of their terrible food, but he couldn't blame the Georgians for his brief imprisonment. It took five days and, he guessed, pressure from Director Drummond to convince them they faced a new enemy called Scorpio, and that he was no part of it.

Maria and this Scorpio group had betrayed him as well. For all his influence, Corso couldn't have persuaded GIS by himself.

After Georgia, the numbers Kay Linh had tracked went quiet. Maria disappeared. They knew almost nothing about Scorpio. He approached the customs office on a hunch that the hijackers had used a boat to shuttle across the Black Sea from Batumi unnoticed. He had nothing else to go on.

Asking around the customs offices for a friend of his named Andrei earned him some strange looks. One official had shouted at him in Romanian and pulled on his sleeve to leave the harbor office. The word American was clear enough. The others spouting from the man's mouth were less polite, he assumed. The following day he had tried again with Nicu and explained that this Andrei owed him money. He offered to share payment—500 lei and promised 2,000 more if Nicu could provide any customs reports on the days after the hijacking.

The desperation of it all nagged him, yet here he sat awaiting delivery of the list. He folded the cash discreetly into a city map and tucked them into his belt. Nicu was past late, even for a cautious official seeking a bribe. He sipped the last of his coffee and left a few lei for the inattentive waiter. He preferred the man's lack of intrusions.

He walked along the promenade among the packs of couples and their children eager to visit the nearby aquarium. Past the facade of swirling fish he spied a woman several yards ahead. Her blonde ponytail swayed as she walked. He glanced again and his blood pumped. It couldn't be Maria. He felt foolish, even more so when he realized he had no idea how he'd react if he saw her again.

"Mr. Pierce," said a mild voice behind him.

He turned, but the mellow voice continued.

"Keep walking. I'm a friend," it said.

The voice was a monotone murmur, clearly American and meant for his ears only. He kept walking while focused on the swish of his own shoes and those of his new companion's tapping on the pavement. The man walked behind him to his left, perhaps fives steps away.

"Ahead there is long pier. Walk out on it, and I'll meet you there."

He heard the steps veer left up a broad stair and disappear onto the street above. He walked on, taking his time to feign admiration for a small monument flanked by white columns. He didn't recognize the man's voice, but it had to be someone from the Agency. It wasn't anyone he had met earlier. *Who was he?*

By the time he walked out on the pier, he felt perspiration rolling down the small of his back. The black shirt warmed in the afternoon sun, but his anxiety and intrigue about his interlocutor was reason enough to sweat. Atop the pier's entrance was an ostentatious restaurant encased in glass. He walked beneath it and out on to the long pier. Pleasure craft lined the sides, and farther down a larger ferry clung to the pier by thick ropes. An old man dangled fishing line from a long rod into the water. Ahead, two more tourists wandered toward him on the concrete walkway.

At the end, he saw a man leaning on the railing overlooking the small harbor and the sprawling beach beyond. The man wore a striped shirt with short sleeves and dull gray pants. He was thin and his long gray hair bristled over his ears and down to his neck. Ethan leaned at the rail a few feet away and surveyed the beach himself.

"I'm Russell," the man said.

Ethan recognized at once the same smooth voice that had approached him earlier. He made a disinterested frown. The name meant nothing to him.

"The SVR is following you," Russell said. He turned about and placed his elbows on the railing, staring back down the pier. A cigarette dangled from his mouth. "Did you know that?"

Ethan winced. He kept looking out at the beach. "No."

"A few days now. I'd say four, maybe five. On the one hand, I can't say I blame you. They've very good." He exhaled a lazy plume of gray smoke. "Very good. On the other, I have to wonder just what you think you are doing."

Russell's voice flowed without judgment, it seemed to Ethan. It neither rose nor fell in its hypnotic sound. Only the cigarette bounced as he spoke.

"Who are you again?"

"Russell. I'm in the Counter Intelligence Center. Paul Corso thought I should check in on you."

"You know Corso?"

Russell nodded. "We go back a long ways, Corso and me. Ask me for a cigarette."

"I don't smoke."

"Humor me," Russell said. His broad mouth smiled and revealed a row of large and nicotine stained teeth.

Ethan took the cigarette and Russell lit it for him. He puffed once and exhaled. It burned his throat. He suppressed a cough while he examined the thing with disdain.

"You get used to it," Russell said.

Ethan doubted that he would, but he played along with the smoldering cigarette hanging from the corner of his mouth. He tried to blow the smoke trails away from his nose. The blowback made things worse, and he coughed again.

"Now that you've established my bona fides, you were saying about your efforts?" Russell said.

"Customs. I'm working a harbor customs officer to give me records for a boat that I think came in after the … incident."

"How's that working out for you?"

Ethan shook his head. It wasn't working. Nicu was a bust. If Russell was right about the Russians, Nicu might be even worse than that. He did seem a little too eager to help. Then again, so did Russell. Ethan bit down in frustration for being so desperate.

"You got someone's attention. That's not the end of the world."

"If you say so," Ethan said.

Russell smiled, baring his teeth once again. His skin was tanned leather with taut lines around his face and eyes. Ethan couldn't guess the man's age. He didn't seem as old as Corso. Then again, maybe he was older.

"When I was just getting started out, I was in Bucharest," Russell said.

"No idea what I was doing. Who does? One day I recognized a man. He seemed familiar to me. I spent a week watching out for him. Not every day, but he was there. I wanted to think it was coincidence. That I wasn't blown. My gut said otherwise."

Ethan leaned out over the water again, squinting from behind his dark shades. "So, I take it they didn't send you home?"

"It was FSK then. Not that it matters. The Russians are still the same. There's always another familiar face. A replacement for all of us. They found me, then I found them. And I'm still here," Russell said, his voice as flat as a lullaby. He raised an eyebrow at Ethan and blew a steady wave of smoke that curled in the breeze.

"Now that I know they're on to me, I can use that against them. Find out why they're here. Is that what you're saying?"

"I'm saying I don't believe in coincidences anymore. I think opportunity is a much better description. They're interested in you for a reason, just like they're here for a reason."

"I'm going to need help. I could use some local expertise," he said.

"You'll get it. Just ask for me with the chief," Russell said. "I've got a couple good people who can work quick."

"I will."

Ethan tossed the half-burned cigarette into the harbor and walked back down the long pier. His eyes danced around looking for familiar faces.

✳ ✳ ✳

Three days later Ethan paced in the narrow space between his hotel bed and the desk and dressers along one wall. He had doubled his offer to Nicu Prodan and now awaited his call from the lobby.

The room phone bleated. He answered.

"This is Sawyer,"

Nicu knew him as Ryan Sawyer, a black-market purveyor of cell phones and electronics. Ethan didn't care anymore if he believed it. The meeting wasn't about Nicu. The Russians would probably abandon him as an asset after this anyway.

Nicu's accented English came thick and distorted through the phone's earpiece. "You have my money?"

"Change of plans, Nicu."

"No change. We meet now." Nicu sounded panicked.

"Yes, change of plans if you want to get paid. I don't like my hotel. The room service here sucks. Meet me in the lobby, and we'll go find a new one."

He hung up and left the empty room. He and Wade had moved everything out earlier in the morning.

He left the elevator, and Nicu spotted him immediately. The man perked his head above the few fellow Romanians in the lobby. Nicu chewed at his thumbnail, then glanced out the window as Ethan eased his way to him with a gratuitous smile. Ethan patted his pocket and pointed to the door. Nicu nodded and followed, his black shined shoes scooting on the tile floor.

Ethan turned left and walked across the intersection. The hotel occupied a narrow street lined with cars packed front to rear like little soldiers. Nicu shuffled along to keep pace, and together they rounded another corner where Ethan ducked into the other hotel, a much older place. A plain looking woman with dark hair fussed in a mirror applying her lip balm. Ethan waved at the clerk and held up his small metal key and fob. Nicu nodded as well, and they rode up to the fourth floor together as Nicu tapped his fingers on the elevator rail waiting for the numbers above the door panels to change.

They entered room 42, a room much like his former place with a bed and narrow floor space to the window that overlooked the street. In a derelict office hallway across the street Wade observed the room and hotel entrance below. Nicu remained near the door and fidgeted with his right hand.

"You have the info I'm looking for?" Ethan said.

Nicu produced a small flash drive from his pants pocket and held it close to himself.

"My money?" he asked. "Please."

They needed time for this to work. Ethan imagined in his head the Russians chattering to themselves, running down stairways and between cars to trail them. He had to stall.

"So polite. What's your rush, Nicu? You seem very nervous here. I'm not a cop. You know, *poliție*? I'm not *poliție*."

"No, I know this. Is no problem. Change of plans no good. Very, how you say? Uncomfortable. You have my money?"

Ethan pulled a roll of cash from under his shirt and began counting. He watched for Nicu's reaction.

"You know, you're in customs. You and I could probably keep working together for a little while. What do you think? If this friend of mine needed some items to sell here, maybe some in Bucharest?"

Nicu focused on the cash and began nodding. "What kind of items?"

"Nothing illegal, no. Electronics, you know. Cell phones, computers, iPads. That kind of thing. Top of the line. Here, we agreed on 2,500 lei? Consider that a down payment on your cooperation with my friend, okay?"

Nicu reached out for the cash and stuffed the tiny flash drive into Ethan's hands. He bit his lip and nodded again

"I'll be in touch," Ethan said.

Nicu nodded once more as he checked the cash.

"Okay, good," Nicu answered. He left the room and let the heavy old door slam shut behind him.

That should do it. Ethan waited for over an hour watching the incomprehensible programming on the room's old tube television until Wade sent him a message that all was clear. He wandered down to the lobby and into a back-room office where Russell waited at a desk observing two video monitors. The dark-haired woman from the lobby—her name was Tereza—leaned against the wall looking bored. She stood when she saw him and gave him a half-hearted smile.

They reviewed footage from the lobby over Russell's shoulder. Ethan watched himself enter the hotel with Nicu at his heels. The images flickered, their faces washed out to bland whiteness. Russell sped the footage forward. A man in dark pants and black zippered jacket waddled into the frame like an old slapstick figure. Russell slowed the video to a standstill as the man scanned the room to find the camera. His face froze as he looked into the lens.

"That's our man," Russell said. "Right on time."

He moved the video forward as a timer in the left corner lapsed on. He watched Tereza approach the man and say something to him in Romanian. He shrugged her off with a wave, but she persisted and wagged a brochure at him. He snapped at her, and she backed away, distracting his gaze from her left hand that slipped a tiny transponder wrapped in a crumpled receipt into his jacket pocket. She was good, Ethan had to admit. He wouldn't have noticed it if he didn't know the plan.

Soon after, Nicu emerged from the elevator. The men exchanged looks, and Nicu gave him a quick nod and raised his thumb and three fingers before exiting the hotel. The man took a seat in the lobby, then approached the clerk. Russell stopped the video.

"He rented a room on the fourth floor," Tereza said.

No coincidences. The device she put in the man's pocket had limited range, but another of Russell's team waited in a Renault outside to follow the man and his SVR comrades to wherever they holed up in the city.

"That was nicely done," he told Tereza.

She shrugged, clearly unimpressed with him. Of late, he had to agree with her.

* * *

Days wasted while he worked with Wade and Russell's team to monitor the Russians. He spent most of his time wandering around the city searching for any sign of the boat or its owners. He reached out to Nicu twice more, but he got no response. It would lead nowhere, but it kept the Russians occupied. They operated from a small house in Coiciu, near the city center. Russell and his team took turns with Wade watching the place from the Renault and a small service van Russell provided.

His frustration grew as the routine wore on. He wandered the docks looking at boats, then would sit for hours watching tourists and checking his phone. He was a decoy, and he felt helpless. He fought the urge to check his voice mail. Under this kind of surveillance, it was too risky. If Corso only knew. He'd had longer assignments than this, but none harder. He wondered if Sarah had called or even left a message. She last called months ago. She'd moved on, but admitting that made him feel even more helpless. He had to let it go for the sake of the mission, and for his own state of mind.

He awoke from a deep sleep to the ghost light of his phone that illuminated the old hotel room like a flickering candle. For a moment he wondered where he was, then he reached for the phone and mumbled a response.

Russell's voice whispered back.

"They moved out of the city. Followed them to a villa north of the DN3. Something's happening here. We may need some help if they split up."

"Where are you? Wade and I will come to you."

"It's a vineyard. Some kind of villa a few kilometers west of the city. It's not just the three of them. They're with several more in two vehicles. I think they're …"

The phone went silent. Ethan called back, but the connection failed. In his head, he replayed the muted monotone of Russell's voice and the hiss of nothingness.

In three minutes he was dressed and in the hallway. He thumbed a quick message to Wade as the elevator descended. He walked out into street between a jumble of parked cars. Quiet seeped into the alleyways. Light from a distant streetlamp illuminated the crass graffiti on the building facade ahead of him. Somewhere in the decrepit office building above Wade slept on an old office couch. Ethan leaned against the building's front and called to rouse him.

"Yeah?" Wade said in an exhausted exhale.

"Time to move. Bring what you need."

"About damn time," Wade answered.

Wade emerged from a stairway door with a long duffel bag slung over his shoulder. He nodded to Ethan and pointed down the lane to the van parked alongside a brick walkway. Wade strode down the street, his sway unaffected by the bag that Ethan guessed weighed eighty pounds. He was alert and watchful, his black skin glistening and wet from a quick rinse in the office bathroom.

Wade had spent more than two weeks in that comfortless space at the top of the stairs or cramped into the Dacia van observing the Russians for hours as they smoked and drank on their patio. He performed this tedious routine without complaint, a remarkable act of willpower for his normally glib friend. Now, his body moved on command, and Ethan became the follower.

Wade sped through the empty streets, careful to note the nose of a police cruiser peeking from behind a blind corner. Ethan navigated on his phone. He found the highway Russell mentioned and scanned around for likely locations.

"What do we got?" Wade asked.

"Russell says the Russians moved in with a bigger group to a vineyard. Some place west of town," he said.

"How many?"

"He didn't say. He mentioned two vehicles, then his phone cut out. I still can't reach him."

The city thinned to petrol stations and auto dealers. The Old-World charm faded as Wade sped on. They passed flat cornfields and scrub. The fields and decaying fences reminded Ethan of his younger days in Missouri —meager spaces and hard earth. It was a road not too different from this one where he learned his first hard lesson in life. A summer night like this, too, with a pair of headlights coming at them fast. He crushed his knee against the dash, but that was nothing. Eric Belcher never drove again. Never did anything again. He was gone, just like Marcus Eldridge. Like Seda. That night and that bad knee had steered him down a different road.

"Ethan, man, you good? You ready for this?" Wade said. His eyes shifted between Ethan and the road as he drove. His hands tightened on the wheel.

Ethan nodded. He still stared out the passenger window. He needed to focus.

"I'm okay. I'm good."

"Look, man. I haven't said one word about what happened in Georgia. That shit wasn't your fault. You can't carry that with you now. You have to be ready for this."

"I know it," he said.

The words rang hollow in his head. What was it Maria said? *They make good liars out of us.*

"I'm ready."

CHAPTER 11

NEEDED INTELLIGENCE

Podgoria Traian, Romania
2:44 a.m., Friday, June 14

ETHAN SCANNED the inland countryside looking for a road that would take them north. Like the whole operation, they had become lost in darkness. Russell had only told him a direction before his phone went dead. They had to find a way to change direction. Ethan tapped his knee anxiously and squinted out the windshield.

"There. Head north," he said pointing at a break in the short scrub along the road.

Wade slowed at an unmarked intersection and steered onto the northern road. The headlights lit up the asphalt like a moonscape, pitted and crumbled in long years of poor repair. Wade veered around the biggest potholes, but the van shook and shuddered as the wheels sunk into the gaps in the road. Ethan looked for any glimpse of the villa. The road rose in a gradual slope surrounded by row after row of low grapevines that clung to posts and wire trellises. Near the peak of the rise another road crossed to the northwest amid a clump of trees. There Wade slowed again as they weighed options. He stopped the car short of the intersection.

"Damn it," Ethan said. He tapped at his phone.

"Now what?" Wade asked.

"The signal out here is terrible. Nothing. That's probably why Russell got cut off."

He felt a little better about Russell's fate, but it meant they would have to find him without any guidance.

"What the hell? We aren't that far out of the city," Wade said. He checked his own phone and frowned, then turned on the car's radio. His finger spun around the tuner as he rolled through the frequencies. The radio returned a steady stream of static hiss. There was no variation, no gaggle of Romanian voices or popular music.

"Shit. That's a wide spectrum signal blocker, my friend. If that was us, something would be going down. Soon," Wade said.

"Or already did. Left. Go left."

Wade cursed the van's lack of power. He floored the accelerator and drove northwest.

Ahead, Ethan spied a pair of faint lights miles ahead.

"Kill the headlights," he said.

He rolled his window down to listen as they approached. There was no sound beyond the hum and thump of the tires on broken asphalt and the stir of wind on the vines as they passed. Wade slowed while he squinted into the dark to keep the car on course. The two distant lights grew into four—dreary yellow dots obscured by trees as they drove. *It has to be the villa Russell mentioned*, he thought. There was nothing else but the rows of vines for miles.

The roadway rose and fell again into a tiny valley, its gentle hillsides arranged with vines. Trees gathered at the road near the bottom, and within these Ethan saw a fleck of orange that reflected their own van's parking lights. He poked at Wade to slow down while he scanned the tree line, looking from the edge of his vision for any traces of movement.

Behind them, a figure emerged from the trees onto the road. He thought it could be Russell, then saw a glowing red cinder head high and knew that it was. A puff of smoke swirled above him. Wade pulled off the road and stopped the car between a gap of small trees that provided some cover from all directions but the road.

"Glad you found me," Russell said. The glow from his cigarette lit his face like a jack o' lantern. Wade scowled at the man for being careless, then looked around for any sign of activity.

Ethan shook Russell's hand. His pants were wet to the knee from walking among the tall grasses growing around the trees. "What's going on?" he said.

"Hard to tell. I watched them at the house in the city. A little before midnight things started to pick up. Four or five tough guys showed up in an SUV. A while later another clown car, same as the first. They and the SVR boys milled around for a while in the courtyard, then packed it in all at once. I followed them out here."

"Where are they now?" Ethan said.

Russell extended his hand, cigarette tucked between his fingers, up the hill toward the lights.

"They're sitting tight," Russell said, his voice a flat whisper. "Don't think they've gone into the villa just yet, but I couldn't get too close. Been maybe an hour now."

"Are they armed?" said Wade.

Russell nodded. "Tough guys, like I said. Trained and serious. Part of why I didn't get too close. Why you shouldn't either. I count ten, maybe more."

"We've got to get up there. Now," Ethan said.

Russell snorted and mouthed an incredulous grin. "Gentlemen, believe me. Whatever they're planning to do, they're going to do. These guys play from a different rule book."

"Who said anything about stopping them?" Ethan said.

He was annoyed and fought the urge to raise his voice. This was their chance. He felt it. If they waited, whatever the Russians wanted at the villa was gone. It was the single strand left, the only thing that tied the future to the past. His only way to reckon for what happened in Georgia.

"You two go up there, and you're as like to end up dead as anything. This isn't cat and mouse. This is international incident. Where does that get us? Don't forget what you're here for." Russell wagged his finger at the men as he talked, his voice atonal.

"You think we don't know that? We can't let this one go, damn it. We don't have time to argue policy," he said.

"Suit yourself," Russell said. "Just remember what I said. And don't get in their way." He pulled a final drag on his cigarette and stamped it in the wet grass before he crept back to his car.

* * *

Ethan followed Wade through a narrow row of grapevines that hung just higher than his waist. They ducked down and strode through the plants, skipping rows as they climbed the rising hill toward the villa. He watched Wade move, planting his feet in Wade's tracks as best he could in the dark. A black rifle wagged from Wade's back. Ethan felt at his hip for his own weapon, a Glock 19 that Wade had given him when they arrived in Constanța. It was a reliable gun, but it felt less familiar to him. He reminded himself these were the tools of last resort. They needed intelligence, not heroics. Russell was right to remind them.

Wade stopped and raised his fist. They crouched behind the vines and scanned around the villa. Its stonework reflected gray in the starlight, a solitary fortress surrounded by the dark silhouettes of trees. They faced the villa's side at a hundred yards or so. An open yard lay between them and the villa, flanked by a trio of smaller outbuildings to their right. Wade tilted his head, listening.

Ethan saw no sign of anyone. He made out a long lane of blacktop and cypress trees that wound to the southwest where it met a stone wall and iron gate to the road. He knelt in the dirt until his thigh ached. He heard only the rattle of leaves in the dark. He saw even less—dark and meaningless shapes. Perhaps the Russians had gotten what they wanted and left. He hated the idea they had outpaced him. The resentment grew in his mind and wandered into an imagined tomorrow where he knew even less than he did now. He would have to tell Corso they had lost the trail all for his vanity—every wasted hour and each drop of blood on his account. His teeth cut into his tongue as his jaw clenched, and in that moment he resolved to meet the sunrise with something more.

Wade remained almost motionless, his head pivoting slowly. He had unslung his rifle and eased it through the vines so he could hold it steady against one of the trellis posts with his left hand. With the rifle tucked tightly into his shoulder, he peered through the night vision scope and scanned again. He motioned to Ethan to come closer, his voice less than a whisper.

"You see them yet?"

Ethan shook his head, and Wade grunted in disbelief.

"Three squads. One in front at the wall. Another opposite us. Third one at the shed."

Wade leaned and let him peer down the scope. At first, he saw nothing but blurry shades of green. Then he found a depth of field that outlined the green glow of four figures near the shed at the edge of the back yard. The Russians were bug eyed creatures in an alien landscape. Gas masks hung like predators' snouts from their faces, dangling under the dark pools of their eyes. They wore black hoods and the dark shapes of gun barrels sprouted from the curve of their shoulders. Their hands made rapid signs, but they remained in place, waiting.

"What now?" he said.

Wade leaned back into his rifle and shrugged. "Get some popcorn. It's going down."

Ethan focused on the shed while his eyes adjusted to the dark. Over the course of several minutes, he convinced himself he could make out the shape of the men there. Wade prodded him with his elbow, and he watched the shadows move into the yard without sound. He felt sorry for whoever occupied the villa. From the corner of his eye to the left he saw more dark shapes slinking across the dim expanse of grass, one after the other in close formation.

Bright fiery light burst from a villa window. The crackle of automatic fire filled the yard. It flashed from four of the villa's second floor windows. The muzzle flashes seared tiny blobs of white in his vision, and before he could look away the soldiers returned fire. A hundred pins of light swarmed in his vision, fading and dancing as he blinked. In the yard the Russians moved like stop motion figures in the strobe of the firefight. One fell in stuttered frames while the others moved toward the house, their rifles spitting fire that illuminated their dangerous advance. He lost all pity for the villa's inhabitants then, knowing at once who they were. Scorpio had anticipated the Russian's assault and met it with harrowing gunfire.

"Got to move," Wade said. "We're in their field of fire."

Wade shoved him from the side as he tried to stand and move away. The blood rushed into his legs. He felt out for the trellis and moved, still blinded by the will-o'-wisp that dazzled his night vision. Still crouched, they stumbled down the vine row until Wade tugged his shirt and motioned to get down. Wade sat with his legs bowed and propped up his rifle in the direction of the battle to observe through the vines.

The fire crescendoed as the Russians rushed the villa. He heard the shouts of the men, barely catching a few words of Russian as they coordinated the assault. Some lay on the ground wounded or dead from the ambush of fire. He thought maybe three fell, but the spots in his eyes confounded the scene. One of the men fired desperate shots from the ground to cover his comrades as they approached. Above, Scorpio's unseen defenders slowed their attack with shorter bursts at the closest group.

"Shit. Can't see the third group," Wade said. "Can you see anything?"

The ripples of gunshots slowed to a brief pause. Ethan raised his head, still dazed by the flurry of violence playing out before him. Whatever the outcome of the ambush, he'd lose any chance to find the connection to Georgia. He and Wade could wait it out, watch these men destroy each other, then sift through the ashes. That would take weeks, if they found anything at all. In weeks, more people could die, and he'd bear some responsibility for it. Patience was the wiser option. But his patience died with Marcus and Seda. He owed them more than that.

Wade snapped at him. "Ethan, man, what do you see?"

"Opportunity," he said.

He stepped through the vines toward the villa.

"Man, what the fuck are you doing?"

"What I came here for. We're not leaving empty handed."

"What the fuck's wrong with you? Get back here. You go up there and you're a dead man."

"I'm going. So watch my back."

He crossed the vine rows and crept closer to the villa. Behind him, Wade cursed in frustration but stayed put. He needed Wade now more than ever. They had run into firefights twice before in Afghanistan, and their immediate action then was withdrawal. Now bullets whistled in the night air, and he walked toward them.

Ahead, the firefight dwindled to a series of shots and rattles of gunfire. He heard a shout, and in a moment a quick and heavier explosion shook his ears. The Russians had breached the house and tossed grenades into the first floor. He caught a glimpse of the nearest team to his left—three men left standing as they barged in the double doors at the front of the villa. The third man in limped his way inside, stumbling at the blasted threshold. More gunshots reverberated from within, now muffled by the stone walls. The windows flashed as though a thunderstorm swelled inside. Two more large bangs popped and there was a respite of quiet.

He waited for a moment at the edge of the yard listening. A burning smell drifted among the trees. Far to his right he saw the wounded operator who had fired from the ground. The man's body lay still and barely breathing. His arms fell flat beside him, his weapon tilted away from his body. Ethan dashed to a tree halfway across the yard and pressed himself against it.

Gunfire from the second floor slammed into the earth and bit into the tree. Scorpio's fighters didn't fall so easily. He froze. The tree trunk was barely his width. He folded his arms across his chest, unable to unholster his gun without revealing his profile. He waited for a pause in the volley, but it came in steady bursts that ripped into his ears. His breath quickened.

He heard a sharp crack from Wade's direction. The gunfire from the window near him stopped. With a second shot from Wade, he heard glass shatter. He dared a glance from behind the tree at a window toward the back side of the house where he had seen the firefight begin. There was nothing but void. He gave Wade a nod and exhaled. Now was his chance.

He ran at the house and drew the Glock as he reached the outside wall. A window at his shoulder revealed nothing but dark shapes—a sitting room undisturbed by the assault. A shadow passed the doorway at the far wall, and at once the darkness gave way to the narrow beam of a light fixed to the muzzle of a Kalashnikov. He ducked away from the window as the light scanned the empty room. They were clearing the first floor with silent efficiency. When the light vanished, he dashed past the window and rounded the front of the villa.

He padded his way across a bed of river rock that clattered and shifted under his feet. He cringed at the sound. With each footfall he slowed, letting the rocks settle before leaning forward. He had to take greater care. If he made a mistake like that inside, Wade would go home alone. The front steps raised before him, and he leapt up in a single motion. One of the double doors hung loose on its hinges into the foyer. He gripped the Glock in both hands and crept into the rustic hall.

He had watched two teams breach the building. That meant he had at least six elite killers to avoid. He had no idea how many defended the place—at least three more on the second floor. Any of them would shoot him on sight. The sitting room to the southeast was empty. He followed the hallway to the right, stepping carefully over the rug-covered wood floor. The gunfire had ended for now, but heavy footfalls overhead and the crash of a broken doorway punctuated the eerie pause.

From the edge of his vision, he caught movement. He spun to face his own reflection aiming his weapon almost tip to tip in a tall mirror hung in the hall. He relaxed his trigger finger, and the reflection chided him with a tense smirk. He resisted the nervous tremors building in his extremities. Ahead the hall turned left, and he saw his destination. He crept toward the sitting room door and pushed it open. The hinges groaned with the slow effort. From his left he saw a dance of light flash on the floor. The Russians were doubling back.

He had seconds to think. The small room contained a narrow couch in the center and a console table behind it that held a tray of wine glasses. He saw the room from their perspective. They would enter swiftly and move away from the door to threaten the spots of cover. The couch. The far corner. Along the near wall. He took the last of these behind a small wooden cabinet along the wall to the right of the door. He lay on the floor with his Glock aimed at the door frame and waited. Too late, he wished he had signaled Wade from the window. He backed himself into this corner alone. *Better that way,* he thought. He couldn't lose Wade like he had the others. Wade didn't ask for his recklessness.

A glimmer of light in the hall approached, a presence without noise. The door burst open. There was no creak from the hinges—only quick and quiet action from the Russian behind the rifle. He moved in coordinated motion, a choreography performed with fluid perfection. The soldier stepped into the room and focused the rifle to the greatest threat. The light froze above the couch, then shifted to the corner. Ethan's position was next. The soldier swung the rifle barrel in his direction.

Ethan squeezed the trigger. Blinded and deafened from the pistol, he fired again from the floor. The Russian's rifle exploded into a star of fire above his head, bullets biting into the plaster walls. His target stumbled back trying to stand as the light bounced across the wall from the recoil. Ethan rolled away and steadied his pistol in both hands at the Russian. His eyes shifted from the man to the door, awaiting another attacker. None came.

The man leaned against the left wall, clutching his side with one hand and his neck with the other. The Kalashnikov dangled from a strap to his side. He slid down the wall no longer able to stand.

From somewhere in the house, above the ringing in his ears, Ethan heard a shout in Russian. More gunfire cut the voice short. Again the battle erupted in a grind of rips and bursts. One way or another, he knew that symphony could not last long. With his gun trained on the Russian, he stood and moved to the doorway. He leaned into the hall but saw no one and closed the door.

He approached the dying man. The light from the rifle illuminated a parabola of floor where motes of plaster dust danced within it. Ethan grabbed the weapon and eased it away from the man. The Russian struggled for a moment, reluctant to lose his weapon but unable to hold his arm without great pain. The man's head sagged, but Ethan could not see his face behind the gas mask. He shined the light on the man. Black and gray covered every inch of him. He wore no insignia, no mark or number anywhere on his uniform. A plastic hood covered his helmet, and rubbery gloves concealed his hands.

They wore protective gear, sealed head to toe in hot plastic. He retraced the assault he had witnessed. They wouldn't need all this just for tear gas. He wondered if they had used some chemical agent in the assault. He smelled the sulfurous tinge of powder from the breaching charge on entering the house, and the same smokeless odor in the room now. More shouts came amid the rattle of fire. His time was running out. He had to find whatever they were after.

What they're after, he thought again. He realized then the gear wasn't for the assault. They protected themselves from something they feared here inside the villa. Something dangerous. He shined the light on the Russian's mask again. *No time to waste.*

He stood in the window and signaled Wade, motioning for him to approach. Then he removed the dead man's gear and waited for Wade to appear at the fence line.

* * *

Ethan stumbled into the villa's foyer. The Russian's uniform and mask fit him well enough. The suit was his height, but the snug boots pinched his toes. In the agonizing minutes he took to stretch and pull the suit on, he listened to the creeping footfalls overhead, a slammed door, a shout, a last muffled burst of gunfire on the far side of the house. Soon those sounds would find him. The Russians were relentless, plodding. Movement above meant they still hunted the last of Scorpio's holdouts. It bought him only a little time. Adrenaline flowed to his fingertips like electric current. He had to be ready.

From within the mask, he could barely see the hallway walls. If there was a deadly chemical here, the suit wouldn't protect him. The bullets he'd fired into the Russian tore three holes in the suit. The mask stank of the Russian's blood and sweat. He leveled the Kalashnikov and its halogen light toward the top of the stairs where quiet had settled in moments before.

He spied Wade hiding just outside the front door when a voice startled him from the top of the stairs. The rubbery hood that covered his ears garbled the Russian's words. His mind panicked to translate. The voice repeated in anger.

"Lieutenant, first floor clear?"

The guise worked. He lowered his head, appearing to scan the hallways as he replied. *"Exactly so, sir."*

From the sound of it, the man standing above him was the unit commander. He looked confused, then leveled his rifle at Ethan. The light scattered on droplets of grime and blood on Ethan's visor.

"Are you injured?"

"It's nothing," Ethan replied. He covered his neck with his hands, then waved at the commander.

"No sign of him up here. Move to the cellar to assist team two."

He released his neck and gave an exaggerated nod. The bright light moved away from him and his eyes adjusted slowly in the dark. The commander disappeared to another hall on the floor above. A second injured soldier slunk close behind him.

No sign of him. They were looking for someone, not something. He had minutes to find out who. Up close, they'd see past his mask immediately. One failed hand signal, one weak Russian accent in reply, and they would kill him without hesitation.

He waited, then signaled Wade inside. Together they moved to the back of the foyer to the cellar stairs. He listened for the other team the Russian mentioned below. No sound traveled up the stairs.

"More of them downstairs," he whispered.

"You lead. I'll cover from behind," Wade said. He'd left the rifle in the field, and now carried his own Glock that looked too small in his strong hands.

Bright light illuminated the stairwell and hallway. This was the working floor of the vineyard with none of the elegance of the main floor. The walls were painted brick and covered in grime, the floor worn concrete that shined under the lights. He leaned out at the base of the stairs to see a hallway in either direction lined with half a dozen doors. The nearest door was across the hall. He darted across and entered the room.

White tile covered the near side of the floor. A solitary chair occupied the center of the room situated directly over a drain in the floor. The far wall featured a large overhead door to the outside. Lights dangled from wires overhead, and he switched them off. He looked around instead with his rifle's light. There was a basin sink on the side wall and some cardboard boxes stuffed with refuse and plastic bags. Pushed up against the right wall was an empty cot. He inspected the chair. Restraints stained with blood dangled from the rear of the chair. Underneath it, he found tiny pieces of dried chicken bones. *They interrogated someone here.* He twisted the shriveled chicken bone in front of his mask. The man the Russians sought had left days ago.

The door slammed into the wall. He swung around to quiet Wade, but instead met a pair of bug-eyed masks like his own hovering over their rifles.

"*Hold fire,*" said one of the unmoving faces from behind a mask. "*Lieutenant, is that you?*"

"*Who else?*" he said, trying to seem annoyed. "*Any sign of him?*"

No response came from the Russians. They were examining him. Something had given him away, perhaps. *Where was Wade?* The barren room afforded him nothing. If discovered, he had nowhere to flee. Turning the lights off may have bought him a few seconds, but he had to maintain his disguise just a little longer.

"*He was here,*" he said, nudging the chair with his rifle.

They approached to examine the chair. He lifted the restraints with his rifle's muzzle.

"*See here?*" he said.

One of the men kicked at the chair. The other soldier faced him at the center of the room. His head shifted as he examined him. Ethan's hand tightened around the grip of his weapon.

"*You are shot. Where are the others?*"

Ethan shrugged. "*Upstairs,*" he said.

The soldier took another step closer, his gun angled down almost at Ethan's feet.

He shouldered his rifle and pointed it at Ethan's face.

"*I'm thinking you're not the lieutenant. What's my name?*" the Russian asked him.

"*What the fuck are you doing? It's me!*" He raised his hand to shield against the bright light, though he did it more so to cover his face.

The Russian's voice shouted shrilly through the mask. "*What's my name?*"

The light from the hallway dimmed as a figure leaned into the doorway.

"Hey, asshole." It was Wade.

The Russian jerked toward the door in surprise. Ethan felt a spasm of shock throughout his body as gunshots fired. He pulled the trigger on his own gun and tried to raise the barrel. The burst sent the rifle upward uncontrolled and the room exploded into a thunderous tempo. He struggled to lower the muzzle with another burst from his rifle and watched as the second Russian staggered, hit by his incautious fire. *So much for hitting my target.* The soldier nearer to him leapt away, still firing toward the door. From the narrow visor of his mask, Ethan lost sight of Wade.

Wade's voice boomed above the fire.

"Dodger, move!"

The Russian had positioned himself between them. Wade had no shot with him in the line of fire. Ethan had to change position. He leaned forward to dive away. It would place him almost on top of the other downed soldier, but he didn't care. The muscles in his legs felt cold and sluggish, like he lived an anxious dream unable to reach his destination.

As he fell, Wade fired a salvo of shots. The deafening thud of the Russian returning fire filled his ears. He heard the rattle of spent brass falling to the floor. The shots ceased. Ethan turned and trained his rifle on the Russian, who lay on the floor, his legs spread toward the doorway.

"You hit? You okay?" Wade said.

Ethan felt around his chest and legs. He pulled off the mask and dropped the helmet to the tile floor.

"I'm good." He panted, breathless. "I'm all good."

Wade entered the room and leaned against the door. His nostrils flared as he tried to calm his heaving body. Ethan trained the light on him to see if he was shot.

"Man, point that fucking thing somewhere else." He shielded his eyes.

"Sorry."

"Check on these guys here. Careful," Wade said as he approached the Russian between them with his gun locked on the man's chest.

Ethan looked at the other soldier on the floor. The man lay on his back, lifeless. His visor bore a single hole where Wade had placed a near perfect shot. He was dead before he hit the floor. Ethan's wild shots didn't matter after all. A sea of black blood sloshed within the sealed mask. The Russian's black and gray fatigues matched his comrades—no insignias, no names or badges. A bag slung over his shoulder hung at his hip. Ethan nudged it open and poked his light inside.

Wade inspected the other Russian. "This guy's still breathing. We got to get out of here."

"Hold on. I think I've got something here."

A mass of crumpled papers spilled out of the bag, uncovering another parcel wrapped tight in black plastic. He teased out the package and flipped it over to reveal a bright orange label decorated with a familiar symbol.

Three crescent shapes arranged in a triangle around a ring. Biohazard. He noticed a long tear near the label. More of Wade's marksman handiwork.

"Give me a knife," he said as he raised up his open hand.

He knelt to inspect the contents. Fabric poked through the tear. Wade handed him the dying Russian's knife, then moved to the back of the room toward the overhead door. Ethan sliced away the plastic cover with gentle cuts, unfolding the wrapping as a pair of trousers and a shirt bulged out of the wrapping.

"No time for this, man. They are headed our way. I don't like the looks of that package you got there. Just leave it."

Ethan held his breath and turned the plastic inside out. The clothes spilled out onto the tile. Stains covered the shirt. Pale yellow at the pits and sides, but ruddy stains of blood darkened the fine shirt along the collar and front. The dark brown pants were likewise soiled with dark stains. He poked them with the knife and felt a subtle resistance.

"Dodger, time to go. Now."

Behind him, a gearbox whined as it lifted the overhead door. Ethan felt the rush of cooler air flow into the room. But the contents of the pants pocket captured his attention. He reached into the pocket with his gloved hand and pulled out a wrinkled piece of heavy paper, white with gold icons scattered across its face. It bore a scramble of blurred ink—a large barcode. Watery ink stains of type covered the thing, including one large word. *ISTANBUL.* It was a boarding pass. He struggled to read the name near the top. *KHORASANI, KAMRAN REZA.* The name meant nothing to him. He scanned for a date.

"Dodger!" Wade grabbed his collar and pulled him up. He held tight to the boarding pass, still trying to read as he stumbled backward to the open door. Far away he heard the compression of helicopter rotors chopping the air.

He looked closer at the pass and found a familiar date. *PC463. 04 MAY 2014. 1930.*

He stared at a boarding pass from the downed airliner. Someone had survived. He had a new target.

CHAPTER 12

STRICTLY CONTROLLED

Brașov, Romania
7:28 a.m., Wednesday, May 28

KAMRAN'S HANDS trembled while he removed his clothes and gold watch. An armed guard looked on, uninterested in his naked body and his obvious shame. The square-jawed man faced him with stout arms crossed over his chest. The guard rarely spoke. He saved his outbursts for curt commands spat out with what Kamran knew was disgust.

This guard and two others had watched him every minute over the last two weeks, even standing outside a windowless bathroom when he used the toilet. They took shifts in the hallway outside the tiny lab room they had converted to his personal prison cell. He spent much of the time in isolation healing from the visible wounds his torturers had inflicted.

The virus was his only power over them. His torturers had learned that power, and word spread among the guards like the fat one staring at him now. They didn't know or believe the power was gone, leeched from his blood by the remedy of his own making. The guards kept their distance, wary of what he carried within him. He found some satisfaction in this, but that was as fleeting as his fitful sleep.

They obeyed the white-haired man called Hector, who had visited him twice. On the return visit Hector provided the last of his antiviral pills. In returning the little white tablets, Hector had restored his life and stolen what little leverage Kamran had left. The remedy came at a heavy price, which Hector extolled from him through the glass panes of his prison. He explained it plainly enough. Hector oversaw his capture, and now he required the virus. He had lured Kamran here for that sole aim. He expected Kamran to grow cultures of the pathogen and verify their efficacy. Kamran had acquiesced. He didn't even bother to inquire at Hector's purpose.

So, it was at Hector's direction that the overweight guard had escorted him this morning from his quarantined cell through a sealed door into this changing room that afforded no privacy. He retreated to a corner of the small room to place his only belongings into an open locker. He knew the process well. At Russia's VECTOR he had prepared to enter a laboratory like this many times. Every painstaking step was a deliberate part of the process to enter a BSL-4 laboratory that sealed the deadliest pathogens known to humanity without releasing them into the world.

Back in the Koltsovo labs, the rooms were bigger, the staff more numerous. This place was different. The procedures were the same, the rooms nearly so, only smaller. But here a solitary stillness filled the vacant laboratory. This was not a research facility. As far as he could see, his captors had constructed this place for him alone and whatever purpose they had for his recklessness. He now knew they wanted him to manufacture more of the deadly virus. Doing so seemed impossible, as if someone had pulled from his mind a nightmare and built this place from it meant to torment him alone.

Across the room were two separate steel doors, each sealed with black gaskets. A shower awaited him in the room to the right. Beyond that, a fitting room for positive air pressure suits that allowed him to enter the secured laboratory within. He would return through the door to his left after chemical showers disinfected his suit and he could shed it like a second skin to re-enter the world, once again a prisoner.

He entered the shower and let the heat wash over him and drive away the ache in his back that had remained since his torturers left him tied to that metal chair for hours. The bruises had almost faded, but his back spasmed no matter how he lay on the cot they provided, looking at year-old Italian magazines for his only distraction.

He dressed in the jade green scrubs they provided. He tucked the pant legs into the bright white socks and realized neither had ever been worn. The green had not faded from repeated sterile washings like so many scrubs he had worn over the years. Wrinkled creases bunched at his thigh. He stood within the airlock passage and let out an anxious sigh.

Standing in the room beyond was a woman dressed like him. Her face was plain and pale, framed by brown rimmed glasses that complimented her brown eyes. She waited for him, and her mouth formed a flat and tacit line of contempt.

"Dr. Khorasani," she said to him.

Only Hector had called him by name. He knew it had been just weeks, but the time weighed on him like years. Her welcome came to his ears unfamiliar, as though she spoke to his father or some other man with his name. He had forgotten himself. Her voice called him back from the shelter of his memories and the life he imagined for himself in the long stretches of boredom and despair.

"Hello," he muttered. He nodded, unsure what to do next.

She dodged around coiled hoses that dangled from the room's ceiling to a steel table that stood between them. She motioned to the rubbery suit laid out there like a deflated man.

"I'm told you are familiar with the suit?"

Again he nodded. He moved to the table and grabbed the blue suit.

"Are you forgetting something?" she said.

He frowned.

"Gloves, doctor."

She held up a pair of thick Latex gloves and handed them across the table.

"Please understand I take this very seriously. I know what you have been through," she said.

He touched his cheek where the trace of bruises was still visible.

"It must be very difficult for you. That is not my problem, however. You must take every precaution. We can continue when you're feeling better, perhaps?" she said.

Is she mocking me? He felt ashamed.

"No, please. It is all right. I'm sorry to have forgotten the gloves. It's just, I didn't expect someone here like you."

"You mean a woman?"

"Yes," he admitted.

"Haven't you worked with women before? Are you going to make this a problem?"

"Yes, of course," he said. "I mean to say, I have worked with many women. It is not a problem for me. I apologize."

"Then let's continue."

She plugged one of the pneumatic hoses into his suit to inflate it. The suit billowed. It quivered as she ran her hands across its limbs and torso. He had done the same many times checking for minuscule punctures or leaks. He stepped into the suit, stretching each of his limbs into the thing. He wiggled his gloved fingers through the thicker rubber gloves built into the suit. Then he pulled his head into the visor, his back straining as he stretched. He felt the rush of air from the hoses that wound through the suit near his head. They filled his ears with a constant swish that drowned out the squeaking of the suit and more instructions from the woman.

What is her name? He watched her lips move, unable to hear her talk. She leaned across the table and tapped his chest where the large zipper seal crossed. He pulled at it and sealed himself within the suit. A valve released the pressure and he was again able to move in an awkward gait.

"Can you hear me, doctor?" she shouted. "You are ready now. Let me prepare, and we'll enter the lab."

"What do I call you?"

"I'm sorry?"

He raised his voice above the stir of the pressurized air.

"What's your name?"

Her lips turned downward, and she gave him a cold look over the top of her glasses.

"This will be easier if we don't share that information. You may call me doctor. Let us leave it at that," she said.

It would not be easier for him. She was as hard-edged and sharp as a broken shard of glass, and just as difficult to see. Even so, he realized he welcomed her presence. He could speak to someone, and she would speak to him. For the first time in days he experienced something real outside the echoes and fantasies in his brain. It gave him hope. If she was here, he could look forward to that above all the dark thoughts he had in his cell. They would kill him eventually. He knew that just as she must know, too. She revealed it in what she did not say. She would not be his executioner, but neither would she save him in the end. But her voice, her standing at his side while he did their bidding? That was enough for now.

She wrestled with her own suit, a mass of blue plastic that enveloped her thin arms and legs. As she struggled to enter the transparent hood, he approached to help. She raised her hand, and he stopped short of clutching the suit at her chest. He backed away and let her wriggle into the suit.

They entered the primary hallway through another air lock. Now they were in the full biosecurity environment. There were BSL-4 facilities like this across the globe, built by governments and universities, each strictly controlled to prevent catastrophe. This place was hidden from all others, a containment within a building within a complex in a place that no one knew. *How did they accomplish this?* It didn't matter. He would do his work as slowly as he could. Then he would find a way out if he could.

He followed her to the lab marked with a black alpha. Work benches with glass hoods covered the walls. Metal stools with plastic seats were arranged neatly in the center of each hood, unused and unmoved. In the corner stood a stainless-steel autoclave, obscured by a half-dozen coils of pneumatic tubes hanging from above. The textured floor scuffed and scraped his heavy rubber boots as he walked.

Everything within the room flowed away from harm. Vents diverted air about the room to avoid the drift of microbes. Somewhere above, filters scrubbed the air free of contaminants. So below, great vats and plumbing drained away fluids, cleaning them with elaborate sequences of filters to prevent microscopic ruin from escaping. The room contained the danger, driving it and controlling it as part of a considered plan. He was part of that plan now, a piece of equipment employed to control the dangerous pathogen they desired. Their interest in him was mechanical, a filter to be replaced once it outlived its utility.

She directed him to one of the hoods. He approached and coupled his suit to one of the yellow hoses. Rushing air again filled his suit. It cooled his back and limbs, and he became aware of the uncomfortable body heat that built up so quickly. He placed himself on the stool and arranged his hands on the hood to balance while he examined the space.

From behind, she grabbed his tether and cut off the air supply flowing into his suit. The sound vanished in his ears and he started. *What is she doing?* He began to panic, but she placed her other hand on his shoulder and shouted into his visor.

"I'm going to retrieve the samples for today's work. Prepare your space," she said.

She released his hose and the flow of white noise again filled the space within his suit. He took deep breaths to relax. She was just speaking to him. That was all. He reminded himself she would not be his executioner.

He investigated the workstation. A centrifuge occupied the left portion of the hood. Pipettes and shell vials were in easy reach. He found drawers with labels and tapes and a marker for samples. All of it was neatly arranged and undisturbed, awaiting his arrival. *How long have they known about me?*

She returned to the room with a small white box that she placed on the hood next to him, then stepped away to attach a pneumatic hose to her own blue suit.

With care, he opened the box. It cradled two slender vials of his own blood. This was no surprise. He recalled Hector draining the blood from his arm what seemed like a decade ago. This was a portion of his blood from a time the virus had resurged in his body. Since, the antiviral treatment had tamed his blood, though not exactly purified it.

They expected great and terrible things from his blood. From these smaller vials—or at most two or three more like them—he must revive the demon his comrades in Russia had created at VECTOR. He had corrupted the data he had access to there. He had destroyed every sample he could, save the one he injected into himself. A desperate act but a necessary one. They would make more, he did not doubt. But it would take time. His efforts were wasted now that he knew the truth. He would not be a whistleblower. He was a prisoner now more than ever before.

He wanted to smash the vials on the ground and let the fluid that was once from his body flow down the drain. But the vials kept him alive, so long as Hector needed them. He regretted ever injecting himself with the virus. He was foolish to think he could develop more of the cure once safely outside Russia. There was no journalist waiting for him in Istanbul. It was these people. They had fooled him all the way along.

The idea wasn't his. At first it was Masoumeh's back in Iran. Kamran lived under the mullah's regime far too long in Iran to misunderstand the man's curiosity about his work. When Masoumeh suggested that he procure a sample as they ate together one fall afternoon in the university lounge, he knew who Masoumeh was. What he was. That was how it happened —Masoumeh calculating his suggestion as one explains an equation. Iran wished to possess the virus. Kamran wished for his family to live as they were accustomed. He agreed seven long years ago to bide his time in the exchange program with Russia and find a way to get a sample out.

The way out was madness. Injecting himself with the virus was never the plan. Defying Masoumeh was never his plan, but that plan ended when he watched his countrymen rise up against the regime. He dared to hope for revolution that summer, then watched it die on his laptop in his Koltsovo dormitory. He worried the Russians would find out and interrogate him. Maybe send him back.

The Basij shot a young woman in Tehran that summer. Her name was

Neda, and he watched the shaking camera as blood flowed from her mouth and her nose, pouring out as easily as one pours out tea. He watched the brilliant red cover her lovely face until his stomach folded in on itself and he wanted to vomit. He later read she called out her last words. "I'm burning," she had said. "I'm burning." He found her photograph and fell in love with her face. He read everything about her. She studied poetry and music. He longed for her, even knowing he would never see her. Each time he watched her terrifying death on his laptop, rage like a cancer grew in his stomach. He wept. He watched it many times while someone said to her over and over "Neda, don't be afraid." He did all of this for her, despite his fear. All for Neda.

Masoumeh's plan died with her. It took him almost ten years to craft a new plan. The Turkish journalist said she could give him protection. Once the opportunity arrived, it took him only three days to book his flights and barely an hour to complete his sabotage in the lab. Injecting the virus was the only way to carry it undetected. He remembered watching the needle enter his skin and feeling the same sick sensation in his stomach. His antiviral treatment would work, or he would die. He had taken only the few pills he had developed for himself, and barely enough for that. Everything fell to the efficacy of his own work. He would carry out the first human test on himself as an act of survival. If it failed, others could die. But what could he do? Days ago, when his despair was deepest, he wished he had died.

It would take the Russians months to recreate the virus. This comforted him. When he planned his escape, he dared to hope it would take years. By then he could tell the world what they were doing. He could hide away and find asylum somewhere. He fancied Paris, where he had studied briefly. The winters there were nothing like Russia's cold and dark nights. But his plan had been for nothing. The world presumed him dead in the jetliner's explosion. Now, it was nothing for them to kill him. He was already dead to everyone else.

Hector demanded he grow the virus. Kamran had fled the greatest scientists in the world who would need months to grow the pathogen again. With a living sample, it would take him a week to restore their work. If there was an Allah, he had a twisted plan for men.

In just over two hours, he emerged from the secure laboratory into a rain of chemical shower. The flashes of heat returned, welling around him in the cloying suit. Perspiration dampened his scrubs. He exited the airlock door and leaned against a table to catch his breath before he struggled with the suit's zippered seal.

His laboratory partner followed and helped him remove the protective suit. She stood facing him, her eyes locked downward on the zipper tab. He stared at her then, his face inches from hers with two layers of visor between them. He admired her features and wondered whether she also faced some ultimatum. Or was she with them?

With the suit's upper half removed, he reached out to help with hers. Again, she moved to keep his hand away from her. Their eyes locked, and he stared at her while he kept his hand firm. He pulled the tab up across her chest as she simply stared back. Then he raised his gloved hands in surrender and offered her a meek smile.

"I am only trying to help you," he said.

"I do not need your assistance."

"I meant no harm."

"Continue on to the showers. You first. You'll need to undress here."

"Here?" he asked while looking about the tiny room.

"Of course. Your clothes must be decontaminated."

He couldn't speak. Undressing in front of his guards was shameful enough for him. For her to see his naked body was beyond humiliation. He felt flush as a wave of nausea rumbled from his stomach to his throat. The sickening feeling transformed into a kernel of resentment within him. His teeth clenched, and his thoughts coalesced into a single realization. They could beat him and shame him. They could even kill him as they almost certainly would. All of this they did with his assent. This was the consequence of his own weakness and fear. He had to shed his old self, his old pride and his vanities. These were the real levers of their power over him.

How could he escape with these things inside him?

He stepped from the protective suit and stripped away the green tunic and trousers. For a moment he stood before her naked with an intensity in his eyes directed at her. His pale and weakened body was pitiful. He knew it. He stood with his jaw clenched and his hands balled into fists at his side. She mistook his anger for shame, but he didn't care. He left her smug look and yanked the next steel door to enter the shower and wash it all away.

CHAPTER 13

WITHOUT TETHER

Bethesda, Maryland
9:33 p.m., Saturday, June 15

PAUL WATCHED couples dance on a parquet floor to a Marvin Gaye tune. He stayed put in a stiff padded chair at one of the large dining tables. Janey left him there so she could chat with friends and donors. Events like this brought out her best. For him, they were drudgery. She flitted through the crowd bright-eyed and smiling. Paul sagged in the chair from too little sleep. He was content to sit and sip his red wine, which was too tart and thin for his tastes. But it was something to do. The meal was much better. To Janey's relief, their dinner companions raved about the beef tenderloin and chocolate torte. He didn't know any of these people, but he did his best to make small talk despite the strong possibility that in eastern Europe a group of unknown killers had kidnapped an Iranian biological weapons expert.

The dinner companions scattered to the dance floor and the bar. They abandoned maroon napkins on the white tablecloth in a ring of Rorschach blots that hypnotized him while he mulled over the last two days' developments. Pierce's discovery in some Romanian wine cellar had escalated the entire affair. With that, Paul's assignment from Harley Gilchrist to root out a sleeper element fell apart in two hours. He didn't have much choice in the matter. He had to share Pierce's report with Suzanne, and up the chain from there. By yesterday's end, more than a half dozen senior officers and directors had read Pierce's report. Three of those were on Paul's mental checklist of candidates for this Scorpio group. But the real truth was it could be any of them.

Before yesterday morning, none of them had ever heard of Kamran Khorasani. Now meetings began with verbal reminders about security and stern faces at the faintest suggestion of WMDs. Khorasani's expertise in biological warfare research got everyone's attention. Even Drummond had stopped suggesting this was all about Ukraine.

He had to focus on next steps for his team. But the inevitable cost was his work on Scorpio. Every little detail, every twist of intel he'd laid out in two weeks hoping to lure out this hidden group's mole dissolved the moment Pierce's report disseminated. Mention of Scorpio didn't come up. He'd removed it from Pierce's report. Harley had a heavy hand in avoiding its mention during two briefings yesterday. Neither he nor Harley could prevent the insider from knowing those next steps. With their secret revealed, he had to assume Scorpio knew what they knew. They'd react and adjust, and again he'd be steps behind them.

He needed some air. He finished off the astringent wine and left his own napkin on the table. A murmur of voices floated over the dance floor music. Masses of people circulated around the mostly empty tables. He passed an older woman who sat alone to touch up her lipstick in a tiny brass mirror. She blinked and smiled at him, then returned to the compact to tend her appearance. He maneuvered through the crowd, nodding at strangers who caught his eye as he pushed past their conversation circles. Pressed in by the crowd, he smelled the alcohol on their breath. He patted a man's shoulder to pass and made his way to a long wall of French doors that faced the green fairways of the club course.

The air outside hung heavy with humidity that remained from the afternoon storm, though the heat had faded since sunset. Clouds rolled by overhead, shifting southeastward toward the coast. He crossed the flagstone patio and stood before a row of privet bushes that fenced off the clubhouse from the empty golf course. At the far end of the patio to his right a group of men smoked cigars and guffawed at one another's jokes. He caught a faint scent of the smoke and the urge to savor one himself came on strong. Janey forgave most things, but smelling like an ashtray would earn him at least one lonely night in bed. She put up with much, but a relapse would earn the wrath of her silent treatment.

"Paul?" said a distracting voice behind him. "I thought that was you. Mind if I join you?"

He turned and saw a vaguely familiar face, a man from the Agency named Brian Crowley. Last he knew, Crowley worked under his counterpart in HUMINT managing a team of collections officers. The man had thin eyes that always seemed to be part of an unserious sneer.

"Be my guest," Paul said.

Brian perched a tumbler of vodka in his left hand and extended his right to him. Paul felt obliged to shake it.

"Nice night out here."

"It's all right. Humid as hell," he said.

"I guess it is. Still better than in there." Brian nodded back toward the banquet hall.

They had that in common, at least. Paul escaped to the patio to avoid the idle chatter and the crowd's drone that grew louder by the drink. Instead, he'd given Brian the opportunity to catch him alone. He barely knew the man. His work overseeing collections in HUMINT meant he'd probably seen reports from Pierce. There was even a chance he'd come across a reference to Scorpio. But this was no chance meeting. With that realization, his mouth dried as he tried to swallow. He had to be more alert.

"I guess our better halves know each other. Alicia says Jane is an inspiration. Says she can barely keep up with her."

"That sounds like my Janey," he said. He put his hands in his pockets and forced himself to stand still. "I'm surprised we haven't bumped into one another before at these things. Your wife been doing this long?"

"No, this is her first event, really. I encourage her to get out and participate. This is such a good fit for her. She loves kids. She's volunteered for the after-school program some this spring."

"Good for her."

"Listen, I'm glad I caught you out here. Just wanted to let you know I'm interested in branching out, taking on a new role. I'd love to shift over to your side of things."

"You know the drill. This isn't the best place to discuss it," Paul said. His eyebrows narrowed, and he must have given the man the frustrated frown that Janey hated so much.

"Right, right. I understand. Just wanted to let you know personally how much I'd appreciate that. I think I can do more, you know?"

"I think I do," Paul said flatly.

"That's great. Thanks for that. And maybe not mention it just yet to my supervisor."

"Well, if we can't keep secrets, what good are we?"

Brian's eyes narrowed to thinner slits. His face tightened as he parsed Paul's response. Then he belted out a laugh. His face and fading hairline flushed pink, matching his bared gums while his laughter grew long and loud enough to distract the cigar smokers at the far end of the patio.

"That's really great. Thanks, Paul."

"I think I need to get myself a drink," he said. "Excuse me."

Brian raised his glass to salute him as Paul returned to the party through the French doors. Three weeks ago, he would have shrugged off the awkward encounter. Now, Harley Gilchrist had him jumping at shadows. *Was Brian putting on an act?* Maybe Brian was just a distraction. There was a time he handled himself better than this, when his confidence kept him alert and alive. He had survived months in Bogotá, ready for anything around any corner. Now a red-headed social climber set him on his heels. It was almost embarrassing. He had to get ahead of this thing. It had always been this way, this competitive urge within him. He could handle faster opponents, stronger ones. God doesn't grant everyone the same gifts, his mother used to say. He had made a career of thinking ahead of better men.

He checked his watch. Almost 2200 hours. The sun was coming up in Romania. He needed to warn Pierce. Scorpio wasn't going to ground. If they really did have someone at Langley—and it was a wise bet they did—their reaction was obvious. They had to cut Pierce out, whatever that meant. Pierce's work increased the pressure against Scorpio's members, so now they had to relieve that pressure. Pierce wouldn't need to seek them out. They would come to him.

He found Janey next to a metal coat rack looking for Father Carson's umbrella. He let her send Father off for the evening, then caught her attention with a wave. She ambled toward him.

"You look tired," she said.

"Just me?"

She yawned, and he warmed a little at seeing the lines in the corners of her eyes. She hated the little signs of her age, but for him it was something dear. Something about her secret and real that these people didn't share—a secret thing for his own keeping.

"Well, you look handsome, too. It's so nice to see you in that suit. You should wear it more often."

She brushed his lapel with her fingertips then clasped her hands at the back of his neck.

"Janey, do you know Alicia Crowley?"

"Of course. She's on the fund-raising committee with me. Nice lady, but kind of quiet. Did you meet her tonight?"

"Just met her husband. He works with me."

"Oh," she said, a little startled. "I had no idea."

He shrugged. "Has she been around long?"

"Just this year. Why do you ask?"

"No reason. Just figured we would have run into them before," he said.

"Well, maybe she's just the thing we needed. Father Carson just informed me we put together around $32,000 just for tonight. And I think there are still a few nonmembers who haven't donated yet."

She paused and moved her hands to his cheeks. Her lips pouted as she looked hard into his eyes. He couldn't recall the last several words she said to him. Success for tonight, he had no doubt. Other doubts swirled in his head, but he had the will to admire her freckled neckline and her lively green eyes. How she kept energy for these events he had no idea.

"You really do look tired, you know," she said.

"I am. I haven't been sleeping well lately."

The smirk on her face reminded him she already knew that. He rarely did sleep well. In younger days, he'd smoke at the bedside while he listened to her dainty breathing. She didn't seem to mind it then, but things had changed. Now he slept in fits and woke earlier and earlier by the year.

"Just give me another hour, and we'll head home to bed," she said.

"Janey, I hate to say it, but I need to head into the office."

It still felt strange to call it that. It was a practiced thing, a euphemism. It was an office in every way. But he convinced himself long ago this was a very different occupation. Maybe it was a kind of bargain he made with himself. A cause to explain away a lucrative career in his father's firm. Maybe it really was different. It didn't matter anymore. He was too far down this path for regret, and Janey with him. She couldn't ask how work was going and expect any real answers. It didn't wash away her worry. It just made her more patient.

Her shoulders moved in a tiny shrug, but she kept her warm hands on his face.

"It's all right," she said. "I'll get a ride. Linda can drive me. It'll give us an excuse to go for a late coffee. Call me before you drive home?"

"All right."

She kissed him good night.

✳ ✳ ✳

Paul entered the operations center. Dark monitors arranged around the island desk absorbed the room's ceaseless light. Kay Linh sat at her station reading from her glowing screen. Another staff operations officer named

Collins occupied the far end of the island desk staring at his own screens in a trance, hypnotized by the thrum of white noise.

"I told you to take the night off," he told Kay. "Don't you ever go home?"

"I did. Now I'm back. Besides, I thought you were going to do the same."

"I'm beginning to doubt you ever having a life outside this room."

"You sound like my parents. But I don't hear you doubting my work ethic."

"No. That I am not," he said.

She looked up from her screen at him.

"Nice suit by the way."

He sighed and dropped into the empty chair next to her station. "How goes the hunt?"

She adjusted her glasses.

"Not much so far. Operations are following up with local assets, but that's slow going. Otherwise, there is no sign of the target. No activity on him. No public transit. If we had known about the villa before, maybe we'd have something. It's definitely the origin of the calls we tracked. Same cell tower, everything. Now, nothing. I think whoever this is, they're operating in a small group. They're not perfect, but they are very good at correcting their mistakes. They could have moved him anywhere by now. That's assuming the target is even still alive."

They wouldn't go through the extraordinary trouble of concealing a virologist's death in a jetliner bombing only to kill the man days later. He couldn't even be sure the guy wasn't part of Scorpio himself. He was alive for now. He had to be. They'd kept him alive for some purpose.

He had reasoned through it a dozen times since yesterday morning. He'd done that twice on the drive over from Bethesda. Khorasani was their link to a bioweapon, but he couldn't see the connection. The Russians sure seemed to think so with all their protective gear at the villa. He had to work on the assumption that Scorpio had a virus. It was too dangerous to think otherwise.

"What about the Russians? Anything more there?"

"The field is reporting a lot of activity since the villa raid. Something definitely has them anxious. They are not being gentle."

What else is new? Khorasani had access to one of their most secure facilities. They would not be forgiving, nor would they share details with anyone else. SVR was a dangerous factor here. It was a miracle Pierce hadn't gotten himself killed.

"Any word from Pierce?"

She shook her head.

"Not since you talked to him last night. They're laying low in a house in Constanța for now."

"I need to talk to him. Get him on a secure line, and get me a headset."

He leaned into the chair and raked his fingers through his hair. The hours wore on him. His eyes strained to stay open. He became aware of a keening between his temples, as if the sound grew from far away and halted inside his head. Kay walked around the island to fetch a headset with a wire-thin mic from another desk. She handed it to him and adjusted her own. She called, and Pierce's voice mumbled into phone.

"Dodger, Hourglass calling. Stand by," Kay ordered.

She opened the line from her screen and gave him a nod.

"Morning, Dodger," he said. His voice came out low and harsh as he adjusted the tiny mic. His thumb rolled over it and sent a scratching wave over the line. Silence followed, and he wondered if they had lost the connection.

Pierce interrupted the pause with a long sigh. "This early morning routine is becoming a bad habit."

"You know what they say, Dodger. No rest for the wicked."

"You would know," Pierce said.

At least Pierce had his wits about him. He'd need that much and more. Paul thought about sending someone to relieve him. Pierce's reports had slowed. His language had become terse, lacking his usual talent for important details and his knack for sharp inferences. Reading his officers' reports was like looking at their portraits. Their voices and their words took shape, and he knew each like a memory. Pierce's reports of late lacked a certain style, he hated to admit it. The weeks had been hard on him since Georgia.

"How's the countryside? I hear you're taking in the sights."

"It's quiet now. Not really seeing anything familiar."

He wanted to share the sentiment. Things at Langley weren't any better after losing all his progress yesterday. From the corner of his eye he noticed Collins leaning into his desk, his hand on his temple. Everything said in the operations center was fair game. He should have nothing to hide. Collins had clearance for this. As Pierce's staff ops lead, Kay Linh should hear every word. He wasn't taking that chance. If he was right, Scorpio was coming for Pierce. They didn't need any more advantage than they already had. Despite everything else, Pierce did get them this far. Paul owed him an honest warning.

"Dodger, hang on one second," he said. He fumbled at a button on the headset wire to mute the call.

"Collins," he said.

Collins' head made a nervous jerk toward him.

"You and Kay take a walk. Now."

Kay frowned and pushed herself away from the desk. Collins shot her a look. She rolled her eyes as she left through the secure door. Collins followed with his shoulders slouched forward, his shoes scuffling the floor as he went.

"Pierce. It's just you and me on the line. I'm alone."

From the earpiece he heard a rustle as Pierce sat up in his bed. Paul broke protocol in saying his officer's name. It got the attention he needed from Pierce.

"Nomad's nearby," Pierce said. His voice hushed.

"Good. Keep him close. Listen carefully. This new target you uncovered? He's upped the ante for us here. It's getting a lot of attention."

"I bet. Staff ops sent me the run down on him already. He's got the kind of résumé that should get our attention. Explains a lot about our friends the other night."

"Those friends of ours have long memories about that kind of thing. You're lucky to be waking up at all this morning. What the hell were you thinking?"

"I was thinking I could use a lot more support than I've been getting, for a start. What did you want me to do, let it go? Let SVR take every lead out in a body bag and leave us worse off than we already are? I was thinking that I would come through. I did."

"And I appreciate that. You know I do. But you don't do me any good dead. You put yourself and your fellow officer at the end of a barrel. Christ, you walked into a biohazard shooting gallery. That's not smart. That's not even brave. That's just dumb luck. I expect you to know the difference."

"So, what now?"

"Same as always. You locate the target. The Russians are a distraction, but you have to deal with that blowback now. There's plenty I can't explain even now, and I'm not going to. You're not the only one who stepped into a mine field. This thing runs deep. Understand?"

"I think so."

"We got their attention. Don't say it. Do not mention their name, not now, not in any of your next reports. Don't get that on anyone's morning briefing. I don't think they want it that way."

"Since when did that stop us? They can't stop us from doing our job. We owe it to the people they've killed, damn it. We're making progress. So, we do our job. I find the target. You get the support we need from seventh floor. And we make them pay."

"It's not that easy. You're going to have to go with me on this. We are now their contingency plan. Get it? You and me. Think about what they've done already. How do you think they stay ahead of us? You think they'll just lay low after this? That they'll just wait it out, let us chip away at them while they bide their time? Is that what you would do?"

"No."

"Then we understand one another. The wind has changed, Pierce. I expect it to blow in your direction."

"I hear you."

"You're right about one thing," he said.

"What's that?"

"We will make them pay for this. I promise you that. Take care."

"You know I will."

He removed the headset and placed it next to its twin on Kay's desk. He stared at the wiry things, his mind lost in the rare quiet of the room. He wondered when it was last empty, when every desk's officer left his operatives without tether to their superiors. It was a room that never knew sleep, no sunrise or sunset. The operatives would not notice. Most of them walked at that moment under a Sunday sun, inconspicuous in their learned surroundings. They blended in with foreign populations like a discolored thread in a vast fabric. If dangerous action unraveled them from that fabric, they did more harm than good for the Agency.

Pierce knew this, and yet he possessed a dedication distinct from his peers. He lacked their fears, which was why Paul liked him more than most. Pierce had purpose as clear and as reasoned as any officer he'd known. The man was no fanatic. There were some within NCS driven by strong and unsubtle emotions for their country or God or a seething need for vengeance in a world teetering from evil acts by evil men. These weren't things Paul tried to sort out for himself, least of all those he had witnessed first-hand. He had faith enough for that, though it never came easy. But with a dozen men like Pierce he'd need less of that faith. For now, he and his teams did their part, and that had to be enough.

In the hall, he found Collins leaning against the opposite wall. He opened his eyes wide at Paul's appearance.

"Kay went for coffee," he said. He fussed for his ID to open the door and return to his desk.

"Anything from your team?" Paul asked as he passed.

Collins shrugged and shook his head.

"Nothing new. They're in Istanbul now. Could go anywhere from there."

Paul nodded and let the door close between them. Maria Hessler's trail was cold. He'd have to reassign the team to something useful soon. They couldn't afford wasting anyone with the threat taking on an uglier shape. He would have no trouble convincing Suzanne. She made no secret of her hope to relieve Pierce, but the call remained his for now.

Kay met him in the hallway. She balanced a tall cup of coffee in her palm and covered the steaming top with her other hand.

"That didn't take long," she said.

She blew on the cup and steam faded into nothingness in the darkened hallway. The coffee's burnt aroma filled his nose and mouth and again he was aware of the tired ache lurking in every muscle.

"I'm headed back to my office to catch up on today's reports. I'll be here for another hour or two."

"All right. See you later."

"Kay," he said. He scanned the empty corridor. "Did anyone else contact you since I've been out?"

She tilted her head sideways as if rewinding the day, separating it from the blur of days just like this one.

"Suzanne checked in a few hours ago."

"Anyone else? What about accessing files?"

"I haven't checked. I doubt it. You want me to verify?"

"Do it. Look for anything. Any modified date that doesn't seem right, any logs of user access."

"What am I looking for, exactly?"

"I don't know. I guess you'll know if you find it. And let me know if you do."

"Okay."

"And, Kay?

"Yeah?"

"Just let me know. No one else."

She gave him a puzzled shrug. He took it as affirmation and headed to his own office to read into the late hours of the night. He thought about Janey, somewhere in the city enjoying a night cap with her friends before she settled into a room as dark and lonely as his office, only far more comfortable. She would be asleep when he crawled into the bed beside her listening to her tiny breaths in the night air. With the rain, she would open the window and let the stir of the city creep in to lull her to sleep.

For now, his eyelids weighed heavy while he read about the world and its constant grind toward calamity. Part of him envied Pierce then. He knew better, but he almost wished he worked independently like Pierce did. As a man dedicated to his work, with purpose and without guilt. For Paul, the guilt was tradition from his Catholic family inheritance. He felt it for leaving Janey alone. For thinking that Pierce was better off out there. He felt guilty for envying Pierce and his dedication.

But that same dedication drove Pierce's wife away. He could tell Pierce about Sarah's visit. That she had moved on and found someone. She wanted him to know that, and that it meant some guilt lived within her as well. Paul was her confessor the night she visited him in the street. She sought absolution and Pierce's blessing through him. Some part of her obviously still cared for Pierce. He hadn't thought much about her since their encounter, and for that he now carried another sin. Someday maybe he could tell Pierce. For now, he'd say nothing after all that Pierce had faced these weeks and what lay ahead.

After 2:00 a.m. when his eyes couldn't focus enough to read anything more, he wandered out to his car. He could use his phone once again to reach the outside world. He started the car and looked at his phone. No call from Janey. He frowned and wondered if he should wake her. She had asked him to, but that wasn't why he did it. He needed to hear her comforting voice to guide his thoughts toward home.

He dialed her phone and listened to the echoing chirps ring without answer. Again he called as he pulled his Lincoln onto the wet blacktop and coursed down the open highway. No answer. She must be fast asleep, drowsy from the wine. He pulled onto their quiet street and crept into the house where the cool air conditioning welcomed him still and silent. Every window was shut tight, the air drained of all humidity. He wanted the smell of and the patter of leaves drying in the dark, a sound to lull him to sleep beside his wife's warmth.

In the kitchen, he emptied some weight from his pockets. His keys, his wallet, his badge. He was eager to rid himself of it all and lay his jacket over the back of one of the kitchen chairs. Janey would cluck at him tomorrow to hang it up, maybe when she returned from mass. He'd have to miss at this hour, though he wouldn't get much sleep despite it. He added the realization to his accruing guilt.

He stood at the foot of the stairs, untucking his shirt, and glimpsed the slick black of the driveway where he'd met Sarah a few weeks ago. Now she stuck in his head like a ghost. He'd tell Pierce when it was all over. Both of them deserved at least that. Janey hadn't inquired why she came to see him. He kept this from her for the Agency's sake, for Pierce's safety. That's what he told himself, but he knew better. Janey certainly did. She knew better than anyone what it meant to wait for someone's secrets, to sleep beside someone while he lay awake thinking of a dozen other people's lives. Now he just needed to surrender to sleep beside her and forget it all for what was left of the night.

Paul crept down the hallway like a blind man feeling by memory the distance from the stairs, past the empty boys' bedrooms, past their bathroom, and to the open door of his own room. He couldn't hear the rhythmic whisper of her sleepy breathing. He dared the light switch.

He stood at the foot of their neatly made bed and called out for his wife. No answer came. She had never come home. A chasm of terror expanded in his chest and he cried out again as he turned on lights in every room looking for her.

His phone rattled in his hands and a strange voice from the sheriff's department told him what his sins already foretold. They had found his wife dead.

TAINTED MESSENGER

Constanţa, Romania
9:51 a.m., Sunday, June 16

ETHAN WANDERED the trash-strewn streets of Constanţa in search of something to eat. He passed a trio of women headed to mass at a nearby church where congregants passed in and out of the elaborate church doorway on their own time. He imagined the three were sisters, each dour-faced and suspicious of an intruder in their decaying neighborhood. They eyed his sunglasses and lengthening stubble as they did the stray dogs that wandered the alleyways sniffing at puddles and empty bottles.

He needed to be free of the cramped bungalow where he and Wade had hidden since their encounter at the villa. Russell provided the safe house, though he scarcely thought of it as a house. Three narrow rooms connected a bathroom barely large enough to hold the toilet and sink. While they waited, Russell's team became their eyes and ears, alert for any sign that the Russians had returned to the city.

Wade needed the fresh air more than he, but they couldn't afford the attention. People stared at his friend like they had never seen a black man. Perhaps some of them hadn't. Wade knew his liability. He heard the muttering comments from a few brazen onlookers these past weeks. Wade sat back in the tiny house surrounded by drab concrete walls while Ethan found them breakfast. Ethan hated the scowling sisters and everyone in the city for confining his friend within those walls. He hated that his superiors sometimes suggested—and sometimes demanded—other officers better able to blend in. They meant someone better suited for the job. Ethan hadn't found anyone one better suited than Wade, an evaluation his friend had proved at least twice for him at the villa.

Several blocks away he found a small corner shop. He almost passed the place, mistaking it for another residence surrounded by scrawny trees that sprouted from the sidewalk. Through a window covered by white bars he saw a case of pastries. He entered the little shop, and a pudgy man wearing an apron greeted him. He nodded at the man who returned his greeting with a shrug. The shopkeeper approached him and spoke again. Ethan pointed to the pastries.

"Four please," he said. He held up four fingers and pointed again.

The shopkeeper wagged his head and stuffed a paper bag with the pastries that were twisted like pretzels. He brushed his fat fingers and thumb on his apron and motioned for Ethan to follow. As Ethan reached for a roll of bread and a salami cooling in an open refrigerator nearby, the man brushed him away and added the items in his cradled arms. He laid the food on a counter and began haggling. Ethan paid the man more than twice what the food was worth, though he bargained for two liters of water and left the shopkeeper to pocket the rest.

He emerged from the shop and caught the glance of an old man sitting on a patio next door. The ashen-colored pensioner sat cross-legged at a small table. In the shrinking morning shade, the old man sipped Turkish coffee out of a porcelain cup and watched him without emotion. Ethan wondered how many mornings he had sat there watching neighbors and the odd stranger like him. There wasn't much chance the man or the shopkeeper were informants. They were simple men living in an old neighborhood. But he couldn't stay here and risk more attention.

He continued on his way closer to the church, switching back on streets and tight corners until he was convinced only the strays could follow his trail as he wound back to the house where Wade waited for breakfast.

Wade hunched in a chair in the front room with a laptop perched on his knees.

"You get lost?" he asked, his eyes still focused on the computer's screen.

"Don't tell me you got lonely without me."

"You were gone over an hour, man. All I got was hungry. What'd you bring me?"

Ethan tossed one of the paper bags into his lap and placed the other in the small sink at the far end of the room. The space was all the house offered for a kitchen. A simple sink and counter shelf where a scorched hotplate rested, untouched since their arrival.

"Nothing but carbs," Wade said. "How do you expect me to keep this physique with the food we eat in these places?" Wade took a bite of the pretzel-twisted pastry and looked at it again. "That's damn good."

"I know, I ate mine on the way back. Perks of the job. Sometimes the food is the best part."

"Take it where you can get it, man," Wade said, grinning as he chewed. "Any trouble?"

"No, nothing. A few stares from locals. We can't stay long."

He leaned against the counter and let Wade finish his meal. Ethan sipped the water. It had turned tepid while tucked under his arm on the meandering walk back. He nodded at the computer pinched between Wade's knees, the lid already covered in pastry crumbs. Wade brushed the crumbs from the laptop and fetched his second pastry from the bag.

"What are you reading?" Ethan asked.

"I started on the dossier for our new target. What do you think?"

"There's not much to go on. This Khorasani guy comes from a wealthy family in northeastern Iran. He studies in France a couple years, goes home and publishes a couple papers. The usual academic stuff. He's there a few years. No wife and kids, maybe he's married to his work. Then he goes to Russia to work at VECTOR. It's their version of the Center for Disease Control. He shows no real political leanings. No security red flags. Up to that point, the guy seems almost boring."

"You mean besides that he's an Iranian working in Russia on killer viruses? He's like the hat trick of orange threat levels."

"No one ever accused you of understatement."

"That's not even the crazy part. The man leaves this VECTOR place and just so happens to board the one plane in Tbilisi that gets hijacked by Chechen militants and explodes in midair."

"It wasn't the Chechens," he said.

"What? It sure as hell was."

"No, I mean they were just hired thugs. A false flag distraction, and an expendable one. They were dupes. All so this Scorpio group could get their hands on Khorasani without anyone realizing it."

"Well it didn't work," Wade said.

"Didn't it?"

"The Russians were looking for him. They figured it out somehow. Now we know, too."

He shook his head and stared at the floor.

"It took us and the Russians six weeks to figure that out. Maybe that's all the time they needed."

"Needed for what? Who the hell are these people?"

"That's what worries me. The Russians sure seemed convinced the vineyard was a hot zone. All that gear and the gas masks? They took every precaution. That suggests Khorasani didn't leave VECTOR empty handed. He may have smuggled out a virus."

"Son of a bitch, maybe he was working with them all along."

"Possibly. But it doesn't explain the restraints on that chair. He was sleeping in a loading dock. Not exactly VIP treatment for the guy."

"True. But we don't know it was him in that chair. Even if it was, he could be another dupe."

Ethan grunted assent. There was much to sort out, but none of it mattered unless they could find Khorasani.

"We have to find him," he said. "Otherwise we're facing a group with a plan. With resources and connections. And they're willing to use extreme force. If we're right about this, they want a WMD that fits in a test tube. I don't see any reason to think they won't use it."

Paul was right. They would come for him. He took it as a twisted compliment. For all they had been through, they were making progress. This was the trickiest operation of his career. It was all he knew to keep pursuing the target. There would be a reckoning for mistakes he'd made and lives lost. He knew that day would come, yet he drove that thought deep within him for another time. The cost wore on him, but they had to perform. He felt it in his grinding teeth and tensing shoulders. He needed more rest and time to think. He had time for neither.

He thought of Russell's advice out on the pier. Scorpio would not act as the Russians had. This was no cautious exchange of looks and radio chatter and calculations. They wanted his operation terminated, which meant they probably wanted both him and Wade dead. They had already killed Marcus.

He needed Wade to make this work. They both needed Russell and his crew, too. Involvement for any of them put them in mortal danger. They had to entice Scorpio's people into revealing themselves. If he did this, he'd put himself in the crosshairs, not the others. The risk was his, and so was the cost.

"Where do we start?" Wade asked.

"We give them a reason to come to us."

* * *

They left for Bucharest in the cool cover of darkness. Russell met them at a petrol station on the west edge of the city, but he reported only the absence of their adversaries. In the course of two days, every contact vanished, everyone replaced by strange faces. The changes seemed to concern Russell as he tugged on his cigarette with his eyes downcast. He waved them off and promised to meet them in Bucharest.

For miles, they traced the same route they had taken to the villa. Ethan looked down the unlit road toward the far-ranging vineyards as they passed his passenger window. The road vanished into the night, trailing somewhere toward the empty villa. In the dark spaces between towns, Ethan's thoughts dwelled on Russell's silent worries. Russell was a worn weathervane that sensed the same shifting winds Corso had warned about. Ignoring his instincts was foolish, even dangerous. He and Wade precipitated that change. They interrupted the motives of a human effort, not some force of nature. That gave him some hope for finding answers—if they could weather the coming storm.

"Always thinking, aren't you?" Wade asked as he drove.

"One of us has to."

"Watch yourself now."

Ethan looked over the shrouded fields where night lay across the slopes. The villa was just miles away in the darkness. He could still see it in his mind like a flashing strobe that stretched moments into hours like the passage of his dreams. He nodded to the north.

"You did some quick thinking the other night. I wouldn't be sitting here if it wasn't for you, and not for the first time. I know you're going to say you're just doing your job. But it's a hell of a job. So, thanks. I owe you."

"Just doing my job," Wade said with a wide grin curled across his face. "And you do owe me. But look, don't get all soft on me just yet. I don't know what we're getting into now, and I don't like that shit one bit. You make good on what you owe me and see that we both keep this lousy job."

Bucharest swelled before them like a swarm of fireflies. A summer's night haze hung above the city. They passed empty car parks and the joyless apartment complexes along E81. Much had changed here for the better, Russell told him. But the city bore old scars. They rode into downtown where it became more beautiful and elaborate. Ahead of them loomed the Palace of Parliament, a massive building awash in electric light that seemed a far-off mountain on the horizon. Traffic bloomed, and they blended into it.

"We're going to need more cars At least four of them," Ethan said.

"I'll take care of it."

"Leave the station office out of it. Do it on your own. Or Russell can help. Pay with cash."

Wade nodded his head as he maneuvered the van around a pack of haggard looking dogs that crossed the street in front of them. A gang of sickly youths walking nearby paid them no attention. They looked gloomy and tired, and the dogs danced among their legs as they stumbled along oblivious to the parade of cars swirling around the city's hub.

Ethan pointed out the side street turn to an office building Russell rented out in the old Jewish neighborhood. A precarious scaffold of lumber and plastic sheeting covered half of the white building. The remainder of the modern edifice rose above the street where they parked, standing erect in bright contrast to the old milky plaster houses and nearby stone basilica. He liked the location—an empty space afforded to them by Romania's unsteady economy. From the looks of the graffiti and shreds of plastic sheeting on the scaffold outside, construction had halted months ago. The place was less secure than either of them would like. But it was near the city center where they could orchestrate a plan, practice it, and await the opportunity to act.

"All the comforts of home," Wade said.

They entered the office suite. The floors were unfinished concrete, the walls painted with white primer. Powdery dust hung in the air and clung to the surfaces of the desks and tables someone had placed inside. Wires bundled with tape sprouted from holes in the ceiling and walls, but fluorescent lights hung from above with a switch that dangled from a hole in the wall.

"It's not much, is it?" Ethan said.

"Maybe you forgot where I've been staying for the last couple weeks? This is the Ritz by comparison, though the decor's about the same. Hope you like sleeping in chairs."

They wandered the office rooms with the single row of lights overhead to illuminate the dark corners and side offices. Wade procured a slender flashlight and a small black scanner from his duffel bag. He paced through the rooms for several minutes.

"We're good," Wade said. He shrugged his shoulders and returned his gear to his bulging bag.

"Good?"

"Either that or they are very, very damn good. It's clean."

Wade left him in the large central office while he patrolled the other vacant office suites in the building. Ethan settled in a black leather chair and began the first step of his plan. If they were coming for him, he needed to see them coming. He thought of only one way to do that. If Corso was right, someone at Langley scoured his reports. His newest dispatch would get their attention.

Reports were his habit, a necessity of the profession that fueled the machinery of intelligence. He had written hundreds of them, often late at night in strange rooms like this one with the weariness of late hours clouding his vision. Now the task took on an unfamiliar form. The report wasn't for Corso, who would—he hoped—recognize it as eyewashed babble. Paul recognized Ethan's work and knew the tenor and tone of his writing. Now he wrote not genuine intelligence but calculated enticement. A lure that balanced the plausibility of his searching with the absurdity of what he sought. He invited his own assassins to parley.

He chose words deliberately, a labor to which he was unaccustomed. Mention of the Scorpio Compact must appear within the text, of course. He mentioned the group in defiance of Corso's directive. That alone would alert someone who would pass it along to another down a chain of someones he could only guess at for now. His report had to prod that chain of colluders to return a signal that would find its way to him. Mentioning Kamran Khorasani seemed too obvious for now. He needed something indirect that they would take as a sign he knew more than he actually did.

This began the fabrication, rooted in his confidence that they now possessed a deadly virus. He filled the report with a trail of leads on medical equipment, providers of specialized filters, or protective suits—anything they might need to contain the pathogen. The idea wasn't far-fetched, but he lacked the resources to pursue each avenue quickly. Worse, he lacked faith in the Agency's special collections to pursue it without inviting more disaster.

The response would take days, he guessed. Or he would write more reports, each subtler than the first to conceal him angling for their attention. They did not know his work as Corso did, but they would sense his desperation if he pressed too hard and too often. He and Wade could spend that time with Russell's team practicing their surveillance and tailing unaware civilians until they mastered every route and street and turn.

By the next afternoon, the skeleton crew of Russell's team arrived at the office building while Wade secured their transportation. Tereza brought him a hunk of dark bread and a cup of ciorbă that had cooled on the way. They sipped the sour broth as they reviewed the nearby streets together on a map. She pointed out the electric rail routes and best times to avoid the heaviest traffic.

Leo, who had tracked the Russians in Constanța, interrupted their planning with a baby-faced grin, a look that every cab driver in the country seemed to share. He teased the pair with his thick accent. Ethan laughed a little and admitted he was impressed with his skills. Tereza had already explained that Leo grew up in Cleveland.

At last, Russell appeared in a long jacket that was far too warm for the June sun. Sweat rolled down his forehead. He sat at the far end of the long conference table they had designated as their operational hub and took his time finishing a cigarette. The others had busied themselves arranging their own quarters in the tiny office rooms.

"Everything all right?" Ethan asked.

Russell leaned down and extinguished the stub of his cigarette on the concrete floor.

"Have you spoken with Langley?"

"Not directly. Not since we came to the city. We're barely settled in. Why?"

Russell eyed him with a vacant look.

"Paul's wife is dead."

"Jane?" he said without thinking. His voice faded as Russell nodded confirmation.

He heard the news as if Russell spoke another language, an accented trick like Leo's teasing. He met Jane Corso a couple times. She was as sweet as her husband was irascible. When he and Sarah were still together, Jane invited them into her home at a time when they knew almost no one in the city. He recalled how at ease Paul was with Jane, so unlike his Agency self. And how generous they were to their guests and to each other as they shuffled around their kitchen preparing an elaborate meal. He envied that comfort in them, even then. Paul would lose all that without her to come home to.

"What are you talking about? What happened?"

"I don't know, really. She was getting a ride with someone late Saturday night. The car hit a wall and she was killed."

"An accident then?" he stammered. It sounded impossible, now of all times.

Russell gave him an incredulous look while he fidgeted with his crumpled pack of cigarettes to fetch another smoke. "Never met her, myself. I hear she was a remarkable woman."

"I did," Ethan said. "I didn't know her well, but she was very good to my wife and me. They invited us into their house a couple times for dinner."

Russell took a long drag on his newly lit cigarette. His eyes winced a little. "Ah, the famous Corso dinner parties. I would have liked to have seen one of those. You're married?"

Ethan took his time to respond as he thought of pleasant evenings that seemed nearer in time than they were. He could see Jane Corso smiling. He heard Sarah laughing as she put her hand on his thigh, relaxed for the first time since she came to the city.

"I was. What about you?"

Russell shook his head. Ethan observed a slight of smile crawl across his lips.

"Not for lack of trying. A long time ago now. Life has a funny way of deciding what you're good at. And what you're not. Here I sit."

Russell's smile flattened once again, and the silence held all of them.

Ethan's thoughts of Sarah remained. She came into his mind like an apparition. It was what Russell had said—that life decided what he was good at. Maybe life decided for her, too. He wanted it to be true. They had what they were good at together, and the remainder pulled them apart like water from the shore. He saw some solace in that. That's what Russell had. The comfort of being good at something five thousand miles away from everything else. The ease of laying blame at the feet of time and chance. But it was a lie, and he knew it. He pitied Russell, but he found no peace in lies he told himself. He bore the blame, but there was no going back to her now.

Everyone and everything around him were a teetering intersection of lies, like the ragged scaffolding outside the window. Sitting there inside the jumble he began to lose sense of things. There were the lies they told to operate, to stay alive, and there was the stack of lies they hammered at that had now pulled the weight down on Jane Corso. Her death was no accident. There was no sense to it, but there was human agency. Someone killed her.

"What now? Without Paul, we can't very well outrun them." Russell said.

Ethan's hands tighten into fists at his side. He wanted to shout, but he kept it within himself, a growing thing that turned his stomach and spun around in his head.

"We can't wait," he said. "You know we can't. That's what they want. Damn it, we're not letting them do that to us. We go on without him."

Russell took the cigarette from the corner of his mouth. "Let's get started then," he said, his expression implacable.

* * *

Tuesday came with no response from Langley. Word would come soon, though Ethan dreaded the call. Paul's absence might spare him the futility of condolences over a secure line. He needed Paul back in the lead, guarding his back from angles he couldn't cover in the field. Even more they needed a sign that Scorpio had responded to his reports. They had to be ready.

He walked along the side streets toward Unirea Shopping Center near the city's heart. Tucked behind the ostentatious building splashed with backlit logos he found what he sought—a large parking garage that spiraled up four floors. Despite its shabby exterior, the garage interior was newly finished. Bright lights reflected off the concrete floor. Newer model cars filled almost every space, and the midday shoppers paced around him on their way to the mall entrance. He noted cameras positioned above entrances, but they didn't cover every corner and curve. Light security would help his plan, but he had to be careful about securing the right spot when the time came.

He entered the mall and browsed the shops as he worked his way to the upper floors to return to the garage. At the top level the spaces were mostly vacant, and he wandered around feigning confusion and impatience while he memorized every pillar and sign. Gaps to the outside air narrowed. All but one faced the windowless walls of the surrounding buildings. With the right angles, he could avoid any field of fire they might position. In all, the place suited him, though the parade of shoppers could interrupt the meet.

They spent two days running his gambit, rehearsing the shifts as each of them drove separate vehicles, trading tails of the oblivious shoppers Ethan chose for them. He picked random people leaving the fourth floor of the garage, then radioed to the team the details. Russell met them at the garage exit and trailed to the Strada Sfânta Vineri, where Tereza could intercept if they went west. Leo pointed his car east. Wade stayed on foot near the electric rail station where he could cover the train route.

With each rehearsal they traded positions, leading each new unsuspecting target into a practiced game of track and evasion. Most were easy marks, but Ethan made everyone learn the bustling streets and the timing of traffic signals and electric rail. With so little he could control, he needed them ready for anything to track their target—with or without him.

On their second run on Thursday, Ethan parked his car in the garage and chose an Audi parked nearby. He lingered, awaiting the Audi's owner. A woman in tight jeans and heels returned to the car after a half hour. She teetered in the heels as two large and glossy shopping bags swayed at her sides. He radioed the team and set them in motion. In the seat next to him, his phone flickered.

"Dodger, this is Hourglass," a woman said. He didn't recognize her voice. "I'm afraid I have some unfortunate news. Your supervisor is away on a family matter."

"So I heard. Took you a while," he said.

"Yes, well, it's been a difficult week. I'm confident we've figured out a solution. You'll be hearing from me for the time being. I'm fully briefed on your situation. How are you holding up? I understand you knew the family."

It was Suzanne Tasker, Paul's boss. He knew her mainly by reputation. She'd risen to command like a diligent bureaucrat. Paul kept her out of his hair, and now he had to rely on her guidance. She was trying to build rapport with him. If this was the call he anticipated, she was a tainted messenger who lured him into a trap while he did the same with whoever sent the message. Whether or not she knew it, for now they were two adversaries dueling over the transom. He could not afford her consolation.

"We're wasting time," he said.

"I thought you'd want to know."

He didn't respond. Out his windshield, the Audi's reverse lights brightened the garage floor slightly as she backed out. He activated his radio to signal the team. He wanted to see how well they'd coordinate without him.

"I've reviewed your newest reports, and I think we found something of interest. One of our assets in country indicates he has information on the kinds of lab equipment you specified in your reports this week."

That was the sign he'd waited for. *Scorpio got the message.*

"What do you know about this asset?" he said.

"I'm told he's been useful in the past. He has contacts in organized crime in Bucharest."

"Contacts?"

"Again, that's what I'm told," she said.

"And he just happened to say he has a lead on HEPA filters? That's convenient," he said.

"No, he did not specify. The agent is cautious, understandably. He wishes to meet. His handler positioned the deal as a payoff for intel on the syndicate he works for. That should put you at an advantage. You can conduct the meet and interview him. Encourage him to tell us what he knows."

"Then I'll need more cash to close a deal with this guy. And I arrange the location."

"It's unlikely he'll agree to that."

"Then he won't find the deal very beneficial all by himself."

"Very well."

"Have the ops officer arrange it. I'll meet him in downtown Bucharest. At the Unirea Shopping Center garage, fourth floor. Tomorrow at 0800 hours. I'll be in a silver Volkswagen. Message me to confirm and send me his file."

"That's incredibly fast. Where are you now? We can arrange for more resources in place to better prepare. You're going to need additional support."

"Just make the meet happen. We've got to keep this operation alive."

I've got to keep myself alive, he thought as he hung up. He had an obligation to keep the team he'd assembled safe as well. He took a risk in shutting down Suzanne like that, but he took a greater one in letting her in on his plan. Whoever they were, they could find him and Wade easily enough. He couldn't give them enough time to disrupt everything.

Through his radio earpiece he heard the team tail the blonde north to the edge of Old Town before he called them off. Without his input, they had traded positions twice and kept her in sight amid a late afternoon rush of cars. They were ready. He had spent the week focused to the point of trance on the plan. He simply pushed away the sorrow he felt about Jane's death. He shoved off any notion that circulated in the back of his mind that he was somehow to blame.

He left the Volkswagen parked in the ramp. The spot was ideal for the meet tomorrow with a clear view of the entrance ramp and an easy course to the exit. In the shopping center he strolled down to the lower floors. He passed a pretty girl with round and rosy cheeks who leaned over her perfume counter and smiled at him. She spoke a greeting to him he couldn't decipher and held up a tiny bottle with a garish gold cap. He waved her off as he walked, but his focus finally broke. In front of him a sign read *Arsis*, and he entered the small store to buy a prepaid SIM card and a cheap mobile phone. The saleswoman babbled at him while he handed over a wad of lei for the phone. Her eyes widened at the bundle of cash he stowed back into his pocket.

Outside amid the honking and thrum of the traffic he assembled the phone and dialed from memory his old phone mail service. The phone was a mistake and against every security protocol he knew. He couldn't help himself from entering his passcode. She hadn't left him a message in months. There was a new message. He heard her voice echoing back from three weeks ago.

"Ethan. It's me. It's Sarah. You know that. I know it's weird to call you now. I hope you're doing okay."

Her voice faltered. He strained to hear her and pressed the phone closer to his ear.

"Listen, I need to let you know something. I'm getting married. I know that's not what you want to hear right now. I'm … I'm sorry I'm telling you like this. It's just, I needed to tell you. Kerim and I are getting married this summer. I'm really happy now, Ethan. I want you to be happy for me, too. God, I just wanted to talk to you and know you're okay. I know it sounds crazy after everything between us, but I'm going to miss you. And you deserved to know. So, I hope you'll be okay. I know you will. Bye, Ethan."

As he walked back to meet the others, he listened to her message four more times.

CHAPTER 15

DESPERATE VOID

Elizabethtown, Pennsylvania
11:18 a.m., Thursday, June 20

Paul SAT atilt in a folding chair draped with crushed velvet. Beneath his feet was a carpet of artificial grass laid over the freshly dug and uneven earth. Janey lay locked away in a casket before him beneath a mound of brilliant red roses. He held one of them in his left hand, its color as deep and red as blood. His son Michael had pulled the rose free with tiny motions until its long stem was free and the bloom drooped under its own weight. Michael freed another and brought it to Janey's sister, who sat next to him. She wept, but Paul had cried all his tears for today. With his other hand, Paul reached out to the lacquered walnut casket and felt its perfect smoothness under his fingertips.

When his father had passed, his mother seemed lost to everyone around her. The loss had so absorbed her every thought that she walked in a foggy stupor able to focus only on the man who left her behind. So, it came as a great surprise to him that his attention now awakened. He remembered every sight and sound, every grieving face that pitied him. Amid their family and the friends standing in the unmowed grass nearby, he heard every sniffle and sigh. He glanced at the trees wagging in the summer breeze that carried the faint aroma of chocolate from the town's factory.

For all of these things, his mind became a chronicler.

Perhaps this was his real punishment. That he would relive every sensation that filled the cavern in his head and echoed against the walls there as sharply as the vision of Janey's face when she last held his hand in hers and said good night. For all the hurt, he held on to that and prayed a silent promise that he'd suffer through any pain and guilt to keep from forgetting her face.

In the last four days he watched Michael transform—as though guided by Janey's spirit—into the gracious family host. He'd become a rock for everyone's crashing waves of tears. He had greeted the guests from his mother's hometown in the entrance at St. Peters and embraced them smiling. Jacob took his mother's death harder. Paul watched his elder son close up as the week progressed. Now Jacob wiped tears and heaved in the chair beside him as his no longer little brother wrapped an arm around him.

What could he tell them? For them this was a tragic accident that killed two innocent women, their mom and her best friend. That they collided headlong into a road barrier became for his boys one of the meaningless tragedies of life. One that for them would shape how they saw the world, and how they would cope and someday tell their children. But he knew better. How could he conceal the truth from his own children? He had no choice. Maybe someday, for their sake he could explain this was a vicious move by enemies he couldn't name. These enemies did it to punish him, he believed. To deter him without raising too much suspicion so that they could visit further evil on more innocents. For now, he contained the anger as simply another sensation he memorized in every detail. Soon he would have to shape and guide that in the direction of those who did this to his wife.

Father Carson embraced him as the crowd returned to their cars along the narrow cemetery lane. "She's in God's hands now, Paul," he said.

Paul heard the words as abstraction, another echo to recall in his head. He had little sense of the sentiment or what it meant anymore. Beside her grave, he hugged his sons together. Their heads touched and he whispered to them.

"She loved you boys more than anything."

Jacob sniffled and slapped him on the back.

"I know, Pop," Michael said.

* * *

By nightfall, Paul returned to an empty house. Janey's friends had cleaned the place for him. They packed away every dirty dish and neatly tucked away each scrap of paper on her desk by the phone. They erased any sign he and the boys had spent the week eating pizza and casseroles or that he made funeral arrangements on the backs of envelopes. Now the kitchen was bare and dim. The weak bulb under the stove hood shed some light on the island counter where the friends left him a bittersweet note and a loaf of homemade bread. They had lost two best friends that night. Linda drove Janey home after the benefit, and now both were gone. The ladies grieved a great loss, but for him and his sons the loss felt limitless.

He left the other lights off and felt his way around the counter to the liquor cabinet. There he stood and stared at the open cabinet lost in thought as the day repeated itself again and again in his mind. He lost track of time. A bottle of vodka stood taller than the other bottles that glinted in the low light. He weighed drinking himself to sleep against making some coffee to fuel the insomnia.

A tap on the back door knocked him out of his stupor. He started at the sound and leaned to look out the kitchen window. A tall bulwark of a man stood on the back step. For a moment he thought to grab a kitchen knife, then shook off his irrationality. No doubt someone had come to check on him. It was too large to be one of the boys. He crept toward the door to take a look. Someone in a tie and dark coat. *Who the hell would come to the back door?* He flicked on the back porch light and revealed Harley Gilchrist squinting at him. Paul unlocked and opened the door.

"Christ, Harley, what are you doing here?"

"I know it's a hell of a time to bother you, Paul. Can I come in?"

He opened the door and let Harley inside. The man's girth filled the door frame, and Paul stepped back into the kitchen to give him room. He turned on the kitchen light and met the ruddy faced giant.

"My sincerest sympathies to you, Paul. I didn't know your wife, but I hear tell she was one of a kind."

Paul nodded a quiet thanks, but the puzzlement deepened on his face. Harley surveyed the kitchen, pausing at the hallways and the windows. He avoided these and settled himself against the counter.

"Looks like you were fixing to have a drink," Harley said. He pointed at the high open cabinet near his head.

"I was until I thought better of it. I was about to make some coffee. Can I get you some?"

"Coffee sounds just fine. Hold up, is that a bottle of Balvenie? A thirty year?"

"Help yourself. It's not my favorite. It was a gift from my father before he passed. That was his kind of thing."

"Oh, I'm sorry. No, sir, I couldn't. That's some gift. Your old man had good taste. The coffee will do me just fine. I shouldn't be drinking that stuff as it is."

Paul set water on the stove, then found the grinder and poured in enough of the aromatic beans for the both of them. Harley asked about the service. Somehow, Paul didn't mind. Harley had no obligation to be there, and he found it oddly comfortable to detail the day as he prepared the coffee. Talk of the funeral put them both at ease as the water came to a boil. Strange as it was to have Harley visit, Paul appreciated that his interest seemed genuine. He knew Harley was a keen observer of details, of course, so he obliged the man. He did it more for himself. He told him about Michael's eulogy and the long procession down Market Street where the old houses and empty porches with flags rolled out for summer saluted a hometown girl.

"I had no idea she was a Pennsylvania girl," Harley said.

Paul stood mute as Harley's voice snapped him out of the raw memory. Any comfort in the telling was fleeting, and he now observed the man who all but ran the CIA standing in his kitchen.

"Harley, why are you here?"

Late in the day, the rasp in his voice was heavy and came almost as a whisper.

"None of this is going to come easy for you, I'm afraid."

Paul shrugged and looked at the floor.

"I'm listening," he said.

Harley stretched his mouth and rubbed the edges of it with his heavy fingers and thumb.

"To start, it doesn't look like this was an accident. Can I take a wild guess that doesn't surprise you much?"

"No, it doesn't."

"It just seemed too unlikely for me to dismiss with what's going on. With respect, nothing like this is timed real well for anybody. But here we've got another thing entire. So, I had some friends of mine at the Bureau look into things."

"I appreciate that."

Harley dismissed the sentiment with a mild frown.

"They owed me a favor or two as it was. The police report says another vehicle collided with your wife and her friend's vehicle. The collision pushed them off the road and into that concrete divider. They're still looking for the vehicle. Maybe a Dodge truck or SUV. County sheriff's team seems to think it's a drunk driver hit and run."

"I already know all of this," Paul said.

He knew the exact spot, though he couldn't bring himself to drive past. It was along his commute from Langley. He could take a longer route, or drive past the scene of his wife's death as long as he worked there. He tried not to think about it for now.

"What you don't know is that two vehicles collided with the car. One at the front right fender, another from the rear. One of my Bureau friends lifted traces of a black vehicle from the rear."

"Did he share that with the police in Tyson?" Paul asked.

"He did, but they chalked it up to all part of the accident. At best, they're looking for another witness."

"They won't find anyone."

"No, sir. They will not. They might find the vehicles, but it's a safe bet that will be that."

Paul poured the steaming water into the French press and let it steep. He stirred the coarse grounds and stared into the swirling murk as he considered the finality of Harley's comment. They ambushed her. He couldn't imagine the terror she had felt, and he didn't want to. He should have stayed at the benefit. He could have been with her then, but all he wanted to do was leave all those damn socialites at the party and that smarmy Crowley guy and get back to his work.

"Paul, you all right?" Harley said.

Paul poured the coffee into a pair of white mugs and slid one toward Harley.

"Do you know a collections officer named Brian Crowley?"

"Don't know him myself. But the name's awful familiar. He works in HUMINT, I think."

"That's right. He was there that night. At the benefit. He came up to me on his own and asked about getting transferred under me at NCS."

"And you think that was a little too friendly?"

"Wasn't it? I don't know what to think any more."

"Is he on your short list for the Scorpio Compact?"

"He is now."

"Don't jump to conclusions, now. He'd have to have some real brass to reveal himself like that. Besides, I don't know how someone like him could pull all this off. It's just as good a bet it's someone else inside."

"Harley, there were two cars, right?"

"So it seems."

"Then what makes you think it's just one mole?"

Harley nodded as he acknowledged the possibility. He took a drink of the coffee. Once he had tasted it, he took another.

"Could be the guy's just climbing the company ladder. Just bad timing on a rough night. Then again, he'd have access to some of the reports that mention Scorpio. And he could coordinate with someone higher up. Jesus Christ," Harley said shaking his head at the possibility.

Paul sipped his coffee and let the warmth spread through him, but he felt less at ease. Nothing about their conversation seemed right. Harley had resorted to sneaking to his back door and checking the windows as if he didn't notice. *Who was out there?* He wondered if they listened even now, invisible intruders prying into his home. They'd taken away everything, and still he jumped at shadows just as he had the night they took her from him.

"Who the hell are these people, Harley?"

"Near as I can tell, it's the same old trouble. Radicals who hate the West. Hackers and nihilists who want to usher in some crackpot new world order. This Scorpio Compact of theirs? It's just a damn manifesto against hegemony or state surveillance. Take your pick. The name's nothing special. Whoever created it released it in November a few years ago. You know, like under the sign of Scorpio, like the Zodiac. All the chatter we pick up, and it's just the same kind of noise it always has been. More secular, maybe. More technologically savvy. But it's the same old bullshit."

"Then what's the appeal? How the hell could they penetrate the Agency? Our people aren't like this."

"Who knows? Money? A threat? Lord knows, you might be next in line if this keeps up. It doesn't matter. With that line of thinking, all you're doing is looking for a way to disbelieve that there are a pack of wolves circling around us. They're circling, and the why don't much matter right now."

He gripped the edge of the counter at his sides and clenched his teeth. His gut tightened. He wanted to scream and yell at them if they were listening. There was no reason to it. Not even despair, but an emotion he couldn't name festered within him, a kind of rage and confusion that he had to exorcise from his body. Instead he stifled it, swallowing it up into himself with a physical effort that kept his body still and rigid, his hands gripping ever tighter. The moment passed as though a white light had left his eyes and he calmed himself again. He took a heavy breath and exhaled slow. If Harley noticed, he just gave him the time to breathe.

"What now?" he said.

"For you? Nothing. You take care of yourself here. Take all the time you need. I'll make sure you have that at least."

"I can't do that. It's only going to get worse. Christ, Harley, this is what they want. They want me off this thing."

"You can't save the world by yourself. Look at you. You can't even think straight. Grieve for your wife. Give it a few days, at least."

"We don't have a few days."

"I wasn't asking," Harley said.

Paul turned and poured half of his coffee in the sink. The taste of it lingered on his tongue, and it summoned memories of mornings with sleepy-eyed Janey. Nothing he could do would change it, just as nothing he could say would change Harley's mind. He was powerless, and that aggravated him even more.

"What about Pierce? They're coming for him next," Paul said.

"You're probably right. Sounds like Pierce can take care of himself. I'll do what I can, but the priority has to be our counterintelligence efforts here."

"Then he's on his own."

With a few more kind words, Harley moved to the back door and fumbled with the switches to turn off the back porch light. Paul shook his enormous hand, and Harley entered the midnight gloom where he stepped over one of Janey's planters at the edge of the patio. Then he vanished from Paul's sight to navigate the neighbors' back yards to the street.

Paul stood in the doorway alone, transfixed by the hesitant chirps of crickets in the night before he went back inside. He wandered the house and shuffled through the rooms where shafts of light fell onto the floor from the streetlights outside. The spaces were all there, but the sensations strange. The ladies had tidied every paper in his study. The dark surface of the old desk lay bare. A weak scent of antiseptic trespassed his favorite retreat. The dining room appeared suspended in time like a museum display after hours. He passed his hands over the padded chairs and their ornamental backs. Janey had them brought over from Columbia. Now they stood erect and unused, all traces of dust and her boxes of fundraiser folders cleaned away. He trundled up the stairs.

The spare bedroom doors greeted him like tombstones. He couldn't explain to himself why, but he opened each and peered into silent rooms where neatly made beds occupied the stillness. Behind one, Janey's white sewing table reflected a little light peeking through the trees from the street. He closed the doors again and crept into his bedroom as he had on countless late nights before. Overhead the ceiling fan spun, flickering and quiet. A glow from her closet door framed a perfect box of light on the far wall. He moved to switch off the light and again without reason opened the door. As his eyes tuned to the brightness of the light overhead, he tasted her scent. The alchemy of her perfume and lotion filled the back of his throat, a smell like jasmine and honey. He stood dazed. His mind fought the sensation that she was just there in the room behind him, waiting for him to come to bed. He closed the closet door and left the bedroom undisturbed.

He wanted nothing to do with sleep, and so he fought with exhaustion. He slouched on the sofa in his slacks and undershirt. Hours passed, and he counted them out of habit. His watch glinted, and he calculated the hours between here and the operations underway. Something about the sense of sunrise elsewhere in the world kept him occupied until exhaustion overtook him and he fell into a fitful sleep. He dreamed anxious dreams where he climbed out of a quarry filled with black water. At each carved ledge he scaled, he found a familiar face who would climb no farther with him. He couldn't remember their names.

CHAPTER 16

RIDE ALONG

Bucharest, Romania
7:32 a.m., Friday, June 21

From the solitude of an empty office, Ethan watched the sun's light spread on the Bucharest skyline. He had slept a little in the office chair, his feet propped up on a desk with a too small woolen blanket draped over his legs. He considered what awaited him in the parking garage. He mapped out by memory the exact space where he left his car, and what to do if the target came alone. He wouldn't come alone, so what to do if he brought friends? He considered one vehicle or two. More? He recounted the paces between his Volkswagen and the lane where the target would arrive. He recalled the placements of every camera and their position. He visualized himself at his most vulnerable, away from his Volkswagen and moving toward the target's vehicle. He imagined all that could go wrong, and everything that he could control. He saw himself from their perspective and imagined a half-dozen ways they could kill him.

From the other side of the office suite he heard the others stirring as they prepared for another day of trailing targets in the city streets. They mumbled to one another as if the reality of their mission weighed down the voices. Wade's baritone grumble echoed across the concrete floors. Ethan envied his partner's ability to sleep anywhere and wake alert and aware.

Wade met the mission like a soldier, his voice stern and serious, his mind focused in the moment without thought of the future.

They assembled in the conference room. The odor of Russell's cigarette wafted in, intermingled with the scent of the fresh coffee Tereza brought from a nearby street cafe where she parked her little blue Renault. It was on the north side of the boulevard, pointed west as they had rehearsed.

Ethan entered the conference room, and they greeted him with a pause in the discussion. Wade nodded to him, and the others turned their eyes his way.

"Morning everyone," he said.

Their murmurs resumed as they mused on the weather and the direction of the summer sun and the intensity of Friday morning traffic. Tereza handed him a cup of coffee and turned back to her section of the table where she toggled her radio and fidgeted with a discreet earpiece. Everyone stood around the table, knights of the round, focused on the gear before them. A crisscross of cables and adaptors that charged their radios and phones splayed across the table amid the steaming paper mugs of coffee. Russell spread a large tourist's map of the city center before him, weighed down by an empty cup he used as an ashtray.

Ethan placed a laptop on the table and rotated it to reveal the screen to the team. A photo on the screen showed a scrawny young man holding up a bottle of liquor and mugging for the camera with a drunken scoff and gap-toothed grin.

"Operations came through," he said. "This is Cosmin Moraru. He likes to call himself *Zmeu*. Some kind of hacker nickname. Everyone outside this room thinks he is our target. Let's keep it that way. Cosmin here is a worm on a hook. We want the group he says he represents. He's ambitious. He started out in computer crime. Mostly scams. Now he seems to have branched out into smuggling unusual goods in and out of Europe."

"So, he's smarter than he looks?" Tereza asked. She sneered at his photo, and the others chuckled at her disgust.

"I think you could say that," Ethan said. "He's clever enough to make friends and not get caught. But his file suggests his ambition is greater than his ability. I'm hoping that means he's eager to make a deal. The last thing I need is a nervous kid playing gangster.

"I'll make contact on the fourth floor at 0800 hours. I'll signal you with radio taps just like I have been all week. One tap for our guy and each of his friends. Hold position until I can confirm the vehicle to you."

"I still say you need someone with you up there, man," Wade said.

"Everyone's assigned for a reason. Stick with the plan."

"Plans don't mean shit if things go south with this guy and his pals."

"No changes. Let's go over it again."

He leaned over the map with Russell and nodded as everyone pointed and pushed on the map, confirming their routes and signals in a robotic cadence. Russell extinguished his last cigarette and dropped it in the cup. He folded the map in sections while the others cleared the table and tucked concealed radios in their pockets and under their clothes.

"You got that new sidearm I gave you?" Wade asked.

Ethan nodded. He'd tucked the compact Glock in the back of his waistline, hidden under his light blue jacket. Wade armed himself whenever he could. But the others had no protection outside of their cars and their wits. If things became violent, he had instructed them to run and not return to the office building.

They took turns leaving, wandering the streets and waiting near their cars. He and Wade sat on the stairs at the northwest exit of the building, awaiting their turn to find their position.

"I don't like this one, man," Wade said.

"It's no different than all the rest."

"You're wrong. This one's different. They know we're coming. They're looking for you. We aren't holding all the cards here, you know what I mean? I'm not questioning your plan. It's just I don't like the circumstances."

"We don't get a choice on that. It's the best we've got with what we have."

"I know it. But I don't have to like it. Just don't get yourself killed. You still owe me."

"More than one," Ethan said.

He pulled the cell phone he had purchased the night before out of his pocket and handed it to Wade.

"What's this?"

"If things do go south, I need you to take care of that."

"What is this, a burner phone? What for?"

"Nothing good. It's personal."

Wade took the phone and turned it in his hand, grimacing.

"Bad idea, man. You shouldn't have this."

"I know. That's why I'm giving it to you. For safe keeping. If I don't see you later, get rid of it for me, okay?"

"This for Sarah?" Wade asked.

Ethan nodded. They clasped hands and Wade returned his nod one last time. Ethan walked into the bright light of morning and left his friend behind.

✳ ✳ ✳

The acrid stench of urine assailed Ethan's senses in the parking garage stairwell. He climbed to the fourth floor and made his way to the Volkswagen. The garage level was quiet and sparsely occupied by eight or nine cars left overnight. To his relief, none were near his car. He situated himself in the driver seat and placed everything he carried for the op in the seat beside him. He checked the handheld radio out of habit, though he had replaced the batteries himself at the conference table. A coil of black wire for his earpiece hung from the device in a clump, and next to that lay the dull black pistol that Wade gave him. He lifted the gun and checked the chamber.

His phone held a message with Moraru's number and his absurd photo. Beside that sat a stack of business cards he kept handy. *Ryan Sawyer, Consumer Electronics.* They were wrapped in a doubled rubber band, the corners folded here and there. Each gave an address in Istanbul, which last he knew was the address of a place to get awful tea and coffee. He took in a hard breath and waited. Over an hour to go.

When the hour approached, Wade activated his radio mic without talking. Ethan heard the rise of the city traffic as a steady hiss. Wade patrolled near the rail stop as they'd planned. From his position on the street, he would see any approach to the garage entrance. The signal meant Wade saw something approach. Three clicks chirped into Ethan's earpiece. Ethan acknowledged the signal, and he tucked the Glock into the waistline at his back. His stomach turned, and he felt the adrenaline radiate into his fingertips. Three cars made things more difficult.

He saw headlights appear at the curve of the ramp. Their light arced across the concrete ceiling as a car approached. An older model Range Rover eased onto the floor like a green-skinned reptile. He made out three figures in the glare of another pair of headlights that followed. Another Range Rover, darker than the first, followed closely behind. He couldn't see how many were inside the second vehicle. He saw no sign of a third vehicle at all.

He signaled the cars with a flash of his headlights, and they veered - toward his parking lot row. The lead SUV pulled close to his Volkswagen's front bumper and parked crosswise a foot away, blocking his path forward. The other car park behind the first. He glanced to his rearview mirror to gauge an escape. It would take time to shift gear and steer out of the lane.

He saw them more clearly now through the tinted windows. There were five in all, their faces young and uneasy. The three in the lead vehicle exited the far side doors and he saw the tops of their dark-haired heads wagging as they strutted around the vehicle. The others in the second Range Rover stayed put and watched. He stretched his neck and opened his door as a trio of them stepped between the Range Rovers toward him.

"Which one of you is Cosmin?" he asked.

"*Zmeu,*" said the one in the middle. He wore a leather jacket and a stylish shirt splattered like graffiti and split at the neck, revealing his hairless chest. While his companion lit a cigarette, Cosmin smiled haughtily and revealed the crooked teeth Ethan knew from the photo. He looked older. *No, not older. More tired, maybe. Angrier.*

"Is that how you say it? I wondered. I'm Ryan Sawyer."

With a flick of his fingers he offered a faded business card. Cosmin looked at the card and scowled before he took it and shoved it in his jacket pocket. He stared at Ethan with eyes almost black.

"Listen, fellas, I hear you can help me out," he said.

"Is that what you heard? I think maybe you hear many things about me," Cosmin said. "I'm not thinking you heard everything right."

Cosmin's words bounced as he spoke in a heavy accent. Ethan knew it was all show and swagger. Cosmin and his friends performed for an absent audience. These scratchy-faced upstarts were too young for the clothes and the Land Rover. Someone supplied them, and that someone led to Scorpio.

"*Zmeu*, I understand you have some very special merchandise. Not my thing, normally. I do electronics. iPads, cell phones, TVs. You know, that kind of thing. But I have an arrangement with a buyer who wants to make a trade."

"What kind of trade?"

"My buyer wants to be discreet, right? Also not my thing, usually. But this is the kind of deal that works in my favor. Our favor. I get him this equipment, he gives me merchandise I can sell easy, and we split the cash."

"Sounds like complicated deal," Cosmin said. His lip curled a little.

"Well, like I said. It's not how I prefer to do business. But it's nothing illegal, right? Just a barter, and we sell the trade. You know how it is. Maybe there is someone else I can talk to if—"

"No, you talk to me. Only me." Cosmin's snarl transformed into a smile.

"All right, so we're talking. What now?"

"Who can say? I'm not sure I like you. When I don't like you so much, we have a problem. If I like you, we both very happy. We make lots of money."

Ethan glanced at the stooge to his right. The dour-faced man said nothing while the other lackey smoked and sneered along with *Zmeu. No, the quiet one,* he thought. That was the immediate threat. Dark circles ringed his bloodshot eyes. One arm hung at his side where his thumb and fingers fidgeted. He hid the other hand in his jacket pocket. Ethan had to make the first move. He gambled that crazy wouldn't get lost in the translation. Ethan spread a wild-eyed smile on his face and stepped toward the man on the right.

"I like your style, *Zmeu*. This guy, though? What's your problem, asshole? What are you looking at?"

He approached with his accusing finger extended at the quiet one. The man's eyes widened, and he raised up his arm to stave off Ethan's approach. Ethan pressed on steadily until the man leaned back on the Range Rover. Ethan moved slowly. Anything sudden would erupt into violence he couldn't handle. The gamble paid off only if he kept the man on his heels, uncertain what to do in the negotiation.

He raised his voice. "Get your hand out of your pocket, man. I don't work like this."

He grabbed the man's arm. From behind, Cosmin and the other man yanked on his shoulders shouting in Romanian. A car door behind him opened. He glanced down and saw the man's hand emerge from the pocket as it let go of a black handled knife. The other two pulled him back while he fumed and stared at the anxious man.

"Is okay, Mr. Sawyer. Everyone is cool," Cosmin shouted. "Is cool. Is okay."

He let go of Ethan and waved off his comrades. Cosmin cursed at them as they cowed back like snarling dogs. He straightened his jacket and closed his eyes while his hands ran a practiced course through his greasy dark hair. The smug grin returned before he opened his eyes.

"Maybe I do like you, Mr. Ryan Sawyer. You are a very crazy man. You have balls. I like this."

Ethan panted. He spread his hands and backed away from Cosmin where he could see all of them. He could push no further, but he had set them off kilter just enough to gain some leverage for himself.

"That's what I wanted to hear. I don't need your friends here to lose their shit. You came with a better recommendation than all this tough-guy bullshit."

"Not everyone is like you. We have to be very careful men. You understand?"

"I wouldn't have made it this far in my line of work if I didn't."

Cosmin laughed. "I think I do like you, Mr. Sawyer. Please, we go for a ride now? We talk your line of work, and make deal. Good?" He gestured at the Range Rover.

Ethan knew they would want this. Most of the scenarios he worked through in his head involved him getting into their vehicle. They wanted him to ride along where they could control him. Maybe take him to an isolated place from which he would never return. If he stayed, any pretense of a deal with Cosmin was off, and with it any thin chance they had of finding Kamran Khorasani vanished. He wondered if Cosmin had any idea what was really going on. These men were not his assassins. He didn't doubt that they could kill him and make a mess of it. They could have done it already, but they had other instructions. Going with them meant meeting his real enemy. Someone who knew the real stakes. He had to make the choice.

"Let me just grab my phone," he said. He turned toward the Volkswagen. Things would work out if he could signal the team.

"No phone," said the one with the knife. He slid around Ethan to block his way, sliding his hand into his jacket pocket. He nudged Ethan toward the Range Rover.

They hadn't patted him down yet. He could explain away the gun. But if they saw the radio in the car, they wouldn't just vanish. They'd leave him bleeding on the concrete beside his car after all. He had to leave the radio behind. Ahead of him, Cosmin revealed his crooked toothed grin again and opened the left side door.

"After you, my friend," Cosmin said.

Ethan climbed into the Range Rover and tugged tight at the hem of his jacket to conceal the pistol at his back. If Cosmin noticed, he showed no sign of it. They left the top floor of the garage and descended the corkscrew ramp.

"So, *Zmeu*, what kind of inventory do you have? My buyer has some specific needs."

"We talk business later, I am thinking," Cosmin said. All signs of amusement had left him. He glanced over his shoulder at the Range Rover trailing them.

Ethan shrugged and waited until the next garage floor to glance back as they spiraled down. The Range Rover trailed close. Behind it he saw a third car that straggled farther behind. He wasn't sure if it was the third car Wade signaled. It could be anyone. In the front seat, Cosmin's friends mumbled to each other in uneasy tones. The one with the knife had spiral of tattoos that crept up his neckline like a ring of spider's legs. The driver seemed more anxious, answering the other in short whispers while the cigarette smoldered between fingers that clutched the wheel.

They passed the garage gate and accelerated out into the shaded street where Ethan knew that Russell waited in his car. He scanned the back street and saw no sign of Russell. He couldn't make out any shape in the car, which sat still with no order from him to pursue. Ethan had to get their attention or the mission would be over before it began. He could signal Wade who roamed the street just ahead.

He coughed, then coughed again while waving his hand in front of his mouth to dismiss the cigarette smoke. He rubbed his eyes, then patted the headrest in front of him.

"Hey, man, can you put that cigarette out for now? Don't you guys know the dangers of second-hand smoke? Jesus."

The driver glared at him in the rearview mirror. "Fuck you."

Ethan rolled the window down halfway and turned to the opening for fresh air. They were about to make the first turn near the electric rail tracks. Wade should be there, and for once he was glad his friend would be easy to spot. He had to get his attention. *Where was he, damn it?* He had to recognize the three vehicles from earlier.

They rounded the corner when he saw Wade leaning against a wall watching a crowd of commuters exit a glossy white tram. He stood alert, and Ethan could see his eyes fix on the Range Rovers. Ethan couldn't signal, but he knew Wade had spotted him just before the tram car blocked his view. Wade would set everyone in motion. Tereza's car was just ahead on the crossing boulevard.

Ethan looked away from the window. Then he saw the gun. Cosmin pointed a CZ automatic at his rib cage. The tiny pistol barely fit his spindly hands. One finger curled around the trigger.

"*Merge!*" Cosmin said. *Drive.*

The vehicle lurched forward. Ethan fell back into his seat. He watched Cosmin's gun and how awkwardly it fit in his hand. Any sudden move, any bump and Cosmin's crooked finger would send a shot into his gut. Reaching for his own weapon might have the same deadly result. He had to play along and give the operation a chance to work.

He held up his hands and focused back on Cosmin's face, trying to read the man's intentions.

"What the hell is this, *Zmeu*? This isn't how I treat my friends."

The man in the front answered instead. This time he revealed the knife and pointed it at Ethan.

"*Mânca-mi-ai pula.*"

"Shut up," Cosmin said to the tattooed man. He turned to Ethan. "As for friends, we will see. We go for a ride to a place and see about deal. Maybe no one follows us, yes?"

"How the hell should I know?"

Cosmin turned to look out the rear window. Ethan took the moment to turn himself and watch for Tereza's Renault. They were headed west, just past her position. As the second Range Rover passed, he saw her veer into traffic. Cosmin cursed and shouted at the driver again.

They turned north into Old Town, weaving in and out of the morning traffic. They wove left, then right around smaller cars, perilously close to a line of steel posts along the roadside. The driver sped through the thoroughfare using the wide lanes to steer around yellow taxis. Outside, the old buildings blurred by. The other Range Rover swerved behind them. For a moment, Ethan caught sight of the Renault's grill maneuvering around the slower traffic. Tereza followed, but she'd need help.

They blew past a wide side street where a car stopped short of clipping Cosmin's passenger door. A horn blared. He jerked instinctively and cursed as it blew past. Ethan ignored the noise and focused his eyes on the gun.

Ahead the road broadened into a wide roundabout. They careened around the flowered circle at the center when the Range Rover struck a car to the right. The side mirror collapsed inward and the Romanians again shouted and cursed one another over the bleating of car horns. The driver kept his speed as they barreled along the main roadway. Cosmin glanced behind them repeatedly, snapping directions at the driver who huffed out smoke as he drove.

Without a glance, the driver swerved left onto a side street. Ethan looked to his window where a black sedan overtook the trailing Range Rover. He recognized Russell's car. It veered hard left with them, swerving sharply to cut off the lead Range Rover. It wasn't supposed to go like this, but he found relief in the faces of Wade and Russell trailing.

They turned right again quickly. *Where the hell is Tereza?* They were blown. He dropped his left hand onto his thigh and slowly began reaching behind him for the Glock. They were running out of options.

The side street narrowed, crowded by buildings on both sides. Pedestrians leapt away from the roadside as Russell's car forced the Range Rover to the road's edge. Russell surged alongside the Range Rover as they sped on north. The passenger window opened, and Wade leveled a black barreled carbine at the Ranger Rover's rear tire. With another command from Cosmin, the Range Rover slammed into the sedan. Ethan felt the collision in his teeth. Cosmin pressed up against him. He grunted. Ethan reached for Cosmin's pistol.

"Nenorocitule!"

Cosmin pulled back, but Ethan had hold of the gun. He twisted forward, wrenching Cosmin's finger in the trigger guard. Cosmin howled while Ethan pressed harder, trying to keep the barrel pointed toward the car door. Cosmin rolled his arm and left the gun in Ethan's hand. It felt light in his hand. Too light—it was an empty bluff. Cosmin punched him twice in the face. He felt a wave of pain next to his ear and motes of light danced in his eyelids. Dazed, he focused again on the glinting tip of the knife from the man in the front seat.

"Don't fucking move again or I stab you," the tattooed man said.

The vehicle lurched again as Russell's car ground against them. Ethan's head snapped to the side from the force of it. In his ringing ears he heard Cosmin shouting again as though from far away. The driver slammed on the brakes. Russell's car flew past, and he lost sight of Wade. They swerved hard right down an alley barely wide enough for the Range Rover. A crackle of sparks popped up by his window. The other side mirror buckled and fell to the asphalt behind them.

The turn put them back on to the main thoroughfare. Ethan let go of the pistol, and it fell to the floor mat where Cosmin retrieved it and put it back into his pocket. He fumed at Ethan, muttering under his breath with his hands still balled into bony fists.

"You really need bullets to have the whole bad guy with a gun thing work for you," Ethan said. He rubbed his sore jaw.

The knife waved again in his face from the front seat.

"Not for mine."

The driver looked at the street to his right as he cruised down the E60, weaving between the broad lanes and the compact cars that seemed to crawl around them. Pedestrians gawked at their speeding vehicle that looked like it had been clawed and chewed by a rabid bear.

"Lose them. Turn here. We go another way," Cosmin said.

Ethan took a last look down the boulevard for any sign of his team. Hope faded. No sign of Tereza's Renault trailed. Russell had missed the turn. For the moment, the entire team had lost track of him. Russell and Wade could catch up. The Range Rover would be hard to miss now.

They entered a large plaza, an expanse of blacktop as wide as an entire block where seven arteries of the northern side of the city entered in a complicated jumble of curves and lanes. The driver barreled through halted traffic and veered northwest on a narrower street surrounded by a city park. Behind them, Cosmin caught sight of Russell's sedan still another block from entering the plaza.

"Did they see us?" Cosmin said, more to himself than his comrades in front. "Go, go. *Băga-mi-aş pula.*"

They passed through the park and stately streets where the trees blurred by in a rush of brown and green. Few cars blocked their way, and they neared an expo grounds where trucks and bright tarps blanketed a vast open market lot.

"*Acolo este,*" the driver said. *There he is.*

He slowed the Range Rover past the expo grounds and pulled under a wide rail overpass where a white van had parked under the concrete bridge. A man awaited them near the van. He signaled at them to stop far from his vehicle, then motioned them to back up several yards. The driver complied and then let the engine idle as the others argued with one another in their staccato Romanian.

Ethan squinted at the man at the van who stood maybe thirty yards away waiting for them to approach. He wore wiry glasses that shaded his eyes and a dull gray jumpsuit. He was thin, his face pale and sunken. He was no delivery man. Something about the way he moved betrayed him. He motioned with one hand in quick motions, his hand darting toward the Range Rover impatiently. The other hand he kept concealed behind his back for some other purpose.

Cosmin shoved Ethan from the vehicle. Ethan stood on the pavement looking over the shoulder of the driver at the man in coveralls. His neck tingled. His instincts alive with the realization that this was no go between. This was the assassin he'd feared, which meant he was also the link to Scorpio. He could stall until Russell and Wade caught up with them. Cosmin and his friends weren't armed, but the man ahead of him definitely was. If anything happened, Ethan would have to shoot the pale man first.

"We brought him," Cosmin said. "As agreed, yes?"

The pale man spoke then, his accent thick. Not quite Russian, Ethan thought. Not Ukrainian. There was a subtlety to it he couldn't identify.

"As agreed. Have you checked him?"

The three men eyed one another like guilty schoolboys, and the pale man spit on the ground, disgusted. He waved them closer. They crowded around

Ethan then and shoved him while they kept a wary eye on his hands.

Ethan stood before the pale man, just paces apart. His head had been shaved recently, and the wiry, bleached stubble stood on end. He had a sallow face, though he wasn't quite sickly. Ethan saw the cords of wiry muscle at his neck and the alert pinpoints of his dark eyes beneath the tinted glasses. He recognized him then, a face he had seen so many times since Georgia. He stared at the sixth man from the hijacking. Seda Alaskhanova's lover.

"Hello, Andrei," Ethan said.

The man's mouth tightened. His nostril's flared. His hands darted out then and grappled Ethan's arms in an instant with a grip like iron. He wrenched Ethan around as he searched him. He found the Glock and pulled it from the concealed holster tucked in his back.

"Hello, Ethan Pierce. My comrade admires your persistence. And now his wait for you is over."

"What did you call him?" Cosmin said as his hands moved in furious gestures. "Who the fuck is this guy? *Zmeu* does not care. I delivered who you wanted. Everything is good. So, pay us our money, and he is yours."

"You want payment?" Andrei said with a mocking frown.

The frown disappeared before Cosmin could reply. Andrei raised the Glock to Cosmin's forehead and the gun exploded. Ethan ducked and raised his hands. From the corner of his eye, he saw Cosmin fall to the shaded street, dead. Two more shots set Ethan's ears ringing. He felt nothing, no pain. The driver fell as he fled. The shots cut him to the ground where he crawled toward the Range Rover before another shot stopped his pitiable retreat.

To his left, Ethan heard a shout of rage. He turned to see the tattooed Romanian lunge with his knife. The glint of steel arced at Andrei's left arm where a gout of blood appeared along his sleeve like a crimson seam. Andrei sneered at the man. He dropped the gun to the street, and with both hands he caught the next attack. His arms and torso sprung into motion then. Before the Romanian could withdraw, Andrei twisted his arm. It bent back at the elbow, and a yelp of pain escaped the Romanian. The knife turned like a thing possessed of its own force. Andrei completed his swift motion. With his palm, he drove the knife in just below the Romanian's chin. The blade stove through his palette, and a macabre grin formed as blood gushed from his mouth and covered the inky tattoos in red. His cries ceased, and Andrei let him fall to the street near his comrades.

Ethan measured the distance between him and the pistol. He had this moment to reach the gun before Andrei. He dove for the pistol on the ground. Andrei moved with him, quicker and more agile. As Ethan wrapped his hand around the gun Andrei's boot pinned down his forearm. Ethan looked up into the barrel of the other pistol Andrei had concealed all along.

Andrei stood over him expressionless, his breathing barely quickened from the ordeal. He stood still and rigid, his gaze fixed on Ethan, daring him to act. Ethan realized then he remained alive by design.

"Your comrade wants to meet. Is that it?" he asked.

From behind him, Ethan heard an approaching car. Andrei's eyes widened as he saw the coming threat. From the ground, Ethan saw a blur of black as the sedan hurdled toward them. Russell and Wade had found him. There was still time.

Andrei pinned his knee into Ethan's back. Ethan squirmed, helpless to move under the man's surprising strength. Andrei watched the car approach. His mouth moved in a silent chant, counting something Ethan couldn't see while he held something slim and black in his hand. His serpentine thumb hovered over a grid of gray buttons.

Russell drove closer, and from the passenger's window he saw the crook of Wade's carbine spitting fire at them. The shots echoed beneath the concrete roof. A crossfire of bullets tore into the Range Rover's windows and ricocheted from the concrete incline behind them.

The car roared closer to the Range Rover. Andrei's chant ceased. His thumb pressed down on the device, and Ethan felt the fires of hell wash over him. A blast from the Range Rover sucked the breath from his lungs. Andrei lay atop him, crushing him down into the gravel as the flames bathed both of them for an instant. He was half blinded and deafened. He heard Andrei cough, then the weight was gone. He gasped for breath and rubbed his eyes, not even realizing the pistol had left his grip.

Flames engulfed the sedan as it slid to a halt.

Andrei pulled him to his feet and dragged him toward the van, past the corpses of the Romanians. He opened the door on the van and gave him a shove.

"Get in."

PART III

The Black Sea

CHAPTER 17

REVOLUTION PEDDLER

Brașov, Romania
11:42 a.m., Friday, June 21

KAMRAN LEANED into his pressure suit's visor and squinted into the micro-scope before him. Peering into the lens became a balancing act he had mastered in longer and longer days in the lab. He perched on the edge of a padded stool, his legs spread to maintain his balance. He positioned the pneumatic hose without thinking. It had become an extension of himself. He could reach it without looking, detach and reattach the coupling as he moved about the lab chamber like he had once moved about his child-hood home.

He made subtle movements, adjusting the focal length from a gray blur to reveal the sickly pink color of tissue beneath the lens. It was a sliver of human lung. A normal thing for this work, but nothing here was normal. *Where did they acquire this tissue?* He asked himself the question again, and his mind dismissed the impossibility that the samples were victims of his captors. Perhaps they had stolen them from a research hospital or bribed a staff worker to ignore the missing cultures.

The misshapen lung cells confirmed his fears about the virus' lethality. He could delay no more. His lady companion had begun to suspect his tiny fits of sabotage, which were explainable for a time but not indefinitely.

She was as capable as him in the lab. She had patience and technique, her methods experienced. She asked him questions as selective and sharp as the instruments she wielded. When he explained his delays with clumsiness, she remedied with precision. His insistence on repeating processes and replication met with her stern reluctance. Now she sat meters away preparing her own examination and would identify the same insidious effect of the virus.

Though he viewed the lung, he thought about the true danger to the liver and the patient's vascular system. The virus destroyed the vessels and produced its notorious hemorrhaging as its victims suffered in fevered agony. This strain was a pantropic nightmare that hijacked the immune system and starved the body's organs within days. A tiny vial could spread to hundreds of thousands. They now had eighteen such vials. He could see no way to destroy them without forfeiting his own life.

His partner, the woman whose name remained a mystery to him, stood and walked slowly and carefully to his station. "Can you confirm the cytopathic effect?" She shouted. Her voice barely carried between the suits and over the rushing air that filled them.

He nodded his head though the bulbous suit around him barely moved. "Necrosis," he said.

He stood and let her peer into the microscope. There was nothing shapely about her in these monstrous suits. In another lab he might have fancied her. She was slim and smaller than he. But here she was cold and distant. He knew almost nothing about her. He stood naked before her every day as they left the lab. It was his ritual of defiance, though he could not measure its effect. Some days she looked at him with disdain. Some she looked away. She never mocked him, never rolled her eyes. She supervised him. She did not share his fear of his captors. She was, like the guards, here out of some kind of duty. But he could not reason why she would foster such a terrible enterprise.

She stood and faced him for a moment, saying nothing. Then she began decontamination. Together they rinsed their utensils with bleach and placed them in the autoclave. They had worked barely an hour, but there was nothing more to do but wait. Kamran dreaded the lonely hours ahead in his makeshift prison. The lab at least occupied his mind. Somehow, he could forget the reality that they had created a kind of torture for him here. He nursed death in a vial to avoid boredom and loneliness, and the work almost made him happy to avoid the extreme solitude of his cell. Loneliness brought him almost physical pain, exacerbated by the guilt of what he concocted in the lab. The cycle continued each day, but each new day he found he could not retreat from it.

"Your work is almost finished," she told him as he undressed.

"If you say so."

"He'll want to speak with you."

"Who?"

"Dr. Korkolis. He knows we are very close to confirming the virus' efficacy."

His ignorance ashamed him more than his nakedness as he stripped. His contact with others for nearly three weeks amounted to a rotation of guards and his lab partner. He knew none of their names.

"Who is Dr. Korkolis?"

"Hector. I expect he'll want to celebrate, knowing Hector."

"What is there to celebrate?" he mumbled.

* * *

When the guard came to his room, Kamran reached for his watch where it lay on the cot beside him. Barely two hours had passed since he left the lab. In the stillness, as he stared off at the tile ceiling recalling the snowfall in the illuminated night sky at Koltsovo, he felt the hours pass as though they were days. The guard carried no meal tray. Kamran gaped at him, then stood and followed the man down the hallway, past the laboratory door and restrooms, farther than he had been in the building since his arrival. *How many weeks has it been?* he wondered.

The guard led him to a cafeteria room with green and cream-colored walls. Long tables surrounded by empty plastic chairs reflected narrow shafts of sunlight that pierced blinds on the windows. He squinted from its brightness after weeks living under the unnatural lights. His aching eyes adjusted, and he recognized the man he now knew as Hector Korkolis sitting at a table in the center of the room reading from a leather-bound folder.

"Dr. Khorasani, I confess it has taken far too long to fulfill my promise to you that we would continue our conversation. But as you will see, I am a man of my word. Please, sit."

Hector nodded at the guard, and the door closed. Two covered plates steamed on the tabletop, each set with a pair of forks, a knife, and spoon. A bottle of wine wrapped tightly in a folded napkin sat between them and next to it a pair of crystal goblets. Kamran sat, mesmerized by the hint of warm food that rose up from the table. Hector set the folder down and poured a glass of wine for himself.

"Do you drink wine, doctor?"

Kamran rarely drank, but he had no compunction about alcohol. His family often drank wine. It was the savory smell from whatever awaited him beneath the plate cover that set his mouth to water. With his eyes fixed on the plate cover, his mind became preoccupied by the meal before him. He nodded.

"Excellent. I've let this warm slightly. I find that is best, though this vintage isn't remarkable. Happily, the food is much better. I have an arrangement with a local chef."

Hector poured wine into each glass and removed his own plate cover. The steam welled up around his white beard and dark eyebrows. Kamran did the same to reveal a filet of baked fish covered in garnish and something like a crepe on his plate. He reached for a fork and took a large bite into his mouth which he chewed in haste.

"I'm pleased you like it. Now, we toast." Hector raised his glass. "To your efforts and your sacrifice, doctor."

Kamran reached for his glass, but his hand froze and quivered. He could not toast the man who tormented him, who forced him to cultivate that terrible weapon. Hector had shamed him. True, he smiled and treated him with some respect, but then he disappeared and let his people defile and beat him. Kamran wanted to escape now more than ever. He felt still more shame for devouring the food. Again, he was weak. Sitting here before this feast, he felt more confined than he had in the sealed laboratory.

"Please, you have many doubts. I understand. And you think we have mistreated you. This I also understand. Much of it was necessary, and if I may say it, a great deal about the arrangement is fair. So, please. *In vino, veritas.*"

Hector raised his glass and drank, and slowly Kamran followed. The wine soothed his tongue and warmed his gullet. He would play along and hope for some alternative to reveal itself.

"You speak of truth to me now? After everything you've done to me? Your men beat me. You keep me here as your slave," he said.

"You are no slave, doctor. Indeed, I intend to give you a kind of reward, most of all your survival should you meet our needs. And today, it appears you have. Your work is nearly complete. Though it is true what you say. We keep you here against your will. But for a greater purpose."

"What purpose could you have for this? The virus will kill thousands. More than that," Kamran said.

"Yes, the box of Pandora, unleashed upon a helpless world. Again we revisit history and myth together," Hector said. He leaned back and dabbed his mouth with a napkin. "Have I told you I am a physician? But I suppose that you have guessed.

"Many years ago, I worked for a time in Liberia. One night, I treated a man with a terribly infected gunshot wound. I knew this man by his despicable reputation as warlord and puppet of the junta. I knew this, and so I entertained letting him die of sepsis. Instead, I operated. In saving his leg, I saved his life."

"If you are a doctor as you say, you have an obligation to save lives."

"In this case, you are more correct than you know. My obligation was to save his life or lose my own. The warlord's soldiers forced me to perform the surgery with their guns trained on me and my nurse. She was also my wife. For a time."

Hector's melodious voice faded. He nibbled a bit of fish and washed it down with the wine.

"Several months later, we came to a remote village devoid of life. Devoid of humanity, you see? Days before, the warlord and his soldiers had gathered everyone into a schoolhouse and burned them alive."

Hector paused again to chew the seasoned fish. Kamran sat silent and stared at his food as his appetite faded.

"Smoke still rose from the school, and in the center of the building's remains were the villagers piled on top of one another. Some at the doorway, some near the blackboard. Twisted and charred bodies stacked like charcoal. An awful sight. My wife cried for hours. I have never felt such guilt. These killers were part of the corrupt government, and I had enabled them. In my way. The Americans funded their killing sprees, all to resist the far reach of the Soviets. Madness fueled by insanity, all for the sake of control of the globe. A tragedy of mythic scale, wouldn't you say?"

Kamran raised his eyes and shrugged. He had no notion of what to say.

"Several days later, we crossed paths again with the warlord's handiwork. In this village, they shot some of the men and took several women. The rest they spared to terrify the neighboring villages. They did the same across the countryside, village after village buckled under their thuggery. Nowhere else did they burn everyone alive. Why? This puzzle confounded me for weeks.

"I found the answer. Or rather, it came to me. In one of these villages, we treated an older man who had visited his daughter. But he left her, believing her village cursed. He told us a sickness had spread among the villagers in just days. A terrible fever that avenged the wicked and promiscuous, he told us. Though he had not seen it, he believed the dead wept tears of blood. Can you guess?"

"Ebola," Kamran whispered.

"Precisely. The daughter's village had perished in the church fire. And with them, all signs of the disease vanished, save one. One of the warlord's men had contracted the disease, and they brought him to me. My wife and

I treated the man, but he died. As did my wife. I pitied them both in the end. As you know, it is a most horrible way to die."

Hector finished his piece of fish and drank more wine.

"I am not sorry for you," Kamran said.

Hector sighed and spoke again in his quiet tone. "You are an interesting man, Dr. Khorasani. Your pity is not the point. Answering your question is. I learned something from the warlord—something that you would do well to learn yourself. You are like the warlord, doctor. You are a puppet on a string, though you believe you act for your own sake. You speak of my obligation. What of yours? It is only to others we are obligated. Those who hold power over the world. We fool ourselves into thinking we act for ourselves. But have you not realized you have simply traded one master for another?"

"I have been lied to all of my life. You are no better than any of them," Kamran said.

"Now you are learning the lesson after all. It may surprise you that I agree. I am no better. But my associates and I offer you a crucial difference. Why is it you think we've gone to such lengths to bring you here? Do you think that chance? Our purpose is yours, my friend, though you do not yet accept it. We speak for the silent. Like you, I look at the world and see only those with power over the powerless. The West. The Russians. Your Ayatollah and his clerics. And we have no aims for such power. We seek disruption. We seek the void of power so that others fill it. Others whose time is long overdue. And you, Dr. Khorasani, are the means to that disruption."

"The means to killing you mean."

"If you like. You think your judgment makes you a better man, doctor. More principled than us. More merciful, perhaps, than the warlord. I once shared your sentiment until the warlord taught me otherwise. I do not judge you for it. I tell you this truly. Understand the consequences of your position. It is a trick of philosophy, and nothing more. You lift yourself above us, but an ineluctable reality remains. You count yourself among the powerless because you are unwilling to act."

Kamran's face twitched at Hector's words. The rage within him had lingered for weeks after every sadistic thing they had done to him. The beatings distorted his face. He sat in agony, unable to sleep. The only void they had created were the endless hours of solitude where his spirit died again and again until the pain of it became as real as the ache in his back. Hector was right that he was powerless, and for this he had felt ashamed since he could remember. Hector offered him something greater, though not as he intended. Kamran hated Hector and his vile comrades more than he hated himself, and this freed him of the last grasp of his shame.

Hector drained the last of his wine and examined the glass as he licked his moistened lips.

"You asked why I do this," Hector said as he held the glass. "A physician should address the source of infection. You agree? The means to combat a pathogen is to ensure it never enters the host. Here it is the same, though the scale is macroscopic rather than microscopic. You see, doctor? I admit the vanity of poetic symmetry. We will administer your virus to prevent the metastatic affliction of those who abuse their power. A difficult preparation for a simple objective."

"What could that possibly be?" Kamran said.

Hector set the wine glass on the table before he answered. "Burn the village down."

"I will never help you do this."

"But you already have, doctor. Only details remain, which your laboratory companion can complete. Did you know she is my daughter? Of course not. She is more than capable, and she has helped me know something very important about you these many weeks."

"What do you think you know about me?"

"Despite your pitiable attempts at defiance, I know you're not willing to die."

Hector spoke the truth. They observed him more closely than he thought. The little black orbs in the lab watched as he worked. Were there more cameras in the room where he slept? Was it his daughter informing them all along? *Let them watch,* he thought. What could he do but play along, much as he had all his life? Hector was another revolution peddler who peered only at him, not within him where something had changed. They had changed him, though not as they believed. It was the same in Iran. Even in Russia. Yes, he feared his own death, though not at Hector's hand. He would show them real defiance.

Lost in thought, he felt a shiver on his neck. Hector raised his thick eyebrows at a man standing in the cafeteria's open doorway. It was Andrei, who Kamran knew would have no trouble at all killing him. Kamran feared Andrei more than any of them. He wore a workman's jumpsuit speckled with dust. His clenched his jaw like a trap and gave Hector a terse nod. Hector arranged his knife and fork at a precise angle on his plate and rose.

"Please, eat your meal before it becomes too cold to enjoy," Hector said.

They left him alone in the cafeteria. Kamran hunched over the plate and stuffed bits of the fish into his mouth. The food had cooled, but the delicate flakes almost dissolved on his tongue. His glands watered at the citrus sting of it, and he chewed the last bites slowly to savor before gulping it down. He reached for the rest of his wine and knocked the glass over, spilling some on the tabletop and onto Hector's leather folio.

His hands shook as he dabbed the spilled wine with the cloth napkin. No one disturbed him. He glanced at the door, but there was nothing. He dabbed again, then peeled back the cover of the folio. The papers within were dry, to his relief. He cocked his head to spy at the contents within. A ledger of figures with notes in pen scrawled on the margins appeared atop a thicker booklet. The arcane figures of business meant nothing to him. He peeked at the booklet's brilliant blue cover with a photograph of a cruise liner in the Mediterranean, surrounded by inset images of the Istanbul skyline and white terraces of the Greek coast. Pristine white letters covered the photos—*Aria.* He closed the book and wiped again at the droplets of wine that covered the folder and tabletop, hoping the sweet alcohol smell wouldn't reveal his blunder and snooping.

Hector returned alone with a wide-mouthed smile.

"Wonderful news, Dr. Khorasani. We have a visitor. Someone I'd very much like you to meet. As I suggested earlier, I have a reward in mind for you and for our new guest as well. He comes to us from the American's own CIA. Imagine them having great interest in you. I assure you he is very eager to meet. The gentleman's name is Ethan Pierce, and you'll have great deal in common with him soon."

CHAPTER 18

HIDDEN MESSAGE

McLean, Virginia
9:20 a.m., Friday, June 21

PAUL CRAWLED along with the mid-morning traffic along I-66 before turning his Lincoln north to avoid the accident site where Janey died. The word accident played in his head, and he frowned. It was no accident. He knew that. He also knew he couldn't sit at home any longer while they were out there. When he saw his own haggard face in the mirror that morning he stared at the face of an old man, wrinkled and worn down by his addiction to the work. The eyes staring back were the last remnants of his youth. Janey always said they were his best feature. He wondered how he had lost the youthful defiance that once kept him alive and alert in the field. *God, I could use a cigarette*, he thought.

He left his car at the far end of the south parking lot where the rows of cars worked like a timepiece, filling hour by hour in the morning. As late as it was, he headed directly to the operations center where he waved his badge and almost fell into the locked door. He pushed again, but the door refused to budge. They had revoked access to his own team.

"Damn it," he muttered aloud to himself. He pounded on the door, but no one answered. Along the hall, the commotion drew the looks of analysts and admins passing by. He pounded louder.

"Christ, people, open the damn door."

His mouth tightened and his forehead warmed as tiny beads of perspiration formed. *How could they do this to me after what happened?* He'd done nothing to deserve this treatment. This didn't happen just for bereavement leave. Someone made this happen. He pounded again, louder than before.

The door opened and a finely manicured hand appeared. Suzanne Tasker held the door open and stood in the door frame blocking his path. She wore a blouse buttoned at the neck that seemed to make her head balance upon her shoulders like a finely dressed mannequin.

"Paul, please calm down. That isn't unnecessary."

"Suzanne, what the hell is this?"

"I can see you're upset," she said. "We thought this the best course of action considering what's happened. I can only imagine what you're going through, but we didn't expect you today. Harley said he spoke with you."

"He did, but not about this."

"I see. Well, I can assure you I have everything well under control. I just spoke with your team. All operations are running smoothly."

Her eyelids fluttered as she spoke. He knew that she lied.

"Like hell they are."

He swallowed the bile rising in his throat. He wanted to shout at her, tell her she was missing the obvious infiltration their new adversary had orchestrated. He wanted to scream and tell her they had killed his wife. She couldn't imagine it. Instead the words caught in his throat in a reflex of self-preservation. Telling her anything informed the enemy that their gambit to discredit him had succeeded.

She crossed her arms and held the door open with her foot. Behind her he saw his officers at their stations doing the work he should be directing. Kay Linh sat up at her desk. She had turned to watch the confrontation at the door in anxious glances that confirmed something grave had occurred. He couldn't interpret much else from her expression. Her mouth stayed flat while her eyes darted between her dueling supervisors.

"Paul, I'm sorry for this situation and for your loss," Suzanne said. "But

I must ask you to calm down. Please, don't make this awkward. We have a great deal in play currently. Your access to the operations center is revoked only temporarily. Why don't you just go home and take more time?"

"Where's Harley now?"

"I'm sure he's in meetings. I promise you, I will manage the situation until you're ready to return."

He glared. Suzanne stood her ground, though he detected her slip toward frustration when she cleared her throat. She outranked him, but she knew nothing about Scorpio. He doubted Harley had updated her, which meant every decision she made played right into their hands at the most crucial time. *Was it her all along?* After what had happened, he couldn't muster surprise at anyone in the building. It could be her.

He glanced again inside the room and sighed. He caught Kay's attention, and for the slightest moment she gave him a nod. He'd almost forgotten what he told her Saturday night. *Look for anything.* Someone had checked the files, and Kay knew it. He took her nod as confirmation. She couldn't debrief him without compromising herself. He had to find a way for her to share.

"I'm going to hold you to that. I'll be back. Don't fuck up my ops," he said.

Suzanne seethed at his outburst, but she didn't respond. She retreated into the room, letting the heavy door close. Paul stomped to the stairway door and headed to his office on the floor above.

His breath came heavy from the climb, and his heart pounded as he unlocked his office door. Dull gray consumed the unlit room within save the indirect sunlight where motes of dust swirled in the quiet air. The window wasn't much—a narrow pane that overlooked a corner of the courtyard outside. The view was just a mirror image of the old building across the way, but it afforded him a little natural light. He closed the door and scowled at the motion sensing light switch that ticked meekly as he entered. He would have preferred a darker room to think, but he left the light alone and sat at his desk.

A banana he'd saved for a snack last week lay in a drab brown heap on a napkin to his left. He had the good sense to lock away the Scorpio Compact files he'd read late Saturday night, but other administrative papers sprawled across the desk in disheveled stacks or tucked out of the way beneath his computer monitor and away from the phone console.

Behind the phone perched a brass picture frame. Janey's smile arrested him from the photo, and he studied her face. Her head leaned on his shoulder. The wind had teased her blonde hair, and it fell across her lovely eyes. They had taken a sailing excursion on Chesapeake Bay that weekend. It was years ago now, and he could still smell the salty southern breeze.

He loved that photo, but now it summoned up an agonizing pang of guilt. *Janey, what am I doing here?* He should have been with her that night, not here in this office. It didn't matter what he thought was important then. She was gone, and here he was back at the same damn place trying to watch over the same damn people that didn't need him as much as she needed him. As much as he needed her.

His admin left a stack of mail at the center of the desk. He shoved the pile aside, but as he did the corner of a baby blue envelope slid from under the white papers and manila packets. He plucked the thing from the pile and examined it. A dainty script on the front read simply *Paul.* It was a woman's handwriting, precise and elegantly penned in ball point. He'd already received several sympathy cards at the house, but this was the only one in his stack of office mail.

While his computer booted, he turned the card in the light. Nothing it could say would trouble him as the old photograph had. Even so, something about its singular presence struck him. He slid a finger into the envelope and tore open the card. It bore an illustration of lilies painted in soft strokes. He put on his reading glasses and opened the card. *Wishing you comfort and peace.* He had read dozens of similar thoughts this week. The messages blurred into meaninglessness for him. Each bore the same pablum of comfort and prayer. This one had no written note, but a pair of names signed in the same delicate handwriting from the envelope appeared below the message. *Kay Linh & David Caspari.*

Paul held the card closer and squinted at the fine script. He didn't recognize Caspari's name. Kay wasn't dating anyone serious. She wasn't dating at all, as far as he knew. His demands of her here at the agency were partly to blame. She pursued her work like he once did—like he still did, out of old habit. He wanted to tell her to stop and find someone and leave this all behind. But he knew she didn't want that. He didn't either at her age, but at least he had Janey at his side all along the way.

He entered the name David Caspari into the Agency directory on his computer. They may have revoked clearance to view anything operational, but he was still a deputy director. David Caspari listed as Collections Management Officer under the Community HUMINT Coordination Center. He couldn't find any connection Caspari had with Kay. She was sending him a message.

He knew what it meant. Caspari had accessed the Scorpio files. He smirked at Kay's cleverness and flair for the old fashioned. He wanted to admire the bleak humor of it all and the absurdity of staring at a hidden message in a sympathy card meant for him. But the laugh came at too great a cost. He tucked the card inside the envelope flap and slid it back under the pile of mail.

He had to learn more about Caspari, like where he had operated and who he worked with. If he worked alone against the Agency, things would be easier. He couldn't imagine anyone that clever after all that had happened. Two vehicles ran Janey and Linda into the concrete divider, not one. *Was it him?* He wondered as he stared at the gray face and dark eyes in the ID photo on his screen. If Caspari did it, he wasn't alone. He doubted Suzanne was involved, but he couldn't be certain. He had to tell Harley all of it, but he needed to be sure. He'd need his clearance reinstated, and that would take too much time with Suzanne prowling the gate for him.

Time was exactly what Pierce needed most. Pierce was still in the field and faced the real danger. He knew that much from Suzanne's confrontation earlier. Something had gone wrong. She was stubborn and headstrong, but not much of a card player. That meant Ethan was in trouble, but it also meant Scorpio hadn't killed him yet. He no longer held any doubt about whether they would try. He couldn't accept losing another officer.

Why didn't they kill me? Janey had nothing to do with it. It should have been me, he thought.

He knew then his misery was a piece of their plan. Someone who knew him was involved. Someone knew how much she mattered to him and how ineffective he would become. The grief and guilt fell onto him like a physical thing, weighing him down in his chair. His despair provided Scorpio the delay they sought. They had kept him alive to avoid suspicion. It was the only explanation he could understand. There was a sinister logic in it—simplicity even. In avoiding suspicion, they spared him and tortured him all in one stroke. But he knew what they'd done. Harley knew it too.

He closed Caspari's file on his screen and leaned back in the chair, hands folded at his face. He peeked between his fingers at the photograph of Janey whose laughing eyes now pleaded with him. He wanted to make peace with her. He longed to tell her goodbye and hear from her that she understood. She said nothing. She never would again. The idea of that left him numb to all emotion save one. It wasn't wrath. He couldn't honor Janey with revenge. This was a need for justice in a complicated game that no longer had any rules. He would set this right, or the deep and desperate void within his heart would erase the last of his soul.

There was no more he could do at his desk but snoop around networked files while these traitors watched and waited. They had tricked the Agency into abandoning him. Abandoning the Agency in turn was the only thing he could do to counter them.

The idea made his stomach flutter. He wasn't sure if he could do this alone. He thought again of Janey, then pulled open his bottom desk drawer and found an old leather shaving kit. The brown leather had cracked over the years. He kept the thing as a sentimental token of his days in the field. He might have some use for his old tools yet. They didn't let him keep his old .45 revolver here in the building, but he wished he had it now. He'd given it to Jacob a few years ago as a kind of family heirloom in place of explaining what his old man really did.

He tucked the leather kit and Kay's sympathy card into his suit pocket and left his office, wondering if he would ever return.

* * *

Two hours later, Paul checked himself in his Lincoln's visor mirror. He'd driven to a townhouse in Clarendon, the most plausible of three addresses he'd found for David Caspari in the area. He studied the address via a map on his phone, memorizing the block's environs.

He'd replaced his tie and coat with a brown button-down shirt he picked out at a uniform distributor an hour earlier. The short-sleeved shirt, which hung from his body at a size too large, had no logo on the breast pocket, but at a glance, he appeared like any delivery man in a drab brown shirt and khaki slacks. He left the Lincoln and pulled on a black cap. The tufts of his graying hair stuck out from the sides above his ears. Under his arm he carried a long and narrow box and a clipboard he'd found in Janey's office at home. He smirked knowing that part of her was still with him, just as she had walked at his side several times when they had met agents in Bogotá cafes years before. She delighted at playing spy, but he stopped all that once he learned she was pregnant with Jacob.

He spent the two-block trek to the townhouse thinking through the difficult contingencies. He plotted his entry from the front and then again from the back lane. If anyone answered the door—maybe a roommate or a family member—he'd feign a mistaken address. He knew too little going in. This wasn't like an operation he oversaw with eyes in the sky and weeks of planning. He reached for his phone and muted the ringer.

At the door he knocked and waited. A little awning shaded him from the bright summer sun overhead. He heard empty silence within—no footsteps or television. He knocked again and looked around the neighborhood street. A woman jogged past. She glanced at him then trained her eyes back on the sidewalk with twin white cords plugged in her ears. His breath came shorter. *Act like you belong here,* he told himself. He tipped his hat as he watched her slender figure disappear from sight.

Through a window he could see a portion of the carpeted floor and the shadowy gloom of an empty house. *Now or never,* he thought. In the old brown shaving kit he found a pair of needle-like tools, one with a hard bend and the other with a crooked tine. He hadn't done this in years, and never with a newer lock like this. Breaking into the flats in Bogotá was child's play by comparison.

He checked the doorknob. It turned free in his hand. He'd have to pick the deadbolt. He inserted the tine and began to turn, feeling for the subtle shifts at his fingertips. Another car passed. He heard the rush of its tires on blacktop, but he kept his focus on the lock hoping they ignored him. He was almost inside. Just another careful turn.

The door pressed open, and he stepped into the cool, stale air within. He checked the door frame and the nearby walls. No sign of an alarm. He exhaled.

"Hello?" he said "Anyone here? Got a delivery for a … David Caspari? Hello?"

No one responded.

He passed the front room and entered the kitchen. As he walked, his footfalls on the wood laminate clattered throughout the house. He sorted through a stack of mail on the counter but found only an Arlington county bill and junk mail addressed to Dave Caspari. He needed confirmation this was the target of his suspicion.

He opened a door along the back wall. The heat of the garage wafted around him like an open oven. A shadow leapt at him from below. He caught the sudden movement from the corner of his eye. His instincts took hold, his body moving without thought. He reached for a weapon that wasn't there. He needed anything. He grasped his keys. The blur moved past his legs and into the kitchen where it let out a long whine.

"Christ almighty, cat," he said. "You nearly killed me. Some field officer I've turned out to be."

The cat growled an achingly hungry reply.

As Paul closed the garage door, he caught sight of the garage's only vehicle. He stepped down into the garage and turned on the light to reveal a black Chevy Tahoe with a mangled front-left bumper. He squatted at the Tahoe's front and ran his hand along the bumper. The plastic had bent and stretched into streaks of white, but flecks of steely blue mixed in with the streaks. His teeth clenched. He stared at Janey's favorite color. The blue streaks on the Tahoe removed all his doubts and replaced them with a flutter in his stomach.

He moved more quickly, sorting through kitchen cabinets and drawers. In the bedroom to the rear he found an unmade bed that still bore the indented shape of his wife's killer. He searched through a dresser containing socks and a stack of old birthday cards. In the closet hung gray and blue sport coats and slacks, a wardrobe rather like his own. He pushed these aside and found a locked rifle case and a stack of boxed .223 ammunition on top.

In the hall he stopped at a framed photo collage of four men in pullovers showcasing their deep-sea fishing catches. Another showed Caspari at some restaurant patio wearing sunglasses seated next to a pretty brunette that had a few years on him. The photos themselves seemed years old, and a rim of dust had settled on the edges of the frame. Paul captured the photos on his cell phone camera and moved to the nearby room.

It was Caspari's office. A tall bookshelf held the remnants of old college textbooks mixed in with an array of books on foreign policy, some on Eastern Europe, the Caucasus, others on the Middle East. Paul had many of the same books on his shelf. There were two worn dictionaries, one Russian and another for Turkish. Hidden behind these he found a Georgian dictionary, and he pulled it from the shelf. He thumbed through the dog-eared volume. Inside the front cover he saw the initials *M.H.* written in tiny capital letters.

He heard the squeal of a door open from the outside.

"Hey, puss, how'd you get in here?" said a woman's voice. "Dave? Honey, are you home?"

Adrenaline shot through his body like an electric surge. He clutched the book and padded his way to the room's closet door. From inside the closet's cramped dark, he pulled the door almost shut. In the crack he saw the box and clipboard he'd left on the desk. He held his breath. Blood raced through his system, and his heart beat like a bird's without release from his lungs.

The woman leaned into the room. "Dave?"

Through the narrow slit of the closet door, he saw the tips of her brown hair and sweat on her puzzled brow. He wondered if she knew her lover was a killer. He waited, each furious pulse just beneath his ears beating like the toll of a clock that stretched each second longer than the last. He could knock her down and run. He plotted his path out the back door. He was old, but he could still run. *Damn it, why was I so stupid?*

She walked away. He heard her steps move down the hall into the bedroom. Behind him, the gush of the shower rumbled through the thin walls. He had to get out.

He crept into the room again and realized he still held the Georgian dictionary. On the shelf he found the gap and jammed it into the empty space that had narrowed from the packed row of books. He wedged the dictionary into place, sliding and pushing the other books for room. As he did, several photographs edged out.

He looked back toward the shower room. No time. Then he tugged at the photos' corners and rifled through the images.

They looked about a decade old judging from the clothes and the quality of the glossy prints. A younger Caspari grinned at the camera. A different woman with shoulder length brown hair leaned into him. Paul knew her. He rifled through the other photos squinting at the faces for others he might recognize. He saw her again. It was Maria Hessler. He remembered the initials in the dictionary.

Some of the other faces he thought he knew. Agency officers he'd seen over the years, now spread out across the globe on assignments. One he had supervised himself briefly. He scanned the last photo. A large man loomed over the lot of them, his great wingspan cradling all. It was the last face he expected to see mugging at the camera.

Panic set in as the shower faucet squeaked. He stuffed the photos into his pocket and grabbed the box and clipboard from the desk. He raced out the back door and trotted down the blacktop lane past two more townhomes where he tore off the brown shirt and hat and tossed them in a recycling bin. He threw the box and clipboard after and ran his hands through his hair in disbelief.

He hurried around the block, then doubled back to his car where he sat and stared at the photo again in the sunlight. The face of a younger Harley Gilchrist stared back at him.

CHAPTER 19

LOYAL DOG

Brașov, Romania
3:18 p.m., Friday, June 21

Ethan cupped his hand to his brow and shielded his eyes from a utility light that blazed white just yards away. The brilliance pierced through his fingers and into his eyes and pounding head. The ringing in his right ear persisted from the Range Rover's detonation the day before. The high pitch had subsided overnight to a monotone that dulled his brain. When the armed men brought him to this room minutes earlier he could barely hear their terse commands, though neither of them touched him.

Andrei had brought Ethan to this industrial facility somewhere in the Carpathians. Ethan did what he could to recall his whereabouts. As Andrei dragged him into the building, he stalled to observe the cameras mounted along the walls and the magnetic locks at every door. He managed to piece together and memorize the straightest route to the loading dock outside.

They first kept him in an empty lab office where he sat alone picking tiny bits of rock from his scalp and clothes. Bruises swelled at his forearms and along his side, and he had a scrape along one shin with no idea how it had happened. It would heal, which was more than he could say for the Romanians he'd watched Andrei slaughter. He feared the same end for Russell and Wade. He couldn't see them after the flames and pungent smoke of the explosion. He wondered how he still lived but realized while sitting in the dark room that they wanted him alive all along. Even Andrei, whose arm had bled through his sleeve, seemed to keep him at a distance, more a shepherd than assassin.

Now he sat in a metal chair, unshackled and blinded by the intense light. It reminded him of the empty chair from the villa cellar where Kamran Khorasani had faced the same captors. As his eyes adjusted to the brightness, he saw a glossy tile floor and a steel countertop along the left wall. The larger room was well kept and clean, much like his makeshift prison cell.

A voice came from behind the light. He squinted and turned his left ear toward the sound.

"Hello, Mr. Pierce."

The voice hung thick with melodious accent, emanating from the dark shape of a man standing beyond the light. A halo of light shone white around his heavy beard and wave of whitened hair. Next to him, Ethan recognized the rigid silhouette and buzzed scalp of Andrei who stood silent and menacing. Between them hovered a red dot and the glint of a camera lens trained directly at him.

"Who are you?" he asked.

"I'm surprised at you, Mr. Pierce. For all your efforts, and still you know so little."

Whoever it was, he led this insane enterprise. Ethan recalled Kay Linh's work to sort out the phone calls from the hijacking. This was the man who made the call that set everything in motion—the call from Cyprus just before the hijacking. That explained his Mediterranean accent.

"Whatever you want, I've got nothing for you," Ethan said.

"That's much better. But your mistake is granting me greater purpose than I deserve. What do we want? That is the question you are asking without asking. I can take so little of the credit. I play my part, but we want something—as you say—you can't provide."

Let the man's ego do the talking, Ethan thought.

His interrogator sat at a small table and peered down at a stack of papers. Ethan could see a little more of his face—twin pinpricks of glint from his reading glasses perched upon his large nose.

"Ethan Allen Pierce, born 1982 to parents Edward and Carolyn Pierce," the man read. "Graduated *cum laude* from Cornell University. Failed to enter Officer Candidate School after an incident with a drunk driver. That must have been very disappointing for you. And for your parents, perhaps? Your patriotic father? A real cowboy, I understand."

"You tell me. I'm sure it's all in your file there."

"So you say. I found your Agency record surprisingly incomplete. That incident in the car. It leaves out many details regarding the death of your friend. What was his name? Eric, I believe? So lucky for you to survive. So unlike your father's pitiful failures."

Ethan showed no reaction. He hadn't seen his dad since the day he married Sarah. If this man wanted some means to rattle him, Eddie Pierce was not the means to do it.

"At any rate, you wandered Europe before taking that fateful leap to the CIA. It seems you excelled. Several times in Afghanistan. Uzbekistan, Turkey. Iraq, of course. What would they say of you, Mr. Pierce? That you are a good soldier. Isn't that the phrase?"

"Not exactly."

"A good spy then, yes? An eager and willing participant in the chronic meddling of the United States. Do you like your work? You seem to. Does it bring you pleasure in an otherwise miserable existence? You are a targeting officer for the CIA. How very official. Do you always get your man?"

Now the man pried closer. Whatever his angle, whatever calamity he hoped to inflict on the world, Ethan couldn't let it happen. He didn't know how Scorpio had infiltrated the CIA or how they had dismantled his team and stripped Paul Corso of everything short of his life. They'd take that too if they wanted. No one was coming for him now, so he had to lean on the one thing that mattered most in targeting work—the patience for his target to make a mistake.

"Not always. Some of them end up dead," he said with a hard look at his captors.

"Like Seda Alaskhanova," said the bearded man. He sought no answer, but merely mentioned her name like an item in a catalog, the parts of a plan he'd pieced together far away from the lives chewed up by his machinations.

"Yes, like her," Ethan answered. He turned to Andrei who stood unmoved, even at the mention of her name. "That was your doing."

Andrei reacted with a shrug. Ethan knew the kind of man he was then. Passionless. Psychopathic. He doubted Andrei even shared Scorpio's aims, content instead to thirst after the adrenaline and spilled blood. It made him dangerous, but in knowing it he also knew Andrei's limits.

"What about your woman?" the bearded man asked. "Do you always get the girl? I neglected a relevant portion of your profile. Married August 16, 2008, to Sarah Manchester. Born 1984 to parents John and Kathleen Manchester. Father deceased. Graduated *magna cum laude* Cornell University …"

The man peeked up from the file with a mocking glance for him.

"That must have been a point of contention, hmm? She attended law school at the very time you—what do they say? Went to find yourself. You backpacked the wonders of the continent. I wonder if she knew what she was getting into with you then?"

He returned to the file with a sigh.

"Sarah Pierce employed since 2013 as a lobbyist for Decker-Reliant pharmaceuticals in Washington, D.C. Divorced in October 2017. I see she kept your name."

He was doing what they had already done to Paul Corso. Ethan felt the first pang of helplessness well in his throat like a sickening gap that ached almost into his lungs. Paul must have felt the same when he realized what they did to Jane. Ethan couldn't explain to his colleagues how he ignored his fears in the field. He couldn't explain it even to himself. He did his job without a sense of fear because he had to. It was the only thing he believed in higher than himself. For the first time in doing what he had to, he felt fear—for her.

"She's got nothing to do with this," Ethan said. "Leave her out of it."

"Or what, Mr. Pierce?"

"Or I swear I will come to kill every last one of you."

The man paused. The light surrounding him changed shape, glowing through the white halo of his beard, beaming. The man smiled

"Such violence, Mr. Pierce," the man said. "And as for your wife, there, too, we disagree. She has everything to do with you, and that has everything to do with me. We have a mutual acquaintance who informs me you are rather sensitive about your ex-wife. Ms. Hessler was quite emphatic on that point, in fact. But I have not finished. Where was I? Sarah Pierce, et cetera, et cetera. Here it is. Married Kerim Osman June 15, 2019. Why, that was just last week. She is currently enjoying her honeymoon, not far from where we sit. What a remarkable coincidence."

He heard Sarah's voice replay in his head from the tin box recording on his phone. *So, I hope you'll be okay. I know you will.* There was no going back to her now. Ethan focused his rage, willing himself to remember every detail about the interrogator's obscured face. *For later*, he told himself.

"Have I said I admire your tenacity, Mr. Pierce? I do. Call it a professional courtesy. After all, you have caused us some complication. And now you alone sit here. None of your peers have joined you. I would not call you heroic. Noble, perhaps. Clever. I do give you credit for cleverness. But you are tenacious most of all. Like a dog who won't let go of his master's prey, even when it is called back."

His interrogator stood up and entered the light, moving his hand as he talked like a toothed maw that clasped onto his other arm. "You bite down and refuse to let go. You refuse to see what's going on around you. You don't even seem to know why, just like a loyal dog.

"Whereas we are like wolves," he said. Now his hands moved in slow circles, fingers snapping together in sequence as he did. "There are many of us. All around you. We bide our time and bite when we must. Until our prey tires, and its demise becomes inevitable. You see? As I said, you alone are here, not the looming threat of your drones. Not your special forces. Only you. And for that I credit my own tenacity."

The man approached him and crouched to his level so close Ethan could smell his musky cologne and bitter breath. He saw the man's face in full, an older man with white hair and darker wild eyebrows with a wedge of a nose stabbing at his face.

"You asked me earlier what it is we want. Despite appearances, this is no interrogation. You have already given us what we want."

He motioned to Andrei, who manipulated the camera. Ethan heard the squawking of his own voice, almost unrecognizable to himself. Then he heard it. *I swear I will come to kill every last one of you.* The voice was someone else, an angry shadow of his. It was so unlike him, but he felt its anger and knew the truth of it. He had said it, even meant it.

"You see?" The man wandered back to his table.

Brilliance again blinded Ethan as the man left the light. He looked away, and the mote of a bright sun followed his vision.

"Your tenacity forced me to alter our original plans. Some would call this my flair for the dramatic. I confess the truth of it, but it is no mere vanity. You have become remarkably convenient for us in your way. You were so very close to everything, after all. Now we have you to thank for providing the means to conceal our current undertaking. We need only advance our schedule and see to it your lost love's honeymoon receives a truly unique gift. Perhaps from a jilted ex-husband? She will be part of my great experiment. A field exercise. Call it a study in human behavior, if you like. I'll leave you to guess the outcome."

At once he knew the depths of it. They were ready to unleash Kamran Khorasani's virus. They would start with Sarah, wherever she was, and blame him as the jealous lover. In a hurried breath, a greater rage filled the emptiness in his throat and consumed whatever fears he held within him. It didn't matter if they killed him. He couldn't let them do this to her.

He leapt from the chair and pulled it from beneath him. To his right, he sensed Andrei's movement as the more dangerous man facing him crouched to intercept. Ethan heaved the chair with both hands. Andrei ducked and raised his arms to bat away the awkward shape of the flying steel chair. Ethan heard a grunt as the thing crashed into Andrei. It gave him a moment to act.

Ethan launched himself at the bearded man.

He knocked over the light as he charged, and the room spun in a spiral of light and shadow. The man stood wide-eyed and frozen, his arms half raised. Ethan dove over the tabletop. He felt the fine cloth of the man's suit and softer flesh beneath. Together they slammed into the far wall and fell to the ground. Ethan's hands felt for the man's neck. He ignored the man's weakening attempts to pull his hands away.

Andrei struck him with the chair. He felt the pain on his back. The agony surged through his body. He couldn't breathe in air. Still he clutched to the man's neck. With another blow, the light exploded like a burst in his brain and the bearded man's gasping face faded from his sight.

* * *

Ethan lost all direction as a pair of men dragged him down the tiled hallways. He had no memory of how he left the room. His vision blurred, and he focused only on the throbbing in his head. His feet dragged along the floor as they passed door after door in the sprawling facility. He had to get out. He heard the voice of the bearded man somewhere ahead of him, but the words joined the keening between his ears in a senseless jumble of noise and pain.

They passed a door that was unlike the others, all brushed steel and framed in black rubber. There they turned one last time into the hallway of laboratories where they kept him earlier. At least he knew where he was.

With effort he lifted his head and found staring back at him through a narrow pane of glass an emaciated man with dark hair and whiskers. The man's breath bloomed on the window as he watched intently from behind the closed door. Ethan blinked to clear his vision, but the man vanished. Only the fading fog of the man's breath remained on the door's tiny window.

The guards left the man in the next room, just a few paces from where he'd caught sight of the fellow prisoner. Ethan lay with a grunt on a cot with his arms and legs dangling over the side. He wanted to throw himself against the laboratory door that locked him away. They were going to kill Sarah, and there was nothing he could do. He groaned at the thought, unable to move from the pain in his head and his back. He needed a minute to breathe. Then he would get out of there.

He awoke hours later in the darkened room to a tapping sound. Forgetting where he was, he squinted at the speckled tiles in the ceiling above trying to make sense of his surroundings. Somehow, he had turned over in the cot. His head swam. The pressure on his back reminded him of the interrogation. He sat up to find the noise ticking somewhere outside of the hornet's nest buzzing in his brain.

Out the door's narrow window, he saw a sliver of one guard's profile leaning against a perpendicular wall. The portly guard wore a dark, nondescript uniform. At his belt dangled a plastic badge and a sidearm holstered tight above his black pants. Ethan backed away from the window and turned to find the tapping that seemed to echo from overhead.

He climbed on top of a counter along the side wall and followed the sound. He crouched along the bare wall where the tapping continued in an unsteady metallic rhythm. Near the back wall he found its origin. The ticking sound came from a vent set high in the wall. He pressed himself into the corner, his ear inches from the vent. A thin, high whisper accompanied the tapping.

"Are you there? Hello?" said the voice.

"Who are you?" Ethan whispered.

"You are there? You are American?"

Ethan heard a pinched voice, and he knew its owner.

"Yes, I'm American. Are you Kamran Khorasani?"

The tapping ceased, and the voice stopped. Ethan waited for the response as his muscles strained to hold his head up to the vent. He watched the door and listened.

"Yes," Kamran said. "What is your name?"

"Ethan."

"It is you. They tell me you are with the CIA. Is this true?"

Ethan considered the consequence of telling an Iranian bioweapon expert the truth, a consequence that he would realize only if he lived and escaped.

"Yeah."

"Then your CIA men will come for us. I will give myself up to them."

"It doesn't work that way," Ethan said. No one knew where he was. Wade and Russell could be dead. And none of them knew about the virus.

"Then they will kill both of us. It is almost over now," Kamran said.

"What do you mean over? Do they have the virus?"

"It is too late. They took the samples today. I think they will use these. I mean to say on people. Many will die."

Ethan strained to hear him through the duct work like a child's game of tin can and string where Kamran pronounced every syllable in his unpracticed English from the other side of the wall and he deciphered the signal.

"Kamran. About the virus. I need to know everything you can tell me about it. How much do they have?"

Ethan waited for answers but heard nothing. In the suspended moments that followed he heard tiny sobs echo from the vent, a sad and human sound very different from the tapping that woke him.

"You still there?"

"You are the first person to say my name since I can remember," Kamran said. He became quiet again for a time. "What day is today?"

"Friday," Ethan answered. He looked for the watch that no longer wrapped his wrist. They took it from him along with his belt. "It's June twenty-first."

"It seems much longer than that," Kamran said.

"I need you to tell me about the virus."

"If it will help."

"Anything will help. What is it? How does it spread? Can it be treated?"

"It is a specialized virus. A strain of Marburg the Russians built. You know Marburg?"

"I've heard of it."

"It is like Ebola. Everyone knows Ebola. But this virus is special. Very deadly and also very quick. But it is not so easy to spread around. This is very difficult. And they do not have much of it. Eighteen vials. No more. But it is enough."

"Can it be treated?"

"No. That is, yes. That was my job. Before I came here. I made a treatment. It is effective. But I have no more of this. I have taken all of it myself."

"You had the virus? And you survived?"

He recalled his blurred view of Kamran through the door's window. He may have survived, but the disease had taken its toll in flesh. He had a cadaver's face.

"Yes. I injected myself. To hide it. But I destroyed the rest at VECTOR. No one should have this."

"So that's how they got their hands on it? Through you?"

"Yes. I mean, no. I did not bring it to them. I thought there was a journalist. Someone who could help me prove what we had created. But these people. They … what is the word? They stole me."

"Kidnapped."

"Yes, kidnapped. That is what they did. You must believe me."

"Can you make more treatment? If we get out of here, can you make more?"

"Yes. But this takes much time. Many months."

Sarah didn't have months. How did it come to this, the entire operation outpaced by something so impossible to hide? Yet Scorpio remained ahead of him at every step, and now when it mattered most to him he could do nothing. He saw her face and the twin corners of her smile. He heard the little laugh she reserved for him when they were alone. She saved that laugh for someone else now. He remembered her in their bed sleeping in her green pajamas the last time he left the country before it all went wrong. He punched the wall. The flesh on his knuckles slapped with a dull thud.

"Mr. Ethan?"

"Months is too long, Kamran. They are going to kill someone I care about."

"I am sorry for this. I would make this right. Who is it you care about?"

"My wife," he said. He shook his head, though Kamran could not see it. "Ex-wife."

"I do not know what it is to have a wife. But I know what it is like to watch someone you love die. Killed by people you hate. I … I am very sorry."

"I have to help her. What else can you tell me? How will they use the virus?"

"I do not know. But I think I know where they will take it."

"Where?"

"A ship. With many people."

"Like a cruise ship?"

"Yes, a cruise ship. I saw a catalog, and I thought this a very strange thing for Dr. Korkolis to have."

"Korkolis?"

"Yes, the man with white hair."

He had a name, which meant he once again had a target.

"What ship?"

"I cannot remember the name. It was like Asia. Or Astra? Aria? Yes, Aria." Ethan clung to his words, desperate for any chance he could find her.

"Kamran, we have to get out of here. To do that, we have to work together."

"I will try," Kamran said.

CHAPTER 20

SHED BLOOD

Brașov, Romania
7:00 a.m., Saturday, June 22

DESPITE EVERYTHING he told himself, Kamran feared his own death. Hector used this fear against him. Kamran wanted more than anything to flee from this place and the stale stink of his little prison. He shed blood for them, then shed his pride. He committed a deed too terrible to admit, and he hated himself for this even more now that it was real. A woman would die, and more after her. This was a debt he could not repay. But more than any of these things he wanted to run from everyone and be free of his fears.

He sat on his cot and ignored the familiar pain in his spine. On the other side of the far wall, this man named Ethan urged him to escape. They would do it together, Ethan told him. He had listened to Ethan explain how the magnetic locks worked and how they were built to keep intruders out, not keep prisoners in. If Kamran could sneak something in his cell to wedge between the electromagnet and the door plate he could get out.

But the guard stood outside his door day and night. Sometimes the heavy man stood watch, sometimes it was others. Kamran couldn't overpower any of them. They had guns. He needed Ethan's help to break free.

Perhaps Ethan was just another of Hector's tricks. But he could do nothing about that. It served no purpose for Hector to fool him now. Kamran had nothing more to offer. They could take his life now that he'd outlasted his usefulness in Hector's plan. No, he had to trust the American. He was the only way out.

Kamran stood at the door and inspected the lock. It was as Ethan had described to him. A box of steel as long as his forearm hung from the top of the door frame. In forty-four days, he had never bothered to look. He hadn't even pressed hard against the door. He ran his fingers along the lock and wondered if he had the strength to wedge something into a seam so tight.

Just outside his room, the guard rubbed his eyes and stared at the floor while he shifted his weight from one foot to the other. Kamran was no threat to the guard. For weeks they saw him only as a coward too afraid to resist. Day after day their senses dulled, awaiting his demise. For weeks he played this part. Now their complacency was his only weapon against them.

The morning hour arrived. The guard shook his head from his drowsy vigil and escorted Kamran to the toilet. On the return Kamran stopped at the containment lab doorway and waited for the guard to open the door.

"What are you doing? You are not working there today," the guard said.

They had different plans for him then. Through the circular window he saw his lab partner's things hanging from her usual spot. Hector had said she was his daughter, and he wondered which parent taught her such predictability. She hung her white lab coat on the hook second from left along the back wall, then draped her scarf so that the tips hung at the same length on either side. Every day the arrangement was exact. She was in the lab now, but he had to risk it.

"I am to help Dr. Korkolis cleanse the lab," he said.

"She said nothing to me."

The guard confirmed it. She was Hector's daughter.

"Yes, but," he stammered. "They said I did not have to. But the risk for contamination is lower. I mean if I help her. Perhaps she thought I would decline. I am sorry. I did not understand I had to inform anyone. I was waiting."

Kamran lowered his shoulders and looked to the floor.

The guard peeked inside and scowled. Kamran had grown used to his grunts of disgust. He waited for the guard to act next. The guard waved his badge over the gray panel to enter the lab. The panel chirped, and Kamran watched as the card retracted on a string to the guard's belt where it dangled above his right hip next to his pistol.

"Do what you want. For now," the guard said.

The door sealed behind him and he moved to his usual spot. The guard did not follow, a bit of fortune he didn't expect. His fingers faltered as he hurried to undress and step into the same jade green scrubs he'd worn for weeks. Overhead, the black orb that concealed a camera recorded his routine.

In the shower he lingered under the hot water to build his nerve. Here was one place the cameras did not reach, a respite from Hector's watching eyes. This was an advantage if he could manage it. For now, the water calmed his tingling skin as he inhaled the steam and cleared his sinuses to breathe deeper.

With effort, he donned the blue containment suit. Once within, it drowned out the incessant hum of the facility with its hiss of pressured air. The sound had come to comfort him these weeks. Like a Pavlovian creature, he associated the rushing air with solitude and a kind of peace. Within the suit, they could not yell at him. Inside the lab, he had no fear of their torture or the unbearable boredom of his makeshift cell. He retreated into a place his tormentors dared not go. Except for her.

He found her in the alpha lab. Seated at one of the hoods she arranged a series of plastic vials, each unpacked from a cylinder container. More than a dozen packages filled her station in uniform rows across the steel counter. Kamran stood and watched her prepare the miniature assembly line where she would soon bottle up the last of his viral samples and place them in the latched cooler at her feet.

He stepped closer. Dr. Korkolis sensed him then. She jumped and pressed herself against the counter, knocking askew the small vials and boxes with her arm.

"What are you doing here?" she shouted over the white noise within her suit. Her eyes flared at him, startled and angry.

"I came to assist you."

She crimped the hose to her suit to deaden the noise. "I gave no instruction for that. Grigore should not have let you in."

"Yes, I realize. I thought I could assist you. Please. It gives me something to do. I can help you."

Her scowl softened. She considered his offer, looking around the lab.

"Very well. Cleanse the hood over there. The instruments as well." She pointed to a station where he had worked many times. "I will handle the samples. You will not touch them."

"I understand."

He snagged the nearest dangling umbilical hose to maintain the pressure in his suit and sat at the station. With a disinfectant rinse, he wiped away any microscopic traces of his work. Her directions could only mean they were leaving the laboratory and moving the last samples. They never meant to destroy them as she once suggested to him. He felt foolish for ever believing the idea. They could move them with ease for more terrible plans, or even sell them to high bidders seeking even worse.

From a panel under the hood, he transported the instruments to the autoclave. In a small plastic tray, he divided the forceps and spatulas from the scalpels. He needed only one. With one slim piece of surgical steel he could escape. He could even defend himself with its razor edge. He placed the tools in the autoclave and spun the door clamp shut.

At her station, Dr. Korkolis returned with the virus samples. She placed each of the plastic vials into a cylinder, six at a time. Kamran moved closer to observe her.

"What are you doing?" She focused on the vials as she spoke, her voice barely audible between their suits.

"So, you are moving them?"

She did not answer. He moved closer to her.

"Why did you not tell me you are his daughter?" he asked.

"As I said then, our work here would be easier if you did not know. He should not have told you."

She turned her stool to face him.

"I am very like my father," he said. It was true in most ways, though he lacked his father's temperament. "But you are nothing like yours. You must be very like your mother."

Her scowl returned.

"How dare you. You know nothing about me. I am like him in every way. My father is a great man. Far greater than a pathetic creature like you. Return to your work and keep silent."

"Or what? You will hurt me? Kill me here? Mock me when I undress as you have every day since I came here? You can do nothing more to me that is not already planned. I am right. I know it."

She stood and pointed with the whole of her hand.

"Return to your work."

He wanted to hurt her. He could think of no reply for her stern words, and his arms tensed as resentment surged through him like a wave of heat. He imagined taking the scalpel and tearing her suit or severing its umbilical hose. He could use the scalpel on her even, if it came to it. He could do this because he hated her in that moment. She was like every woman he had worked with. All of them thought him pathetic. It was the same in Koltsovo. Their pity was worse than the contempt the guards had for him. He hated them for it.

But it wasn't true. He could not hate them. He desired them. He wanted to be with them, to possess them and they him. They had such intelligence. How could a woman like her be part of infecting thousands? Perhaps she was like him, swayed by the words of her father. Hector brainwashed her, just as his own father's tirades had made him like he was now. *Don't let her do this,* he thought.

He could say nothing to stop her. He could only escape. Let someone else stop her. He obeyed her command and returned to disinfect the other areas of the lab while the instruments sterilized in the autoclave. He needed only twenty minutes more while she bundled up the last of the vials into innocuous little boxes labeled as insulin.

The autoclave's timer counted away the minutes while he disinfected another hood's workspace. Overhead he felt the watching lens of the camera that seemed to domineer the sterile whiteness of the laboratory. He kept his eyes from the camera. *Just a few minutes more.* Once the instruments cooled, he could hide the scalpel in his hand. But if they left the lab together, she would see. He hoped whoever manned the cameras would not notice the thing in his hand. The timer moved too fast for his thoughts.

He had to leave before her. She would never leave him alone in there, not after what he had said to her minutes earlier. Even if she did, she would wait for him. He could conceal the scalpel if he was alone.

He'd have to fool Grigore as well. He never wanted to know his captor's name, and now he couldn't forget. She was right after all. Not knowing names would have been easier.

The timer expired.

He freed the instruments from the pressure and heat of the autoclave. He couldn't feel the heat through the thick rubber skin of his blue suit, but within the suit he felt his own body heat. The pressure within his head increased. His heart raced. For a moment, he wanted to return the instruments to the cabinet and do nothing, to forget everything and return to his cell. Let them do what they would with him. His father shouted at him from a deep and dreaming part of his head. The voice shouted at a coward. *No more.*

He picked up the scalpel and turned from the camera. With a careful slice, the blade cut into his sleeve. Air seeped from the tiny slit into the lab's low-pressure atmosphere.

Behind him, Dr. Korkolis moved the boxes into an insulated crate. He stumbled toward her with his sleeve outstretched. In the other, he tucked the blade along the inside of his arm, clenching it with his fingers.

"My suit is breeched," he said in a panic.

Her eyes widened.

"Get out!" she shouted, though her voice was impotent and frail within the suit. "Sterilize immediately."

She pointed to the hall. It was her instinct to do this, but she had no real concern for him. She did not pause to think or question. What did she care if he lived or died? This was her training, nothing more. Still, in her eyes he glimpsed a vulnerable reaction to the surrounding danger. She was for a moment, like him—a weak child.

He ran to the air lock and waited for the pressurized seal to release the steel door. Air flowed past him like a sucking breath, and once inside the nozzles doused him with chlorine bleach that sterilized any trace of disease. His risk of contamination was low, even with the puncture in his sleeve. The lab served its singular purpose well. She saw to that for her own sake. She could not enter behind him while the nozzles rinsed away chemicals that disappeared into a steel drain.

He still held the scalpel along his arm, ready to conceal it from the camera in the room beyond. There he stripped from the blue suit and laid it like a deflated skin on the epoxy floor. He hurried through the process, making a fist to calm himself as he shed his scrubs and stood naked in the changing room. At each step, he focused on the scalpel. He concealed it on the table within the wad of scrubs. Then he clutched it in his left hand where the blade fell along the bare skin of his forearm.

In the shower, he scrubbed himself with one hand while the other hand grasped the scalpel. He dropped it. He leapt to avoid the blade from puncturing his foot. The scalpel clattered on the shower floor, and he muttered to himself as he examined it. The blade was intact. He clutched the steel grip tighter in his hand

Grigore awaited him in the locker room beyond. Kamran's stomach turned. *Did she alert him?* He crossed the room naked and dripping wet. He dared not look at Grigore, but from the sides of his vision he saw the guard take an uneasy step back as he entered. Kamran dropped the blade into his bundle of stinking clothes and dressed. Grigore watched from across the room.

"Where is Dr. Korkolis?" Grigore asked.

Kamran nodded his head toward the containment. "I had to leave the lab. There was a tear in my suit."

"Is that dangerous?"

"Only for me. But I have sterilized everything. This can happen sometimes."

He shrugged and sat on the bench to put on his socks and slippers.

Grigore's shoulders drooped, a sign Kamran took for relief. The guard rubbed his mouth and looked to the shower door. Kamran used the moment to put on his shirt and again tuck the scalpel along his arm. Without any force at all the blade cut through the sleeve, but he ignored it and made an effort to button his shirt.

"She will be out to yell at me soon," he said.

Grigore chuckled and shot him a malicious sneer. Unfazed, Kamran stood with his arms at his side and waited for Grigore to move first.

"You clumsy fuck," Grigore said. "You buttoned your shirt wrong." He prodded with his chin at Kamran.

Kamran looked down at his worn shirt, its buttons askew. He tugged at a one of the buttons with one hand and shrugged. *Don't look at him. If he can notice that, he can notice the scalpel.* He shuffled across the tiles toward the door.

"What do I care? Back to your room," Grigore said. He stood at the door waiting for Kamran to exit, unaware of the scalpel.

Kamran pushed the door latch and entered the bright hallway. Grigore trailed behind and passed his badge over the sensor to open the prison cell door. Kamran thought he could reach out and take the card, cut it loose with a flick of the razor-sharp scalpel in his hand. For that matter, he could cut the man's throat. The scalpel's edge would slice through his flesh before he knew what had happened. But it wouldn't kill him outright. Kamran's arm froze at his side. Grigore would fight back, and Kamran could not fight. He couldn't even run. Fear stole his breath. The vice in his chest returned. He entered his prison once again as Grigore backed away to avoid any risk of contact. The door slammed shut with a metallic *thud*.

Kamran sat on his cot and stared at the wall. He still clasped the scalpel at his side, but the fear paralyzed him as he lost track of time. He heard a faint tapping, a tick at the base of his brain that he realized came from without rather than within.

He had no sense of how long it had been—how long the random beats of tapping had sounded in his ears. Minutes or hours, it did not matter. He was the pawn of everyone here. Maybe the American was just using him. All he had to do now was remain in place. They would free him, or they would kill him. There was nothing he could do to change that. There never was.

The tapping ceased. From the vent where he spoke to Ethan the night before he heard a sound like a voice. Dazed, he made no sense of the words. The sound was faint and desperate, a kind of pleading mantra. He stared at the wall until the pleas also ended.

A crash shook him from his trance. The force of something heavy and loud on the other side of the wall sent tremors into his quiet space. He stood. More banging sounded, like a hammer on a rock. From his doorway, he watched Grigore run to the room next door, shouting at the American. From within his cell, the American screamed back.

Kamran turned his head to hear more. On the counter next to him he spied his watch curled in a coil of gold and glass. He took the watch in his hand and gripped tight. His skin shivered. All sense of fear left him. It was time.

Overhead, he found the metal bar of the magnetic lock. He jammed the scalpel once, twice into the tiny crevice and shoved through to the door frame. He pulled the scalpel's handle away from the door, pleading to himself for it not to break. His weak arms strained, and the surgical steel seemed to bend. *Please let me be strong enough.*

He heard a tiny crack and stumbled back into the room with the scalpel still in his hands. He thought it broke, but the door opened slightly into the hallway. The nearby shouting and banging became louder. He examined the blade. Its tip had chipped away, but a gleam of razor edge glinted in the hallway light. He stepped out into the empty hall.

More shouting came from the room where Grigore's voice screamed at the American. From the American came an anguished cry that Kamran recognized. He'd made that sound himself in the cellar where they beat him. It was a cry of anguish, much like the ones he kept inside himself while they made him part of their killing. Grigore stood over Ethan, reaching for his gun.

Unnoticed, Kamran stepped into the room. He wrapped his free arm around Grigore's wide girth. With the other he pulled the scalpel hard across the man's neck and felt the warm blood cover them both.

CHAPTER 21

DEEP WOUNDS

Brașov, Romania
8:49 a.m., Saturday, June 22

ETHAN CRIED out as the guard threw him to the hard floor of his cell. He couldn't overpower the heavyset man who stood over him shouting in words he couldn't comprehend. His ears thrummed from the pain. He fought to keep one battered eye open. He had thrown himself at the door, then at the guard in desperation to get out. Now he wasn't sure he could stand. He had failed.

The shouting stopped. A pale dread overtook the guard's expression. The guard clawed silently at a pair of scrawny arms that quickly vanished. In their place, smears of bright red spread down the guard's shirt. The man's eyes went wide in shock. His life blood fell from a gash across his throat. The guard turned to the hallway where Kamran Khorasani backed away from him. He fumbled at his hip for his weapon. Wounded as he was, the guard could still kill either of them.

Ethan forced himself to his feet. Blood rushed from his head and sent the room atilt. He threw himself again at the guard, clutching at the pistol before the man could free it and fire. They fell to the floor together wrestling over the weapon.

Ethan struggled to speak. "Help me."

He tugged at the man's stout fingers, prying them one at a time from the pistol's grip. He tried to breathe through the pain. He had little strength left to fight. His lungs burned. The guard's breath gasped and gurgled, and slowly his fingers weakened as Ethan pried them away.

Ethan freed the gun and crawled away from the dying guard with the weapon trained at his dying body. His forearms stung from exertion, and the pistol hung heavy in his hands from the effort.

Sweat dripped into his eye, and he blinked away the blur. Kamran faced him, sitting against the far hallway wall with his bloodied arms raised in surrender. In one hand he clutched a gold watch. The other held a slim scalpel.

"Do not shoot please," Kamran said.

His voice trembled, high pitched and weak. Ethan saw terror in his soulless eyes. Scorpio had stripped everything from him. His station, his dignity, his hopes and fears, any sense he had of his former self had crashed in the Black Sea weeks ago. All of it was laid bare now with only his instinct to survive remaining. This was their aim. They inserted themselves like a parasite in his mind, driving him to become a killer.

Ethan lowered the weapon.

"Are you hurt?"

"No." Kamran lowered his arms and pointed at Ethan's face. "But your eye …"

"It's all right. We've got to get out now. Down the hallway to that door."

He stood again. A steady sting of pain swelled in his left eye, but his balance returned and with it his senses. They had no more than a minute before other guards would arrive. He stepped out into the hallway over the guard's body. Down the long hall, he saw a sliver of daylight under the steel door. He pointed with the pistol toward the exit, but Kamran crawled back into the room where he reached at the dying guard's belly with the scalpel.

"He's gone. There's no time for that. Let's go," Ethan said.

Kamran snipped at the guard's belt and held up the guard's ID badge. "We may need this."

Ethan nodded. He moved to the other end of the hall where it turned deeper into the building. He knew more guards would come from the doorways and twisting halls beyond. He checked the pistol and peeked around the corner. He heard nothing—no shouts, no running feet. No one came. Not yet.

"Go now," he said.

Kamran ran ahead of him down the long hallway. Just a straight sprint to daylight, and then they could find a vehicle or escape on foot. Their footsteps reverberated down the empty hall. If the guards didn't hear, they could see. Ethan spotted the camera exactly as he remembered, hanging from the ceiling like a watchful eye.

Kamran reached the door and wagged the handle. He looked frantically for the security panel and waved the badge across it. With a tiny click the lock released, and Kamran shoved the door into bright morning sunlight.

Ethan turned to check behind him as they exited onto the loading dock outside. He squinted into the gloomy hallway, but nothing moved. Still no footfalls of pursuers bounded down the hall. They could escape.

He spun around and watched as Kamran fell mutely to his knees with the scalpel jammed into his shoulder.

Andrei came for him next. He had waited for them at the entrance. Kamran hadn't even seen the attack. Now it was Ethan's instinct that drove him to kill or be killed. His vision narrowed so tightly that he saw only Andrei's empty hands moving in a blur toward him.

He lunged left and pulled the trigger with the pad of his finger. Just as Wade had scolded him to do again and again in training. Once, twice the gun kicked in his hand. Andrei swatted his arm away, and the shots fired wide into the open lot.

Andrei wrapped his hands around the gun and shoved Ethan back. A shiver of pain shot up his arm, and the gun twisted away from him. His fingers tensed, but the more he grasped it, the more his fingers bent to the point of breaking. He let go.

Andrei clasped the gun with one hand awkwardly, unable to fire. With the other he struck Ethan's neck in a swift jab like a snake's bite. The blow dazed more than hurt, and he stumbled back. Andrei positioned the gun in his left hand and sneered at Kamran who knelt nearby clutching at the scalpel.

"Fucking coward," Andrei said.

He shot Kamran in the back and kicked him to the ground.

Ethan saw his own end. Andrei moved quicker than him, each movement the practice of a trained killer. Now he'd die at Andrei's hand, just like those Romanian fools who didn't know what they had bargained for. He remembered the tattooed one with the knife and Andrei's bleeding left arm. The memory was his last advantage.

He reached out before Andrei turned the gun on him. He didn't want the weapon, but Andrei would expect that. It bought him the fractional second he needed to grab Andrei's forearm. He dug his thumb into the deep wounds along his left arm. Andrei jerked in pain and a grunt escaped his sneering mouth. The pistol clattered on the concrete as they struggled.

Ethan drove the tip of his thumb deeper. Andrei howled, then struck Ethan again and again with his fist. Ethan held ever tighter, trying to shake off the rapid blows to his chest. With each, his lungs tightened, and he struggled to breathe. But Andrei squirmed in agony.

The punches stopped, and Andrei shoved himself toward Ethan, twisting his arm to break Ethan's grasp. Ethan held tight and opened the cut along Andrei's arm. Warm blood soaked through his gray jacket sleeve.

Andrei shifted his weight again and kicked. The pain Ethan tolerated, but his old weakened knee buckled beneath him. Andrei freed himself, and with a shove knocked Ethan to the ground.

Andrei rubbed along his forearm and winced. "I should have killed you before. When I killed your CIA friends."

"But you didn't. Because you do whatever you're told."

Behind Andrei, Kamran's body moved. Blood covered his shoulder, and below that a darker stain grew on the back of his shirt. He rolled to his side, and Ethan saw his face. Light faded from his eyes. His mouth moved like a dying fish gasping for breath. Ethan would face the same fate if he didn't do something. For now, he could only stall and hope for some chance to fight back.

"Isn't that it, Andrei? You're just Korkolis' bitch."

Andrei kicked him hard in the side. Ethan coughed from the force of it. He fended off another kick, but the effort drained the strength from his limbs. Andrei loomed over him while he gasped for air.

"You think I give a fuck what you say?" Andrei said.

"I think you don't believe their bullshit. They'll throw you away for the cause. Just like you used Kagirov. Like you used Seda."

Andrei mocked him with a snort, and a twisted smile replaced his cruel sneer.

"I'll take my time with you. You die alone. No one will ever find the pieces of you," Andrei said.

Kamran slid over the coarse concrete, inching himself along within reach of the pistol that lay a few feet from his grasp. Ethan cowered from more kicks from Andrei's heavy boots. He absorbed the heaviest blows with his arms, trying to protect his ribs.

Andrei stopped to smirk at him again and gather his breath. He wiped away a froth of spittle from his mouth, unaware that behind him Kamran had reached the gun. Andrei kicked again, slower this time, more forceful.

Ethan endured the pain and took his turn to mock. He forced out a laugh at Andrei who paused enough for Ethan to lower his arms from his head and speak.

"You of all people know what they say, Andrei."

"No, you tell me, you little wretch of a whore. Tell me while you bleed out your asshole." Andrei raised his boot to stomp again.

"*Tebe pizdets*," Ethan said. *You're fucked.*

Kamran fired. He shot up at Andrei, pulling the trigger in slow succession. Each shot rose from the recoil that he struggled to contain in both of his feeble and blood-soaked hands. The first shot tore through Andrei's back and out his stomach. The rest rose up through his lungs as Andrei twisted away from the gunfire. The last shots missed altogether and lodged into the nearby wall. But Kamran had his revenge.

Andrei took a step toward Kamran, then staggered off the edge of the loading dock where he fell onto the gravel below.

Quiet washed over the open lot like a calmed sea. In the fleeting moment, Ethan wanted to close his eyes and wake in his bed next to Sarah. That was a fleeting dream, but cold reality kept him awake. He pushed himself up. More guards would come for them.

Kamran mumbled something Ethan couldn't understand. His hands still held up the emptied pistol, his fingers tugging at a dead trigger. A miserable whine escaped his throat, but Ethan ignored his delirium. They had to move. He reached for Kamran to drag him to the edge of the dock. Kamran's eyes fixed on him in horror.

"No," he said, "do not touch me." The pistol fell away, and Kamran raised a blood-soaked hand. His voice stuttered and shook from his wounds. "I could still infect."

"Can you make it?"

Kamran nodded. He dragged himself to the edge and swung his legs over the side to stand.

Ethan climbed down to find Andrei's contorted body on the ground. In his pockets he found the van keys he'd hoped Andrei still carried. He searched again and found his phone, but no weapon. As much as Ethan wished for a gun now, it meant they were lucky to make it this far. Their escape caught Andrei off guard. If he had found time to grab a weapon, both of them would be dead.

Ethan glanced along the long building and its many doorways. The doors stayed shut. No guards pursued them, but it was only a question of seconds now. He hobbled to Andrei's white van across the lot. Behind him, Kamran limped along as he pressed his hands against the hole in his chest.

Shouts erupted from a doorway down the far length of the building. Men emerged from the door like scattering black ants, all dressed like the guard that stood outside his cell door overnight. They brandished side-arms, and one signaled to the others toward the van.

Ethan started the engine and jerked the gearshift into reverse. He maneuvered the van between Kamran and the guards. They opened fire. The first shots drummed along the van's side like a crash of hailstones. Ethan ducked and leaned over to open the passenger door where Kamran fumbled with the handle.

"Get in!"

A bullet struck Ethan's window. He raised his hands in a desperate reflex as the tiny pieces of glass rained upon him. The cadence of gunfire increased, and Ethan floored the accelerator. Gravel churned beneath the back tires, and the van rocketed toward another parked vehicle. He swerved around it to block the gunfire, then sped toward the boom gate at the lot's perimeter.

Kamran slumped in the seat next to him, unable to lift his wagging head.

"Stay with me, Kamran. Hold on."

The van burst through the boom gate and onto a narrow lane of cracked blacktop that ran out of the mountain valley into a maze of industrial buildings. He leaned to check the far side mirror for pursuers. He rounded a corner, then took several narrow lanes and hard turns to find a wider avenue into the city.

Kamran sputtered something next to him. He spoke in Farsi, but to Ethan it was the ravings of a dying man. His clothes had soaked through with dark blood. Ethan pounded the steering wheel in frustration. He didn't even know where they were. It was a city large enough to have a sprawling industrial neighborhood that slowed their escape, which meant it had a hospital.

A car appeared in the mirror far behind. It sped closer. He turned hard into a walled yard behind a massive white warehouse and looked for a way around the building. The wall trapped them in with no route to the warehouse's front. He reversed the van along wall where he could see the opening. But the car rolled by, leaving them alone in the empty yard. He stopped to check on Kamran.

"I think we made it. We've got to get you to a hospital."

Kamran's breathing slowed. He faced Ethan with a pained look as he fought to speak.

"Did you love her? Your wife?"

How could he ask this now? He knew the answer without doubt, but it changed nothing. She was lost to him, and he bore the blame. He let the Agency become more important somehow, and when she left he drove himself deeper into the profession. Now people all around him were dying, and he began to doubt everything else.

"I never stopped," he said.

Kamran's face eased, as though he'd let go of the pain and embraced the inevitable. "I never had a woman."

"Just hold on. I'm going to get you help."

If Sarah ever was his, she wasn't any more. He couldn't tell Kamran that. The man who just saved his life sat there dying, just like Marcus Eldridge and Seda Alaskhanova had. He'd watched the dullness in their eyes as they died. He'd lain helpless when flames engulfed Russell and Wade. Now he would add Kamran's face to his fitful dreams, and he'd wake knowing he didn't do enough to save them.

Kamran held the gold watch to his mouth and kissed it, streaking its crystal face with red. He repeated something quietly over and over, and Ethan wondered what it meant. He knew the words were not for him. Maybe for someone Kamran had loved, some last solace for a terrible death. He hoped so.

"I'm burning. I'm burning. I'm …"

The words became a thin rasp, and then he was still. Ethan sat helpless, afraid to touch Kamran's bloodied body. He let out a frustrated scream that filled the van's confined space. He pounded the wheel again with his fists with such force the van shook. Nothing he could have done would have saved Kamran. No matter how fast he drove or how hard he fought, he couldn't have saved the man who saved him. He told himself this, but the voice in his head rang false.

He had to abandon Kamran and leave the vehicle. Scorpio would not give up on finding them both. If he drove into the city and found the police, they'd detain him longer than he could afford to wait. They might even suspect him. Worse, whoever found the body here risked infection.

Ethan leaned over Karman's remains and searched the glove box. Beneath a stack of papers he found an orange road kit with a bundle of flares. He lit one and set it back into the glove box, then exited the still running van.

Through the shattered driver side window, he watched the flames grow on the dash until the dark gray smoke obscured Kamran's lifeless body.

"I'm sorry," he said. "You deserved better."

* * *

Ethan wandered the alleys and streets of the industrial yards where not a soul appeared on a quiet Saturday. At each street he crossed, he checked over his shoulder for his pursuers. None appeared, so on he shuffled between the buildings. The sounds of his own feet dragging over the gravel lots echoed around the rusting ghost town. He kept the pine covered hills to his left to stay on a course to the city. Behind him a tendril of dark smoke rose from the burning van.

The city spread under golden sunlight below. He strode down through hedges and around the black metal fences of a housing district.

The pain welled in his ribs, and he slowed to a lumbering pace. His breath eased once the adrenaline thinned. His fingers and feet trembled from the ordeal. A woman smoking a cigarette observed him from a balcony above. He squinted up at her where she perched behind striped sheets hung to dry in the morning sun. He rounded her building's corner just as the wail of sirens wound through the narrow streets heading off toward the smoke.

He leaned against the apartment building under the cool shade of a balcony just over his head. He wouldn't get far on foot with no identification and no money. Andrei's phone had a signal, but calling the U.S. Embassy invited Scorpio to follow. He needed Wade's help, but he last saw him engulfed in flames. He dreaded calling his friend for fear he wouldn't answer.

He dialed the number of the phone he'd bought himself in Bucharest. If Wade had any sense—if he was still alive—he'd answer. Ethan hoped he kept the phone after what happened. He hoped Wade had made it. The tone chirped as he waited. No answer could mean anything. That Wade had discarded the phone like he should have. That Wade was busy trying to find him. But with each ring his thoughts fell to the worst option—that Wade was dead and he was alone after all. *Please pick up that phone, man.* He never questioned Wade's loyalty, and Wade followed him into fire. Wade had given him a trust he no longer could justify. *Pick up.* They had shared a bond beyond that of officers. Wade was his only friend. *Pick up.* That was gone now, too, and he was to blame.

The phone clicked in his ear, and a baritone voice answered.

"This better be who I think it is," Wade said.

"It's me. I thought you might be dead."

"God damn!" Wade whooped in his ear. "I thought the same about you. Where the hell are you? You okay?"

"I've been better, but I'll make it. Just a little banged up. I think I'm in Brașov."

"Listen, man, you go to ground and sit tight. We'll come get you."

"We?"

"I'm with our people. And a few others. The rest of us from the op are here. Everyone except Russell. He's in the hospital. He got the worst of it in the blast, but it looks like he'll pull through it."

"So, Langley knows what happened?"

"Chief of Station handled that, yeah. We can't keep up this off-the-reservation shit forever. We had to call it in to track you down."

"I wish you hadn't done that."

"What the hell were we supposed to do, man? The op was a bust. Russell was hurt bad. We thought you were dead."

"They know everything now," Ethan said. He bowed his head and rubbed his eyes. No matter what they did, this adversary stayed one step ahead.

"Look, it doesn't matter right now. We'll figure it out. I'll gather up a team and come get you."

"No. Just you." Ethan checked the streets in both directions. "I don't trust anyone else now. They're after Sarah."

"You sure?"

"I'm certain. Come get me, and I'll explain. Tell Hourglass we need a paramilitary team to move. Right away. We need transport to sea."

"Wait, what? That's not going to be easy. Chief's going to freak."

"Do whatever it takes. We need this. They've got a bioweapon in play." He thought of Kamran's corpse amid the smoke. "They really did it. Just get here fast. Call me when you're here, and I'll guide you to me."

"What's all this got to do with Sarah?"

"Like I said, I'll explain."

"Roger that. Sit tight."

"And, Wade? Way to follow my instructions on ditching the phone."

"Told you it was a bad idea. You'll be thanking me later, you lucky motherfucker."

"I'm thanking you right now."

CHAPTER 22

INFERNAL REVELATION

Vienna, Virginia
8:10 p.m., Saturday, June 22

PAUL SAT on his side of the bed and wiped a layer of dust from of his father's shotgun. He kept it high in his closet where it had rested out of sight for years. He never fired the thing. Like most of his inheritances, it was a relic for which he had no real fondness. His father had loved the gun—an Italian masterpiece he had spent considerable money on when Paul was a boy. Paul admired the etched scrollwork on the lock plate and the long lines of the over-under barrels. That beauty had tarnished under the grime and dust these long years in the closet where the humidity rose and fell with the seasons. He had no need for its decoration, nor any wish to sell it. Now it was just a gun, the only one in the house.

A box of Janey's things from the accident still sat on the bed behind him. Her side. He slept—when he slept—on his side, barely disturbing the bed she'd made last Saturday. He ignored the box each morning and night. It remained on the bed's edge undisturbed, a reminder of things he didn't want to remember. As he ran a washcloth down the length of the shotgun, he knocked the box from the bed with the stock. He leaned the gun against his side of the bed and walked around to gather her things.

Janey's possessions spilled out onto the floor. Her lipstick rolled onto the carpet. A little vial of perfume tumbled out of her sequined wallet. He held the vial between his fingers and savored the fragrance. Alongside it all were her black heels, which she'd traded for a pair of flats like she always did after her benefit dinners. He righted the box and placed the heels inside along with the items from her purse. In the purse he found her iPhone. Its face had cracked in the crash like a portrait of dueling spider's webs. He stared at its inscrutable surface and heard a ringing. But no one could call her anymore.

The ringing came from his phone. It was Michael.

"Hi, Pop. How you holding up?"

"As well as I can be."

"Did you get yourself something to eat?"

He hadn't bothered. Janey's friends had stocked the refrigerator with more food than he could eat in a week. But he hadn't thought about food after spending most of his Saturday at Langley trying to find anything to explain away the photograph of Harley and the others. What he found only strengthened his suspicions.

"I'll get myself something here soon. I was at the office the better part of the day catching up."

Michael knew better than to ask more. He couldn't tell his son he had spent hours studying the men who killed his mother.

"Well, you've got to eat. Mom would want us to take care of ourselves. We've just got to keep on going."

"I know what you mean, son. Don't worry about me," he said. He looked at the cracked phone, then at the shotgun propped against the bedpost. "I'm keeping myself occupied."

"That's good. Don't overdo it. Work will be there when you get back. I hear the house is in good shape. Just take it easy. I'm worried about you."

"I'm the one who's supposed to be worried about you boys. You heard from your brother?"

"Yeah, we talked today. He's doing okay."

"Doesn't sound like you mean it."

"He's pretty broken up. He said he's worried he won't remember what she looks like. Isn't that a weird thing for him to say?"

"He just misses your mother. I know the feeling," he said. He put Janey's phone in his pocket and went to the window where the last bits of daylight peeked through the maple trees. "How are you holding up yourself?"

"I don't know. I'm just getting through it for now. Emily's been here a lot this week, so that helps. Listen, we were thinking we could come over for lunch tomorrow. Jacob can come with us. We can get some steaks and grill out. How's that sound?"

He wanted to say yes and tell Michael how proud he was of him for staying strong. He was so much like Janey. He had her patience, and Paul needed that now more than ever. Paul's attention dwelt only on her killers. They were the same people who drove to headquarters every day like him. They put on neck ties and kissed their loved ones. They passed through the same gates he did, and they ate the same cafeteria food. Their likeness ended there. They betrayed the Agency and killed their own. He had attention only for them, and he didn't know where that would take him by tomorrow. Neither did he much care.

"Pop, you there?"

"I'm here. How about I take a rain check on that, Michael. I just need to be alone for the next couple of days. There are a few things I need to sort through by myself."

"You're sure I can't change your mind?"

"I'm sure. You look after your brother."

"I will. See you soon, Pop."

"Goodbye, Michael."

He took the gun downstairs to the kitchen, where he loaded two shells into the breech and set it by the door to the garage. The gun did nothing to ease his growing paranoia. If they wanted to eliminate him, they would, just as they had Janey.

Under the light at the sink he studied the photographs again. Caspari he knew, and Harley and Maria Hessler. One of the youngest faces was Brian

Crowley. He scowled and held the photos close to his nose, remembering the names of some he knew and others he thought he recognized from the Agency. Maybe he imagined seeing them, but he couldn't be sure. They could be anyone.

They were just old photos. They were evidence only that Harley knew the others, not that he'd gathered them up for some traitorous cabal years prior, long before the Scorpio Compact even existed. He couldn't believe they'd take part in their radical politics. But the faces smiled back at him, and now he knew they were connected. He needed more. Until he had it, he was on his own—with one reliable exception.

He called Kay Linh and prayed she was home for once on a Saturday night.

"Paul?"

"Where are you?"

"At home," she said with a mouthful of food. "Is everything okay? What happened this morning?"

"You alone?"

"Thanks for reminding me. Yes, I'm home and alone. Again."

"Good," he said. "I got your sympathy card. Nice touch."

"It was the best I could think of. Tell me you took that home with you. I don't want anyone seeing that and getting the wrong idea."

"Or the right one. Yes, I took it home by way of your new friend's place, where I found something interesting."

"Like what?"

"Like he has friends, too. Several, in fact."

Paul heard a fork plink on her plate. Silence followed while she considered the implications, running down the possible collaborators in her head.

"There's something else," she said. "It's Pierce."

"Is he dead?"

"We don't know. I shouldn't be telling you this on the phone."

"Then don't. If there's a chance, that's enough. We can't help him unless we handle things on this end first."

"What do you need me to do?"

"This isn't exactly official business. You need to know that going in. If you don't want to do this, you need to say it now. This could end either of us. Our jobs. Our ..."

"Paul, maybe I was unclear. What do you need me to do?"

"I'm going to send over some photos I found. Hold on to them for now. Then I need you to be my ears. I'll call from a different number later tonight. Stay quiet and record everything you hear. If anything happens to me, take everything to the Director. Only the Director. No one else. Understand?"

"Affirmative. Just don't let anything happen to you. Suzanne is driving me insane."

"I'll do what I can."

He hung up without saying more. He doubted he could stop what would happen to him. They had killed Janey, and for reasons he only suspected, they hadn't killed him yet.

He didn't believe in fate. He'd seen too much of God's absent hand to think men had no choice. But he made up his mind the day they took Janey from him. Pierce faced the same odds, he guessed. If Kay didn't know anything, that meant he disappeared hours ago. *God, let him be alive*, he thought.

He had one more call to make. Ethan's disappearance meant time had run out. They'd made their move in Bucharest, and worse would follow. He dialed Harley Gilchrist's number.

"Evening, Paul. You doing all right?" A rabble of restaurant voices bubbled under Harley's drawl.

"We need to meet. Tonight."

"Sounds urgent. What's got you all shaken up? I hear from Suzanne there was a little trouble yesterday. I was hoping you'd stay home and take some time for yourself."

"No, it's not about that. It's that top priority we discussed. It can't wait."

"All right then. I've got something for you myself. There's a place over here in Georgetown called Montrose Park. I take the dog for a walk there from time to time. As good a spot as any."

Harley picked the place a little too quickly for it to be mere convenience.

He lived in Georgetown, so the park was familiar ground for him. It would be a public place, but out of the way and probably dark. If Harley wanted him dead, the place didn't matter much. His knowledge of Harley's involvement was his only leverage.

"I'll be there in an hour," he said.

"Make it two," Harley replied. "I'll see you then."

* * *

Paul drove over the Key Bridge into Georgetown where the waterfront lights stood tall on the still Potomac. The city came alive there at night in the trendy clubs and invitation-only cocktail parties. Janey had dragged him to a few of those over the years in the same streets he drove down now. He had no cause or desire to return, and yet there he was driving the narrow lanes where the row houses and old brick mansions closed in on an endless parade of parked cars that claimed space for the lucky. People strolled in groups on the sidewalk so close he could hear their mundane conversations as he drove by.

He found his own luck at an open spot along R Street near the hedges of Montrose Park. Under his dark pullover, he wore an old neck wallet. It was a tourist's trick to protect passports. Janey bought the thing on their second trip to Rome. He didn't have any use for it until now. He knew how to avoid the pickpockets whose tricks weren't so different across the continents. Now it held Janey's iPhone flat against his sternum. He tapped Kay's number and spoke into it, then patted down the tiny bulge in his shirt.

On the floor of the back seat behind him lay the shotgun and a box of buckshot shells. He had covered both with a dusty blanket from the garage —one Jacob had used at summer camps years ago. The gun was a last resort, but now he regretted ever bringing it along. The phone would be enough. He could leave no room for regret now.

The summer night air hung perfect and still. An older couple walked ahead of him holding hands while the old man whistled, but the drone of cicadas drowned out his tune. The sound hummed above Paul's head like a warning not to enter the darker foliage and open grass of the park. He strode down the brick sidewalk to the open path at the park's entrance and let the couple on the sidewalk carry on their stroll.

The park appeared empty. In the corners of his vision he watched for movement as his eyes adjusted to the dark. He wandered past an old tennis court worn past repair with cracks of moss pushing up through the dark asphalt. He followed the smell of grass deeper into the park. Harley lurked somewhere in the shadowy grays ahead waiting for him. He walked like he did in his dreams. He was alone but steady and unhindered by the small voice in his mind that warned him of his demise. He floated along, his head swimming like a drunk's, carried by his determination to hear Harley admit his part.

Ahead he saw a flash of lighter gray. A dog paced in a quarter circle, leashed to a figure standing still under an oak's branches. He recognized Harley standing in the dark waiting for him. Harley still wore a sport jacket without a tie and a white shirt that reflected the scant light down his heavy torso like the pallor of a mushroom.

"Hey there, Paul. Hell of a nice night, isn't it?"

"Harley." He nodded while his eyes scanned the park beyond the path where they stood.

"This here's Cicero. Not exactly a killer attack dog. Are you, boy?"

The dog snorted and brushed its body along Harley's leg. He reached down his heavy hand and scratched behind the mottled dog's ears.

"You got a dog?" Harley asked. "Cicero's what they call an American Staffordshire terrier. You should get yourself one. It'd do you some good. Keep you company."

"Very loyal. So I hear."

"Nothing more so," Harley replied. He stood and nodded to the eastern side of the park. "Let's walk a little."

They strolled farther into the park. Cicero trotted between them, claws clacking on the blacktop path.

"I don't know that I should tell you this right now, but I got word today Ethan Pierce may be involved in all this," Harley said.

"Not possible."

"Are you so sure about that? Looks like he may have staged his disappearance. We've got some bits of video and now a credible threat on his ex-wife. The whole god damn thing's a mess. We've got a good officer in the hospital. An old friend of yours, I hear. Walt Russell. We should at least consider the possibility that Pierce is involved."

"No. Not a chance. I put him on that assignment myself. It's a smoke-screen."

"Suzanne isn't so sure about that."

"Then she's wrong, for Christ's sake. Pierce is the only reason this mess isn't worse."

"Look, it's been a long week. Things on the ground have changed. I'm just saying keep your mind open to the idea. Like I mentioned, maybe I shouldn't have told you just now."

Paul shook his head in disgust. Harley didn't believe it any more than he did, but no one else would know it. He had to get Harley to reveal himself before Pierce became a scapegoat.

"Now, let's talk about what you have for me." Harley said after they'd walked a few yards more.

"I found one of them."

"One of what now?"

"Someone inside the Agency. One of the drivers who killed Janey."

"I'll be damned. You're sure? You're accusing a man of murder here. One of our own."

Yes, one of our own, Paul thought. He wondered if Harley even considered his role and the hypocrisy of his smug Southern charm. Harley believed himself untouchable, peering down from some unassailable height in his climb to power. Paul realized Harley saw it all as the justified means to an end. He began to understand why Harley had sold his soul.

"I'm very aware what it means. I'm sure," he said.

"Have you gone to the police? What about the Bureau?"

Paul thought he heard a hint of anxiety in Harley's voice. His pitch raised a minuscule amount, like the changing speed of the cicadas chirping in the cooling air. Harley would protect himself at every turn, and Paul had to be ahead of him to witness it.

"No, I'm talking to you first," Paul said. "As much as I want justice, there's more at stake here. There are others. If I want real justice, I'm going to get all of them."

Including you, he thought.

"Well I appreciate that. Could mean the difference in cleaning up this mess once and for all. It's a good damn thing you came to me first. I can give you all the access you need to identify everyone involved. Now, just who are we talking about here?"

"Do you know David Caspari?"

"Can't say that rings any bells for me. He's your suspect?"

Paul hummed assent. He almost admired Harley's response. Not a trace of hesitation betrayed his reaction. Paul knew he lied, of course. He had the photo to prove it. Paul took his mendacity as confirmation of Harley's role as handler for the traitors who killed his wife. But he needed more. He needed Harley to say it.

They stopped at the edge of the park where the ground eased into an old city graveyard. Gravestones hovered like ghosts in the faint light. Cicero sniffed the ground between them.

"You used to train recruits at the Farm," Paul said. "What was that, about eight years ago?"

Harley shrugged. "Give or take. Why do you ask?"

"Just that I thought there was some chance you ran into him. You had to see a lot of our officers go through the program. Must be a good way to learn names and faces. I looked up his file earlier today. He actually went through the program about that same time. You don't remember him?"

"Afraid not. Caspari? That what you said his name was? He must not have trained with me."

"I guess not. What about Brian Crowley? He trained at the same time as Caspari. You didn't seem too familiar with him the other night."

"No. He's involved too? Looks like your hunch was right about him after all. They may have trained together."

"It looks that way. A coincidence like that made me curious. That's intelligence work. That's all it ever is. One coincidence after another until you can see the shape of things."

"I'm not sure what you're driving at," Harley said. He shifted his stance while they stood side by side overlooking the rise and fall of the cemetery hills that folded down out of sight. Harley let Cicero's lead drop on the ground while he fiddled with his pocket.

"Maria Hessler. You remember her. She trained with them, too. It's all connected. The three of them and more. I can tell you what they had in common, but you already know. I found an old photograph of you, Harley. Looks like you knew them after all."

Harley turned to face Paul.

"That's a hell of an accusation. Just who do you think you are?"

"I'm the guy who hounded after more than you really wanted. You thought you could control all this, didn't you? Christ, Harley, people are dead. You killed my wife, you son of a bitch."

"Not me. Never me." Harley raised a compact semiautomatic and pointed the gun's long suppressor at Paul's heart. "But maybe they should have killed you instead."

"So why didn't you? Why her, Harley? Janey had nothing to do with this. You killed an innocent woman for nothing."

"Turn around," Harley said. With his free hand, he searched Paul's pockets and ran his meaty hand down his body from arm pits to ankles. He took Paul's phone and tossed it into the graveyard. Cicero started at the sound of it in the grass and barked once at the spot where it landed. Harley hushed the dog with a kick.

"They didn't kill her for nothing. Look at you. Master and commander of everything halfway around the world. But take away your comfy little home life and you fall apart. I hate to see it come to this. Truly I do. If you would have just done what I told you, we wouldn't be here right now, would we?"

"I'm right where I need to be," Paul said.

Paul raised his head and turned slowly toward Harley. His eyes locked on Harley's face. The shadows crawled into the crevices of his eyes and jowls, and Paul saw the age and wear deeper than before. His lips quivered and Paul sensed weakness. Whether doubt or regret, he couldn't say.

"I thought you were smarter than this, Harley. Did you think I'd meet you out here, knowing what I know, without a plan? Without some insurance? You honestly think I give a damn whether you pull that trigger?"

Harley raised the barrel to Paul's forehead. "You're bluffing."

Paul's eyes narrowed. He felt no sense of fear, no pulse pounding rush. It was a feeling unlike anger, unlike any he had a name for. He wanted Harley to face an anguish worthy of his misdeeds. He wanted it more than he desired life, and he would fulfill that wish alive or dead. He already had fulfilled it.

Paul moved his hand toward his chest. Harley's fist tightened. The pistol's tip shook, moving in nervous circles at his forehead. Paul tapped the slight bulge at his chest.

"They've heard every word."

Harley's face fell. The shadows fell longer on his open mouth and sagging eyelids. He lowered the pistol.

"I'm a dead man," Harley said with a whisper.

Harley looked at the gun in his hand as though realizing for the first moment what he held, like an infernal revelation of his self-constructed torment.

Paul had nothing more to say. He turned and walked away, awaiting the bullet to strike him at any moment. He crossed a walkway and continued on toward the streetlights far away when the shot came. His body jerked, startled by the sound. He felt no pain. He waited for a second shot to take his life, but nothing followed the echo of the first loud report. The shot came from farther away, from someone else—a rifle's report unmuted by a suppressor that shook the night. And then nothing. Scorpio had taken care of its own failures. He wondered if it was Caspari or Crowley who pulled that trigger. Or was it someone else? *Why didn't they shoot me?* But there was no one to answer for him.

He turned back toward the darkness and saw Cicero trotting toward him, his leash trailing behind without a master.

CHAPTER 23

KILLING STROKE

MSC Aria, The Black Sea
4:50 p.m., Sunday, June 23

FROM THE air Ethan watched the *Aria* cut against the waves with a great arcing tail of white wake on the sea. The massive ship curled westward toward the afternoon sun on a course the crew no longer steered. The ship's second officer had established contact with the helicopter's pilots and explained she had lost control of the ship's helm.

As they flew two hundred miles over the Black Sea, he had heard the officer's voice in his headset. She had no idea what was happening or why. She knew that just hours before the ship strayed uncontrollably in aimless circles, her captain had fallen ill.

To her, these two misfortunes had no connection. It was the kind of bad luck that gave her a chance to prove her mettle to the cruise line bosses. He admired her calm, though he could hear the frustration grow as she snapped orders at the bridge crew. Things would only worsen for her because she didn't yet see the common thread that hung at her neck like a garrote wire. She faced a planned malevolence. Once she realized what was happening she could only minimize the damage.

He wondered again about Scorpio's plan. If the captain had already succumbed to the virus, then there were others. Korkolis had chosen the ship to spite him. He called it an experiment, though the idea of that seemed to Ethan as petty as it was insane. *Please let her be okay*, he thought. The updates he heard over the radio suggested that she wasn't.

The Sea Hawk helicopter circled the massive ship that towered over the waterline like a white palace. Wade sat across the helicopter's cabin from him, next to one of the two Navy corpsmen that flew with them. He occupied the harness seat hanging from the cabin ceiling like a man born into it. In the seat he was both at ease and ready for action with hard grimace partially concealed by the Oakleys that hugged his temples.

Ethan had him to thank for getting them both this far, though they'd lost valuable time coordinating between Langley and the captain of the *USS Vella Gulf*. In the morning something changed, and somehow Wade convinced Suzanne Tasker that he needed Ethan to assist. They had boarded the Sea Hawk to contain the situation. But Wade knew why he was there. He had to find Sarah.

With a nod from one of the corpsmen, Wade pulled on a thick pair of leather gloves.

"You ready for this?" Wade asked.

"I don't really have a choice," he said.

"It's like we talked about. Control descent with your feet. Don't let yourself go too fast, or your hands will burn like a bitch and a half."

Ethan nodded.

"And don't let go."

The crewman opened the door, and the roar of the rotors slicing overhead drowned out all sound. They dropped the heavy ropes to the deck below, and with a tap on his helmet, Wade descended.

Ethan stood and watched him descend. He held fast to the harness overhead. His muscles ached. Every movement sent stiff pain through his sides and his legs. He saw Wade clear the zone and wave at the cruise ship crew waiting on a lower deck.

The chopper crewman signaled for him to descend. He gripped the braided ropes and swung out into the open air. He felt nothing below and kicked his legs frantically. The downdraft spun him around, and he felt like he'd fallen free of the rope. The rope became a blur in his hands. Heat surged through the rugged gloves like a warming oven. He hit the hard deck out of breath and fell in an awkward roll.

The corpsmen followed, and the Sea Hawk ascended away from the ship.

"That was damned ugly," Wade shouted over the thunderous noise from above. He picked Ethan up and patted his shoulder, then pulled him toward a stairway where a ship's officer greeted them both with a salute.

"Are you the officer in charge?" Ethan asked the woman saluting.

"Second Officer Lucia Ranieri," she said.

He recognized her Italian accent from the radio. She met him in height, and her face was as calm as her voice. She wore an orange jacket over her white uniform with her hat tucked under one arm.

"The first officer is with engineering trying to restore the helm. Is this all of you?" she said.

"There are more on the way. But the helm is the least of your problems right now. How many are sick?"

The question confused her, and her dark eyebrows closed together in frustration.

"I don't understand." She held a hand to halt Wade as he dropped gear on the deck and checked his weapon. "Are the firearms necessary? We don't normally allow that. You'll frighten the passengers."

"I don't think you do understand, lady," Wade said.

"Ma'am, please. The outbreak is extremely serious. This is no ordinary illness," Ethan said.

"What do you mean? How do you even know that?"

"Because you're facing a biological weapon attack."

Her once serene face fell into a pained look. Her eyes danced from him to Wade to the ship decks beyond where passengers lounged, many watching the spectacle of the helicopter drop.

"How many are sick?" he said.

"Around twenty, I think."

Kamran had said the virus didn't spread easily, but Scorpio had managed it in two days. More would contract the disease from the twenty alone. More still would become infected if they didn't find how Scorpio brought it on board.

"You need to get these corpsmen to the infirmary. Then we need to review anything brought on board in Constanța."

She nodded. At her command another officer escorted the corpsmen away. They lugged packs of protective equipment. The heavy biological warfare gear could protect them and the ship's medical staff. The equipment wasn't enough for everyone on board who needed it, and the corpsmen knew it. They waved at Wade and headed down the stairway.

"Follow me," she told Ethan and Wade.

She led them past the opulence of swimming pools and waving pennants strung along the upper decks of the ship. Sunbathers gawked at them as they strode by, alarmed by Wade's stride and his automatic rifle pointed at the deck. Rumors would spread faster than the disease and compound Lucia's problems.

They passed sliding doors into a lavish hallway and strode on for a hundred yards before reaching an elevator that took them to the inner workings of the ship. There they found a narrow security office with monitors hung on the wall above a command desk. It reminded Ethan of the operations center in Langley. The operations staff would be waiting for an update from him, just as the security officers here scanned the ship on a dozen screens watching for unusual behavior.

"Show me everything from Constanța. Supplies, passengers, crew. Anything," he said.

Lucia prodded a security officer who pulled open lists of events on a monitor at eye level.

"We often take on supplies and new crew. And many of our passengers go on excursions. This will take a while, and I need to return to the bridge," she said.

"We don't have a while. The virus came aboard in Constanța. If we don't find who or how, you're going to have more sick. And most of them will die."

"Do as he says," she told the security officer.

They wasted nearly an hour reviewing the recorded faces of passengers as they boarded. Their cruise badges appeared on the screen as they scanned their identification. He recognized none of the sun-weary faces that boarded half drunk or exhausted from a day at the Riviera. Nothing about any of them suggested they carried certain death on board. No nervous glances, no obviously incriminating packages. With every new face, he hoped to see Sarah. She never appeared, which meant she could have stayed on board. Or maybe she wasn't here at all.

Lucia showed him the ship manifest. The galley had taken fresh fish and produce aboard, but not much else. They took on no medical supplies, nor any large palettes or containers to hide the small vials Kamran had described to him.

"What about the crew?" he said without taking his eyes off the screen. The faces began to repeat in front of him.

"Some took shore leave. You saw most of those return with the guests. There are a few who came aboard for new positions."

"Does that happen a lot?" Wade asked. He leaned against the back wall, his great arms crossed at his chest. Ethan sensed his growing impatience.

"It's not unusual. And they have to pass a security inspection to board."

"Who came aboard for new positions?" Ethan asked.

She reviewed the manifest on screen. "Four cabin stewards. All women who worked with us before, it appears. A butler and two cook crew, all for the main dining room. Look, all of their names are here."

"These last two have the same last name," he said. "Ramil and Marco Dimaapi."

She shrugged. "We have many Filipinos on staff, though I don't recognize them specifically. They could be related."

The security officer glanced away from his many screens. "Brothers. Vikram checked them in Friday. He said one of them was a diabetic."

"Diabetic?" Ethan said, still staring at the men's security photos.

"Yeah, yeah," the officer said. "One of them had a bunch of insulin in little boxes."

Little boxes. With little vials, he thought. Labeled as other medication, they could easily conceal the vials Kamran told him about.

"Where is Vikram now? I want to talk to him first," he said.

"I'll call for him." Lucia picked up a phone and dialed. She spoke with someone and placed the phone down. Her face paled, and the calm retreated from her now unsteady voice. "He's in the infirmary."

Wade stood away from the wall and nodded at Ethan. "That's our boys right there."

Ethan saw Lucia's gaze wander. She would lose the confidence to command if the uncertainty and fear contaminated her thoughts.

"We'll detain them quickly and quietly," he said. "Provide us a security detail. You can call it a random inspection. Then we can search for the virus."

Her stare lengthened, her confidence returning as she spoke. "Yes, exactly. We must keep the guests calm. I can arrange a security detail." Her eyes refocused, and the stern calm returned to her voice. "I need to return to the bridge."

* * *

Ethan followed Wade and two security officers through the white service hallways to the main galley. Crew in white smocks stared as they passed. The officers stood out in their light blue shirts and black shoulder stripes, conspicuous with their sidearms and radios scratching transmissions from all over the ship.

At Lucia's insistence, Ethan and Wade both carried radios as well. He convinced Wade to abandon the rifle. In trade, Wade forced the M9 Beretta that he'd stowed in his pack into Ethan's hands.

"Just like your old one. Don't lose it this time," Wade told him with a smirk.

He thought of the one he'd lost in Tbilisi. He had lost much more since and wanted that trend to end here. Sarah was here somewhere. That thought alone drove him to finish what they had started.

The show of force wasn't his first choice. If the targets saw them, they'd slip away into whatever contingency Hector Korkolis had plotted for them. But there was nowhere for them to run on board Korkolis' crazed experiment. He reached for the Beretta as they approached the galley doors.

They opened to the clamor of preparing food for more than two-thousand guests. Ethan marveled at the size of the sprawling galley. The impossible space within the ship was an organism in constant motion as men and women in white hats shuttled carts of desserts between rows of counters covered in sliced fruit and long knives. The staff nearest them gawked at their entrance, but activity continued unabated across the galley.

One of the security officers asked a loitering dish washer who stood off to the side awaiting more work. "Marco Dimaapi?"

The scrawny dishwasher frowned and shrugged.

A crash of steel erupted from the galley. Ethan jolted from the sound and turned to see a wave of scalding water splash on the officer. Steam rose up like a smokescreen and a steel pot clattered on the floor. The guard screamed and fell to his knees as the steam rolled off his body. Through the haze Ethan caught sight of a black-haired man as he scrambled over a counter and out of sight behind a massive cooler.

The orchestrated order of the galley dissolved into chaos. Galley staffers scattered, yelling at one another and running away from the spot where the officer knelt screaming in agony. The boiling water had scalded his arms and neck to a pale pink. His eyes widened in shock as he stared at his hands where the skin sloughed off. The other officer called into his radio for aid, trying to calm his comrade as he did so.

Wade leapt over the counter in pursuit. Ethan followed, then hesitated. They had to find both brothers. He surveyed the chefs and stewards. Most moved farther away from him, pressing into one another to find some shelter behind the steel counters and cook stoves. Some stood gaping at the guard's gruesome injuries, unsure how to help. He scanned the kitchen staff, but he lost track of the terrorized faces as they scattered in a confusing swarm of white uniforms and hats.

He heard the shout. One of the staff unleashed a burst of automatic fire at the security guards. The drumbeat sound ripped through the steel galley. Just behind him, the gunfire struck the guards, silencing the injured man's screams.

Ethan dove behind the end of the counter. The shouts erupted again as the panicked staff fled the room. Another quick burst rattled the galley like a chainsaw cutting steel.

He shouted for Wade. No reply. Ethan raised his pistol in both hands and peered around the edge of the counter. The brother with a lean and pock-marked face plodded toward him. It was Marco, not that it mattered now.

Marco ignored the galley workers who ran past him and raised a machine pistol no bigger than the Beretta that Ethan held in his hands. In the close quarters of the galley, the weapon would tear him apart.

More gunfire muffled by steel doors and angled corridors echoed into the galley from the dining hall. He knew Wade could handle himself. But it only took one misstep and he'd lose another fellow officer. He couldn't accept that. He owed Wade more than that. Again he peeked around the corner to see Marco who looked toward the great hall, distracted by the gunfire.

Ethan had the opportunity to act, but not the angle. His sides hurt. His arms ached with dull pain. Every part of his body resisted motion. He sat against the counter, his arms on his bent knees, and willed himself to move. A streak of red along the wall caught his attention. He could buy the time he needed, but he'd have to move fast.

He aimed and fired.

A plume of white streamed from the fire extinguisher on the opposite wall. The white filled the air like a dense fog that began to settle as quickly as it came. Marco shouted at him, and a burst of gunfire tore into the white cloud.

Ethan heaved himself around the counter. He steadied his pistol on the countertop. The smoky white thinned, and he saw the standing shape of

Marco peering into the white. His enemy fanned away the foggy haze and pointed the machine pistol at the counter's end. He sprayed a roaring burst of bullets that punched holes in the counter where Ethan had sat moments ago.

Ethan wanted to question the brothers. He had to find the virus and how they had spread it. There was no intelligence to capture from Marco now. That opportunity died with the guards that lay at Marco's feet. Maybe for Ethan it had died with Marcus Eldridge many weeks ago, lost with Seda and with Kamran, gone with Jane Corso. They all stood in the path of a killing stroke set in motion before they knew their fates. He had failed all of them, and now he held the sole recourse left to him firmly in two hands. He gripped the pistol just as Wade taught him—a practice with which he had become too comfortable in these weeks.

Ethan fired. Four rounds struck Marco before he could react. Marco stood for a moment, propped up perhaps by his fanaticism. An expression of shock that his work could end here and now, unwilling to accept that as he exhaled he would fall to the floor and bleed out like the dead guards lying next to him.

A trio of shots fired again from the dining room. Ethan ran to the doors and looked out the round window into the ornate room. He saw no sign of Wade.

He entered the hall and crept between round tables draped in white tablecloths and perfectly placed settings that awaited evening guests. The tang of smokeless powder from Wade's weapon filled the air as he moved around the perimeter. The hall's center opened to rising floors where a grand chandelier spanned the levels above like a rain of diamonds.

Something moved to his left. It was Wade crouched low, creeping between tables toward the curving staircase with his pistol raised to the level above. Ranil Dimaapi must have escaped to the upper dining floors.

Ethan circled around the main floor. He moved quickly and silently. He tried signaling Wade as he approached the opposite staircase. But Wade's wide eyes tracked above, searching for any sign of their quarry.

Wade reached the far stair and scanned with his pistol at the balconies above, creeping up the plush stairs. On the balcony behind him, Ethan saw too late the face of Ranil squinting down the iron sights of a gun.

"Wade!"

His friend spun around, but the shot struck him somewhere below the waist. Wade fell back firing his weapon. But Ranil had disappeared.

Ethan raced up the steps, his aim focused on the other side of the hall. Ranil slunk between tables to another part of the floor. His white smock blended in with the white tables, but Ethan caught glimpses of him as he moved.

Lucia's voice crackled from the radio at his hip, interrupting the sounds of Wade swearing between gasps of pain. The radio awoke with chatter. They were coming, but not fast enough for Wade's sake. Ethan had to end it.

He ran to a wide support column at the balcony's edge and pressed himself against it. He lost sight of Ranil who had moved to somewhere in the middle of the hall, stalking closer to him.

"Hold on," he shouted at Wade, but he did not look down at his friend. He set the radio at the base of the column, tucked just out of sight along the balcony's baseboard. Then he crawled back the way he came. His knee shot out pain with each deliberate step back. He stifled a grunt and held his breath, creeping back until he reached the cover of a tablecloth and waited.

The radio bleeped and crackled again. Metallic voices spoke to one another about the bodies they discovered on the galley floor. They were close. Ethan sat on his haunches and raised his weapon at the column.

Ranil came from the left, farther away than Ethan had expected. His target rose up and moved fast to aim his shots at the source of the sound. Ranil's mouth opened in an angry sneer, then jerked his head in a panic at finding the lone radio.

Ethan adjusted his aim to the base of Ranil's sternum.

"Drop the gun," he said.

Ranil spotted him at last and brought his pistol around to shoot. Ethan returned with a quick cadence of fire. Ethan's shots struck Ranil, but by instinct he flinched away from the flash and explosive force of Ranil's gun shooting back. A high pitch filled his ears, and he fell forward to his knees. Ranil's wild fire missed its mark.

Ethan stumbled forward gasping for breath. He stood cautiously, gun raised at the spot where Ranil fell. From behind a tablecloth, a pair of legs writhed on the ground. Ethan moved around and saw Ranil clutching his chest, his face contorted in pain and shock. For a moment, Ethan's finger tensed on the trigger. He wanted to do it. No one would blame him, if they ever knew. Ranil lay there, minutes away from his last breath. Ethan could take those moments from him, just as he and his brother had already stolen time from so many others. From Sarah. *No, not her.* He kicked the pistol away from Ranil's grasp and backed away.

The threat was over, but he cursed himself for coming too late. He ran to Wade, who had crawled down the steps to a table and pressed a white cloth napkin soaked through with blood onto the side of his thigh.

"You're bleeding bad."

"I'm all right. Asshole hit me in the leg." Wade said. "Hurts like hell, though."

"Let's get you some help. Can you stand?"

He helped Wade hop up to one leg. He draped his arm over Wade's shoulder and helped him hobble back to the galley.

"You got him?"

Ethan nodded.

"Damn. That's one less you owe me," Wade said. He almost seemed impressed.

* * *

Ethan hauled Wade to the lowest level of the ship. They walked from the elevator across the steel deck that seemed balanced like a beam along the keel. Beneath them lay the rumble of the engines and below that the depths of the sea. Ahead they met a rank smell of human waste wafting from the infirmary.

A nurse wearing a surgical mask stood at the reception desk and waved them away. Blue Latex covered her hands, and she had tucked her long shirt sleeves into the gloves at her wrist.

"Get him the hell out of here," she said.

"He's been shot. Where can I take him for treatment?"

"I'll see if someone can treat him out there. He can't be past this point with an open wound like that. Just go back."

Wade lifted his head and curled his nose from the stink. "Looks bad."

Ethan helped him sit on a palette of supplies wrapped in cellophane. Minutes passed. Wade's blood dripped onto the plastic down to the white steel deck. His eyes drooped.

"I'll go get someone," Ethan said. "Sit up. And stay awake."

Ethan approached the infirmary desk. The smell worsened with every step. The hospital staff's voices overlapped in a frantic chorus. They spoke in urgent tones, talking about fluids and symptoms that he knew were signs of the virus.

A lone patient lay in a gurney in the infirmary hallway. A slender hand gripped the gurney's rail. Layers of blankets swaddled her body, but she shivered uncontrollably.

"Hello? I need help here," Ethan said. He stepped closer. "Can we get some help?"

Sweat matted the woman's brown hair. A pouch of fluid hanging over her head fed into her arm. She groaned pitifully, and he stepped to the foot of her bed. She rolled over moaning weakly for help, and he realized his greatest fear. Sarah's eyes watered. Her face twisted in pain, flush from the fevered heat of her body. She didn't seem to recognize him.

He stood immobilized, unable to speak. He wanted to cry out to her, to hold her hand and comfort her. But he knew what it would mean for him, and he hated his sense of self preservation. She had left him for his overly rational mind and his dedication to his job. He hated all of it in that moment.

"Sir, I need you to step back. Now," said the nurse who'd greeted them.

She jogged to him and waved her hands, motioning to shove him away without touching his chest.

"That's my … I know her," he said.

"I'm sorry. This is a very contagious area. Please, we don't have enough people. You have to get away from here."

"Is she going to be all right?"

"We don't know. Please," she said.

Sarah's feeble voice croaked, and he heard his name.

"I'm here," he said. "Sarah, I'm here. Hold on."

He backed away to wait with Wade, unable to look away from the gurney where he could just see the lump of Sarah's feet. He wondered where her new husband was, and knew he probably lay in another bed somewhere inside the infirmary.

An anxious corpsman came out to tend Wade. Ethan helped him cut away Wade's canvas pants, and he held a flashlight as the corpsman stitched up the wound on his thigh.

"That's Sarah, isn't it?" Wade asked.

He nodded. There was nothing he could say and nothing more he wanted to.

"They're going to take me upstairs. You stay here with her," Wade said.

He remained with her for two days, covered in the pale blue scrubs with mask and gloves the nurses provided. The sterile barrier between them was the price he paid for her presence. He held her hand while she slept.

When she woke, she asked him to check on Kerim, her new husband. He fared much worse, but he couldn't tell her the truth. From an infirmary room doorway he watched Kerim vomit blood into a bedpan. She wanted to see her new husband.

"I'm sorry," he told her.

Twice he left to eat. On the second night, he stood on deck alone under a night sky without stars breathing the humid sea air. She wasn't getting better, and he didn't want to see the awful end. He'd forgotten everything else around him—the disorder of the ship and his duty to his work. His mind occupied only the nightmarish stupor of stink and misery as nineteen people wasted into putrefied wretches around him. He willed himself to return to it for another hour with her.

At the end of the two days, when she too had vomited blood, he watched her slowly slip away into delirium and pain. He told her he was sorry again. She couldn't hear him, let alone know the totality of why he said it. And then she was gone.

CHAPTER 24

BAD HABITS

McLean, Virginia

7:55 p.m., Tuesday, July 10

PAUL TRUDGED to the seventh floor and entered Director Drummond's office. The wood paneling seemed darker in the evening, more aged and more severe. It was a trick of age and absence. The room was the same. Paul had aged since his previous visit. He met with Drummond alone, and the room's emptiness seemed to close in on the two of them standing there without their peers.

"Paul, thanks for meeting me so late. Take a seat."

Drummond sat on the front of his desk with a leather-bound folder tucked under his arm. "I've read the latest. We have a few loose ends, and that doesn't give me much confidence to ease the President's mind."

Paul walked the length of the conference table and sat at the end near Drummond's desk.

"The Navy team recovered twelve of the vials," he said. "Two of them had been emptied, apparently in the kitchens by the two brothers Pierce eliminated. They used them on trays of fruit. Just poured it over the top. Apparently if you cook this stuff or do much of anything to it, the virus isn't effective."

He let out a little cough, and his voice rasped with phlegm. He'd taken to sleeping on the couch, when he slept at all. In the evenings, his old bad habits caught up with him.

"And the second outbreak in Tunisia is contained?"

"So far. No new cases reported after the numbers we received yesterday. Fifty-three dead and six survivors."

"Could have been a damn sight worse. But let's assume that's just one more vial. So, you're telling me none of our people know where the rest are?"

"Yes, sir, that's what I'm saying."

"You don't need to sir me, Paul. I think we're well past the bullshit now."

"I'd say we're very much in the thick of the bullshit at this point."

Drummond chuckled, and his posture eased. He stood and took the chair at the end of the table next to him. Paul sat at his right hand, the very chair Harley Gilchrist had occupied every time he'd visited the room. The realization unsettled something in his head. He'd lost so much, and he spent the last ten days trying to piece together the damage Harley had wrought. Paul cleared his throat again and swallowed.

"Pierce indicated there were eighteen vials. There could be as many as five more out there," he said.

"And how does he know there aren't twice that or more still out there?"

"That's the intel he received from Khorasani. The Romanians have taken over the facility in Brașov. Scorpio won't be producing more of the stuff any time soon."

Drummond went quiet. He folded his hands and stared at the empty table space.

"This thing really snuck up on all of us. You suffered the worst of it, and I'm sorry for that. But Harley left all of us in a hell of a tough spot. You know, I have no illusions about my liability here. If the virus hits stateside, my tenure will end faster than a shit storm tornado. After what's happened, I'd say I'm a notch closer to the exit, wouldn't you?"

"Those politics are above my pay grade."

"Don't kid yourself. My predecessor lasted nearly ten years. If I make it to a fourth year, I'll consider that a good run. I'd like to say I left the place better than I found it. Right now, I can't. How the hell did it go this far? You're a smart guy. How in the holy hell they did this to us?"

Paul had asked himself the same question every day since he found the photo of Harley and his protégés. It was a ghost's enigma that would haunt him every time he considered it. With Janey gone, he would never stop asking himself why it had all happened and what more he could have done.

"I know this much. Harley wasn't some revolutionary," Paul said. A true believer, maybe, but he didn't share politics with this damn Scorpio Compact. Maybe he did it for the money. But I think it was something more for him. Maybe he did it for power. For the freedom to operate and do what we can't do and run his own kind of agency. That's the only sense I can make of it."

Drummond frowned with his chin pushed up as though he'd eaten something spoiled.

"Maybe he was right," Drummond said.

Paul glared at him. It was a callous thing to say, but Drummond continued unfazed by his expression.

"Right about the freedom to operate I mean. This Korkolis character ran circles around us. He used our own limitations against us. You know that better than anyone. We're facing a new kind of asymmetry here. And the hell of it is, he's still out there. I think a little latitude is in order here."

"We have a good idea how to track him down. Once Pierce gets back on his feet, he'll be more than eager to target him."

"Do you really think Pierce is the right officer for this? After all that's happened?"

"No," Paul said. "I think he's the right officer because of all that's happened."

"Don't make that the wrong decision for the both of you. I don't want to know where the target is or what the target's going to do next. I want to know when he's no longer a target, and you've moved on to the next one. And the next one after that. Understood?"

Paul nodded. He had no confusion about Drummond's intentions, though he hated the political undercurrents. Despite Drummond's insistence that things had changed, the consequences hadn't. He and Pierce would be hung out to dry with any misstep. But that was the genius of Drummond's directive. He wouldn't decline. Neither would Pierce. And Drummond knew it.

"I understand you perfectly. Sir."

He left the seventh floor but reconsidered a visit to the operations center. Pierce slept in quarantine somewhere on the Black Sea where it was close to four in the morning. They could both use the rest.

He descended the stairway, and his voice echoed as he spoke aloud to himself. "No rest for the wicked."

He drove home as the summer sun set late, and for the first time since Janey left him he passed by the site of the crash. He slowed to see the concrete slab, but it bore no mark of the collision that he could see. It was as though she never existed and had never been there to leave a mark. He had to face the reality of a world that moved on while he could not forget.

He entered the house's unwelcoming silence. He opened the first-floor windows to hear the rustle of leaves in the cooling night. He fixed himself a turkey sandwich and devoured it while standing at the sink. The crumbs fell down into the drain, and he washed the bits away still craving something more. He went to the garage to find an old pack of Marlboro Lights he'd hidden away from Janey in a locked drawer of his tool bench. They had dried out through heat and cold and humidity after two years since he last snuck a smoke. He walked back and forth in the unmowed grass of his back yard, pulling on the old cigarette that burned fast and bitter in his mouth. He watched the smoke drift up into the maple leaves and stared at his empty bedroom window above.

CHAPTER 25

NO RESERVATIONS

Ayia Napa, Cyprus
7:10 p.m., Friday, October 19

ETHAN KILLED the engine and let the small fishing boat slide to a stop a hundred yards from Nissi Beach. A flock of blue umbrellas and empty lounge chairs on the shore caught the last beam of sunlight, and behind those the hotel gleamed white. Tourists trotted inside to change into their evening wear for a night of drinking and dancing. He heard the early revelers at the hotel bar. The music and their laughter carried over the water where he and Wade had other evening plans.

Here the sea calmed, and the tiny islet to the west sheltered the shallow waters from the wind. Wade chose the spot four weeks ago, and each week they had launched a different rental around the eastern horn of Cyprus to anchor at the lively resort. Each week, they saw fewer tourists as the temperatures cooled. Each week they fished for their target but caught nothing.

Wade sat behind him in the rear facing chair. He wore a bucket hat and tank top, every part the tourist fisherman. A pair of great deep-sea rods angled up like antennae at the aft, but Wade ignored them. He kept still in the seat and focused on the hotel that rose up ten stories at the water's edge.

"This is good. Right here. I can handle this," Wade said.

Ethan dropped anchor into the shallow sands below, and the boat glided almost imperceptibly until the prow faced the resort like a compass arrow. He played his part. He wore a linen shirt, and his skin had tanned under the Cyprus sun.

"You think he's here?" Wade asked.

"Kay says he is. I don't see the car, but the agent in place confirmed him at the dock in Larnaca."

"Then he's here."

They waited out the hour, adrift on the rising tide that flooded the white beach sands. The western glow waned and gave way to a starry night sky. He and Wade had waited too long for those stars to align, and he wondered if Wade now had any doubts. If so, he said nothing as he rolled out a towel to lie between the boat's forward cushioned seats.

For himself, Ethan held no reservations. He had lost any doubts before Paul Corso called him months ago. In the tiny crew's cabin aboard the *Aria* where he waited out those sorrowful days in quarantine, he had spent hours remembering every misstep he had taken and every weakness they had used against him. Against all of them. Paul's call was permission to act. It wasn't revenge. It wasn't even justice for Sarah or for anyone else. He saw it in a way that Kamran Khorasani would understand. This was strictly remedy, like the painful pinprick of inoculation.

Through binoculars, he scanned the beach side for workers in white shorts who scurried around a row of wooden boxes sprouting wires along a concrete dock. As he watched them, he heard Wade open the latches of a long case and load rounds into the rifle with a quiet clack as the bolt slid into position.

"Time to call," he told Wade.

Wade leaned into the forward cushions and propped the rifle's bipod upon the boat's prow. The sizable scope atop the rifle swallowed up light, and Wade settled into it, breathing slower as he waited.

Ethan reached into his pocket and emptied a cracked cell phone from a plastic baggie. He'd kept Andrei's phone for the occasion, though Kay already confirmed the number he dialed had remained active. He recognized the sonorous voice that answered and pictured the white hair and beard of Hector Korkolis.

"I was wondering when I would hear from you, Mr. Pierce. I'm even a little disappointed it's taken you this long. So many things could have happened since our last encounter."

"I hear you're losing more and more friends these days," he said.

"Then we have that in common. Although you do go about it in a much more severe fashion. Tell me, how is your estranged wife? Did she receive my gift? It's so difficult to return."

Before he could answer a string of little meteors shot up from the ground and burst over the water in a brilliant shower of purple and pink sparks. The popping sound travelled through his phone at a delay to Hector's penthouse. More fireworks followed from the dock side.

He waited for a sign from Wade before he replied. Another volley exploded overhead, and Wade gave him the slightest nod.

"Just think of me as a loyal dog who learned a new trick," he said.

Wade's rifle fired under the crackle of the fireworks overhead. The shot rang loud in Ethan's ears, but at the beach the tourists cheered along with a wedding party at the display overhead and the crackling pops and reports of the show.

Wade cycled the bolt without lifting his head and waited. Ethan crouched awaiting a second shot. None came.

Wade exhaled. "Target down."

His friend returned to his chair and pulled his hat down low over his eyes. Together they watched the firework display of brilliant orange and fiery reds. The electric blues and whites lit up the dark water like a mirror made of darkness and light. Ethan closed his eyes and felt the thunderous bursts from above like an invisible weight he would carry with him from then on. He thought of Sarah. He saw in his mind her beautiful face and her sickly one, overlaid like a trick of the light that never settled. He knew he'd carry that forever as well.

When the skies darkened again, he pulled the anchor out of the sand, hauling it up hand over hand. He started the engine and steered the boat past the islet out into the deeper water where they sped along the coast into the trackless night.

ACKNOWLEDGEMENTS

No one writes a book alone. I owe much to my wife Canada Snyder, who read along and cheered me past doubt. Thanks to my kids, Kate and Riggs, who wondered where Dad was many nights. My hat's off to the Gateway Group: Tracey Kelley, Nate Granzow (my partner in crime), Chad Cox, and Thad Smull. This book wouldn't exist without them and their superb writing advice and fellowship. Thanks also to the Des Moines Writers Workshop group. Big thanks to Erin Johnston, Amy Lillard, and Julie Stone, great writers. Their advice shaped this book as well.

Special thanks to Gayle Lynds, whose professional guidance made this book better. And special thanks to Vincent Racaniello, whose expertise in virology and willingness to share his thoughts made my unusual ideas more plausible.

Finally, teachers never get the just credit they deserve. What I know and what I write is because of many great teachers along the way. Thanks to: Pat Fife, Bruce Hukee, Barb Lang, Linda Unser, Thisbe Nissen, Richard Thomas, Steven Wright, and most of all to Brooks Landon and Carla Lawson.